A FOREIGN AFFAIR

A FOREIGN AFFAIR

Colin Mander

Book Guild Publishing
Sussex, England

First published in Great Britain in 2011 by
The Book Guild Ltd
Pavilion View
19 New Road
Brighton, BN1 1UF

Typesetting in Baskerville by
Keyboard Services, Luton, Bedfordshire

Printed in Great Britain by
CPI Antony Rowe

A catalogue record for this book is available from
The British Library

ISBN 978 1 84624 620 3

Education and travel open up the world. I dedicate this book to the memory of my parents who, despite losing everything to a Luftwaffe bombing raid, ensured that my sister and I received a first-class education. We have received full benefit.

1

Matthew Boston was getting frustrated. 'Why the hell is the motorway always so crowded when you're in a hurry, eh Tom?' he barked irritably at the chauffeur.

'Why don't you just give your wife a ring, sir, and let her know we're on our way?' replied Tom, hoping to calm him down.

'Yes Matt, just try to relax,' his father added from the back seat. 'You know there's nothing you can do about the traffic. There was probably an accident earlier.'

Matthew pulled a mobile from his pocket and pressed some buttons. 'Hi darling, it's me, thought I'd let you know we're a bit stuck on the motorway, so could be later than expected. With a bit of luck I should make it in time, though. Mum and Dad are with me but will be staying round the corner at The Ritz as we have a full house. I am going to drop them off there so they can change before the party.'

Anna muttered her acknowledgement and slammed down the phone. 'You'd have thought he could at least make the effort to get here on time for my thirtieth birthday,' she said to herself out loud. 'The bloody business always takes pride of place!'

The annual general meeting of Boston and Wood had taken place that morning and Matthew had expected to have plenty of time to get to London for Anna's birthday celebrations. Unexpectedly, his father Gerald called a special meeting of the board for the afternoon, as all the directors were in town for the AGM. Since the main topic on the agenda directly affected Matthew he had no alternative but to attend.

Boston and Wood was a pharmaceutical company based in Northampton. The firm of Boston & Co. had been started in the early fifties by Matthew's grandfather. Initially they made precision instruments for the medical profession and had prospered well with the growth of surgical operations. In the mid sixties they merged with Wood and Wellcome Ltd, manufacturers of pharmaceuticals and medical supplies, who were seeking a partner to inject money and expand the business. The new company had grown rapidly under his grandfather's chairmanship. Gerald Boston had taken control in 1985 and instigated the opening of their own research laboratories. This had led to the successful pioneering of several drugs which are now household names.

It was seven o'clock before the chauffeur stopped the car outside the Boston residence in St James's Square. The square is one of the finest in the West End of London, with many imposing eighteenth-century buildings, and a large private garden in the centre. A wide road, invariably busy with traffic, surrounds the green. Matthew's grandfather had acquired the house on the south side nearly fifty years ago.

Matthew burst hurriedly through the door and was greeted gleefully by his two children, Mark and Louise. Anna's reception was more frosty.

'You've got less than an hour before the guests arrive,' she barked at him. 'Couldn't your board meeting have waited?'

'You know what was being discussed, Anna, and Dad wanted everything agreed by the end of the meeting. A couple of directors were a bit awkward – you know, they like to hear the sound of their own voices – which made the meeting run on a bit. By the way, Dad wants to propose the toast this evening and would like to announce what went on today, if that's all right with you? He feels the family at least should know before they read the business news tomorrow.'

'I suppose so,' said Anna grudgingly, 'so long as he keeps it short.' She and her birthday party were going to play second fiddle again! 'Mark and Louise are going to stay up to say hello to everyone but are not having dinner as there is school in the morning,' she continued as they walked from the room.

Entering the bedroom, Matthew put his arm round her and pulled her to him. 'By the way, a very happy birthday, darling,' he said handing her a small box wrapped in gold paper.

Anna took the box without a smile and removed the wrapping. Opening the box she saw a beautiful diamond and emerald brooch. 'Oh Matt, this is so pretty!' she exclaimed and immediately felt a little guilty for the cold reception. 'I can't wear it tonight though, I'm afraid; it won't go with the dress,' she added as she moved to give him a kiss.

Having stripped to his underwear, Matthew walked to the bathroom for a shower. Anna followed him with her eyes. 'He's no longer the gorgeous creature I married ten years ago,' she muttered to herself. Too many hours spent at a desk and too many business lunches had added a paunch to his midriff. His shoulders, previously so broad and muscular, had sagged, further revealing a puffy neck. She had mentioned it a few times with little positive response.

When Matthew returned from the bathroom he found Anna peering into a wardrobe. She had, of course, already chosen her dress for the evening, but that did not prevent her from staring again at the rack just in case another idea struck her.

'I'm going to wear that apricot outfit I bought in Milan last month,' she remarked.

'That sounds absolutely perfect,' replied Matthew, trying to appear both knowledgeable and enthusiastic.

Matthew finished tying his bow tie and waited for Anna to complete her make-up. He walked over to an occasional table at the side of the room and picked up a photograph of their wedding. Staring at him was the man he no longer resembled. Pictured here was a debonair figure just under six feet tall with a handsome smiling face. His blue eyes portrayed intelligence and the smile a real tenderness, but his face had since become hardened by the tough business world. At twenty-seven years old his light brown hair had been thick, naturally wavy and with a hint of auburn that appeared more pronounced in the photograph. He instinctively ran his fingers through his receding hair, replaced the photo wistfully and turned to see that Anna was ready.

'You look simply stunning, darling,' Matthew complimented her. 'That dress is such a pretty colour. No doubt who will be the belle of the ball tonight, eh?'

Anna smiled appreciatively. On her feet she was wearing matching shoes with three-inch heels to elevate her height of only five feet three inches. Her features were so reminiscent of her Mediterranean birth place. She had jet-black hair that glistened in every light. She had deep-brown eyes and a fine nose above perfectly shaped lips. Her firm chin gave her a resolute look that belied a genuine shyness. Considered pretty rather than attractive, her olive brown shoulders tapered to a slim waist but curvaceous hips warned of an increasing problem in later life.

'We'd better be downstairs for when they arrive, and I've got a little more arranging to do.'

'And how many are we expecting?' Matthew asked.

'I've told Nina to set the table for twenty-four but there could be the odd dropout.'

'David says he's so sorry he can't be here tonight and sends his love. He believes he has made a major breakthrough and can't possibly leave the laboratory overnight.'

'I shall miss him,' replied Anna. 'I wanted him to come.' She omitted to mention that David, a researcher at Boston and Wood's laboratory and old friend of Matthew's, had phoned her earlier in the day for a chat and to wish her a happy birthday. She knew he hated parties but felt he could have made an effort, for her.

The first guests to arrive were Matthew's parents. Gerald Boston was the same size and shape as his son, but weary eyes and a bald head made him look older than his sixty-five years. Having been chairman of Boston and Wood for the past twenty-five years he had added greatly to the family fortune, but success had come at a price. His wife Linda was only a year younger but looked considerably more. She was tall, trim and wore spectacles that gave her a schoolmistress appearance, but soft brown eyes hinted at a kindly manner.

Anna appeared from the dining room where she had been arranging the seating. She was greeted by her in-laws and Gerald gave her his usual crushing hug.

'How's my favourite daughter-in-law?' he enquired. 'And a very happy birthday to you – quite an important one, eh?' He had always had a soft spot for Anna and was looking forward to proposing the toast. By contrast, Linda was cordial but lacked warmth when they embraced. She already had her suspicions about Anna, though as yet, nothing concrete.

As the various guests were shown in, Anna busied herself ensuring they knew one another and that the waiter hadn't missed out anyone with the champagne.

The next to be announced were the Italian ambassador, Alberto Destefano, and his wife, Carla. They were everything that epitomised his profession. He was tall, distinguished, with swept back grey hair. She was slim, dark haired, with a sensuous mouth and laughing brown eyes that suggested she thoroughly enjoyed the high life. The position in London had been Alberto's first choice and the couple had settled into the social whirl with consummate ease. They were old friends of Anna's mother. Being very fond of Anna, they often used the Boston residence as a bolt-hole from the world of official functions.

They were followed through the door by Anna's parents, Paolo and Bella Medina. Paolo's presence was immediately felt in the room. He was powerfully built, swarthy, with a deep penetrating voice that lacked the musical lilt typical of his native tongue. His bushy eyebrows gave his face a noticeable character but a pug nose and a mouth that turned down at the left corner produced a sullen appearance. He had often in the past been likened to Robert Maxwell. Laughter in his presence was rarely an option unless he was making the joke. His wife, Bella, had been lithe and attractive in her youth, but had become a little overweight. During her days at university she was an ardent and active supporter of the Italian Socialist Party. It was there that she met Paolo, a leading Socialist politician, who was a prominent speaker at many of their rallies. Motherhood had left her looking weary, although alert brown eyes suggested an intelligent mind.

Anna received her second bear hug of the evening. Although still rather afraid of her father, she was delighted he had made the effort to fly in from Rome for her party. Paolo strolled across the room, making straight for the ambassador. They were old acquaintances but diametrically opposed politically. Alberto groaned inwardly at seeing Paolo approach, but greeted him with his well-rehearsed flourish.

'*Buona sera*, Paolo! And how's life back in the old capital?' he enquired.

'You know as well as I do,' Paolo growled. 'We've got another bloody Nero fiddling away at the senate whilst Rome and the rest of the country disintegrates!'

'It will probably be all right without your interference,' stated the ambassador defensively. 'Don't worry; the powers that be in the EU are getting to grips with it.'

'Oh yes – getting to grips with what?' snorted Paolo.' What on earth makes you think the EU is going to do anything to help Italy out of this financial mess? Especially after all the money that has been poured into Greece and other countries.'

The two wives, who were chatting apart, heard the temperature rising and interrupted the men's conversation. 'Come on, darling, this is meant to be a pleasant evening for Anna,' said Carla. She knew it would be easier for her than for Bella to prise her husband away from an argument. 'Let's leave politics alone for tonight, shall we?' Alberto took her arm gratefully and made to circulate the room.

'We'll have to continue this chat another time,' he said with obvious relief, leaving Paolo to find another victim for his opinions.

The noise level, which had gradually risen as the room filled up, dropped suddenly as Anna's younger sister and her latest escort were ushered in. Gina Medina had flown in from Rome that day, where she had waved a relieved goodbye to the Italian paparazzi. Her appearance, though not unlike Anna's, was more sensuous. She was slightly taller, bustier and much more vivacious. She was wearing a coral pink dress that, unusually for her, was high at the neck. Her handbag and slingback high heels in a light cream leather were stylish but almost understated. She had no doubt chosen carefully as her father was not a fan of her society playgirl reputation. It was also conceivable that on this occasion she had decided not to upstage her sister. Her other accessory, Andrea Scarlatti, was a suave and well-known couturier from Milan. He stood head and shoulders above Gina, which helped to make his light brown ponytail stand out. His black velvet dinner jacket fitted impeccably but white patent leather shoes displayed an inexplicable lack of taste. Once they had crossed the floor, the guests returned to their conversations and the hubbub resumed.

Gina went over to her father and received one of Paolo's trademark bear hugs that ruffled her hair.

'Lovely to see you Papà, Mamma, how are you both?' she enquired, trying to kiss her mother and rearrange her hair at the same time. She continued without waiting for an answer. 'I thought we might be on the same plane but you must have come earlier.'

'I booked a flight early enough to prevent him from going into parliament today, otherwise I doubted we'd ever get here,' said Bella, obviously pleased she had managed to do something positive.

'And who's this?' Paolo demanded, flicking his head rudely towards Andrea, although he knew full well who he was.

'This is Andrea Scarlatti, I'm sure you've heard of him. He designed the new Hemline fashion that everybody's wearing.'

'Well, I'm not,' replied Paolo shaking Andrea's hand and drawing him to one side. 'Any chance you could take my daughter somewhere quiet for a time and keep her out of the media? Preferably for a very long time,' he added.

'Not much I can do there, sir, she does as she pleases,' came the tame reply as Andrea tried to rejoin the group. In any case, he was also a beneficiary of the attention Gina garnered from the press.

'Well, I'm fed up with seeing her photograph in every glitzy magazine. It's not doing my image any good.'

'I'm sure you'd get a better reaction from her yourself, sir,' came the unconvincing reply. 'I don't have any influence.'

'More's the pity – she needs a firm grip, but I don't have the time.'

Their conversation was interrupted by the appearance of the last guest, Lieutenant Col. Philip Boston, Matthew's younger brother.

'I knew my brother would be the last to arrive,' Matthew whispered to Anna, who nodded her agreement. Philip always arrived late. To arrive ahead of the political wing of the family would have meant loss of face. As far as he was concerned, the military was far more important than politicians.

Snapping his mobile phone shut in full view, he made his entrance. Philip liked to appear busy to dispel the assumption that, being an army officer, he rarely was. Nevertheless, he cut a fine figure in his dress uniform of the Welsh Guards. He had joined the army straight from school as, in his considered opinion, the life of a university student required being either decadent or studious. He was neither. Steady promotion had moved him through the ranks and now at age thirty-five he was wondering what the future had in store. His regiment had recently completed a tour of duty in Afghanistan and he had no desire to return. Taller and slimmer than his brother, his eyes were a steely blue and his fair hair bleached further by outdoor life. As he walked through the room the eyes of the ladies followed him admiringly. Unfortunately for them, apart from the occasional fling, he preferred the sporting life and the company of men.

'Anna, my lovely,' he said loudly to the audience of ladies, 'hope you are having a wonderful birthday.' He lifted her off her feet, held her high and gave her a long kiss on the way down. He pressed a present into her hand and she moved aside to open it. 'Matt. How are you, you old sod? Still working too damned hard? You should give it a break sometime. Come up to the big city and we'll have a couple of nights out on the town. Do you a power of good,' he added in his clipped manner of speech.

Anna made sure Philip had a drink in his hand before checking with the kitchen that dinner was ready to be served. When the announcement came she took Matthew's arm and made for the dining room.

'I've sat Papà and the ambassador as far apart as their political opinions,' she said with a grin.

'And kept him away from Father Kennedy as well, I hope,' replied Matthew. 'We don't want any heated religious argument, either.'

The dining room was not in the same elegant regency style of their home in the Midlands. This was pure Rennie Mackintosh. High-backed oak chairs surrounded a long narrow table. The curtains were William Morris design and three Pre-Raphaelite paintings by Burne-Jones, Millais and Rossetti adorned the walls. The two chandeliers were also a Rennie design and a deep burgundy carpet added warmth. The ladies in their finery added colour. 'All very elegant in its own way,' thought Matthew as he admired his wife's choice of decor. Anna had recently spent a great deal of her time redecorating the entire house.

The party was a mainly Catholic gathering and the guests waited to take their seats until Father Kennedy had said grace. Matthew picked up the menu and studied it. Anna had chosen two Italian wines and one French. A Gavi di Gavi to accompany the sole paupiettes and a 1998 Sassicaia with the rib of Scotch beef. Anna's absolute favourite was saved for the tarte Tatin. An old Château d'Yquem was, in gourmet terms, going to be her highlight of the evening. At least she managed to avoid Italian food this evening, he thought; he hated pasta.

When the meal was finished and everyone looked replete and relaxed, Gerald rose from his chair to toast Anna's health. He was an accomplished speaker, rarely humorous but always well prepared and fluent. The toast portrayed his genuine affection for her whilst thanking her for providing Linda and him with two lovely grandchildren. Paolo and Bella nodded their agreement. When the guests had noisily wished Anna a happy birthday and a welcome into her thirties, they sat down again. Gerald remained on his feet.

'Anna has kindly allowed me to interrupt her evening with a special announcement,' he said. 'After our AGM this morning I called a special board meeting, and before the Stock Exchange opens tomorrow they will have received this information. I have decided, with immediate effect, to stand down as chairman of Boston and Wood.' A ripple of surprise circulated the room. 'Despite it being a public company nowadays,' he continued, 'I have always tried to retain the business as a family affair. It is, therefore, with a great deal of pleasure and pride I can tell you that, with full board approval, Matthew here will be taking over the chair from me. I know you will join with me in wishing him the very best of luck.'

When the messages of good luck had died away, Gerald glanced round to sum up the impact. Only Philip seemed genuinely surprised and gave a thumbs-up sign to his brother. Paolo was nodding his head knowingly; he was pretty certain he understood exactly why Gerald had decided to pass the responsibility over to his son.

Some guests started to move around the table for a change of conversation. Paolo took the opportunity to place himself beside Alberto before the ambassador became aware of the danger. Paolo was looking flushed and more expansive in his manner.

'As I was saying earlier, what makes you think anything is going to come out of those idiots in Brussels that will make any damn difference?' he said in a loud voice that made others turn in his direction. Alberto had no other choice than to pay attention but preferred not to offer a reply; so Paolo ploughed on. 'Why do you believe that waiting on the whims of the European Central Bank will solve any of Italy's problems? The government is going to have to act now and positively if we are not going to face financial ruin and international embarrassment! The way we're going, we will end up like Greece; completely bankrupt.' He glared hard at Alberto, demanding a response.

'If you think we can get out of this global recession on our own, you must be crazy,' retorted Alberto. 'We must all work together, collectively, to get everybody's economy moving forward.'

'That's just the sort of response I expect from you bloody conservatives! Pretend nothing's wrong, do sweet fuck all and hope somebody else will get you out of a mess. Are you completely unaware of the massive rise in unemployment and the despair of the workforce at most of our factories?'

'Of course I know what's going on but it's happening everywhere. It's not just Italy that's suffering.'

'I told you ages ago we should never have gone into the euro. That's what is stultifying our economy. We are being manipulated by the Germans and the French who are controlling the European Bank and setting interest rates and policies to suit their own individual economies. Why do you think the British are doing better than us? It's because they kept their own currency and didn't rush to embrace the euro,' Paolo said, answering his own question.

'Well, we can't get out now, so the argument's fatuous,' responded Alberto, getting more than a little irritated. 'Anyway, what makes you think the British economy is in any better state than ours?'

'Whether it is or it isn't, at least they have their destiny in their own hands. They are not kowtowing to the Germans and French as we are forced to all the bloody time.'

The ambassador shrugged his shoulders diplomatically

by way of response. He moved his chair backwards and started to stand up to end the conversation.

'That's right, walk away when you know I'm right and you can't think of any excuses for your right-winged government's inertia,' shouted Paolo, flourishing his left arm and sending a glass of red wine flying across the table.

Alberto eyed him in a disparaging manner and moved away as a waiter arrived with a cloth to soak up the damage. Those nearby, who had been listening with amusement, turned away pretending nothing had occurred. Anna glared at Paolo and joined her mother at the other end of the table.

'Couldn't he give it a rest just for one evening, just to please me?' she complained to Bella. 'Everything pleasurable in my life seems to get ruined by either business or politics.'

'That's what happens when you're married to a powerful man. That's all they think about so, as I know only too well, you've just got to get used to it and do your own thing. Once I resigned myself to taking more of a back seat, I've been a lot happier. Believe me, there are worse situations in a marriage than having a husband preoccupied with his work.'

'I hardly get to see Matt these days,' Anna pointed out, 'his father seems to monopolise him totally.'

'Well, what do you expect when you spend all week in London?' Bella added unsympathetically.

'Mark, Louise and I go up to Northampton every weekend,' Anna protested. 'The kids love it up there but half the time Matt disappears off to the factory to see everything is running smoothly. It will probably get even worse now he's the chairman.'

'Well, you seem to me to have a pretty good life,' replied Bella reassuringly, 'and the children are so lovely. You must be getting a lot of enjoyment out of them.'

'Yes of course I am; it's just that I get a little bored at times stuck here by myself. I love London but I suppose that really I miss the Italian lifestyle. And you of course, Mamma,' she added.

'You're better off here for a while; I dread to think what is about to happen back home. Your father thinks the government is about to collapse and, between you and me, I know he is hoping it will.'

Anna spotted an empty seat next to Gina and moved quickly round the table for a chat. The two sisters rarely saw each other these days but still enjoyed exchanging confidences.

'What's happened to your boyfriend tonight, then?' Gina asked in a voice louder than Anna would have wished.

She glanced round the table furtively to check if anyone heard. 'If you mean David, he's got too much on the boil at the laboratory and couldn't get away. In any case, he doesn't like large parties. I sometimes get to see him at the weekends when he's not working.'

'So it's the same problem as you have with Matt. Perhaps you should find yourself something in London,' she added dismissively.

'I'm not like you,' Anna countered, 'changing men every month. Basically I love my family, but as you know, I've always had this thing about David.'

'I don't blame you for that. I remember at the wedding all the women were giving him the eye – including me.'

'Well, you can keep your eye off him, Gina. What really irritates me is not just that Matt is tied up so much with work – it's that he's allowed himself to get very unfit. I mean, you can see for yourself. He's looking very middle-aged and I don't want to get like that yet.'

'I'm afraid I had noticed, but you told me David is a keep-fit fanatic.'

'He's certainly the more fanciable at the moment,' Anna

confirmed. 'Now, tell me about your latest conquest. I'm sure I've seen him before at a fashion show in London.'

They were interrupted by some guests wishing to depart. The party was beginning to break up and Nina was busy sorting out the ladies' coats. It being a warm evening in late June, the men had arrived with no coats and were giving a helpful hand to the ladies. Gerald and Linda had reserved a room at The Ritz so that he could be available early the next day to deal with the press. They set off to catch the warm night air as it was only a short walk to the hotel. Gina and Andrea had a rendezvous with some younger friends and were dying to get away from the family environment to party elsewhere. A chauffeured car arrived to take Alberto and Carla back to the Italian Embassy

Philip, who was in no hurry to leave, decided to stay and have a nightcap with his brother. Paolo, who had clearly enjoyed the dinner to the full, remained in the drawing room with them, while Anna and her mother went to their bedrooms.

The three men could hardly have been more different. Matthew now had the burden of a million shareholders on his back. He slumped down heavily in an armchair. Paolo was already seated but appeared alert despite his heavy indulgence at the table. Being a politician he was always seeking an audience. Philip's only problem amounted to uncertainty about his next assignment. He had recently received an exceptional proposal which he wanted to discuss with Matthew; but not in front of Paolo.

'Hey Matt, you managed to keep that news pretty quiet,' remarked Philip.

'To be honest, it was a very sudden decision by Dad to quit,' replied Matthew. 'It certainly took the board by surprise. He only told me of his plans a few days ago.'

'Probably a tactical move not to give the rest of the board time to oppose his proposal of your taking over,' proffered Paolo, who was well versed in political manoeuvre. 'By the way, Philip, what's going on with the British Army today? I read that numbers are slowly dwindling despite the fact that more troops will be needed in Afghanistan for a long time.'

'I could even end up there again myself,' Philip answered. 'A lot of chaps out there are due to be relieved and our special training puts us back in line for another tour. I'm afraid the army is finding recruitment very difficult. After training, all the lads want an operational posting. They want action and not to sit around the barracks here. On the other hand, because of the adverse publicity over Iraq we can't persuade enough young chaps to sign up. So we have very few spare troops if there's an emergency.'

'But what about all the troubles Europe is having with the Russians at the moment?' Matthew queried. 'Aren't we going to need to strengthen NATO?'

'That's something we'll just have to worry about later; we certainly won't be able to offer anymore troops ourselves. In any case, it's time some of the other European nations made a bigger contribution. A lot of them are just loafing around in non-combat areas, maintaining a useless presence.'

'The Russians aren't causing any problems that I can see,' countered Paolo. 'It's the Americans who are threatening the Russian borders with Poland and causing eruptions elsewhere!' He turned to Matthew and changed the subject. 'Do you have any more news on your factory expansion yet, Matt?'

At this point Philip decided it was time to leave as he detested entering into any business discussions. He bade farewell to Paolo, and Matthew rose to see him to the door. The brothers' paths had taken very different routes since they were young but they had remained close. Philip was still fancy-free but the days of beer swilling at the rugby club and bawdy evenings together were distant memories now. They gave each other a brotherly hug and Philip went down the steps. He turned. 'You be careful now Matt,' he warned. 'Dad says he wouldn't trust that man any further than he could throw him. By the way, I wanted to have a chat with you and get your opinion on something important. I'll phone you over the weekend. Ciao.' Matthew waved farewell and went back inside.

Returning to his seat Matthew proceeded to answer Paolo's question. 'There is just no prospect of getting more space in the immediate vicinity. I think we should look seriously at your suggestion. Do you still believe we could do a good deal with Donati's in Turin?'

'I assume this is why your father decided it was time to retire,' Paolo observed. Like all politicians he gave himself a little extra time before answering the question.

'What he told the board was that he felt the company was moving into a new era and he believed it would be better served by a younger man,' countered Matthew. 'I know he is uncomfortable with the idea of opening up a factory outside the UK. He accepts it's probably a good idea, but doesn't want to be party to it, particularly if it could mean the loss of jobs here.'

'I am reliably informed that Donati's problems are insurmountable and he will have to sell,' said Paolo. 'My contacts assure me we are in the driving seat if you are ready. Being Italy, there are always a few palms that will need greasing, but I can take care of that. Will you be able to get board approval to move quickly?'

'Now that Dad has gone I would not expect any opposition,' replied Matthew. 'I've already sounded out some of the other directors. I'm going to be busy for a few days getting myself organised, but should be able to fly out to meet you at the end of next week, if that is convenient? The bank is all prepared to provide the necessary finance, despite the current credit squeeze.'

'Okay, I'll carry on with things from my end then.'

Realising the conversation was at a close the two men stood up, shook hands in agreement and Paolo went to find Bella.

Matthew walked over to the window and stared at the traffic that was still tearing round St James's Square. His mind wandered to his new position in life. Here he was, about to take over the reins of a large public company. He was confident they were about to perfect a drug that would be beneficial to hundreds of millions of people all round the world. The company and the family would become extremely rich and powerful. He would be the darling of the City. Or was it just a pipe dream?

He looked round the room, once again admiring Anna's taste. He spent little time in London as he preferred the country life, but tonight he felt totally at home.

As he returned to his armchair and stretched out his legs, a feeling of contentment mixed with apprehension overcame him. He was now the complete master of his own destiny. 'Nothing can possibly go wrong,' he assured himself.

2

Matthew and Anna were up early the next morning. Despite having an exhausting day ahead of him, Matthew was keen to have breakfast with the family before setting off to the factory. Mark and Louise, aged nine and seven, had managed to spend some time with their grandparents before dinner the previous evening. They already had a strong relationship with Gerald and Linda as they saw them regularly at weekends. By contrast, they found Paolo intimidating and were also inclined to avoid Bella, who smothered them in typical Italian style. They were busy gathering their books so that Matthew could drop them off at school on his way to the M1.

The company chauffeur arrived; he was solely at the disposal of the new chairman and he helped the children into the car with a mock salute.

'I suppose I'd better get going now and present myself to the staff,' said Matthew as he bade farewell to Anna with a hug. 'They will have seen the notices in the press by the time I arrive so let's hope I get a good reception.'

'Yes, good luck,' came the reply, 'and we'll see you at the weekend.'

Matthew waved goodbye and climbed into the front passenger seat. He would have preferred to drive himself but, from now on, that was not an option. The car came to a halt outside the private school; Mark and Louise jumped out and raced each other through the gates. Anna would normally have walked with them but after a tiring evening had taken the easy option.

Back at the house, Anna closed the front door and walked into the dining room where Paolo and Bella were sipping coffee. Matthew had informed her of the prospect of the company acquiring a factory in Turin and she was excited at the possibility of returning to her old haunts.

'I shall suggest to Matt that we sell or let the house in London,' she said to Bella, her mind already scheming about the next move. 'I could bring Mark and Louise out with me and they could continue their education in Turin. Their Italian is not good, but kids learn quickly and they would soon pick it up. Being fluent in two languages is a great asset.'

'That would be lovely,' replied Bella, 'and I shall be able to see so much more of you. We do miss you, you know. By the way, did you get a chance to mention to Gina how much her antics infuriate Papà?'

'I did try to say something discreetly, Mamma, but it just falls on deaf ears. She won't change and has no intention of trying. I'm afraid in that respect she's her father's daughter.'

Paolo, who up to then had kept out of the conversation, glared at his daughter. 'And what exactly do you mean by that?' he demanded.

'You know perfectly well what she means,' interjected Bella, coming to her daughter's rescue. 'When have you ever listened to anyone?'

Paolo decided he'd had enough of this irritating conversation and preferred silence over the breakfast table. He made his excuses and left the room, saying gruffly, 'Don't forget we have to be at Heathrow by ten-thirty. The car will be here in less than an hour.'

The two ladies watched him leave and relaxed. 'He does have an awful lot on his plate at the moment,' Bella said in his defence, 'and I worry he is taking on too much by himself. As I was saying last night, the economy is in freefall and he claims the government is totally incompetent to deal with the situation.'

'Oh well, I expect it will all sort itself out somehow,' replied Anna optimistically. She took no interest in politics and was always keen to avoid the subject.

Bella ignored her daughter's reluctance and continued, 'Papà says the financial situation in Italy is so serious that the collapse of the banking system is almost inevitable. What concerns me is that he is openly enjoying the government's discomfort. I'm not sure I want him taking on the problems at the moment. His blood pressure is not good, you know. He, of course, sees it as his big chance to take over. He has the unions behind him and a lot of support from the left all over Europe.'

'It's no use my saying anything, so just try to stay calm,' Anna replied. 'You probably won't be seeing much of him in any case. Better make sure you're ready to go – you know he gets bad-tempered if you keep him waiting.' Bella hurried out of the room, leaving Anna to contemplate what promised to be a lively few months ahead.

The factory gates opened to allow the chairman's black Jaguar saloon to glide noiselessly through. Matthew leaned over to release the lock but the chauffeur was there first. He held the door open and Matthew climbed out, realising that he had better get accustomed to this extra attention.

'Thank you, Tom,' he said with an amused smile, and this time waited while the door to the offices was opened to let him enter. The chauffeur, Tom Bailey, had been with his father for the past ten years and was as close to a friend as Gerald allowed any employee to get. He was a trusted confidant and had occasionally warned Gerald of impending problems with the workforce. Tom, a former policeman, had joined the company when an injury to his left leg whilst on duty had made life difficult in the force. He had originally expected to work in the security department but had seen the advantages of a sedentary existence to protect his damaged leg; an unnecessary limb in a car with automatic transmission.

'I won't be needing you any more today, Tom, so why don't you grab some food and take a break? When Dad rings to let me know his whereabouts I'll give you a shout and you can pick him up at the station.'

'Very good of you, sir,' replied Tom, 'and I hope you get the best of luck in there!'

As Matthew entered the office the staff looked up from their desks and a hush descended; someone started clapping and the whole place erupted. The news of the change of chairman had circulated fast, as had the news of his arrival. Matthew waited for the noise to subside a little before raising his hand.

'I suppose you would like me to say something,' he shouted, trying to make himself heard. Silence returned and Matthew continued, 'Thank you all for that kind reception; it is much appreciated. I would firstly like to pay tribute to my father, who has chaired this company for the last twenty-six years through both good and difficult times. During his tenure the company has gone from strength to strength and we have been able to increase the staff by over three hundred. As you can see we are now bursting at the seams. My father always had the welfare of his workforce as his main priority and your loyal support has been his reward. He will be here next week to say his farewells and I shall be arranging a proper send-off shortly. I hope that I can fill his place with the same confidence and enthusiasm; I will certainly try. This decision has come rather suddenly but I see no reason for making any immediate changes, so it will just be business as usual. Finally, I would humbly ask for your support whilst I strive to get to grips with my new job. So if you will now excuse me I think I have work to do,' he added with a smile. His plans with Paolo were not yet in the public domain.

Matthew's own office had all the trimmings of the modern executive. Wires ran in all directions and stand-by lights of various colours stared or winked at him. This was his home from home and the realisation that he would have to move hit him hard. The chairman's office was so different, with its antique furniture, plush carpet and heavy curtains. It was cosy but not practical in today's world; he would have to get it up to date without offending the previous incumbent. *I won't move until I'm ready*, he thought as he surveyed the pile of papers that surrounded the computer on the desk.

Matthew sat at his desk and pondered his first task. *I'd better go and have a word with Jane*, he decided, *she'll be wondering what her position is now*. He rose to leave but was intercepted by David at the door.

'Congrats and all that, Matt,' he said, pushing his way into the office and grabbing Matthew's hand. 'I certainly didn't see that coming yet. Did Anna have a lovely party last night? You're not too hung-over, I hope?'

Returning to his seat, Matthew waved David into a chair. 'Thanks, David. Yes, we had a super evening – you know, everything ran to order, no family rows, the political arguments didn't get out of hand, no ladies sick on the carpet. Dad caused a bit of a ripple when he announced his retirement, but all in all we had fun. So, how are things going in the lab?'

David sat back in the chair to relax and give the latest report. He was the same age as Matthew but had managed to retain a more youthful appearance. He was the son of Joseph and Becky Steinberg, a Jewish couple, now retired and living on the south coast. Joseph had been sent as a baby to Britain just before the outbreak of war to escape the Hitler regime. He had been brought up by wealthy relatives in north London and well educated. He never knew his parents who had died at the hands of the Nazis and this loss still haunted him. A trip to Cologne to see the old family home had only served to increase his angst. His marriage to Becky had helped to relieve his obsession with the past and when David came along a greater enthusiasm for life got into him. He and Becky were inclined to lead their lives through their son's achievements and were delighted when he won a place at Cambridge.

As Matthew waited for an answer he studied his old friend. David was a similar height but more slimly built. He had a handsome face with dark curly hair and thick eyebrows. His deep-brown eyes were intelligent and piercing. He had a strong jawline with a cleft chin and a winning smile. A white laboratory coat, almost a permanent fixture, disguised an athletic body.

'So far so good,' replied David. 'We are seeing no adverse reaction from the monkeys and all the tests so far are negative in that respect. The chemical is definitely getting into the bloodstream so it looks as if the new coating is the answer. Hopefully, we can press on with just the animals now. It's going to take a fair time yet before we can be sure it actually works this way. It certainly has with all the monkeys that were treated, and they're still not showing any signs of distress.'

'Fantastic news,' shouted Matthew, jumping out of his chair and slapping David on the shoulder. 'What sort of time scale could we be looking at?'

David waved Matthew back to his seat. He was not surprised at his friend's impatience. The two had first met at a staircase party at St John's College in Cambridge during their first term. Sharing similar sporting interests, they had become friends. Matthew had even persuaded David to join the college choir, despite the Christian influence of the repertoire. David was studying chemistry and graduated with a first-class honours degree. Matthew was taking a course in modern languages, but too much time spent attempting to win a rugby blue had left him struggling to get a third. The friendship had blossomed through university and they had kept in regular touch after graduating.

Their two lives quickly diverged as Matthew joined the family business and David, who had developed an interest in forensic medicine, went into the laboratories at the Wellcome business in Kent. David had become frustrated at his progress and, when he discovered a combination that had beneficial effects on blood clotting and atherosclerosis, he was anxious to develop it secretly under his own banner. He persuaded Matthew and Gerald to allow him the use of their laboratories on the understanding that if he developed the drug successfully, they would have the licence to manufacture. He was prepared to operate on a minimal allowance plus all expenses. As such he was not directly employed by Boston and Wood, but his personal connection with Matthew gave him full access to the factory.

'Hold on a bit,' responded David with a wry smile, 'we have a long wait yet to determine whether there will be any reaction with the rhesus monkeys. Then we will have to get authority from the Medical and Healthcare Regulatory Agency to dispense the pills. We are still at least a year away. The hardest task will be getting authority from the USFDA but, if and when we do, you can expect practically the whole world to follow,' he added confidently.

Matthew had not previously mentioned to David his expansion plans but felt it advisable now to seek his reactions. 'As you know, David, we just don't have the room here to increase production to the extent you will need if this drug materialises. I have looked around locally without success and now something has turned up which could make a lot of sense. Paolo is sure he can acquire a factory in Turin at minimal cost, that would be ideal in many ways for our requirements. We would need to spend a lot of money getting it up to our specifications, but once done there are some obvious benefits.'

'Oh yes, such as?' retorted David aggressively. This had come as a bombshell, and he couldn't see any 'obvious benefits'. 'We can't move all our research abroad, just like that.'

'The advantages are,' replied Matthew in a calm voice, intending to diffuse the atmosphere, 'that, firstly, we can get the factory for a song. Secondly, the workers out there come a lot cheaper. Thirdly, we won't have to disrupt the workforce here, who can continue uninterrupted with the existing output.'

'They don't sound good enough reasons to me. We should be looking to give more work to our own people. There has got to be somewhere we can find a suitable area to build on.'

'Don't think for one moment that I haven't been looking around. In any case, half the workers in this country are coming in from the Continent, so what's the difference? Another advantage that will interest you is that the Italians are less bothered about animal welfare and animal rights than we are. Your experiments won't be so threatened.'

David accepted that point. They had managed up till then to keep their animals in a remote farmhouse near West Haddon, a few miles to the north, and animal rights demonstrators had no knowledge to date of its existence. No experiments with animals took place at the factory and only a few trusted employees were aware of the farmhouse and its purpose.

'What's your timescale then?' he questioned Matthew. 'How long is all this going to take?'

'By the time we've acquired the place and got permission

to operate, it probably won't be much different from yours,' he replied. 'We don't have to rush things and we're not having to find too much up front.'

'Are you going to be in charge out there?' David asked, thinking about who he might have to work with.

'I will have to put a senior director out there to run the factory as I will need to stay here. You would of course be in charge of production. We can't have anything going wrong on the manufacturing side.'

'So what will happen to my laboratory and the animals?'

'No problem there – I promise you can have everything you want and take anyone you need with you.'

'And suppose I don't want to work in Italy?'

'David, look, this is a golden opportunity to turn the company into a truly international business that's known all round the world. Distribution from Italy will be quicker to most parts of the world. Anyway, once things have been running for a year or two you can always come back.'

'So you and I won't be working together then?'

'No, but I'll be making regular trips out, of course. Anna is already making overtures about moving back to her old home and taking Mark and Louise with her. She thinks it will do them good to spend some time at an Italian school.'

'So Anna is likely to go too,' said David thoughtfully.

'Well, that's about all I can say at the moment,' said Matthew, 'and please will you keep our conversation under your hat for the time being. It's not concrete yet and we don't want a lot of rumours flying around. I'd better go and see Jane now, but if you have any further thoughts or objections, just get back to me.' The two men left the office together. Matthew went in search of the secretary and David returned to his office in the laboratory.

Glancing at his watch to check that Anna would not have left to collect the children from school, David picked up his telephone. 'Hallo my lovely, it's me again,' he started clumsily. 'Has the headache gone now?' Without waiting for her response, he continued. 'I've just been talking to Matt, who wants me to go and live out in Turin if they acquire a factory there. He also tells me you want to take the family back there. Is that correct? You haven't mentioned it to me before.'

'Matt swore me to secrecy about the factory. I'm sorry, I've been dying to tell you, but I knew you would soon find out. You're not cross with me, are you?' she contrived to say in a plaintive voice.

'How could I ever be cross with you, Anna? I didn't particularly like the idea to begin with of working in Italy, but if you are thinking of moving that's a different matter. What were you ... oh damn, Alec is waving to me, I'd better go. I'll make sure I get away at the weekend and pop round to see you, cheerio.' He replaced the receiver and sat deep in thought for a moment before leaving to sort out his assistant.

Jane Healy got up from her chair, crossed the floor, and gave Matthew a hug and a kiss on both cheeks. She was in her early thirties and had been private secretary to the past chairman for the last eleven years. She was average height, with long blonde hair that covered her shoulders. She had retained an hourglass figure and a sexy walk that turned the heads of all the men. Matthew watched her return to her seat before speaking.

'Dad sends his love,' he said, watching for her reaction, which gave away nothing. 'I assume you have been wondering where we go from here. Well, so far as I'm concerned I would love you to stay as the chairman's secretary. That is, if you will have me,' he added.

Jane smiled, 'I'll have to think about it; I know it will be tougher working for you. Your father was such a sweetie.

I could read his every mood and we never had a cross word. I shall miss him, you know.'

'I've no doubt he'll miss you, too.' Matthew was not the envious type but he had always looked longingly at Jane. He had even found her devotion to Gerald a little irritating. Well, now she was going to be his secretary and that gave him a very smug feeling. Jane was more apprehensive.

'I've arranged a press conference for you at two-thirty this afternoon in the boardroom,' she continued, 'and I got in touch with your father after his meeting in the City this morning. Everything went okay but he mentioned a couple of points you need to prepare for; I'll get the details out for you before the meeting.'

Matthew had not bothered with a secretary before as he was perfectly able to type his own letters and keep his own diary. This had given him a large measure of independence. The tone of efficiency in Jane's voice woke him up to his new life. He belonged to everybody now; the secretary, the staff, the stock analysts, the shareholders, the press. He'd better get used to it!

Sunday arrived and with it an invitation to lunch at Gerald's manor house, situated along a private lane on the outskirts of Northampton. Matthew still loved the feel of the house he was brought up in, and was delighted to hear that Philip was able to join the gathering. Linda was especially pleased to get the whole family together. She had given the maid the day off. Anna and she could get the meal while the children were out riding and the men sorted out the world's problems. Gerald opened a bottle of champagne and the ladies assembled promptly on hearing the loud pop.

'I never thought it would feel so good. I woke up on Friday to realise I hadn't a care in the world; I've just passed them all over to Matt and, boy, what a relief! I thought of waiting till Matt was forty before handing over, but I believe now that I've got it just right. The family's interests should still be in safe hands.'

They all drank to that and the ladies returned with their refilled glasses to the kitchen.

'I'm glad you're here as well, Dad,' said Philip. 'There's something I was going to discuss with Matt, but I'd appreciate your opinion, too. The fact is, I've been approached by General Williams, Chief of Staff of the Armed Forces, to head up the British contingent for this new European Army. You've probably heard already that the French are very keen to set up an army based on a contribution of soldiers from all the EU members.'

'And how would you come in?' interrupted Matthew.

'Just hold on and I'll tell you as much as I can, but you must realise it is very embryonic at the moment. The idea is that each nation provides a minimum of fifteen hundred soldiers to the pool and training grounds will be set up. I gather France and Germany are prepared to offer more troops and the training grounds will probably be in those countries.'

'Sounds like an interesting project for you, Phil,' suggested Matthew with enthusiasm. 'Why have you been picked on?'

'General Williams thought it would be nice if someone from his old regiment took the post. He also liked my being a bachelor boy as there won't be much accommodation for women or wives in the initial stages.'

'So there won't be any female soldiers then?' enquired Gerald.

'The idea will be to keep life as simple as possible in the first instance. There will be enough complications bringing twenty-seven nationalities together. For a start, the language difficulties will be enormous.'

'Well, I think you should go for it, brother,' said Matthew. 'Just think – a Boston in charge of the European Army!'

'Steady on, Matt; I would only expect to be in command of the British forces, although I dare say they will suggest we also train the troops from some of the smaller states.'

'So who will be the commanding officer,' asked Gerald very suspiciously, 'and who the devil will have the authority to press the nuclear button?'

'That decision is a long way off, but it's not likely to be a Brit. Of course, the army commander would not have the power to do anything without the permission of the various heads of government.'

'Well, I still think you should take it,' interjected Matthew. 'We definitely need someone there at the start to keep an eye on what the French are scheming.'

Gerald was more circumspect. With age comes caution and he instinctively disliked the formation of any army; especially one that could have no obvious purpose.

'So you're talking about forty thousand soldiers in training for what?' said Gerald. 'I mean, what are you going to do with them after they have completed their training?'

'There's a lot of policing to do round the world that needs our expertise,' responded Philip, already using the possessive pronoun.

'I thought that's what the UN forces are supposed to be for,' retorted Gerald, 'and they are a bloody toothless bunch. Tell me where they've ever managed to get a situation under control; and I bet any EU force would be just as useless.'

'Okay Dad, I hear where you're coming from,' said Philip resignedly, wishing now he hadn't involved his father. It wasn't the response he had come for, but he always had a sneaking respect for Gerald's opinion.

'You don't have to take any notice of me, son,' said Gerald. 'I realise my views on so many things are getting out of date. That's one reason I decided to retire. I'm joining the grumpy old men; there's a whole army brigade of us,' he added with a smile.

'I'm behind you, Phil,' Matthew contributed. 'It could be a lot of fun, and what have you to lose? Another trip to Afghanistan, eh?' He suggested poignantly.

The sound of an old-fashioned gong called them to lunch and they set off for the dining room.

'I'd rather you didn't mention this to the girls,' said Philip, 'my involvement is very hush-hush at the moment.'

Two hungry children raced past them to the dining room and the family sat down to eat.

3

The following Thursday Matthew took the afternoon flight to Turin. He was sitting in the business class section, although, so far as he could make out, the seats were as cramped as anywhere else. He had left the factory in the more than capable hands of the deputy chairman, Peter Woolidge. Peter had been the deputy to Gerald for a long time but was nearing retirement age. Matthew wanted to use his experience for as long as possible before making any changes. He had received a call from Bella that morning with an offer to collect him at the airport. A friendly face is always welcome and he was soon on the road to the Medina residence.

'The flight arrived nicely on time,' said Bella just to make some conversation. 'Did you have a good journey?'

'Got a bit bumpy over the Alps but otherwise quite pleasant. A director of Fiat was sitting beside me and we had an interesting chat. He's extremely unhappy with the way the car market is going.'

'And how are Anna and the kids?' continued Bella, not wishing to get into a discussion on the problems of the motor industry. 'I'm looking forward to seeing them in the holidays.'

'They are looking forward to coming, especially as you've opened up the old house near Rome,' replied Matthew.

'We'll have to see about that. It's a matter of getting the pool operational or they'll get bored very quickly. I've told Paolo to get it fixed but he always has something else on his plate. Parliament's summer recess starts soon and I'm hoping he'll take a break.' Bella fumbled for the remote control and pointed it at the pair of iron gates at the entrance to the house. They opened with a clatter and the car crunch noisily over the gravel driveway. 'At least any burglars would have a job making a quiet entry,' she joked, as the car stopped and Matthew lifted out his suitcase and laptop.

The house had been in the possession of the Medina family for the past four generations. It was situated in the commune of Marentino to the east of Turin. The front door opened and Maria, the long-serving family maid appeared and offered to take Matthew's case. He was too embarrassed to accept as he was twice her size. Carrying his own case, he followed Maria to his allotted bedroom, while Bella spelt out her suggested plans for the evening.

'As you know, Paolo can't get here till tomorrow morning, so I thought I would book a table at Franco's for just the two of us and we can have a good natter. There's always a good atmosphere there and the food is always fresh.'

'That's fine with me,' responded Matthew rather more cheerfully than he felt. 'I'll have a shower and freshen up and it will be about time to go.' He closed the door and sat on the bed. He actually didn't mind too much having dinner with Bella alone. She said very little when Paolo was about but one could get much more information from her when he wasn't. Given freedom of speech, she wasn't always very discreet.

Unsurprisingly, Matthew was ready first and went into the lounge to await her arrival. He just loved the feel of the open aspect both within the room and the view from the picture windows that were pulled aside to allow the cool evening air to circulate. Facing the windows were a couple of sofas and an armchair in pale cream leather. These had been chosen to replace the cloth-covered furniture that had been badly discoloured by the children after swimming in the pool. The old oak furniture contrasted well with the expensive Carrara marble floor. A scattering of carpets and rugs from the East added brightness to the room, as did several paintings of Tuscan landscapes.

He walked out through the glass doors and looked out over the estate. There were about five acres in all, mainly comprising natural woodland. A garden had been laid out with a swimming pool on the right side. As the family were often away for long periods there were no flowers but bushes had been carefully chosen to provide colour for most of the year. He could see abelia and oleander in flower. Pittosporum and photinia were also in evidence, whilst jasmine and bignonia clung to the arches surrounding the patio. A couple of olive trees were overshadowed by a spreading albizia in full blossom.

Matthew heard the sound of high heels on the marble floor and retreated to the lounge. 'I like your new leather furniture,' he said warmly, 'I sat on it just now and it's very comfortable.'

'Well, it can easily be wiped over after the kids have dumped their oily wet bodies all over it,' replied Bella resignedly. 'The car's waiting, so if you're ready we can get going.'

Helping Bella into the taxi he couldn't help noticing how much effort she had made over her appearance. He had the courtesy to compliment her whilst wondering why she looked so much more radiant than at Anna's party. He came to the conclusion that she, like so many politicians' wives, preferred not to upstage their husbands in public. Those who did made themselves vulnerable to snide comments from the tabloids.

They were given a warm welcome by the proprietor and shown to a table on the side of the terrace overlooking a deep valley.

'This is Paolo's favourite table,' Bella said as a glass of Asti Spumante was automatically placed in front of each of them.

'I'm surprised Paolo comes to a restaurant named Franco's,' remarked Matthew mischievously, 'I would have thought it against his religion.'

It took Bella a few seconds to see the point. 'It obviously hasn't occurred to him. He certainly wouldn't be seen at a restaurant called Mussolini's,' she added with a smile.

The meal was as delicious as Bella had predicted and a shared bottle of Barolo loosened their tongues. She was anxious to find out what the family might do if the negotiations went ahead.

'I suppose you will all come out here to live,' she ventured. 'You could have the house here as we spend most of our time in Rome these days.'

'There is no way I would be able to live here,' countered Matthew. 'Our head office will always be in England and that's where I must remain. I know Anna has expressed a wish to come to Turin if we acquire the factory, but in many ways I would prefer to have her and the kids with me.' In fact, he had already seen the advantages of having the family away for a time while he consolidated himself in his new responsibilities. He was going to be working long hours. Nevertheless, he didn't want Bella organising their lives and changed the subject.

'How is Paolo faring as leader of the new socialist movement?' he asked. 'I get the impression that there is a strong move to the left in Italy at the moment.'

'You know that's how we met,' said Bella with a look of nostalgia, 'at a socialist rally at Milan University. Paolo, of course, was one of the speakers and I just fell for him immediately. He was so committed and intense and very good looking. Since then little has changed with him but I have lost that youthful enthusiasm and commitment. You might say I have grown a little weary of politics and now I am worrying about his future ambitions.'

'What do you mean by that?' asked Matthew, who was keen to find out as much as possible about Paolo's ambitions.

'He believes he can unite all the left-wing parties into one and take on this government, who are currently so unpopular. That worries me to hell; you know, of course, what happened to the last man who attempted to do the same.'

Matthew had no idea what she meant. 'No, what did happen?'

'Oh, a bit before your time I suppose. It would have been in the late seventies. A Christian Democrat named Aldo Moro tried to form an alliance of the left. When he attempted to include the communist party, he was kidnapped and eventually murdered by the Red Brigade. They were an extreme left-wing organisation who didn't want to see any democratic ideals introduced into their communist agenda. That's why I worry about Paolo.'

'That was a long time ago and things have changed a bit since then,' replied Matthew, putting a comforting hand over her arm. 'There aren't the extremists around today. I'm sure he's quite capable of looking after himself.'

'He's doing an awful lot of travelling, too. He only got back from Greece yesterday.'

'The socialists are also getting very strong there,' Matthew remarked. 'Is he expecting to get some support from them?'

'I think he was actually there to meet some Chinese. He is hoping to get some funding and if he went to China the press here would be asking all sorts of questions.'

'So he's hoping the Chinese will bankroll his campaign.'

Bella fell silent, suddenly realising she had said far too much. Matthew read the signs and quickly announced, 'I'll get the bill and we can go back and give Anna a ring.'

'No need for the bill, we have an account here. I'll sign it on the way out. Won't Anna be in bed by now?'

'Don't forget the hour's difference; she should still be up. She'll want to know we had a nice evening.'

Paolo arrived sharply the next morning just after nine o'clock. He had taken the early flight from Rome and joined the others for breakfast.

'I've arranged a couple of meetings for this morning,' he said as he finished his coffee, 'one with the bank and then on to the attorneys' office.'

'What is the latest information you have on Donati's problems?' Matthew probed.

'Look, the bank manager is an old friend and has kept me pretty well up to date with the crisis. He has perhaps confided more than he should but he is hoping to recoup some of the bank's money if a buyer can be found. It appears that Donati has been borrowing large sums of money against the collateral value of his company shares. The business of making components for the motor manufacturers has hit rock bottom and the share price has gone to next to nothing. The factory is closing down with the loss of nearly a thousand jobs and the bank will be left holding a bundle of worthless shares.'

'But what's happened to the money Donati borrowed?'

'The bank is still trying to find out but Silvestre, the manager, tells me that he has no doubt a major scandal is about to materialise. I don't think they expect to make any recovery from him.'

'So how are we going to play this?'

'Better leave the negotiations with me for a start and if you're not happy we can always get back later. After we've seen the latest balance sheet, which will almost certainly reveal that the company has no worthwhile assets, other than the ground the factory stands on, I shall make this suggestion. I believe we are talking about thirty acres of land, which, without planning permission for housing, is worth no more than six hundred thousand euros. We can argue the site will be expensive to clear and offer to pay three hundred and fifty. They won't accept that immediately but anything under half a million will be a good deal. What do you think?'

'Nice to see you thinking like a capitalist,' mocked Matthew, 'but surely they'll prefer to hang on to the property and hope to get planning permission for housing or the like?'

'Not a hope in hell, Matt. For a start, I'm the local member of parliament and the city council is strongly socialist. With the loss of jobs the bank will be looking for a way out that pleases the community. It is a local bank and already under fire from the press for reckless loans that have helped Donati to bankrupt his company. A headline that they have arranged for the set-up of a new factory to save a lot of jobs could also save a lot of faces.'

Paolo omitted to mention that he would make sure he got all the headlines and all the credit for the employment prospects. Why else would he be spending his precious time away from Rome?

The meeting with the bankers went completely to plan and Matthew left feeling he had a very good prospect. After all, if the new drug turned out as anticipated, the costs of setting up in Italy would be pennies against the huge potential profits. Alternatively, if the drug was a failure, they would not have lost an amount the company could not reasonably afford.

'So will Donati himself be in this meeting?' asked Matthew as they made their way over to the attorneys' office.

'Donati has disappeared for the moment but no doubt the bank will catch up with him shortly. Of course, there's always the possibility that one of the workers has found him and, as the mafia would say, he is already sleeping with the fishes. But we don't need to deal with him; bankruptcy procedures are well on the way. The attorneys are basically co-ordinating matters between the bank and the other shareholders. They are looking to get the best deal for all concerned, but as there's very little money in this deal they will be looking for a quick fix. I'm going to suggest we appoint them to look after your interests after the negotiations; that will get them to speed up the deal!'

The attorneys were totally in Paolo's pocket and he could get any deal speeded up whenever he wanted. By making them Matthew's legal representatives he would be kept informed of all of Boston and Wood's activities in Italy.

As at the bank earlier that morning, Paolo dominated the discussions. Matthew sat back quietly as Paolo spelt out the deal that had been agreed at the bank. The attorneys listened patiently, though the bank had no doubt already been on to them with the details.

'The other shareholders are not going to be happy when we tell them the shares are worth less than ten per cent of their value a few months ago. We can't guarantee their reaction, Signor Medina,' pointed out Aldo Borgia, the senior partner.

'Well, the bank is the biggest shareholder now and they are happy with the deal,' Paolo responded. 'So the others will just have to like it or lump it.'

'Happy is hardly the word, signor, but we obviously realise that in the end the shareholders have no option than to go along with the bank.'

'We can leave you to sort it out when we give you the word. Obviously Mr Boston will have to report to his board first before anything can be finalised,' Paolo pointed out.

'Of course, and we are looking forward to a long

association with you and your company, sir,' said Aldo Borgia, turning to Matthew with a contented smile.

When the meeting concluded, Paolo was also beaming. As they walked out of the building he turned to Matthew and said, 'How about having some lunch? I gather you went to Franco's for dinner last night, so I thought we could eat at some little place I know in the old town.'

'That's fine with me,' Matthew readily agreed. 'I thought the meetings would take much longer, but you just seemed to steamroll the bank and attorney into quick submission.

'Ah, here we are,' announced Paolo soon after. 'I think you'll like this place, they do some delicious scampi.'

The two men were led to a table, with Paolo as usual getting obsequious attention. Two Martinis arrived and they sat down to review the morning's events.

'Thanks for all your efforts this morning, Paolo, I didn't think that every part would go so smoothly.'

'I had done quite a bit of bargaining beforehand, and, you may have noticed, when I get my teeth into something I don't take "No" for an answer. Anyway, I am deeply concerned about the unemployment in this region, and I intend to take the problem on head first. The workers are right behind me and we're going to take back the initiative from these capitalist bastards. They have left the country bankrupt and now even our prime minister is being accused of corrupt practices.'

'But it is not just Italy that is in a financial mess,' Matthew reminded him. 'As Downing Street keeps insisting, it's a global problem.'

'Your government is in the same denial, but few are in as bad a financial mess as Italy. Our debt is now well over a hundred per cent of our gross national product. We and other eurozone countries are being absolutely impoverished by the richer states to the north. Greece is in an even worse situation than we are, and Spain and Portugal are in desperate straits. I can tell you the socialist parties all over Europe are amassing and waiting to take over. And they will.'

'I gather you've just got back from Greece.'

Paolo deliberately ignored the remark. 'I'm going to do it, you know, Matt. I'm going to get all the left-wing parties together and take on this government at the next election. And I will win.'

'And when is the next election due; have you got enough time to get organised?'

'Constitutionally, not for over three years, but Italian governments are seldom able to last the full term. With the current political turmoil, we can put a lot of pressure on them. I have already secured the support of the federation of left-wing parties called Sinistra Arcobaleno, or the Rainbow Left as you would know it. They did very badly at the last election and want me to take over the consortium. I actually owe my seat in the house to the union of the Left Party.

'I don't think I can win without the support of the Democratic Party, which is also to the left. As it happens I have just been approached by them to see whether there is a way forward to unite all the parties. This is what frightens Bella, but it is a wonderful chance for us to get rid of a corrupt capitalist government. With a united left it won't be long before we win a vote of no confidence in the government. President Carlo Salvatore will be forced to call for another election, which we will win; I'm supremely confident about the result.'

'My spies tell me you're certainly the man with all the political clout and charisma, so I guess one day I shall have a prime minister for a father-in-law. One good reason, I suppose, for maintaining a business here. Presumably there won't be any difficulty getting planning permission to demolish the old buildings and put up a modern factory?'

42

'Absolutely none, you can assure your board that it will be a very smooth ride. By the way, what's the latest regarding Steinberg's experiments?'

'David is growing more confident by the day. He really believes he has the formula right now and it's just a matter of waiting. It all takes time and patience, which I must admit is not one of my virtues.'

'Nor one of mine,' confirmed Paolo, 'but this will certainly be well worth waiting for. You obviously realise that if this drug hits the world stage, your company could be right up there with the big boys; AstraZeneca, GlaxoSmithKline and the like.'

'In some ways it's quite a frightening thought,' replied Matthew, 'but it will be a fantastic challenge.'

'What about Steinberg?' queried Paolo. 'Is he happy with the plans?'

'He's only just been told and his initial reaction was not favourable. He was concerned for the workers in England, but when I assured him that the factory there would still be in full operation he seemed to accept the plan. I don't think he minds where he works so long as he has a first class laboratory. He's not at all interested in financial detail.'

'Anna tells me his politics are somewhat to the left of Lenin. Is that correct? If so, he and I should get on famously.'

'He was certainly a member of the communist students association at Cambridge but fortunately didn't follow in the footsteps of Burgess and Maclean and others. I don't think he is particularly active now, but he did recently give a talk to the staff association. That was more to do with a cause célèbre he has regarding the behaviour of the banks.'

'He'll find plenty of people to agree with him about them at the moment; even, I believe, among the most ardent capitalists.'

'David never ceases reminding me that Karl Marx always said capitalism would inevitably destroy itself one day. It has eventually to implode and take the whole financial world with it. His attack on the banking system is that it is grossly weighted against the poor. It is they who, at the end of the day, are being called upon to provide the cash to bail them out.'

'And that is exactly what I am saying to my supporters. It is the working class people who are being laid off work. It is they who have been enticed into borrowing money they will almost never be able to afford to repay. And they are the ones who will doubtless bear the brunt of taxation imposed to reduce government debt.'

'You can't altogether blame the banks for lending money. Those individuals who have been accepting credit greater than their ability to repay are just as culpable.'

'I'll accept that argument up to a point,' retorted Paolo, 'but to wave money in front of men who have very little puts them in a situation they find impossible to resist. That's just human nature. The governments of the rich nations around the world should never have allowed it to happen.'

'They couldn't really have stopped it; it's freedom of choice that makes the world go round today. People don't want to be told by politicians how to run their lives.'

Paolo was beginning to warm up and he had just the man in front of him for a heated discussion. This capitalist had no choice but to listen to him.

'I've been doing a bit of research into banking history; do you realise that in England over three hundred years ago there was a law known as the Law of Usury, which prohibited moneylenders from charging excessive interest? Some fool had the law finally repealed in 1854 when sterling was still the world's standard currency, and it seems nobody has had the common sense to reintroduce it. In my view, it is criminal for the banks to be charging several times the lending rates set by the Bank of England or the European Central Bank.'

'But you can't really expect the trading banks to give unsecured credit without a high premium.'

'Look, Matt – I recently read of a major credit card company charging in excess of forty per cent APR to borrowers, when even the current London Interbank Borrowing Rate is at an all time low. This is tantamount to theft, and as usual it will be taken from the poor. How on earth can you expect poorer people ever to get out of debt when they are being screwed to the floorboards? I tell you that I, along with the socialist movement across Europe, am going to stop this attack on the proletariat. Jurisdiction over the banking system will be a major part of the agenda for my manifesto.'

'So you are going to stop poorer people from borrowing money. They won't be very happy about that, will they?'

'It's a matter of stopping the banks from lending money to people willy-nilly without first determining their circumstances. If they are made to lend with a ceiling at, say, no higher than double the base rate, they will have to be much more cautious. This will enforce a discipline that would prevent another global banking disaster in the future and not put poor people into unmanageable debt.'

'You're a brave man to take on the financial tycoons, but I understand where you are coming from. Nevertheless, I don't think the right-wing parties would actually oppose your views as much as you might think. Everybody wants to see the bankers taken to task.'

'Maybe, but they wouldn't have the balls to take them on. Believe me, unless we get a complete change of thinking, the next recession will be even worse. That is, if we ever get out of this one!'

'So, Mr Prime Minister Elect, what are your plans for the banking world?' Matthew enquired with a cynical smile.

'That you will have to wait to see,' Paolo replied, 'and don't go asking Anna because I won't be telling her either. Not that she's at all interested.'

'I shall watch this space with great anticipation, sir. Anyway, thanks again for sparing me your time today. It all went very well. Let me sort out the bill this time; Bella insisted on paying yesterday.'

'Okay, then we'll drive back to the house, pick up Bella and we can all go to the airport together. I'll let her know we're on our way.'

4

It had taken Matthew nearly five months to get his new office up to his own requirements. He had waited for the dust to settle on the changeover before having the antique furniture removed. Some of it had gone to his father's home to furnish a study for Gerald to escape into. The chairman's office was now fully equipped with state-of-the-art electronics and Matthew at last felt at home there.

There was a tap on the door and Jane entered without waiting for a response. She had several documents for Matthew to sign and sat herself down in a chair beside his desk.

'David Steinberg was trying to get in touch this morning while you were at that meeting. You have a pretty free afternoon so I suggested he comes over from the laboratory about three o'clock; if that's all right with you.'

'That's fine. He's probably spent the morning with his monkeys, so I hope he'll have had a change of clothing. Last time he came he stank like a polecat and I had to spray my office after he left. Hopefully he will have some positive news for us.'

'I got the impression he had something important to say as he was even more abrupt than usual. His communication skills need a lot of polishing. Don't ever let the press loose on him or we shall all be out of a job. He's lovely, though,' she added as an afterthought.

Having got the signatures she required, Jane got up from her seat and walked to the door. Matthew watched her perfectly shaped legs disappear and let his mind wander for a minute. What sort of relationship had she really had with his father? Did they have an affair, as he had always suspected? If so, they had managed to keep it very quiet. Nobody on the staff had ever suggested to him that anything had been going on. But then, perhaps he was the last person they would tell. He looked across at the empty space where a large sofa had previously resided. *That might be able to tell a few stories*, he mused. *I wonder if that's why Dad insisted on moving it to his new study?* His reflections were interrupted by a ring on the telephone with confirmation that David would be joining him directly after lunch.

'And I told him to smarten himself up,' Jane said triumphantly, though she knew that in reality it had gone straight over the top of David's head.

David burst in through the door without bothering to knock. He walked straight over to the desk and held out his hand. Matthew got up a little irritated but shook hands and offered him a chair. David had taken no notice of Jane's request but fortunately had not been at the animal farm that morning.

'Well?' Matthew enquired apprehensively. 'I hope there aren't any problems.'

'Absolutely not, Matt, in fact I think I can now say that the experiments are completed and we can apply to have the drug fully registered. The authorities have been kept up to date as much as possible, except for anything too sensitive. We should be able to call them in to substantiate our methods and verify all the findings. We're there but it is likely to take another six months at least to get full approval and certification. Will that coincide with the rebuilding of the factory in Italy?'

Matthew allowed himself a few minutes to sit back and take everything in. This had been a long haul and the stakes for winning the race to produce this drug had been high. He had put a lot of faith in his old friend to come up trumps but had so often had reservations. The experiment costs had been greater than anticipated and had required more loans from the bank. This had been seen as unhealthy by some City analysts and the company's share price was still a little depressed. Some directors had become a little nervous and he had not had the easiest of rides at the last few board meetings. Nevertheless, his confidence in the project had allowed him to persuade them to purchase the factory in Italy in advance of completion.

A huge feeling of relief rather than exultation came over him as he went over to give David a massive hug. The two men stood locked together for some time before Matthew broke away and stood looking admiringly at his chum.

'I always knew you'd do it!' he burst out, after he had recovered enough energy to speak. 'David, I love you. I can't wait to tell the board and all those doubting Thomases. Let's get Jane in and tell her the news. Then I'll phone Dad and tell him we're celebrating tonight. Make sure he's got some champagne on ice. Pity Anna won't be able to get up here before the weekend.'

'Why not save the celebrations till the weekend? I'm sure Anna wouldn't want to miss out and she's always shown enormous interest in our progress.'

'Perhaps you're right, I need to calm down, take this more slowly and be a bit more professional. The whole matter is going to require some very careful planning. I shall need to have a board meeting as soon as possible. Let's get Jane in and see what she can arrange. I'm sorry, David, but I've got to tell somebody.'

'I'll leave you then; perhaps we could have a drink together this evening. Just the two of us; just like old times.'

'Good idea. I'll see you later then. Have a think about exactly what we should announce to the press – it mustn't be too technical or they'll make a mess of the reporting.'

Matthew called Jane back to his office and gave her the news. For the first time since the occasion of his chairmanship announcement, she walked over and gave him a warm hug. And this time, he thought, she seemed much more reluctant to pull away.

A little unsure of himself and his feelings, he returned to his desk. 'How quickly do you think you could get a board meeting organised for me?'

'I'll email all of them and hopefully get a meeting arranged later next week.'

'No, don't do that; anyone can read an email. Contact them personally and impress on them the urgency without giving too much away. I'm insisting they are available for no later than next Thursday. Tell them, also, that under no circumstances should they buy any company shares. I want no scandals about insider trading.'

'Okay, Matt, I'll get on with it straight away,' she replied, but lingered at the door for a moment before giving him a smile and leaving the room.

Picking up the phone, Matthew dialled his parents' home and heard his mother's voice answering.

'Hi, Mother, it's only me. How are you? I'm just ringing to find out what you're doing this weekend,' he continued, without waiting for her answer. 'I'm thinking of arranging a little party.'

'What's this in aid of?' she probed. 'So far as I know your father and I have nothing special on.'

He proudly told her the news. 'So David and I thought we should have a little celebration at the weekend,' Matthew concluded.

'This is wonderful news, Matt, your father will be thrilled,' exclaimed Linda joyously. 'How many people do you expect to ask?'

'There will be Peter Woolidge and Jane, and probably a couple of other directors. David and his chief assistant will certainly be there and of course the family. Probably there won't be any more than a dozen; we're having to keep it under wraps till after the board meeting. I'm so excited I just had to let off a bit of steam with you both and a few close friends.'

'Better have it here then; I've got much more time than Anna to organise a party. I'll pass you over to Dad now – see you Saturday.'

Matthew talked to Gerald and received a few tips on dealing with the press. The company had previously pioneered a few drugs but nothing with the same potential as this. Some City analysts had recently given poor reviews on the company, stating that their debt position was worse than other companies in the pharmaceutical sector. This had led to a depressed share price, leaving the company vulnerable to a potential takeover. All that was about to change and those ignorant analysts were going to have red faces.

Jack Edwards, the marketing director, watched patiently as his champagne flute was being filled. He had joined the company late in life, having spent twenty years in the RAF. He had lost none of his squadron leader exuberance and still sported a bushy moustache. A ruddy complexion portrayed his bon viveur lifestyle and a loud voice identified his whereabouts.

'You always know where Jack is,' Gerald use to say, 'but he could sell ice cubes to the Eskimos. That's why we employ him.'

Jack moved over to talk with Matthew, who was in conversation with his mother. Having noticed Anna deep in conversation with David, Linda decided to join them. Their conversation changed rather abruptly to an embarrassed silence, so Linda hurriedly interjected, 'David, as you know, my knowledge of chemistry and medicine combined adds up to about minus fifty. I'd like you to explain to me in words of one syllable exactly what this new drug is capable of doing.'

'Actually, it's all really very simple, Mrs Boston.'

'"Actually" has four syllables,' Linda pointed out with a smile, 'and I'd much rather you called me Linda.'

'Let's all sit down while I go through it and I promise to keep it simple. Basically, it is a drug that we believe will drastically reduce the risk of a heart attack if taken regularly from, say, the age of forty.'

'I understood a while back that you had developed the formula. Why has it taken so long to get to this stage?'

'Because, before our recent experiments, the only way possible to administer the drug was by self injection into a vein. We know from experience that nobody will do that on a regular daily basis.'

'But people with diabetes have to inject themselves with insulin all the time,' interrupted Anna.

'Yes, but that is a necessary curative action. They have no alternative. What we have here is a preventative medicine and people have to be encouraged to take it. They won't do it if they have to use a needle. The only way forward was to find a method of producing the chemical in the form of a pill, so it is easy to take.'

'And why has that been so difficult?' Linda enquired.

'The problem is that some of the ingredients are protein and get destroyed by the stomach acids, and that makes the drug impotent. What we have been working on is a method of getting the drug past the stomach. I can assure you it has proved no mean task, but we are now sure we have found the answer.'

'Are we allowed to know all about it?'

'The straight answer to that is "No, it must be kept secret, at least until all the tees have been crossed at the patent office." But I can tell you roughly how it works. We have managed to coat the pill with a mixture of various compounds that will take the pill past the stomach intact but break up afterwards. The drug is then released into the small intestine and absorbed into the bloodstream. The arteries in that region are invariably free of clogging, so we get good circulation.'

'But don't modern statins have the same effect?'

'Yes, to some extent they do and this drug has some of the same ideas incorporated. However, it is further advanced and will completely remove any possibility of the arteries clogging up, provided it is taken regularly. In other words, it will be far more efficacious than statins.'

'So what are you calling it?'

'Well, we haven't got full agreement among ourselves yet, but the likely name will be Bosteinex 1. That will ensure it is not linked with other drugs like the statins; it is a completely new product.'

'Aha, I see – a mixture of Boston and Steinberg. I'm certainly impressed, David. If this really works, you will have achieved something for mankind as important as the discoveries of scientists like Fleming or Pasteur. Quite frankly, I'm struggling to get my mind round it.'

'It's not quite the super drug penicillin is,' David said with a grin, 'but it will certainly help to keep the hospital beds clear for other ailments. We believe there is another great advantage to the drug in that it appears to slowly dissolve the fatty acids that might have already built up in the arteries. So it could also act as a cure as well as prevention. We have not been able to test this fully yet as we really need human guinea pigs. It would take far too long to build up arterial blockages in the monkeys to test them. If the drug is approved, we shall find out quite quickly enough once humans are taking it on a regular basis.'

'Well, I'm impressed too,' said Anna, 'I don't think Matt has been giving me the full story. No wonder you will need to expand the factory.'

At that moment Philip came through the door and Linda leaped to her feet. 'We're so glad you could make it, darling. Come along and have a drink. Matthew, give Philip a glass. How were the roads; did you have a difficult journey? You're looking very tired; have you been overdoing it?'

'Slow down, Mother,' Philip replied jovially, 'no need to worry about me, I'm fine. Just dying to hear about all the latest developments.' He walked over with Linda to join Matthew and Gerald.

'I think you know everybody here so I won't bother to take you round,' Gerald said, shaking Philip's hand. 'Have you seen the kids yet?'

'Yes, they jumped on me in the hall when I arrived. I think they've gone back to the television room.' He peered round to make sure he recognised everyone in the room and groaned inwardly on seeing Jack Edwards in conversation with Jane. The two men rarely saw eye to eye on military matters and Jack would no doubt have plenty to say on hearing Philip's own news.

The other director in the room was Alasdair Brodie, the company secretary. He had joined the company in that capacity nearly ten years ago, but was still the most recent executive director appointed. He noticed Jane finishing a call on her mobile and went to find out whether the proposed meeting was now complete. Alasdair was tall and thin, with an angular nose and receding hair. He was in his early fifties, with an arrogant appearance and an educated Edinburgh accent. He was not Matthew's favourite member of staff, but worked hard, and had been very supportive of his father.

'Are we all okay for Wednesday, then?' he enquired.

'That was the last one,' Jane replied, 'I had the usual problem with the two non-execs but they've agreed to drop whatever they were supposedly doing and will be there.'

Alasdair took Jane to a quiet corner to check if she had been discreet regarding a conversation he had had with her a couple of weeks ago. He had been worried about the drop in the share price. He was sounding her out as to whether other directors might feel the same, and if so, whether there might be a move to change the chairman. He was now extremely worried that this action might be seen as disloyal.

Jane eased his mind by confirming that she had not betrayed his trust, and had no intention of doing so. She pointed out that, in any case, his thoughts would not now receive any support. There was something about him that made her feel uncomfortable, and she knew Matthew shared her concern. She was smug in the knowledge she now had something on him that she could store away for the future. As anyone in the business world will tell you; power doesn't come from 'what you know' but from 'who you know'. But the most power comes from 'what you know about who you know'.

Having filled his glass, Jack decided to catch up on the gossip with his old chairman. He appeared just as Gerald was asking Philip what the latest news was regarding the European Army.

'We've decided to go ahead, Dad, and support the French and German initiative. We will be sending a British force for the new army. It was only agreed yesterday by the MOD and the papers will be full of it after the minister announces the details to the House tomorrow. I see it as a big challenge.'

'So you will be commanding our forces. My heartiest congratulations, Philip, even though that won't change my own misgivings. Still, Matt's on your side and you both have plenty to celebrate. Your mother and I are extremely proud of the two of you.'

'I had heard rumours that this was being mooted,' Jack interjected, 'but I didn't realise you were in the thick of it. Frankly, I share your father's misgivings.'

'I assumed you would,' Philip replied bitterly, 'how often do we agree on military strategy?'

'Exactly, and nothing you say will make me believe this a sensible idea. This is going to infuriate the Americans, which is probably precisely what the French intend. We shouldn't be party to it.'

'You can't stop progress, Jack. We are moving inexorably towards a federal Europe and it will need its own military force. You realise that France and Germany already have a combined army brigade over five thousand strong. They have had for twenty years, since Mitterrand was president. Why should you expect Britain to stay out?'

'Isn't that the chap who had an army of illegitimate children?' Gerald chipped in, hoping to lighten the conversation.

'Because this move will inevitably destroy NATO,' Jack almost shouted, ignoring Gerald. 'If the Yanks perceive that Europe is channelling its military resources into a separate army, they will be tempted to just pull out completely. And if you think Europe is capable of defending itself without American support, you are crazy!'

'But we can't and shouldn't rely on the Americans forever. Life moves on; Europe combined is now richer and potentially stronger than the United States. If we get ourselves properly organised, we could be a force even the Yanks would have to respect.'

'You must be mad if you think we can rely on the French and Germans to defend us. They won't even do their fair share in Afghanistan. They are putting caveats on their own troops' deployment to prevent them going into combat.

They are just a bunch of cowards. Personally, I'd rather rely on the Americans; wouldn't you?'

'I can see we're poles apart again, Jack, so we'll just have to wait and see who's got it right.' He turned to his father, 'Don't forget that Grandpa used to say that before the war Europe was more worried about the rising power of the Far East than about the antics of Adolf Hitler. What I believe he referred to as the Yellow Peril. Now look at the financial and military strength of that part of the world today; Europe should not leave itself unprotected.'

'I don't agree Philip, and I'm sorry to hear you are taking up such an important role in this new army. Mark my words, this is a move you will live to regret.'

Matthew decided he'd heard the same argument before from Gerald and moved over to where Anna and David were still talking. Linda was watching them with some consternation. She had mentioned earlier that she knew nothing about chemistry, but her feminine instincts told her there was definitely some between David and her daughter-in-law.

'Do I get the impression you won't be joining me and the kids in Turin for half term next week, Matt?' Anna enquired. 'David tells me you're having a board meeting.'

'Jane is trying to arrange one for next Wednesday. Unfortunately, I have to inform the board and have an agreed strategy before all this leaks out to the press. On Thursday the press will have it so I shall have to be around to answer their business editors. I might be able to catch a flight that evening and join you for a long weekend.'

Anna feigned a sigh and continued in an offhand manner, 'David says he would love to see how the factory is progressing. I thought it might be a good idea if he comes whilst we're there, so he can stay at the house and I can show him around Turin.'

'I would really like to see the laboratory area,' David added. 'I have only seen the plans but it would be useful to get a full impression on the spot.'

'I thought he could come down with me on Monday if he's not needed for the press meeting,' Anna suggested.

'Matt knows I avoid the press like the plague.'

'I think it makes sense,' said Matthew, 'and I'll try to join you on Thursday or Friday. We can all have a good time.'

'I suggest you come back with me to London Sunday night, David, and we can fly out together on Monday. I'll get Jane to arrange a ticket for you.' Anna left to find Jane and inform her of the arrangements. Jack joined the two men.

'You should make sure you enjoy the board meeting next week, chairman. If I were you, I'd arrive a little late to savour the applause. David, you and your assistant should take a month off in the sunshine and get some colour back in your cheeks. Working half the night has left you a little pale.'

'You're the one who will be expected to work half the night now, Jack. Marketing the drug will take some doing,' said David. 'It might even keep you off the booze for a while.'

'It would take more than a world beating drug to do that,' Matthew added mischievously.

'Perhaps I'd better have another one then,' Jack said gruffly and wandered off in search of the champagne bottle.

The evening drifted to a close after Gerald had made his habitual speech.

'I wish he wouldn't insist on saying something every time we have a little party,' said Matthew. 'It's so embarrassing; especially when it concerns me or Philip.'

'Well, he does it so nicely and he means well, so just humour him. He's a kind man,' said Anna. 'Oh David, before you go, I'll get Tom to pick you up with the car around five tomorrow, so have your case ready.'

David left a little unsteady on his feet. He hardly touched a drop these days, but in future he thought he might find more time away from the laboratory to enjoy some of his old habits.

Anna was hanging on to Mark and Louise as they left the airport in Turin. David was struggling with the cases as no trolley had been available. The taxi rank was fifty metres along the sidewalk and they eased their way past other harassed travellers. Anna gave instructions to the cab driver and they set off for the family home.

'I want Daddy to be here,' Louise whined, 'he always comes with us at half term.'

'He's hoping to get here on Thursday, darling, so you'll see him then. Anyway, Uncle David is staying with us. We'll all have a lovely time.'

Mark pulled a face in the back of the car. He had never known Uncle David to be much fun. He always seemed very distant. David perceived their disappointment and turned his head.

'Your mother's right, we can have lots of fun. We can play in the garden and go on outings, and you can choose whatever you like,' David said, trying to get on to their wavelength. It didn't come easily to a man whose head was generally absorbed in chemical equations.

The journey by road to the house in Marentino was 20 kilometres, but took less than half an hour on a route that avoided the city centre.

David had not visited this part of Italy before and had enjoyed the ride through the countryside. He now eased himself into the villa and immediately felt at home. Maybe it could be very pleasant living out here for a while, he thought to himself.

'Are you expecting your parents this week?' he asked Anna.

'Mamma wants to see the children, but can't get here before the weekend. God knows whether Papà will make it.'

'I hope he does, I would like to see your father again. I find him quite fascinating and we got on well last time. So you've just got me to amuse you till Matt arrives.'

Anna smiled. 'I'll just have to put up with it.' She put her arm round his back and gave a squeeze. David instinctively knew he should pull away; this was his best friend's wife. But he didn't. Their eyes met; he gave her a quick kiss on the cheek and picked up his case. Anna walked on ahead and directed him to his bedroom.

'This room has a terrace on to the garden, an en suite bathroom and a double bed, so you shouldn't be cramped. I'll leave you to change while I sort out Mark and Louise. They are on the next floor and have their own rooms these days.' David sat down thoughtfully on the corner of the bed with some trepidation. His attraction to Anna had started years ago when he had been best man at the wedding. How was his conscience going to cope with this situation?

David slowly unpacked, had a shower, and returned to the sitting room. By that time Anna had everything arranged.

'I've organised a babysitter for tonight,' she informed him. We are going to have dinner in town and Freddy Lucca, the works' manager, is joining us.' David didn't know whether to be disappointed or relieved by the intrusion. 'He's going to give you a full tour of the factory tomorrow. He speaks perfect English.'

'I have been taking Italian lessons, you know. I ought to make sure I get a bit of practice this week.'

'I can help you there, *caro*. We'll speak Italian at mealtimes with the kids. It will help them, too, as they may be going to school over here.'

'*D'accordo*,' replied David, 'and there will obviously be plenty of ways you can help if you come to live here, too.'

As promised over dinner, Freddy Lucca arrived early the next morning to take David to the factory. At Anna's request they had avoided talking shop, so there was plenty to discuss now. Matthew had advised David that, in reality, Freddy knew almost nothing of the real plans. He had been led to assume that Boston and Wood were going to move their entire operation to Italy, that they would, in other words, be closing the factory in England. This deception had been necessary to avoid revealing the existence of the new drug.

'So how far on with the building are we?' David asked. 'Do you have a completion date yet?'

'The shell is there already; we are now waiting on your requirements for the internal fittings.'

'You should be getting those very shortly now. What do you think, then, about another six months?'

'Could be less, depending on how complicated your specifications are. Shouldn't be more than six, but things have a habit of being late in Italy,' he added apologetically.

'Not just in Italy, I can assure you – with the building trade that problem is universal. The good news is the chairman says I can have everything I want, so get your pencil ready. I am, of course, only here to discuss the laboratory, but I intend having everything right up to date; state of the art.'

'I'll take you to the area designated for the lab and you can work out how you want the various divisions laid out. I gather you are expecting to have a zoo.'

'Hardly a zoo,' replied David laughing, 'but we will be keeping animals. They need to be kept well apart from the lab, with separate sanitation and high security.'

Freddy showed David round the entire new factory buildings, ending up with the laboratory. They spent most of the day there discussing the layout until David was satisfied he had the most suitable plans. By the time Freddy dropped him back at the villa his mind was in a whirl.

'Did you have a nice day at the office, *caro*?' Anna asked mockingly.

'I'm a bit out of my depth when it comes to building specifications, but he and I think we're mostly on the right lines. My God, I could do with a drink! By the way, where are Mark and Louise?'

'I took them over to Aunt Rita's house; that's my mother's sister. She's soppier with them than Bella is, and they asked if they could have a sleepover. I jumped at the chance. So I thought we would have a peaceful evening here and I'll rustle up something from the kitchen.'

'Sounds fine to me; shall I pour a couple of drinks? Gin and tonic for you as well?'

'Yes please; I've got some fresh penne here and some veal escallops, will that do?'

'My absolute favourite,' replied David, stretching the truth a little. 'What wine do you think we should have?'

'Pop down to Papà's cellar and you choose something. I believe he's got some lovely old reds down there,' she added, by way of a hint.

The warmth from the food and wine enabled them to stroll out on to the terrace without feeling the chill. A number of spotlights lit up the trees and a crescent moon was visible occasionally between passing clouds.

'Won't it be lovely when the leaves are back on the trees?' Anna sighed, slipping a hand inside David's. 'I can't say I enjoy the winter.'

'And by the spring,' he replied, squeezing her hand, 'we could both be living out here.'

'I think Matt is now in favour of my bringing the family here,' Anna said, but then regretted mentioning his name when David released his grip on her hand momentarily. She moved closer and rested her head against his shoulder. The couple stood there pensively, looking at the illuminated trees and feeling the cool breeze brush their cheeks.

David suddenly turned to face her and she felt his eyes slowly penetrating her mind. She returned his gaze unflinchingly. He engulfed her in his arms and they stood locked together for several minutes before kissing passionately. He lifted her gently from the terrace and walked towards his bedroom. Anna offered no resistance; after all, wasn't this what she had planned? She was still kissing his neck as he eased along the corridor and into the bedroom.

David lowered her carefully on to the bed and removed her shoes before lying down beside her. Anna began to unbutton his shirt while he fumbled for the zip on the back of her dress. Neither of them spoke while their consciences were put aside. She helped him with her bra before sliding her hand inside his briefs. Easing them carefully over his erection, she pushed them towards his ankles before moving her hand slowly up the inside of his thigh.

David was now running his tongue over her nipples and she relaxed back to take full enjoyment from the sensation. Her breathing was getting deeper as she felt his hand moving firmly between her legs, making her back arch. She climbed on to him impetuously and bent forward to lick his face. She felt him penetrate her and they both groaned in ecstasy. Their breathing reached a climax and they fell slowly apart.

Anna ran her fingers through the hair on his chest and

then over the fresh stubble on his chin. 'Perhaps next time we can take it a bit slower,' she said, turning to see his reaction.

David stayed silent while he tried to clear the guilt from his mind. 'I'm sorry,' was all he could bring himself to say.

The next morning Anna was a mother again. 'I promised the children we would take them to the mountains today,' she remarked as she arrived with fresh croissants from the kitchen. 'We can pick them up at Rita's and go on from there.'

'I've decided to go back before Matthew arrives tomorrow,' David announced, 'I really need to check out the animals.'

Anna understood. 'There's a flight early in the morning. I'll phone through and book you a seat. We can have one more night together.'

David nodded his agreement, finished his coffee and went to get dressed.

5

It had taken eight months and the arrival of summer before Bosteinex 1 was finally approved by the MRHA. The factory was ready to start production. David and his team were fully installed and the necessary workforce employed. Approval from the European Medicines Agency and the American authorities was expected shortly as no obvious snags had come to light during the final testing. Once the factory moved to full production a larger workforce would be required.

When David had moved to join Matthew at Boston and Wood, there had been a tacit agreement between them regarding the ownership of the drug if it were perfected. The consensus at the time was that David would be the sole owner of the patent and Boston and Wood would have the exclusive right of manufacture. This agreement had never been put into a proper contract, but when the patent had been applied for, it had been done just in David's name.

Matthew now felt that this was not a very satisfactory situation as it left his company vulnerable to a change of circumstances. He decided to make an offer for the patent and had a lawyer draw up proposed details. He was now flying every weekend to Turin to be with his family and arranged to meet David at the villa. He had agreed with the board that he could make an offer David 'could not afford to refuse'.

The two men were sitting comfortably in a room with large French windows overlooking the garden. Matthew explained his concerns for the future and laid out the details of the legal agreement he had brought with him. David listened calmly at first but, as Matthew proceeded, he became more and more agitated.

'I have taken advice,' Matthew explained, 'and everyone thinks it is not advisable for the company not to own the patent. Since we are going to do the production it makes sense that we are in control of all aspects. I have spoken with the board and they agree I should make you an offer to purchase the patent.'

'But that is not what we agreed when I allowed you to talk me into joining you.'

'Come on David, you were just as keen to branch out. You felt you were being far too restricted where you were.'

'Well, maybe, but I know what we decided when I joined you. It was quite clear that I would retain all rights to the patent.'

'And I'm not disputing that; it's just that it makes more sense for the company to be in complete charge. We just didn't think it out properly in the first instance. I must say my father mentioned at the time that things were a bit loose, but I argued then that we trusted one another implicitly.'

'I'm quite happy to have a proper agreement on this, Matt, but the patent is mine and I want to keep it that way.'

'I think you should at least hear what the company is prepared to offer.'

David shrugged his shoulders irritably and sat back to allow Matthew to continue.

'We are prepared to give you fifty million pounds spread over two years.' He waited while the number sank in. 'That will make you a very rich man and you will be free to continue your research in any way you like.'

'Look, Matt, I'm quite happy to sign an agreement that

gives you licence to manufacture the drug for as long as you like, but I want to retain the patent; full stop!'

Matthew leaned back in his chair and the two men eyed one another. *The first one to flinch is a coward*, thought Matt, and he suppressed a grin. But he knew they had never looked at each other in such an aggressive way before. He decided on one more roll of the dice.

'I could probably persuade the board to increase the offer, say up to sixty or seventy million.'

'I'm a chemist, Matt, not a bloody banker; that's my interest and my life. Can't you get it into your thick head I don't want your bloody money? I'm quite happy with the arrangement we have. I'll just stick to taking a percentage of the profits as we agreed. As far as I'm concerned you can tear up that agreement and stick it right up your arse. Tell that to the board.'

'All right, David, we'll leave it there then,' he replied, not wishing the meeting to get out of hand. He decided, however to get all the ends tied up. 'So there's no way I can persuade you to part with the patent, but you are happy to give us a long licence?'

'That's right; that's what we always assumed, and I, personally, have no desire to change anything. If you get the lawyer to draw up an agreement along those lines, I'll be happy to sign it.'

Nothing more was said. David got out of his chair, walked over to Matthew, patted him roughly on the shoulder and left the room.

Matthew was left to contemplate the encounter. The board would be disappointed with his failure, although one or two directors had considered even the lower offer too generous. They at least might be relieved. In any case, as far as he was concerned, he had the next best thing. A long-term agreement with priority on renewal was enough to satisfy the stock market. He was going back with everything he needed, if not everything he wanted. But he was saddened that his relationship with his old friend had become tarnished.

David found Anna in the kitchen and exploded. 'Your husband has just tried to bribe me into parting with the patent. I will never do that.'

'It sounds like you told him so,' she replied. 'I hope you two haven't been having a row.'

Ignoring her remarks, he continued, 'I got the impression he was definitely trying to get rid of me. You don't think he suspects anything, do you?' he added, lowering his voice.

'He knows absolutely nothing, *caro*. I wouldn't suppose for one minute he was trying to get rid of you. I expect he's under pressure to keep the shareholders happy as usual. Don't take it personally. If I know Matt, it was purely a business matter.'

'Well, I'm glad I'm just a chemist – the business world is too cut-throat for me.' He stole a piece of freshly made pizza and hurried away.

Anna started to chase him but he was too quick. She thought back to a conversation David had been having with Paolo the previous week. Wasn't that also about the patent? Her father had certainly been giving him some advice. If he had it would more likely have been to Paolo's advantage than David's. She dismissed it from her mind; it was the men's affair.

It had taken some time for Anna to persuade Matthew into her taking Mark and Louise to live in Italy. The main opposition to the move came from Gerald and Linda, who understandably were upset at getting less chance in future of seeing their grandchildren. At Matthew's insistence, Anna had agreed that they would, at age thirteen, go to an English boarding school to get the better all-round education and sports facilities on offer there. As he pointed out, they were first and foremost English even if they would also be able to benefit from dual nationality.

Paolo had ensured that the factory opened to a full political fanfare. He now wasted no time in furthering his political ambitions. His face appeared almost daily in the left-wing newspapers and the right wing knew they had plenty of reasons to be alarmed. Paolo Medina was a charismatic leader and had enormous support not only in Italy, but all around Europe.

The political scenario in Italy and, indeed, in all the Mediterranean countries in the eurozone, was chaotic. The European Central Bank had been putting in vast sums of money to support the governments of the Mediterranean zone states. Domestic debt was at an unprecedented high, initially causing depression, but now producing rampant inflation. Unemployment was running at levels never experienced before, even including the great depression of 1930. Tourism, upon which their economies relied heavily, had dwindled to a trickle. They were being easily undercut in the export markets for both manufactured goods and food products. Wine sales were now almost confined to the domestic market as previous importers looked to the New World for better value. These weaker European countries, including the Eastern bloc, were, not without reason, making accusations of protectionism against the major economies. For all but the richest nations, the euro currency had become a complete disaster.

It came as no surprise when the Democratic Left party, despite their misgivings about the extremists, finally decided to invite Paolo to lead a combined opposition to the government. The newspapers had been predicting this probability for several months. He set about his new responsibilities with relish and started to make his plans for the downfall of the government.

Paolo's first act was to seek the financial funds to launch his campaign. With the deepening recession that was not going to be any easy task. The socialist parties of Spain and Greece were unable to provide any meaningful contribution but he was surprised to get some substantial offers from Germany, France and the Netherlands. The United Kingdom had gone into recession under a socialist government which had been thrown out of office. There were no funds left in the Labour Party's coffers to help him.

With the majority of the press now firmly behind him, Paolo decided he would get little opposition to seeking political and financial assistance from China. He flew to Beijing where he received a warm welcome. Although the economic situation there was little better than that of the West, it would suit China to support a major political rift in the European Union. He procured the promises of the financial support he desperately needed to launch his campaign. Part of the agreement with the Chinese was that he must attempt and eventually succeed in uniting the socialist parties of the major European countries. This, he confidently assured them, could be done.

Paolo's ambitions made him blind to the political advantages the Chinese might seek to achieve in Europe from this alliance. He returned to Italy and in his own words, 'Set about the destruction of the capitalist society.'

The groundswell of opinion against their respective governments was growing stronger even in northern Europe. Marches and demonstrations by the workers were also becoming weekly events in the Mediterranean bloc. Paolo was in touch with all the socialist factions around Europe and attempting to incite them to revolution.

In France, persistent rioting by ethnic minorities over poverty and maltreatment was giving the police and security services a permanent nightmare. In Germany, unemployed workers were in regular conflict with the police, who were also having to deal with an upsurge in support for the neo-Nazis over immigrant workers. There were now regular clashes between the two factions. The Netherlands was experiencing the same problems.

The socialists had at last found a champion. He would lead them out of the capitalist stranglehold that had suffocated them for the past sixty years. Left-wing parties had disintegrated over the years, but the cause had not gone away. They would all unite under Paolo Medina and destroy capitalism.

The broad equivalent of MI6 in France is known as the Direction de la Surveillance du Territoire (DST). This secret service agency has offices in Levallois-Perret, just outside the Paris city boundary. The offices are situated in a modern building that is also occupied by the Renseignements Généraux (RG), an agency that deals mainly with internal subversion and terrorism. The two agencies are known to be tribally opposed and mutually suspicious. The idea of joining the two agencies under one roof had come from the very top, but mutual collaboration was still to be manifested. They continued to spy on each other as a matter of habit.

The supreme head of the DST was Baron Henri de Courcy. His whole demeanour screamed aristocracy. He was tall, heavily built, but without an ounce of spare flesh. His expensive suit, bought in London's Saville Row, fitted impeccably and, unusually for these days, he wore a stiff detachable collar. Although in his late fifties there was no sign of grey in his light brown hair.

The Baron was finishing a conversation with one of his agents when his secretary announced the arrival of Albert Von Meissen. He suggested that she wait until the agent had got out of sight before bringing Von Meissen into the room.

Von Meissen was the Baron's counterpart in the German

secret service, the Bundesnachrichtendienst, known as the BND. He was also a burly man but, unlike the Baron, had allowed himself to become grossly overweight. His head was shaven and his blue eyes hid behind thick horn-rimmed glasses. The crumpled suit he was wearing had seen better days and would no longer button at the waist. Despite his slovenly appearance, he was constantly on the alert.

'Ah, Albert, lovely to see you again, and thanks for coming so quickly. I invited you here so you could see our new offices. Hope you didn't mind making the trip.'

'Not at all; I get out very rarely these days, so you gave me an excuse. Now, what is it you want that cannot wait?'

De Courcy instinctively glanced at the door to assure himself it was tightly closed. 'I have been talking at great length recently to Monsieur le President, who is getting paranoid about the left-wing insurgents. I'm not just speaking about the damage being done by rioters. Demonstrations fuelled by foreign infiltrators are getting out of hand in both our countries. He has a fear that anarchists are controlling much of this subversion and the whole continent could come under the threat of communism. I know he has been speaking to your Chancellor about his concerns.'

'I'm not as close to the Chancellor as you are to your President, but the concerns are being well broadcast by all the media. You may have noticed that in Germany it is not just about foreign infiltration. We have, in addition to the communists, some very active neo-Nazis and the Baader–Meinhof Group is rearing its ugly head again. Are you suggesting there is something we could do about it?'

'I have been giving the matter a great deal of thought and I believe there could be a solution. There is one man who seems to be at the forefront of all this unrest. The President has made several hints lately about the dangers of letting him loose all over the continent. Let us just say I know when to take a hint.'

'I assume you are talking about Paolo Medina.'

'Quite so,' replied the Baron, nodding his head with great deliberation. 'If we could get rid of him, I believe the whole socialist impetus would be halted. He's nothing but a red revolutionary and if you look back in history such men always leave a trail of death and misery behind them. Look at Lenin and Castro and even Mugabe today. These sort of men need to be stopped before they get too powerful.'

'If you mean what I think you mean, then I will have to take this away and give it a lot of consideration. I assume your President agrees with this idea.'

'I haven't mentioned it to him; nor would I. It is much better he knows nothing. He wouldn't be able to give consent and any action we take could embarrass him. It's better he's kept completely in the dark.'

'How many people have you discussed this plan with already?'

'Apart from you and me, only the agent I would trust to carry out the mission. I have been discussing the feasibility with him and, in his view, the sooner we do something the better.'

'Why is that?'

'Because, as leader of the opposition in Italy at the moment, Medina doesn't get the same level of security enjoyed by the prime minister. Also, to achieve his ambitions he is subjecting himself to a lot of exposure. There's bound to be a good opportunity.'

'I take the point, but I obviously can't give you an answer immediately. I shall have to sleep on it,' said Von Meissen nervously. 'I must say, from the urgency in your voice, I was expecting an important discussion, but this has come as quite a shock. I'll get over it in a couple of days and get back to you with an answer. I may have to talk to the Chancellor before I can come to a decision.'

'I'd rather you didn't do that without contacting me first,' the Baron objected. 'We would need a change of tactics. If it is any comfort I can assure you the Chancellor shares my President's opinions. If you feel you cannot make a decision on your own I quite appreciate your position; but the fewer people who are in the know about this the better.'

'How many people will be involved?'

'I think we can initially keep it down to four. That would be you and me, plus the two agents who will perform the operation. I was about to come round to this point. The agent I mean to employ is Pierre Lavalle and I have already been talking to him.'

Von Meissen raised his eyebrows at this. 'I know his reputation well. That gives me a little more confidence.'

'The thing is, he has specifically asked that one of your agents works with him. I understand he is known as The Rook.'

'That will be Fritz Vogel. Well, he couldn't have made a better choice.' Von Meissen was aware, nevertheless, that by involving one of his agents, he was being deliberately reeled deeper into the plot.

'I believe the two worked together in Kosovo a while ago.'

'Don't mention Kosovo to me, that was a big embarrassment,' said Von Meissen, shaking his head. 'One of my agents is still the prime suspect in the murder of the chief of the armed forces there.'

'Vogel is ex-Stasi, isn't he?' the Baron enquired. 'You're certain he's one hundred per cent trustworthy?'

'Absolutely; we've taken on some of the old East German agents, who were first class. They were exceptionally well trained; but look, I haven't agreed to anything yet.'

De Courcy decided he could play his trump card. 'I hate saying this to you, Albert, but there is no doubt that if a certain individual had been taken out seventy odd years ago, a huge number of lives would have been saved.'

Albert said nothing for a minute while he allowed the point to sink in. Not wishing to be reminded of that period in his nation's history, he changed the subject. 'Obviously you decided not to speak to Stephen Johns at MI6.'

'I was tempted, but we really need to keep this to the smallest number possible. I don't think in this instance the Brits would be opposed, but why take the chance. You know, of course, Medina has strong family links in England.'

'Quite right, better to keep them out of it. In any case, my sources tell me MI6 are already keeping a close watch on him.'

'That's my information too, so I hope they don't end up getting in the way.'

'Okay, I'll let you know what I think as soon as possible. I won't take up your kind offer for lunch if you don't mind. It is probably better we're not seen together in public; so I'll take the next flight back to Munich.'

'Thanks for coming at such short notice. My secretary will show you to the door so we're not even seen together in private,' the Baron added with a grin.

When he had departed, the Baron sat down to review the conversation. Towards the end, he thought, Von Meissen had been warming to the idea. He felt confident the response would come in the affirmative.

It took a full week before the Baron received the phone call from Germany he'd been waiting for so anxiously.

'Von Meissen here. Are you alone? Is the line I'm on safe at your end?'

'Good to hear from you at last, Albert. Yes I'm on my own and this line is perfectly safe, even from the RG. I have it checked every morning. You never know these days who is trying to tap in.'

'Right then, listen to what I have to say,' Von Meissen began. 'It took a couple of days to get The Rook back here from an overseas assignment. I have been questioning him hard on his opinion regarding the potential success of this operation. I also wanted him to be able to assure me that there could be no comeback on either of our agencies.'

'I doubt anyone could give that assurance,' interrupted the baron.

'Quite so, but this is what he thinks will happen after the assassination.'

'Hold on a minute, Albert, are you in fact telling me that you are agreeing to this plan?'

'Well, yes, I'm prepared to go along with it if you think The Rook is right in his assertions.'

'And what exactly are those?' the baron wondered.

'He's quite certain that whatever happens we could get the blame pinned on the Mafia. As you know they detest the communists even more than we do. So who else would attempt an assassination in Italy?'

'I think he's absolutely right; the Mafia would make the perfect scapegoats,' the Baron concurred. 'I'll have a word with Lavalle and see how we can best incriminate them.'

'With them in the frame I can't see how we could possibly come under suspicion.'

'So I take it that is a YES, then, is it?'

'We are with you, but God help us if it goes wrong. Like you I've decided not to mention it to higher authority. It's better for them if they know nothing.'

'We can get things moving then?'

'Yes, I've taken The Rook off of his assignment and told him to report to your office tomorrow, if that is all right with you.'

76

'As I said before, the sooner the better. By the way, we are giving the operation the code word SHERGAR.'

'Right; that's a strange title, how do you spell it?'

The Baron spelled it out. He was a horse-racing fanatic and Shergar was an exceptionally fast Irish stallion that had won him a lot of money, so he'd always had a soft spot for him. Unfortunately, the horse was kidnapped, supposedly by the IRA, and killed. At the time there was huge outrage as he was worth millions.

'Well, hopefully it will bring both of us luck. I doubt we can swing this assassination on the IRA, though,' said Von Meissen with a chuckle.

'We'll keep in touch via our agents then,' said the baron. 'I'll only contact you if something very urgent crops up.'

'Okay, I'll leave it all in your capable hands. Au revoir and the best of luck.'

'Auf Wiedersehen, Albert, and just keep your fingers crossed.' He replaced the receiver, picked it back up and asked Pierre Lavalle to come to his office.

'We are on, Lavalle,' said the Baron, 'I've just had confirmation from Germany.'

'I thought they would agree; The Rook was very enthusiastic when I had a chat with him.'

'So you know the plan will be to make it look like a Mafia killing. How difficult will that be?'

'Shouldn't be difficult at all – there are a few obvious ways.'

'So you'll just leave a pointer or two at the scene.'

'Certainly not; that would be more likely to arouse suspicion. We'll just use a typical Mafia method and leave the rest for the media to speculate. I doubt they'll even need prompting.'

'All right then, I'll just leave you to make plans. I won't need to hear from you any more until you are ready. By the way, The Rook is arriving here tomorrow so you can get straight down to it. Nothing else matters, do you hear?'

Pierre Lavalle left the office with a very satisfied expression. He hated the communists and this was going to be the most pleasurable task he'd undertaken so far in his murderous little life.

6

In the heart of the city of Siena lies the Piazza del Campo, considered by many as the most beautiful square in Italy. The fan-shaped piazza is surrounded by tall medieval buildings on the higher part, from where the clientele of the surrounding cafes can gain a full perspective. The lower, southern flank is dominated by the beautiful Palazzo Pubblico, built in the early thirteenth century. To the side of this building, the striking Torre del Mangia rises high to over three hundred feet.

On most days students and tourists are seen sitting lazily around the Fonte Gaia fountain watching an active but peaceful scene as the locals hurry about their business. On two special days each year the atmosphere changes when the Palio, the famous horse race around the square, attracts a tumultuous crowd. On these occasions the square is packed with excited, rowdy contestants and their supporters. Heated exchanges, not always good natured, escalate as vast sums of money change hands when the results are announced.

On this particular day in late September an expectant crowd was gathering for a different reason. A rumour had circulated that Riccardo Orvetti, the mega star of Italian football, was going to launch the latest model of the Lamborghini Murciélago. The gleaming car stood, cordoned off for protection, in the centre of the square. The men in the crowd were passing their eyes admiringly over the sleek lines and imagining the awesome roar and pace generated by its V12 engine. The ladies were dreaming of speeding through country lanes, their hair trailing loose, with (depending on their age) Brad Pitt or Robert Redford behind the wheel.

Cables ran across the paving from several large vans parked on the edge of the square. Technicians were running, seemingly in all directions, to get the lighting organised. Cameramen were shouting their instructions to the technicians. Managers were shouting instructions to the cameramen. The complete chaos was keeping the good-humoured crowd amused.

At around eleven o'clock a buzz of excitement went round the piazza, sending the pigeons flying for the safety of the rooftops. The cafes around the top end of the piazza suddenly emptied as people left their seats to get a better view. There was spontaneous applause as Rico, accompanied by a glamorous model, eased his way through the crowd, which was being held back by security guards. The couple waited for their instructions from the organiser before taking up their positions.

The Lamborghini was a powder blue colour in which the surrounding buildings were reflected by the morning sunlight. The seats and interior trim were in an ivory shade. Rico was being positioned by the driver's door and the cameramen were moving in. He was wearing an ivory-coloured shirt that showed off his deeply tanned arms and face. His beautifully tailored light-blue trousers had matching shoes and leather belt. He stood slightly under six feet tall, but a handsome face surrounded by long curly black hair made him immediately conspicuous. At twenty-six years of age, he was a model of physical fitness.

'Rico scored another two goals for Roma last weekend,' a spectator whispered to his wife. She tried to appear suitably impressed, and replied. 'You know who that model is with him, don't you?' The man tried to think but finally shook his head. 'I'm pretty certain that's Gina Medina – Paolo Medina's daughter.'

With Rico seated behind the wheel and Gina draped over the nearside wing, the cameras were flashing continuously. She was wearing an ivory-coloured dress with a pale blue trim to match the colour of the car. The design of the dress left a great deal of leg and cleavage on display. The couple were moved around for various poses, smiling pretentiously for the cameras, and trying hard not to show their boredom with the whole procedure.

Some heckling had already started among the crowd, which had eventually begun to get restless. 'Well proportioned for a communist's daughter, ain't she?' one wag shouted. 'Hey, Rico, in that outfit you should be playing for Argentina,' cried another. 'I wouldn't mind scoring a few times with her,' caused a ripple of amusement.

The couple were relieved when the experts were satisfied they had sufficient photographic material for the promotion. At over €300,000 the car would take some hard selling, even though they had received a promising number of advance orders. When the official photographers had packed away their equipment, the paparazzi pushed their way to the front. The security guards led the couple past the fountain to the inside of a cafe where champagne was being passed around.

Rico was in training and had one quick glass. Gina was looking forward to a bit of a party but changed her mind when Rico asked her how she was returning to Rome.

'The promoters provided a chauffeur driven car to get me here, so I assume it is still waiting.'

'Why not let me take you back and we can stop off for some lunch on the way?'

'I think that's a lovely idea,' Gina replied, trying to appear nonchalant.

'I'll tell them to dismiss your driver, then, and if you don't mind, I'd quite like to leave as soon as you're ready.'

'We can go now then,' said Gina, placing her half empty

glass on the table. 'Anyway, I find that drinking at this time of day can give me a headache.'

They left the cafe and were besieged again by the paparazzi and surrounded by security as Rico made his way casually towards the Lamborghini.

'We are not going in that, are we?' Gina asked, putting her hand to her hair in a futile gesture of keeping it in place.

'Your hair might get a bit roughed up', Rico teased, 'but we'll have lost the photographers by then.' He helped her into the car and stood for the cameras again, flashing his white teeth. Climbing into the driver's seat, he started the engine and gave the crowd a full blast of the engine; they responded with a loud cheer. They were waved enthusiastically out of the piazza, accompanied by the exaggerated gesticulations of the local police.

'The paparazzi won't follow us in the car. Since that awful tragedy in the Paris underpass, we have a tacit arrangement with them not to chase after us.'

'So, have you bought the car or is it just on loan for the day?' Gina enquired.

'Neither of those,' replied Rico, 'They have given it to me; or rather, it is my fee for promoting the beast.'

Gina, who had previously been quite content with the €20,000 offered her, suddenly felt a little undervalued. She consoled herself with the fresh cooling air in her face and the anticipation of an interesting lunch. She had not previously met Rico officially, but had attended the same function a few weeks before. She had noticed him watching her, and would have liked to make contact. On that occasion they had both had a companion with them and no opportunity had arisen.

Rico headed southwards from Siena towards Rome but pulled off the main road in the direction of a village called Casciano. 'There is a discreet little restaurant up in the hills where I'm known and there will be no fuss,' he said. Gina nodded her head in approval; she was in the mood to agree to anything.

He turned into the car park and reversed the car under a mimosa tree to shelter from the sun. Recognising and expecting his guests, the proprietor rushed out and helped Gina alight from the car.

'Your table is ready, signor,' he greeted Rico, letting slip to Gina that Rico had planned the lunch before the invitation. 'Follow me,' he said, leading them into a private corner.

The restaurant was spacious and opened out on to a large terrace with panoramic views. The wooden tables were covered with pale yellow tablecloths with dark-blue scalloped edging. The floor of both the interior and patio was laid out with metre-square ceramic tiles of white with an intricate royal blue pattern.

Since it was too windy to sit on the terrace, the few diners were seated inside the restaurant. In a corner diagonally opposite, three ladies were talking and laughing noisily. They stopped for a short while when Gina and Rico appeared, but quickly resumed their chatter. Near the sliding glass doors, closed to keep out the wind, sat a distinguished looking older man holding the hand of a young lady who may, euphemistically speaking, have been his niece. In the centre of the restaurant, two smartly dressed men and a lady were holding what appeared to be a business conversation.

The proprietor, Vito Mascagni, accompanied by a waiter in casual attire, came to the table. Rico ordered two freshly squeezed lemon juices and the waiter hurried away.

'I have some beautiful fresh soles brought over from the Adriatic coast today, Signor Rico.'

'Do you know I was hoping you might have; I had some last time I was here and they were absolutely delicious.'

Gina nodded her approval and Rico ordered some salad and rice to go with the fish.

'No antipasti, Rico?' asked Vito. He looked at Gina, who shook her head.

'We'll just have that for a start, Vito. Maybe a little light dessert later if we feel like it. And no wine, thank you, just a bottle of San Pellegrino.'

'Si signor,' said Vito crisply, and went to inform the chef.

Rico turned to Gina. 'I asked specially for you to be the model to accompany me today,' he said with a broad smile.

Gina returned the smile. 'That was very kind of you, I didn't realise you knew me.'

'That's the point – I didn't, but I saw you recently, as the song goes, across a crowded room. I thought: I would love to get to know that girl.'

'I saw you, too, but there were too many admirers around you.'

'The agency said they had difficulty contacting you, so I thought you may not be available.'

'I have been abroad in Africa; I only got back last week.'

'Were you taking a safari holiday?'

'Unfortunately not; I was doing work for a charity. A while ago my father was asked to be a patron of the National Society for the Blind. He didn't want to get involved and persuaded me to take it on. Of course, it suited him to have the Medina name on the list of patrons without doing anything himself. As it happens, I have got thoroughly involved with the work of the charity, and I'm loving it. I hadn't understood before, the satisfaction one can get out of helping others.'

'So what were you doing in Africa?'

'An offshoot of the charity arranges clinical work in Uganda. The majority of blindness there comes from malnutrition and cataracts, both of which can be cured just with the help of money. Did you know you can have a cataract removed there for as little as ten euros? And if we can get the funds to feed the poor population better, there need be very little blindness. Most of it is just a matter of proper organisation. I went out there to see the money was being used properly. There is always corruption, if you're not careful, and the money ends up in the hands of the wrong people.'

Rico became pensive. *This lady has a heart*, he thought to himself. She wasn't like the countless, publicity-seeking, selfish bitches that followed him around.

'My grandfather is blind,' Rico eventually admitted ruefully. 'He was caught in a bombing raid by the Americans during the war. And he was fighting for the partisans. He's still very bitter, but I suppose you could say that he survived.'

'We still deal with a lot of war victims; I'm amazed at how resilient and courageous they are.'

'It's no fun being bombed by your own side. My grandfather told me it was well-known joke that, when the British bombed, the Germans hid, and when the Germans bombed, the British hid. But when the Americans bombed everybody hid. He prefers not to talk about it any more.'

'Doesn't your grandfather get any help from the NSB?'

'No, he's too independent, but my grandmother is still alive and very fit. She looks after him. I send a car to take him and several other blind people to the stadium every week, whether Roma or Lazio are playing. They love the atmosphere and we have a man giving them a commentary on the match. It's ironic to think they probably have the best seats in the house. After the match they are taken to a bar near the directors' box and given a drink. They get a chance to discuss the game, often with some of the players, before being taken home. It is a lovely outing for them every week and they grumble like the devil when the season finishes,' Rico added with a grin.

'Well, don't forget to tell them we are here to help at any time.' Gina was warming even more to this man. She liked the compassionate side of him and the fact they both had a common interest. Not many people understand or care about the agonies of the blind. 'You still haven't told me anything about yourself,' she added enquiringly.

'There is not a lot to tell, really. Football has completely dominated my life, and it's all in black and white in the newspapers since I was fifteen. Pretty boring to you, I would suppose.'

'I confess I don't know much about the game, but I'm willing to learn.'

'What about your father, does he support any team?'

'His real love is motor racing, but I believe he is seen at the occasional football match if it's politically advantageous. To be honest, the family have been attending the rugby internationals, both in Rome and at Twickenham. My sister married into an English family and they are keen supporters. I'm beginning to understand the game and find it very exciting. But to answer your question, I believe he supports Juventus, as it is our local team in Turin.'

'I'll arrange for you to have a seat in the directors' box for the next game, if you would like to come, that is?'

'Yes, I'd love to, thank you; now tell me, how much of a burden is being captain of the national team putting on you?'

'I can get a little wound up by the publicity and it means I am never out of the limelight, but the pressure is only really there on international days. Being captain of AS Roma is not difficult, as the management take all the decisions, on and off the field. I have learnt just to take it all in my stride,' he added, shrugging his shoulders.

'Very modest of you,' said Gina, laughing. 'I shall look forward to seeing you play.'

'So long as you don't put me off. What about the man I saw you with last time?'

'Oh, you mean Andrea: we are just good friends really. I don't see him very often. He spends most of his time at fashion shows in Milan or Paris or New York; you name it and he's there,' she added dismissively.

Satisfied with the response, Rico called for the bill and they prepared to leave. 'No wonder we got catcalls in the piazza; you realise we are wearing the colours of Roma's deadliest rivals.'

'That will be Lazio, won't it?' said Gina, proudly displaying just about her full knowledge of the game.

'In that case you probably know we share the Stadio Olimpico with them. Ours is the next home game, so put it in your diary. Now, look, don't be frightened to ask me if you want any help raising money for your charity.'

'I expect you get a lot of requests to appear for some cause or another. I would hate to bother you.'

'That's true, and I have to be very selective or I'd be out every night. But for you, that's different,' and he gave her a smile that sent shivers down her spine.

They decided to skip a dessert and finished the meal with a large espresso coffee. The proprietor waived any suggestion of a bill and accompanied them out of the restaurant. He opened the car door for Gina and helped her into the deep padded seat. When the two were settled, he passed over three copies of the menu.

'The three ladies sitting in the other corner would like you to autograph their menus, if you would be so kind,' he said, handing Rico a Montblanc pen. 'Apparently they each have a son who is a fan of yours,' he continued with a knowing wink.

Rico grinned, signed the menus and passed them over to Gina, who glanced nervously at the proprietor. 'I'm not so sure they'll want mine as well,' she commented.

'Of course they will, signorina. Just think, when you two are married the menus will be worth a fortune.'

Rico laughed while Gina, looking suitably coy, added her signature and returned the menus. The engine roared into life and they eased gently toward the road; Vito was waving goodbye with one hand, and waving the menus in the air to dry the ink with the other.

As they approached Rico's home, he warned Gina that the paparazzi would almost certainly be waiting for them again.

'I'm beginning to feel a bit stupid in this outfit,' she said. 'I'll be glad to get into the old jeans I brought with me for the journey home.'

'Me too; a quick change and we can have a sundowner and relax on the terrace.' He pressed the remote control and the wrought-iron gates swung open. It was easier to pause for a moment and allow the photographers plenty of time, before driving the car through the gates.

The house was situated in the hills near the small town of Rocca Priora, to the south-east of Rome. There were panoramic views to the south and the dome of St Peter's was clearly visible on the north-west skyline.

The couple changed into less formal clothing and met again on the terrace. Rico opened a bottle of Asti Spumante and they sat contentedly admiring the view.

Outside the house, two members of the paparazzi remained to get a photograph or two of Gina when she reappeared. By midnight it was apparent she would not be coming out and they moved off toward their pitched tents.

'I wish now I had brought my pyjamas, don't you,' Marco 'I wonder if Gina is thinking the same,' came the reply. The two men sniggered.

* * *

Their patience was hardly rewarded the next morning when the gates opened and a dark grey Jaguar XF saloon with tinted black windows passed quickly through. Rico and Gina were barely visible behind the windscreen and the vehicle sped off in the direction of Rome.

'I didn't want to drive the Lamborghini into Rome today. For a start, everybody will know by now who owns it, and we'll get hooted all the way. Secondly, if it is seen parked beside the practice ground by a Lazio supporter it will probably get scratched. I expect you noticed the marks on the Jaguar already.'

'Yes, such a shame; did Jaguar give you this one, too?'

'No I paid for it myself,' Rico replied indignantly. 'Now where exactly do you want me to drop you off?'

'My apartment is in the Via Veneto, just near the American Embassy. Go to the Piazza Barberini and it leads off from there.'

'Would you be offended if I just dropped you off and made a dash for it, as I'm running a bit late already? I'd prefer to take you to the stadium myself on Saturday, but we have team talks before the match, and you'd be hanging around for ages. What I'll do is arrange for a car to pick you up and get one of the directors to take you into their box. I'll make sure you are very well looked after till I can get there after the game. If you let me have your mobile number, we can sort out the exact arrangements before the match.'

'I'll wait to hear from you then. If you just pull in over there that will be fine.' Gina leant over and gave Rico a long kiss on the cheek. 'That is for last night,' she said, and hesitated while he squeezed her knee before climbing out of the car. She heaved a holdall out from behind the seat, crossed the road, and tapped in her security number before disappearing through the door of the apartment block.

Rico sat for a moment watching her disappear. He had

never before experienced the feelings running through him. This was something new and, still deep in thought, he fired the engine and eased the car away from the kerb.

Gina's first thought on entering the apartment was to share her experiences with her sister. She rang Anna on the landline for better reception and was pleased to get an immediate response.

'Hi, Anna, how are you and the kids?'

'No need to tell me why you are ringing, sister, it's all over the national press. What's he like?' she asked, coming straight to the point.

'Absolutely dreamy, I think I'm in love for the very first time.'

'And I think I've heard that more than a few times before.'

'Don't be catty, I really mean it this time.'

'Are you going to see him again?'

'He's invited me to the Stadio Olimpico on Saturday to watch the match.'

'You are going to watch a football match? You must have it bad! According to this morning's newspaper you spent the night with him.'

'I spent the night at his house,' Gina prompted. 'That's all the press knows and all I'm admitting to.'

'Aren't you going to tell your big sister about it, then?'

'Not just yet, I only phoned to tell you I'm in love.'

'Well, the best of luck with this one; he's quite a bit younger than you, isn't he?'

'Only three years, and I really think he likes me.'

'No doubt the media will keep me informed, if you don't. You've certainly hooked a big fish this time. What do you think Papà will say about it?'

'Normally I'd expect the usual blast, but on this occasion, he might like his name linked with the captain of the Italian football team. He's looking at all the angles for publicity now. I think he might see some advantage here, if I know how his mind works. I'll wait and see if I get a phone call from him. Actually, I really phoned to see how your affair is getting on.'

'It's a bit difficult at the moment. David is having to work very late during the week, so I don't get much chance to see him. Matt has taken to coming down every Friday evening and not returning until Monday morning. Sometimes he stays even longer and then Papà arrives, usually during the week, without any warning, to visit his constituency. So there isn't really very much I can tell you. Quite frankly, it is all very frustrating.'

'Does Papà know about your relationship with David?'

'Good God, I hope not; you know how straight-laced he is about these matters. The strange thing is, he has struck up a friendship with David, and sometimes even stays for a night at his apartment in Turin.'

'I think you told me they had the same political sympathies; they are bound to get on well together.'

'I don't want Papà involving David in his socialist dogma. Sometimes it really frightens me.'

'So you still haven't told Matt?'

'I don't dare at the moment; I'm not even sure how David would react. The drug is becoming so successful and the orders are piling in. I try to stay out of business matters but I do fully understand that they need each other's cooperation at the moment.'

'It's usually best to get things out into the open. Once you've done that you will feel a lot better.'

'It's not just my feelings that matter now, Gina. And there are the kids to think about. They will be devastated if and when it all comes out.'

'Sounds like we both need a bit of luck then, Anna. Well, I suppose it's time I was getting on; I'll be in touch again soon. Ciao.'

91

As Anna had mentioned in her telephone conversation, the drug had become a universal success. As anticipated, its sale had been additionally ratified by the European and US drug administrations. Production was in full swing and the company was struggling hard to keep abreast of all the new orders.

A subsidiary company, under the name of Boston Pharmaceuticals (Italia) Ltd, had been set up and a managing director appointed. He was Martin Ford, who had been a director of the parent company for about ten years. He was in his mid forties, with a bubbling personality and a workaholic nature that was infectious. He was a trained chemist, but his management skills had been quickly identified and he was lured away from the laboratory. He was the perfect choice for the job.

Accepting that Jack Edwards needed a high-flyer to help market the drug overseas, the company had poached Alain Baugniet from a major Swiss competitor. He had come with a very expensive contract, but his credentials were impeccable. He spoke the three Swiss national languages of French, German and Italian, plus English and Mandarin. Since Jack had passable Spanish they could cover nearly the entire commercial world.

David and his team were working at full stretch to produce Bosteinex 1, whilst the management was busy expanding the workforce. This had risen to more than two thousand employees, completely bucking the trend of rising unemployment being experienced around the industrial world.

Paolo had made great political capital out of the factory, as though he, singularly, was responsible for its success. At the very beginning, he had persuaded Matthew to employ Bernardo Totti as personnel officer. He was a political confederate of Paolo, and a known agitator. The company was unaware of his political history, having taken Paolo's recommendation as bona fide. Totti was in charge of the workers and Paolo was in charge of Totti. It was just as he had planned from the start.

The success of the drug could not, of course, be attributed to Paolo in any way. Large loans from the bank were almost repaid in a few months. The staff at the factory in Northampton, having got over the disappointment of not manufacturing the drug there, were enjoying the rewards of a thriving business. Matthew had been oiling their cogs well; as he put it to the board, the workforce, if hard working and competent, was always your biggest asset, whatever the business.

The shares of Boston and Wood were going up in price almost daily and the company secretary was, it seemed, in almost permanent discussion with stock analysts. It was anticipated that if the business continued to expand at the current rate and the profits with it, the company would make it into the FTSE top 100 within a year. Nobody, not even Matthew, could have predicted that situation a few months ago.

Gerald, perhaps with a slight wish that he hadn't relinquished the chair so abruptly, was still a contented man. There had been mutterings about nepotism from some shareholders when he appointed Matthew to succeed him. It was obvious to all he had chosen the right person, and nobody would dare to criticise him now.

7

In the offices of the DST in Paris, Pierre Lavalle and Fritz Vogel were busy planning the assassination of Paolo Medina. The two men would probably require at least two identities, and so having previously had false passports made up while clean shaven they were now growing beards. The Rook had cut his fair, receding hair short and dyed it and his beard black to blend in better with the local inhabitants of Sicily.

They preferred not to be seen together in Italy during the initial organisation, and had split the various tasks accordingly. Lavalle would take the job of following their victim to establish his normal pattern of movement. The Rook would be in charge of logistics. They anticipated the preparations would take a minimum of two months and arranged to meet again in Paris after six weeks. The less contact they had between themselves the better; they could always make indirect contact through their respective agencies if a difficult situation arose. Whilst they were in the field they would know each other as Shergar 1 and 2.

The Rook was fully experienced in the art of bomb-making. He was also a first class shot if they decided to use a sniper's rifle. His first assignment would be to go to Sicily to seek out the kind of explosive most popularly used by the Mafia and to acquire a small arsenal. Meanwhile, Lavalle would go to Rome to establish Paolo's daily routine and work out the best way to get to him.

Although under the terms of the Schengen agreement they would not be required to produce passports at either end, they decided not to travel by air. They could not avoid the CCTV cameras at the airports. Travelling individually, they were taken across their selected borders by cars driven by female agents. The women were not informed of the reason for the exercise, but would probably be required again to escort the men out of Italy.

Lavalle was taken over the French/Italian border by a minor crossing on the edge of the Mercantour National Park. He was driven the short journey to Ventimiglia where he bought a second-hand motorbike. He had always wanted to drive a Vespa scooter and found one at a backstreet dealer. He paid cash with Italian-marked euros and started his journey southward towards Rome. By the time he reached Lucca, he decided the Vespa was far too vulnerable and uncomfortable. He abandoned it sooner than he had originally planned. He continued his journey on a more comfortable motorcycle and arrived in Rome shortly after midnight.

It took him a while to locate the apartment he had rented in the northern outskirts of Rome. He had arranged a six-month contract and paid in full in advance. The keys had arrived in Paris a few days before via four separate couriers, none of whom knew the other's identity. A set had also been given to The Rook and they would eventually be returned in similar fashion. The apartment had an allotted garage and Pierre's first act was to get the motorcycle out of sight. He then entered the furnished accommodation which would be his home for as long as it might take to carry out the assignment.

He was wearing surgical gloves, a discipline he would maintain the whole time he was at the apartment. It was probable that his fingerprints were in the files of other secret service agencies. It was impossible to live in a place without leaving traces of DNA, but he was fairly sure nobody, other than his own agency, could possibly have any records. However, you could never be one hundred per cent certain; after all, the DST had surreptitiously taken samples from both The Rook and Albert Von Meissen on their visits to Paris.

The Rook crossed into Italy via Austria and was dropped off in Padua. Here he also purchased a second-hand motorcycle for which he paid cash. He would abandon it nearer his destination, destroy the registration plates and purchase another for the final part of the journey. He expected to be picked up by CCTV at the port of Messina after the ferry crossing to Sicily, but, with his new disguise, he believed there was absolutely no chance of recognition.

The Rook had rented a small flat in the old town of Palermo, near the port area. He had also hired a garage about a kilometre away. He was less bothered about concealing the motorbike as he would be repeating the entire process again after returning to Paris for the final approval. It was his intention to use the garage as a workshop and to store necessary equipment. His tasks should take less time than Lavalle's, so he would be returning home sooner; he just had the more tedious journeys.

Pierre had already done some reconnaissance on Paolo Medina. He had confined his surveillance to Paolo's movements around Turin, and had been initially encouraged by what he considered very slack security. Obviously, the man considered himself inviolable in his own constituency. However, since becoming leader of the Left Alliance, his trips to Turin had become scarcer and more unpredictable.

Having arrived in Rome, Pierre allowed himself one day of wandering about to get the feel of the city. He had been to Rome on several occasions in the past and felt no need to visit the famous tourist spots. Instead, he just wandered aimlessly along the Via del Corso, staring into the shops and watching the tourists mingling with the local population. He eventually arrived at the Spanish Steps and installed himself in a cafe to rest his tired feet. A feeling of loneliness suddenly overcame him on the realisation that he would be making no personal contact with anybody for six weeks.

The following day he got down to work. It was a Tuesday and he arrived early at a parking space for two-wheeled vehicles, a short walk from the parliament building. He strolled along the Via della Stelletta and made his way round to the spacious Piazza Montecitorio. On the northern side of the square stands the massive Palazzo Montecitorio which houses the Chamber of Deputies.

The Italian parliament consists of two Houses, which, unlike the British equivalent, are both elected. In total there are 945 elected members. The Chamber of Deputies has 630 members and is termed the Lower House. The Senate of the Republic is the Upper House and has 315 members. The main prerogative of the parliament is the exercise of legislative power. New legislation may be proposed by either House, but must be approved by both Houses to become law.

The electoral system is complex and different for each House. The Chamber of Deputies is voted for at a national level. Candidates must be over the age of twenty-five and the electors at least eighteen years old. For the senate, the candidates must be over forty and the voters at least twenty-five. The senate is elected on a more regional basis. Paolo was an elected member of the Lower House.

Pierre had decided to wait in the Piazza Montecitorio in the hope of seeing Paolo arrive. It was seven-thirty and the morning sun was sending a pink glow across the ancient buildings. He was wearing an outfit designed to appear as much like a casual tourist as possible. He had blue jeans, a nondescript, crumpled light shirt, with a loose fitting gilet. On his head he wore a round, floppy cotton hat, and large sunglasses protected his eyes from both the sun and easy recognition. He was a thin man of medium height with a swarthy appearance suggesting some Algerian blood in his ancestry. He had jet-black hair and narrow, deep-brown eyes, above a long thin nose made even more prominent against the newly grown black beard.

His main difficulty was keeping watch over the entire palace, which stretched back for over a hundred metres, where the rear of the building faced another square. This was the Piazza del Parlamento from which several entrances to the palace were in constant use. It was possible for visitors to watch the proceedings in the chamber and, after waiting all morning to no avail, Pierre contemplated getting a ticket. Seeing how much security was involved, he gave up that idea and left the area. Tomorrow he would watch from the rear of the palace first and hope to get a positive result.

The following day he was wearing dark jeans, a crumpled navy blue shirt and a baseball cap with no insignia. He again arrived early and this time waited first in the Piazza del Parlamento. Quite suddenly Paolo Medina, accompanied by two security guards, appeared from around the side of the palace, walked briskly along the side of the square, and disappeared through a rear entrance. Pierre checked his watch; it was four minutes before nine on a Wednesday morning. He left the piazza and went to find a cafe for some coffee and rolls. At least today he would get some breakfast. He returned to his apartment to determine his next move.

What he wanted to discover in particular was Paolo's residence in Rome. He had been a little surprised at Paolo's sudden appearance, as he had expected him to arrive by car. This may mean that Paolo had a place quite close to the parliament building. He returned to the square in the late afternoon in anticipation of catching Paolo leaving. He waited in the side street from where Paolo had emerged in the morning and got immediate success when he appeared with his guards. Pierre turned away as they passed and started to follow them at a safe distance. He checked his watch again; it was five twenty-three.

The three men turned left, crossed the Corso and carried on along Via della Mercede till they came to the ancient church of Sant' Andrea delle Fratte. To Pierre's surprise, the two guards waited outside while Paolo entered the church. He would have loved to follow him in and watch his movements inside. Had Paolo gone there to pray; had he gone there for confession; or had he just gone there to admire the beautiful angels carved by Bernini? Pierre waited over ten minutes before Paolo reappeared and followed him until they reached a doorway in the Via Gregoriana. A security guard took out a key and entered the house; he reappeared and waved Paolo inside.

It was obvious to Lavalle that Paolo did not take his own security very seriously. He had seen photographs of him attending and speaking at rallies, where security had been practically non-existent. It was not going to be too difficult to get to him. The real difficulty would be to avoid detection.

Pierre followed him through a similar routine the following day, except he did not go into the church. On the Friday, he appeared as usual in the morning but not in the afternoon. He had either left early or was still in the building till late. Pierre did not hang around; he had learnt quite a bit already. On the Saturday he walked past the house in Gregoriana on several occasions but saw no sign of movement. Paolo may have gone elsewhere for the weekend and Pierre decided to have a quiet time for a couple of days.

On the Monday he was back waiting in the Piazza del Parlamento. A large black Mercedes drew up on the side of the square and Paolo, accompanied as usual by his two henchmen, got out and strolled purposefully into the palace.

This appeared to confirm Pierre's assumption that he had gone away for the weekend.

In the same pattern as the previous week, Pierre waited outside on the Tuesday but Paolo did not appear all day. 'What's so special about a Tuesday?' he wondered; next week he would need to follow Paolo from the house in Via Gregoriana to his destination.

On the Friday he saw the three men arrive as usual just before nine o'clock. He went for some breakfast and then moved his motorcycle to a discreet position near the palazzo. At around half past twelve the Mercedes arrived and the driver went into the building. Pierre, having noted in which direction the car would have to leave the square, went to fetch his vehicle. Twenty minutes later he was following the car northwards as far as the ring road, where it turned left. At junction three they exited the ring road and swung north again towards the Lago di Bracciano. About 3 kilometres short of the town of Bracciano, which sits on the edge of the lake, they turned left up a winding country lane.

Pierre stopped and studied his map. He knew he would have difficulty keeping the car in sight without being spotted. He waited a few minutes and then drove at a high speed along the lane. If he caught up with the car he would have to overtake and decide the next course of action. As it happened, he was just in time to see the Mercedes passing through electrically controlled gates on the right side of the road. He sped past, deliberately not glancing in that direction; after a few kilometres, he pulled over, studied his map and made a few more notes. He stayed to enjoy the view toward the lake before driving back more slowly past Paolo's weekend residence. With Paolo safely installed, he could enjoy a full weekend to himself and decided to visit the wine-growing region of Orvieto.

* * *

Meanwhile, The Rook was having a more relaxed existence. His small frame normally allowed him to pass unnoticed, but the black beard he now wore made him feel more conspicuous. From his appearance nobody would have believed his record of political assassination on behalf of his country. Behind his steely grey eyes there was neither a conscience nor any compassion.

He had spent several evenings visiting various nightclubs in the centre of Palermo. His main plan was to chat to the girls until he found one able to introduce him to a discreet, under the counter arms dealer. Although his budget was unlimited, he was fortunate to find such a contact after less than two weeks; evenings in the clubs was proving to be a very expensive exercise. He had avoided any sexual encounters with the girls as he obviously didn't want to take them to his own flat. In Palermo it would be too dangerous to accept an invitation to the apartment of a nightclub hostess. Once he was armed he might be tempted to take the risk!

At the crack of dawn on Monday, Lavalle took the road again to Bracciano. He stopped short of the lane leading to the Medina home and tinkered with his motorbike. Just before eight o'clock the black Mercedes with tinted windows appeared. It turned right out of the winding lane and drove past him. As Paolo was probably returning to Rome, Pierre did not attempt to follow but decided instead to investigate the countryside. He motored slowly along the country lane until he came across an opening to a wooded area on the left side. He drove up a narrow path and found a place to hide the bike. He then set off on foot with a hiker's rucksack on his back.

He had walked less than a kilometre in the direction of the Medina's house when the woodland petered out into a field of rough grass and gorse. He could make out the roof of the house through some cypress trees, about a kilometre to the south. He took out his binoculars and surveyed the landscape. The narrow lane was quite close to the spot where he was standing and he could clearly see its route winding away from a sharp bend. It was lined in both directions by an overgrown hedgerow of oleander and variegated laurel. He was on the side of a hill with the lane below him and more trees rising up behind. On the other side of the lane the land fell away quite steeply, allowing an uninterrupted view toward the lake. 'I wouldn't mind a little place here myself,' he muttered to himself as he proceeded to take a number of photographs from different angles.

He picked his way through the gorse down to the lane and walked briskly in hiker fashion toward the house. After about half a kilometre he decided he had seen nothing more favourable to his mission. Not wanting to get any closer to the house, he retraced his steps. He walked past the spot where he had joined the lane until he came to the opening he had taken the bike up. He checked it was still securely hidden and walked on to see where the path led. It was a narrow path about 2 metres wide running through a wooded area of pine trees and scrub. The surface had been worn fairly flat by the wheels of a farm vehicle; probably a tractor that in the past had dragged logs to be cut up. Pierre was pleased to find, after about 2 kilometres, that the path led into another country lane. He studied his map and realised that this lane would return him to the main Bracciano road.

After returning to collect his motorbike, he drove along the path to ensure there were no potholes he could have missed. This could be a perfect escape route. He spent the rest of the day touring around to familiarise himself with the district, before dining beside the lake.

Pierre needed to discover where Paolo disappeared to on a Tuesday. Perhaps he had a mistress locked away somewhere in the city? He waited early in the Via Gregoriana for some action. To the disappointment of his fertile mind, he watched as the two bodyguards arrived and waited outside for Paolo to appear. He followed them in the direction of the Piazza Montecitorio and assumed they were going to the chamber. However, when they came to the Corso they changed their normal route by turning left. They crossed the road further down, cut through a narrow alley, and past the church of Santa Maria Maddalena. It suddenly dawned on Pierre what their destination would be.

On the east side of the famous Piazza Navona is the Palazzo Madama, built in the sixteenth century for the Medici family. Since 1871 it has been the seat of the Upper House, the Senate of the Republic. Pierre watched as the three men disappeared through the door cut into the beautiful facade. He was now satisfied he had Paolo's normal weekly routine covered.

For the next month he kept occasional checks on Paolo's movements, including several trips to the country lanes. The only times Paolo changed his routine was when he attended a rally in Milan and visited his constituency in Turin. Pierre was, of course, unable to follow him on those occasions but learnt of his movements from the media.

Satisfied that he now had enough intelligence, he left Rome. That day the Baron received a coded text message that read; 'Shergar 1 returning to stable.' Lavalle crossed the border into France near Menton, disposed of the motorbike in a forest near Cannes and took the TGV to Paris. He would be home well in time for the Christmas celebrations.

* * *

The Rook had completed his assignment a week earlier and returned to Germany. He had acquired explosive, remote systems and wiring essential for making a bomb. He had also acquired two Armalite rifles and two revolvers in case they had to shoot their way out of a corner. He had taken as much as he could reasonably carry on the motorbike as he left Sicily. This he deposited in Lavalle's garage in Rome without making contact. On hearing of Pierre's return he flew immediately to Paris.

Lavalle and The Rook had not seen each other for nearly seven weeks and they sat down to devise an undetectable plan for the assassination.

Pierre opened the conversation. 'It would be the easiest thing to gun him down near his house in the Via Gregoriana. There is an alleyway to escape along where you could be ready with the motorbike at the other end. We could be away in seconds.'

'Where do we go from there?' The Rook enquired.

'We drive about three kilometres north where I have found a disused building site. We dump the motorbike and equipment and continue by car. We should be well away before the police come across the bike.'

'What are the snags, then?'

'There will obviously be immediate police action, particularly when they realise who the victim is. The search for us will be on quite quickly and we will have to shift to keep ahead. But I think it would work.'

The Rook looked dubious. 'If anything goes wrong, we won't get a second chance; any other suggestions?'

'I didn't think you'd be too keen on that, and I think there is a much better way. I have been watching Paolo's house in the country where he goes most weekends. There is a narrow lane leading to the house, which would be perfect for an ambush. He is driven there with his bodyguard in a Mercedes with tinted windows which we can assume are also bulletproof. We will require your expertise with explosives.'

'Go on,' said The Rook, sitting back in his chair; this was more up his street.

'Paolo usually leaves Rome on a Friday afternoon, although on one occasion it was not until the Sunday morning. But on every occasion he left his country house on the Monday morning around a quarter to eight to return to Rome. I would suggest we hit him then.'

'And that happens every weekend, does it?'

'Except on one occasion, when I learnt from the press that he was in Turin. If we go to the area and he doesn't turn up, we just abandon and go the next weekend; nothing lost.'

'So what is your full plan, then? How do we get to him and how good is the escape route?'

Lavalle produced a map and photographs he had taken. He explained the position where they could look down on the approaching vehicle and where it slowed noticeably to take the sharp bend. He showed him the path through the woods where the motorbike would be waiting to speed them away.

'So what hitches do you see with this plan?'

'None, really, except you are going to have to run about six hundred metres through the woods back to the bike.' He glanced teasingly at The Rook's stomach. He had obviously eaten well during his stay in Sicily. 'The big advantage here is that we should be hours ahead of the police. I have watched that lane for ages after Paolo leaves and have not seen another car or individual come along for at least an hour.'

'All right, I'll make sure I get myself fit again! So you reckon that, by the time the police sort out the mess, we could be a hundred kilometres or more away?'

'Exactly, and I have worked out how we can best return home. We'll need the girls again.'

'Have you shown this plan to the Baron yet?'

'No, but I don't think we will have any trouble convincing him. It is his baby and he's very keen to get the job done.'

'Better let him see it first and get him to sell it to my boss. Believe it or not, he's still a little troubled with his conscience.'

The Baron agreed the plan and flew to Munich to put it to his German counterpart in the BND. In the two months since they first met, political problems in the whole of Europe had escalated. Extremists of both the right and left were gathering strength and their supporters getting more aggressive.

Albert Von Meissen welcomed the Baron to his offices and they started by discussing the political scene across the European Union. There was no doubt that in Spain, Italy, Portugal and Greece the socialists were topping the popularity polls by a wide margin. France and Belgium were also beginning to move strongly in that direction. Germany was still maintaining a middle-of-the-road attitude, although the factions from either end were getting aggressive. Poland and the Eastern bloc countries were moving strongly in the opposite direction towards a fascist doctrine, having had a torrid time with communism in the past.

'We have got to stop this extremism from going too far,' the Baron stressed, banging his fist on the table. 'We have to start somewhere, and I believe knocking out the leaders will take the steam out of the movements.'

'You may halt the socialists for a bit if you take out Medina, but that won't stop the fascists. What do you propose doing about them?'

'Like I said – we have to start somewhere. Weakening one set of extremists will probably have the affect of dowsing the opposite view. I have always looked at it this way: that the politics of the centre can be determined by a point anywhere on the circumference of a circle. Take a pencil and the further you move away from that point, going either left or right, the closer you come back together again, until you reach totalitarianism. At the point where they meet you have the dictatorships that permit no opposition, resulting in imprisonment and the mass murder of political opponents. Socialists, fascists, communists, nazis – they are all the same. This is what I believe we should be trying to prevent.'

'I accept that the socialists, or communists if you like, have found a champion and the fascists haven't, so at the moment, their momentum is more forceful.

'Are you happy we just take on one thing at a time, Albert?'

'I suppose I shall have to be; I hope you haven't got something else up your sleeve, have you?'

'Calm down, Albert, we are just going to take things step by step.'

Albert seemed mollified, and continued, 'Now, I understand from The Rook you are totally satisfied with the plan of action?'

'I'm convinced it will work and there is no chance we could be implicated. It is a very straightforward plan and the means of getting away are quick and uncomplicated.'

'Then if you're happy, Baron, so am I. The less I know, the better, so far as I'm concerned. Presumably you want to get cracking immediately?'

'I promise you will get your man back in a few weeks with the job done. Goodbye, Albert, and thanks for your invaluable support and cooperation.'

'Best of luck, and I expect to hear good news from you shortly. Oh, there was just one question I was going to ask. How do you think the British will react to the news?'

'With a fair degree of equanimity, I expect. They are in enough political turmoil themselves. For a start they are still deeply suspicious of the socialists since the unions wrecked their industries. They've had a left-wing government that has destroyed their economy, so I can't see them shedding any tears over Paolo Medina. But they are also fearful of a fascist backlash and their extreme right is clashing with a multicultural population that hates them.'

'That was my interpretation of events there. Just for once we can ignore them, eh?'

The two men parted grinning, and the Baron took his waiting car to the airport.

On his return to Paris he gave Lavalle and The Rook the all clear and wished them 'God's speed'.

8

To the amazement of both family and friends, Gina had become a regular visitor to the Stadio Olimpico. They were more accustomed to seeing photographs of her on the catwalk, at the opera or at society dinners. She had now become a celebrity among the hierarchy of the football world and was thoroughly enjoying her change of lifestyle.

She was getting used to the earthy, rough manner of the players and their humorous banter, of which she was often the target. There was a convivial atmosphere here not generally experienced in her old circle of acquaintances. In the directors' box she was somewhat sheltered from the uncouth chants of opposing fans, but she decided in any case to ignore the bad language she found all around her. She even gained some personal comfort from this environment. These were the class of people her father was dealing with every day; and she began to feel a little closer to him.

Her relationship with Rico was becoming more intense in every way. For his part, he made sure he was not seen anywhere without her, and their mutual adoration was evident in every photograph. The paparazzi loved her, too. She made Rico no longer just a face for the sports pages or women's pin-up magazines; with the voluptuous Gina by his side, the couple were sought after by practically every gossip publication in Europe.

Gina had moved into Rico's villa at the start of the new year. In his more remote house the couple could get a little respite from the paparazzi, with whom they had more recently made an agreement. They would keep the press informed of their intended movements in return for no cameramen on permanent watch outside the gates.

The demands on their time from travel and functions left little opportunity to relax. There were also the training, the football matches and countless interviews to contend with. After a couple of months Rico's game had started to deteriorate and the possible causes were being aired daily by the media. Needless to say, Gina was getting some of the blame, and a few of the more despicable columnists were suggesting the various ways in which she was wearing him out.

It was true that when the opportunity arose to get to bed early, they did not let it pass. They were young, virile and deeply in love. Rico regularly had difficulty reporting on time at the training camp, which did not pass unnoticed, or commented upon, by the rest of the team.

Nothing could alter the fact they were the most photographed and popular couple in Italy. Paolo used it to his full advantage. Despite his previous indifference to the game, he was now a regular visitor to the Stadio Olimpico. He would even fly to Turin to watch Juventus play. His publicity agents took every opportunity of using football to enhance his popularity; being seen regularly in the company of the Italian captain could not have come at a better time.

Pierre Lavalle and The Rook returned overland to their rented apartments in Rome and Palermo to prepare for the final assault. The Rook got rid of the two Armalite rifles, which he now considered superfluous. He had taken the explosives and revolvers to Rome already and now only needed to pack the wiring and remote control system. It was a relief this time to be travelling light and with no incriminating possessions. Pierre had already been in Rome for three days before The Rook arrived. They now had all the necessary equipment, plus their two motorbikes, stored in the garage.

The following day they drove the bikes to Orvieto, just over an hour's ride to the north from the apartment. They disposed of them in a large pond, having first removed the registration plates. They walked into the town and purchased a powerful Suzuki motorcycle, which they would need for a quick getaway. On the drive back to Rome they veered off towards Bracciano for The Rook to get acquainted with the intended assassination spot. Satisfied that all seemed exactly as he imagined it, he gave Pierre the thumbs-up sign and they returned to the apartment.

'Do you think we are on for this weekend?' he asked Pierre. 'There's nothing to hold us up, is there?'

'I would just like to keep an eye on Paolo for a few more days and check out his routine again, which may have changed a bit now he's gone football crazy. I noticed Juventus are at home this weekend, so he could easily go up to Turin. Roma are playing at the Olimpico next weekend, so he'll probably watch that match and go to his country house on Saturday evening,' Pierre explained. 'Let's make it Monday week, the twenty-fifth; it's my birthday, which is a good omen for us.'

'So is there anything you want me to do?'

'Only get the explosives set up, keep out of sight, and stay away from loose women.'

'Okay, but I think I'll give the bike a good service. It looks in good condition but we don't want it packing up on us.'

Pierre nodded in approval. 'I'm going to take a close look at the press each day. My only worry is that there will be a clash shortly in the chamber between Paolo and the prime minister. If a vote of no confidence is called, it could change his whole routine, so we mustn't hang around.'

'Just wait till Monday week and he won't be worrying anybody,' said The Rook, ominously. 'I reckon the Italian prime minister would pay us a million euros or more each for our services, if he only knew. The two men have the reputation of being bitter enemies.'

'Yes,' Pierre agreed, 'let's think of it as our present to the whole of Europe.'

'What day have you arranged to get to the hideout?' asked The Rook, returning to the matter in hand.

'My plan is for you to drop me there on the Saturday morning so I can keep an eye on the comings and goings at the house. I'll stay the night in the woods and you can come and take over on Sunday morning. I'll take a break and return in the evening, by which time we should know exactly what is happening. That will also ensure the bike is not left lying about during daylight hours. On Sunday night, before it gets light, you can set the explosives.'

'It's going to be a long ten days, Pierre, but I can promise you, the grand finale will be spectacular.'

To the Agents of Death the time did pass slowly while Lavalle checked again on what he expected to be the final movements of the leader of the opposition. He continued to be intrigued by Paolo's visit on each Wednesday to the church of Sant'Andrea delle Fratte. He had toyed with the idea of going into the church some time ahead of him to avoid the bodyguards, but in the end decided it could be dangerous to show his face. One day in the future, he told himself, he would return and speak to the padre just to satisfy his curiosity.

They made certain that Paolo stayed in Rome on the Friday night and was taken the following day to the Stadio Olimpico. Whilst he was at the match, The Rook drove Pierre to the woods and returned to the apartment, where he completed the manufacture of the two explosive devices. Just one would have sufficient velocity for the complete destruction of the vehicle and its contents, but two would give the added protection against an unlikely failure.

Pierre settled in to watch the lane for the whole of the Saturday but it was not until late evening that he saw the black Mercedes. Through his binoculars he could just make out three passengers and a driver; exactly what he would expect. Twenty minutes later the car went back again, this time with only three people in it. 'That's Paolo where we want him,' Pierre muttered to himself. 'So far so good.' He settled down for a night's rest.

He was relieved of his duties early Sunday morning by The Rook, who was brought up to date.

'So you had a pretty good rest since I dropped you, Pierre?' he remarked, mischievously.

'All that happened was the arrival of Paolo at the house about nine o'clock in the evening,' he replied, ignoring the sarcasm. 'With a bit of luck, you should also have a quiet time and I'll be back around six this evening. I've never noticed anyone wandering about in the vicinity at the weekends, but if you get disturbed just let them think you are a lone hiker. For goodness sake don't go slitting any throats, in case you start a hunt.'

The Rook grinned malevolently as he watched Lavalle disappear through the woods. The day was not going to turn out to be quite as peaceful as he expected.

Matthew had flown to Turin, as usual, to be with his family for the weekend. He was getting tired of the persistent travel between the two factories and was beginning to wish he had insisted on them remaining in London. Anna picked him up at the airport and they drove to the house with hardly a word exchanged. At least he always received an ecstatic welcome from Mark and Louise.

'I've arranged for us all to go to the coast near Savona tomorrow,' said Anna as they came into the front room. 'We are going to meet some school friends of Mark whose parents have a villa there. I know the family well and we should have a lovely time.'

'Well, I've arranged to meet Peter at the factory in the morning,' replied Matthew irritably, 'we have a number of problems to sort out.'

'I've promised the kids now, so you will just have to cancel the meeting. The other thing is that, on Sunday, we are all flying down to my mother's. Mark and Louise are on half term holiday next week and I thought they would enjoy staying with their grandmother.'

'I can't go to Rome; I have an important meeting in London on Monday and can only get there in time by catching the early flight out of Turin.'

'So you are not coming with us on Saturday or Sunday, then?'

'Look, what I will try to do is change my meeting with Martin to Sunday and come to the coast with you tomorrow. I just can't do both days, and flying to Rome on Sunday is too much for me.'

'I'm getting fed up with weekends being constantly disrupted by your business. Mamma was hoping to arrange a big family get-together on Sunday. Even Papà has agreed to be there.'

'Well, I'm sorry, but why the hell don't you tell me your arrangements in advance? I might then get a chance to alter my plans. If you've already got me a ticket for the flight on Sunday, you will have to cancel it. You and your mother are always organising things without checking with other people first. Then you get bad-tempered when they don't conform to your plans.'

'Why can't you just forget the company occasionally at the weekends and give some time to your family? After

114

all, you are the chairman; you should be able to do what you like.'

'You know bloody well it doesn't work like that! I'm at everybody's beck and call practically day and night.'

'Your father managed to find plenty of time for the family. When did he work at the weekends?'

'I think he did when he first took over. Anyway, the company is more than twice the size now.'

'It's useless talking to you, you obviously don't give a damn about your family. As far as I'm concerned you can go straight back home and don't bother to come here again!'

Matthew was about to point out that he regarded this house just as much his home, but Anna swept out of the room, slamming the door behind her.

The tension between the two had hardly abated the next morning but Matthew was determined at least to stay friendly with the children. He helped them pack up a few things in case they wanted to go swimming and promised to take them to the funfair. Anna was particularly irritated by the way they clung to their father and practically ignored her when he was around. Having found some computer games to keep the children amused on the car journey, they set off for the coast.

The children of both families had an exciting day at the coast where they were able to run wild and swim in the heated pool at the villa. They had a long lunch at a restaurant overlooking the sea at Torre di Mare. Matthew noticed that Anna was drinking more than usual and he would definitely have to do all the driving home. They left the coast early evening in a lighter mood, which unfortunately did not last the journey.

'Why didn't you tell me the kids had a week off school?' Matthew demanded gruffly. 'You could all have come to England for the week and saved me coming out here.'

'I thought you wanted to see Martin; so you were coming in any case.'

'I could easily have got him to come to me, if I'd known. Mum and Dad are going to be very upset; they haven't seen Mark and Louise for ages. They are missing them terribly.'

'Well, my parents want to see them too, and yours saw much more of them than mine until recently. So everything is evening itself out.'

'I have a damned good mind to take them back with me on Monday and you can come or not,' spat Matthew, angrily.

'Don't you even think about doing that; they are coming with me to Rome tomorrow and that's final,' Anna shouted, her face looking flushed.

The traffic was getting thicker now they were approaching Turin and Matthew decided to back off from the argument and concentrate on the driving. He could see from the faces of his children in the rear-view mirror that they were extremely agitated by the constant tension between their parents.

Arriving home, Anna fled into the house and burst into tears.

'Now what's the matter?' Matthew asked naively, putting a hand on her shoulder.

She shrugged it off, contemptuously. 'This just isn't working, Matt, we are not a family any more. You just come and go as you please, and then expect me to jump to your every demand. I've had just about as much as I can take.'

'I thought you said you'd be so much happier in Italy, that's why I agreed to your coming out here with the kids. Now you're saying you are dissatisfied again. What the hell do you want?'

'You just don't understand, do you? I want a life of my own; not just waiting around while you and the children make demands on me.'

'I bet this is all about your sister and her depraved lifestyle. You want to be like her; is that what this is all about?'

'This has nothing to do with Gina and don't you dare call her depraved. I'm going to see her tomorrow at Mamma's and she will have her new boyfriend, Rico Orvetti, with her. I thought you might like to meet him.'

'Well, I'm not going to Rome, and that's final,' Matthew barked out, but then, in an attempt to diffuse the atmosphere he added, 'I'll drop you all off at the airport in the morning and then I'll be meeting Martin.' He walked out of the room leaving Anna drying the tears from her eyes.

The Rook settled down for a long day. He was dying for a cigarette, but didn't dare light one up for fear of the smoke being spotted. It was just as well he remained alert, for, at about ten o'clock, he heard in the distance the sound of the iron gates opening. He trained his binoculars on the lane and noted an Alfa Romeo 156 winding its way along. It was, in his estimate, about eight years old and was driven by a lady alone in the car. The windscreen was quite clear and he recognised Bella, Paolo's wife, as the driver. Probably going to church, he thought, as he made a note.

Two hours later, he heard the sound of a car approaching from his right and recognised the Alfa returning. This time there were four occupants and he tried to identify them. Sitting in the passenger seat beside Bella there was a lady, and in the rear there were two children. *They must be her daughter and grandchildren*, The Rook surmised, making a further note on his pad.

In the afternoon, the distant sound of children shouting and splashing in the pool helped to justify his assumption. It wasn't until about five o'clock that he heard the roar of a powerful engine. He watched as a blue Lamborghini screeched round a bend in the lane. The passenger and driver were both wearing black crash helmets with tinted glass visors. He listened and heard the car stop at the gates to the house. He made a note to ask Pierre if he recognised the vehicle and the passengers.

At six o'clock precisely Pierre returned to the hideout. The Rook explained the day's events and waited for any reaction.

'I know exactly who the sports car belongs to,' Pierre said in a low voice. 'That will be Rico Orvetti, the Italian footballer. He is seeing Paolo's daughter. So that would almost certainly have been Gina in the car with him. I'm surprised you haven't read all about it.'

'I have, of course, but I didn't know he owned that fantastic car. It looks like they are having a family reunion today. That could complicate matters,' The Rook pointed out.

'I don't see it makes any difference, provided Paolo leaves for Rome at his normal time tomorrow morning. If not, we shall just have to abort and wait for the next opportunity.'

'Let's hope he does then; I'd rather not spend another weekend watching the house. Not a lot goes on, really.'

'That is true, but that's the beauty of this location. We've been able to observe the comings and goings without getting disturbed. You should be able to set the explosives at first light and, with a bit of luck, we should be away about eight with the mission accomplished.'

'You take first watch, then, when it gets dark,' The Rook suggested, 'and I'll relieve you at about two. That will give me plenty of time to prepare everything while you are having a rest.'

'That sounds sensible to me; so go and get some sleep. I'll wake you up around two.'

* * *

118

At the house the family was beginning to gather for dinner. The property, set in just over one acre, had been acquired originally by Bella's grandfather. It had been left to the family by way of a trust on his death so that there would not be a dispute among his four heirs over future ownership. It had been leased out to several tenants before Bella persuaded the trustees to grant her a lease while she and Paolo were spending most of their time in Rome.

Bella's preference on a Sunday would have been for a relaxing lunch, but Rico had been unable to get away until the afternoon. He and Paulo were by now well acquainted and strolled out to the front drive to admire the Lamborghini.

'Sadly, my racing days are over,' Paolo said wistfully. 'I would have loved to take a car with this power round the circuit at Monza.'

'Gina told me you were an enthusiast, but I didn't realise you raced yourself.'

'I only raced as an amateur, but had a lot of fun. Did Gina tell you I have in the garage a 1929 Bugatti 35B? It's identical to the car that won the French Grand Prix that year.'

Rico whistled. 'Wow! That must be worth a fortune now, I'd love to see it.'

'It is not in running condition at the moment, but if I find time to get it up to scratch we could take both cars to Monza. I imagine we have enough contacts between us to get us on the track,' Paolo added with a grin. 'Would you like to see it?'

It was Rico's turn to look with admiration when the garage doors were opened. 'Just look at that,' he exclaimed. 'Do you mean to say you can actually drive that machine? At least mine has got some protection for the driver.'

'This could do up to a hundred and twenty-five kilometres per hour. That doesn't sound much at all these days, but when you can see the ground slipping past beneath your feet, believe me, it appears mighty quick.'

'I hope you can get it running again soon, sir, I'd love to give it a whirl. Isn't that Gina calling us?'

They sauntered back to the house where the ladies were already refilling their glasses. The children were still playing in the garden and had opted to eat their dinner in the summer house by themselves. Mark had already obtained Rico's autograph on his football, but Louise had kicked it into the pool and spoilt the signature. Rico obliged for a second time and ruffled the youngster's hair as he promised to keep the ball out of the water.

'You're very good with children, Rico,' Gina remarked with a smile, as she took his arm on the way to the dining room.

Rico returned her grin. 'Just part of the job,' he said, but after a moment's contemplation added, 'Actually, I think I get on better with the kids than I do with most of the adults around me. At least they appreciate me, whereas the others are just interested in what profit I can make for them.'

'I heard what you said,' Paolo interjected, as he waved Rico into a seat at the table, 'and that's what is so wrong with people's attitude these days. All they ever think about is money, money, money.'

'We are keeping the global financial problems and politics out of the conversation this evening, Papà,' Anna stated emphatically, 'there are plenty of other subjects we can discuss.' Bella and Gina added their support.

'Okay, you are right, I promise to keep right off them. Tonight we are going to let our hair down and have a riotous time. I've got out some of my best vintage Barolo which I took the trouble to decant a couple of hours ago.'

Maria, the family retainer, came into the dining room carrying a large plate of mixed salad which she placed in the centre of the table. 'What else have you arranged for us this evening, Maria?' Paolo enquired enthusiastically.

'After this,' she replied, 'there is some vermicelli with mussels and clams. Then I have prepared your favourite: escallop of veal with a creamy mushroom sauce. The dessert is a surprise!'

By the satisfied looks, the menu appeared to suit everyone. 'You know I can't drink red wine with shellfish,' Bella pointed out.

'Don't worry, my dear,' Paolo replied, 'I have plenty of your Soave in the chiller. I'll go and get some right now.'

'Papà is in a good mood,' Anna remarked as he left the room. 'Let's hope we are going to have a lovely evening without any of his aggressive outbursts for a change.'

The food was devoured with relish and the wine glasses refilled continuously. The noise level rose and had reached fever pitch by the time the dessert was laid on the table. It was a home-made cassata, which Maria knew was just about everybody's favourite.

Mark and Louise came in to say goodnight to the rest of the family. Mark was now eleven and had grown considerably since living in Italy. Like his mother, he was dark skinned with black hair and deep-brown eyes. He was more thoughtful and subdued than his sister. Louise was more like her father, with light brown hair and grey-green eyes. At nine years of age she was already noticeably pretty. She was much more extrovert and vivacious than Mark and a permanent tease and irritation to him.

Having spent more time of late with their Italian grandparents, they had become more relaxed in their company and lost most of their initial trepidation. They circled the table to give everyone a kiss. Rico put his arm round Mark and gave him an additional hug. Getting a hug and a kiss and an autograph from the most famous sportsman in Italy sent a warm glow through him; his schoolmates were going to be very jealous.

Louise reserved a special kiss for Auntie Gina, who of

late had shown much more interest in her. On her ninth birthday, Gina had given her a trendy red dress, with white lace trimmings, which she had shown off to the full at her party.

The children escaped to their rooms, pleased to get away from the group of adults, who were becoming more than a little intoxicated and boisterous.

'I have just had a brilliant idea about what you can do to please the people of Rome when you get to being prime minister, Papà,' Gina said. They all looked at her expectantly. 'Why don't you completely restore the Colosseum and reintroduce the ancient Roman games?'

'Good Lord, what a suggestion! And what sort of games are you thinking about, Gina?' Rico enquired with anticipation.

'We could bring back the gladiators. I'm obviously not suggesting they should fight to the death, but it would create a lovely atmosphere. It would bring back the old Rome to the rest of the world.'

'We could have real chariot races again. That would make the Palio chases round the square in Siena look very tame,' Bella chipped in.

'What about restaging the famous naval battles?' Anna suggested. 'We could get boatloads of all our wonderful politicians involved. The crowd would love to see them all take a thorough soaking.'

'Why restrict it to our own politicians?' Rico interjected. 'We could also get all those useless members of the European parliament in Brussels and give them some old-fashioned broadsides.'

'And make sure the water contains a lot of poisonous snakes and crocodiles for when they topple in,' Bella added, giggling.

Paolo was not sure he liked the way the conversation was heading, although he too hated Brussels.

'I've got an even better idea,' cried Paolo. 'Why don't we bring back the lions? We could get all those fucking greedy bankers into the arena and bring on the lions. The whole world would love to see them being torn to pieces!'

'I think we should drink to that!' shouted Rico, and they all raised their glasses and burst into uncontrolled laughter.

Paolo suddenly felt the need for a cigar; he left the table and walked out on to the terrace. Rico decided to follow him to get a bit of fresh air. He was not a smoker and had recently appeared in an anti-smoking campaign on television. Paolo mischievously offered him a cigar, which he sensibly waved away with a grin.

'I know that in the past I have had a bit of a reputation with different women,' Rico began nervously, 'but that has all changed since I met Gina. I never felt the same way towards the others as I do towards her.'

'Are you trying to tell me you are genuinely in love with my daughter?' Paolo asked, coming straight to the point.

'Well, yes, I suppose that is what I'm trying to say. As you know we have been living together for several months and I think Gina feels the same about me.'

'She has had enough publicity with various men, too,' Paolo pointed out, more to relieve Rico's opinion of his own background than to highlight Gina's reputation.

'We've both lived a bit, signore, but I just thought I would let you know that my feelings towards your daughter are genuine and that our relationship is serious.'

'My generation has had to get used to the modern trend of living together rather than marriage,' Paolo ventured.

'I understand what you are saying, and Gina and I have discussed it. We have decided to wait a bit longer yet; there is no need to be precipitate.'

'I wasn't really suggesting anything,' Paolo interrupted,

slightly embarrassed. 'So long as Gina is happy, then so am I. But thank you for letting me know your feelings, no other so-called friend of hers has ever been so courteous.'

In the meantime the women had decided to move to more comfortable chairs. They each picked up some items from the table to take to the kitchen, to save the busy Maria a few journeys. There was a large crash as a pile of plates smashed on the tiled kitchen floor, followed by shrieks of laughter.

'I think it would be better if you left this to me, ladies,' Maria said in a scolding tone. 'Why don't you all just return to the lounge, and I'll clear up the mess.'

The two men could hear the ladies still giggling as they left the kitchen. They looked at each other and raised their eyebrows to the heavens; nothing needed to be said.

Bella took the opportunity of questioning Gina about her relationship with Rico while he was on the terrace.

'We are both very committed to each other,' she confided. 'I have never been so happy and he says the same; and I believe him.'

'Do you really think that being a footballer's wife is the right thing for you?'

'Wait a minute, Mamma, we are not making any decisions about marriage right now, and in any case Rico doesn't intend staying in the football world all his life. He thinks it is a sordid business and wants to do more with his life. He has got a lot of brain, you know, and we want to start a charity together. He wants to use his wealth in a compassionate way.'

'Well, I think he's gorgeous,' Anna remarked, 'you should do everything to hang on to him.'

Paolo and Rico came back into the lounge and the conversation went dead.

'Talking about us?' Paolo asked. 'Which one of us has done something wrong now?'

'Nothing of the sort,' Bella replied, 'we were just having a little chat.'

'I think it's time for bed,' Paolo said, 'we have all got to be up early in the morning.'

'Anna and the kids don't,' Bella corrected.

'I'll give Anna a kiss then, in case I don't see her tomorrow, and then I'm off.'

Rico also made his excuses and left the room with Paolo. They climbed the stairs and parted in opposite directions. Paolo turned and watched Rico enter the bedroom. He still could not get used to his unmarried daughter sleeping with a man under his own roof. 'I would never have got away with it in my father's house,' he said to himself, shaking his head.

When Bella came to bed, she was curious to know what the men had been discussing on the terrace.

'Only that he is very much in love with Gina and they are very happy together.'

'Did he say anything about marriage?'

'He said they were not thinking of rushing anything.'

'So he did mention it,' Bella said, waiting for further confirmation.

'Yes, but that's all he said. He just wanted to let us know that he is not messing about.'

'Gina says the same; it would be nice to see her settle down for a change. Have you noticed how much more interest she is taking in Mark and Louise lately?'

'Is she?' replied Paolo yawning. 'Now look, I'm tired, I'm going get some sleep. I have a very busy day tomorrow. Goodnight darling.'

Bella laid back and stared pensively at the ceiling for a few minutes. 'Do you think we should hold the wedding in Rome or Turin?' she whispered, but Paolo was already asleep.

9

It was around two-thirty in the morning when Pierre Lavalle took over the watch from The Rook.

'Get some sleep and I'll wake you up just before daylight,' he said. 'I presume nothing has happened on your watch to cause a problem?'

'Thank you Pierre, I haven't seen or heard a thing apart from an inquisitive animal or two.' He climbed into the vacated sleeping bag and had no difficulty falling asleep.

The night air had cooled more than Pierre had expected and he sat hugging his knees for warmth. This was the final phase of his mission and he was looking forward to getting home for a while. He was always a little concerned about The Rook who, he believed, could be over enthusiastic at times. He hoped The Rook hadn't prepared some special effects to make the show more spectacular. But they had previously worked together on several occasions with successful results in their nefarious missions.

At the sign of the first light appearing in the east, he woke The Rook. A haversack containing the explosive devices was retrieved from its hiding place and The Rook gently removed the contents.

'I'm taking these down to the road, Pierre, and for God's sake don't touch those remote controls while I'm down there.' He carried one device down to the road and covered it with a small amount of brushwood after setting the remote receiver to positive. He returned for the second, which he placed on the other side of the road. He again activated the remote receiver before concealing the explosive with brushwood. Before climbing back up to their viewpoint he stuck a white stick into the ground.

'All we need to do is this: you can see I have placed that white stick a couple of metres to the left of the explosives – at the precise moment the front of the car passes that marker we both press our remote controls,' The Rook explained. 'Either device is capable of blowing the car to smithereens, and with two separate controls operating both, it will be absolutely fail safe.'

'What if it doesn't work?' Pierre asked, more for something to say than out of any belief that such an event could possibly happen.

'Then we are back here again next week, but don't worry – I can promise you a very loud bang!'

It was now six-thirty and the two settled back for the indeterminate wait. They had plenty of experience from the past to maintain their patience and composure. To help the time pass they went through, hopefully for the last time, the procedure for their immediate escape.

Pierre leant back on his elbows and contemplated the last few weeks. He had been following Paolo almost daily and had learned a great deal about his lifestyle. He had also been listening to his political speeches on the television and radio and often found himself more in agreement with some of his opinions than he might have expected. But, as the Baron had pointed out, when you are dealing with extremists, they invariably appear very plausible and conciliatory in the early stages. It is only when they get into power that the ogre in them becomes apparent, and by then it is too late to oppose them. This man showed all the signs of being a dictator and taking him out now could save a lot of bloodshed in the future. Nevertheless, he had grown a little attached to Paolo and had some regret over his impending assassination.

The Rook was having no second thoughts. To him, this was just another job at which he was an expert and the complete professional. He intended to enjoy the spectacle to the full. The satisfaction of a job well done did not require the luxury of a conscience.

After a little over an hour's waiting they heard a car turn into the lane to their right and watched it drive in the direction of Paolo's property. Pierre studied the vehicle through his binoculars as it passed.

'That was Paolo's Mercedes, just as I expected, and I could make out the three passengers inside. So far so good; they must have arrived to take Paolo to parliament.'

In the still morning air they could clearly hear the sound of the automatic gates opening and the car running over the gravel drive up to the house.

'They are usually out again within twenty minutes, Fritz,' Pierre warned.

At eight o'clock precisely an engine started up and Pierre listened intently. He turned to The Rook. 'That's not the Mercedes,' he whispered, 'it's much too throaty; that has got to be Rico's Lamborghini.'

They listened as the huge V12 engine was revved up to the full several times before dying down as the vehicle slowly eased through the gates. This followed by a mighty roar as the car took off at breakneck speed down the narrow lane.

The two assassins watched as the sports car raced down the lane. There was a loud screeching of tyres as the Lamborghini took the bend below them and accelerated away.

'Did you see that mad bugger take that bend?' Pierre exclaimed. 'He must be crazy!'

'I was terrified he would slide off the road into the explosive; didn't you see me duck instinctively?' The Rook remarked with an obvious sign of relief on his face.

'I wonder what the football club chairman would say if he saw him driving like that down a country lane!'

'Or the national team coach, come to that,' The Rook reminded him.

'It's just as well they are wearing crash helmets. They at least have the common sense to do that.'

'Yes, but he could damage any part of his body in a pile-up at that speed. His legs are far more valuable than his brains and probably insured for a fortune. I bet the insurance company isn't aware he drives like that!'

'I reckon Gina's got a lot of guts sitting in the other seat. Anything could have been coming in the opposite direction when he took that bend.'

'That's true love for you,' The Rook pointed out, and the two men grinned.

Peace returned to the valley as the car sped away into the distance, and they strained their ears for any new sound. At that moment the sun appeared over the treetops and the colours brightened. Pierre noticed how much browner the valley had become since the start of his vigil. A pair of greenfinches had settled on the brushwood on the far side of the road and he had difficulty preventing himself from attempting to frighten them away. Again he experienced a moment's sadness that Paolo would never again see such a beautiful morning.

The sound of another engine starting up reached them and they both stiffened simultaneously.

'This is it,' Pierre whispered, and held the binoculars to his eyes. A minute later he could clearly see the Mercedes coming sedately down the lane. It passed several high bushes before coming into sight again.

'I can definitely make out four people inside, so here we go then.' He put the binoculars gently into the rucksack and picked up his remote control.

'Make sure the front bumper reaches the white stick,' The Rook reminded him.

The chauffeur of the black saloon changed down a gear to take the bend. He rounded the bend and started to accelerate away. At that point the front of the Mercedes passed the white stick.

'Now!' the two men said aloud to themselves, and pressed the remote controls. They flattened themselves on the ground as the shock wave from a mighty explosion rushed passed them. They waited about ten seconds before looking up to see piles of debris still descending to the earth in a large radius from the bend. Some of the lighter debris had gone over 50 metres in the air and they watched until it had all fallen to the ground. Pierre shuddered at the thought of its grisly contents.

'Well, we must have got him!' shouted Pierre, who was still quite deafened from the blast. 'Nobody is going to walk away from that!'

'Of course we got him,' The Rook shouted back, 'what else did you expect?'

'Time to get out of here,' Pierre said, unnecessarily glancing at his watch.

They made sure everything was safely stowed in the rucksack and nothing incriminating had been left behind. They ran through the woods, occasionally stumbling over protruding tree roots in their haste. They changed quickly into the black leathers they had concealed near the motorcycle and packed the rucksack in the saddlebag. With The Rook driving, they went as fast as they dared along the narrow path through the woods, and turned on to the road. Pierre glanced at his watch again; it had taken just seven minutes to get away from the scene, exactly according to plan.

Their escape route took them up the western side of Lake Bracciano and past the town of Viterbo. They continued driving north towards Montefiascone and Orvieto. About 10 kilometres along that road, Pierre decided they had left the scene of the crime far enough behind. He tapped The Rook on the shoulder, who slowed the motorbike down to a crawl. Pierre took a mobile phone from his pocket and punched in a text message.

Sitting in his office in Levallois-Perret, Baron Henri de Courcy heard his own mobile phone vibrate and knew immediately who it was. He pressed the button to bring up the message which read, quite simply, SHERGAR IS A WINNER.

The Baron allowed himself a satisfied smile and reached for his landline telephone. He dialled the prearranged secure number which was answered in a matter of a few seconds.

'Von Meissen here, is that you, Baron?'

'It certainly is Albert, and with the very best news. I have just received confirmation that the project has gone completely to our satisfaction,' the Baron said, avoiding any reference to the actual deed.

'I'm delighted to hear it and might I say how much I appreciate your handling of this little matter. I think we can say, without doubt, that the EU will be a safer place.'

'Perhaps in a few months, Albert, when the dust has settled, we could meet up for the lunch I still owe you.'

'Good idea, but even if you insist on paying, I'd still like to entertain you in Munich for a change. I'll be in touch and thanks again for all your efforts.'

The Baron replaced the receiver and thought for a moment. 'I'd better wait for a while before making an innocent call to our contact in Rome to see if everything is quiet at his end,' he said to himself. He leant back in his chair and allowed himself a deeply satisfied smile.

* * *

Matthew Boston and Martin Ford were sitting in the business section of the British Airways direct flight from Turin to London, totally unaware of the tragedy unfolding beneath them. They had several important meetings arranged which would take up the rest of the day. They were going to see their lawyers first, to get some advice regarding the legal restraints on setting up a subsidiary company in the US.

'We managed it fairly easily in Italy, Matt, and the States are supposed to be very keen on free trade, so I don't see any difficulties,' commented Martin.

'I'm told it's not as simple as you may think. Pharmaceutical companies come under particular scrutiny and we haven't had any experience to date of operating on the other side of the Atlantic.'

'That is your father's fault – he was terrified of getting involved with the Americans. He always said he had no desire to lay the company open to their culture of suing anybody at the slightest pretext. We are going to have to tread very carefully in that respect.'

'Very true, but we didn't really have any products before that the Americans needed. His opinion was that they had equivalent drugs manufactured there, so it wasn't worth our while trying to compete and exposing ourselves to their legal system. But they are extremely interested in Bosteinex 1 and I believe we should take the risk now the drug has the approval of the USFDA.'

'Well, you've been chairman now for a couple of years, and times have certainly moved on fast and become more exciting, so I'm with you on this.'

'I have been doing a lot of research into the various options and I know which one I tend to favour.' Martin looked at him quizzically but decided to let him continue. 'I'm all in favour of going the whole hog and starting up a wholly owned subsidiary of Boston and Wood in the States, just as we did in Italy.'

'But surely you don't intend to open a factory there as well, do you?'

'Not at the moment, but who knows? I've no doubt the drug will be a winner, so we might contemplate manufacturing a number of our lines in the US in the future. I'm only talking about enough to satisfy the American market if we can break into it; home production won't be affected.'

'I accept, Matt, that if we get a large demand in the States, we won't be able to cope for much longer at the Turin factory, especially with the enormous increase in sales we are getting in the Far East and China. But I would still question the wisdom of exposing the company to American jurisdiction.'

'Well, let's wait and see what adverse advice we get, if any, from Pitt and Stainer. I haven't used them before but I am reliably informed they are about the best on US regulation. If they think we should take the bull by the horns, I shall rely on your support. Nothing ventured, nothing gained, as they say.'

'If you are considering taking chances, you might have difficulty persuading the board next week,' Martin replied, with a strong hint of caution in his voice.

'Leave me to worry about that, Martin, I wouldn't dream of going into a full board meeting unless I knew I already had the directors behind me. My father gave me very sound advice. Never, he said, chair a meeting unless you are completely versant on every item on the agenda. Never allow a director to surprise you, and keep discussion down to an absolute minimum. As far as I'm concerned, a board meeting is purely for rubber-stamping matters that have already been debated and approved. So believe me, I won't be laying myself open to any opposition.'

'Yes, Matt, I accept that Gerald and now you have always run very carefully contrived meetings, but this is going into the realms of the unknown. Just make sure you allow the directors plenty of time to consider whatever you intend to propose.'

'I detect that you feel this may be a bridge too far, Martin,' surmised Matthew.

'What about the non-executive directors?' Martin continued, ignoring the observation. 'They are bound to make a number of comments; they always do, if only to prove they've read the board pack.'

'Yes, and what a bloody great waste of time and money they are! Do you realise how much we have to pay them? It is only to go along with all this compliance nonsense that we have to put up with them in the first place. You know only too well, they come to the meetings and try to appear intelligent, when it is quite apparent they are bored to tears. They understand fuck all about the business and waffle on about irrelevant matters to hide their ignorance,' Matthew fumed.

'I agree with you, Matt, and every businessman I talk to is of the same opinion. All companies are now grossly over-regulated. It is the way the politicians protect their backsides – by distancing themselves from the realities of the hard world.'

'Have you noticed that every time there is a problem, the government can't wait to set up an enquiry? It may be referred to as a public or private investigation, or even a Royal Commission, but they all have the same outcome. I go into fits of despair whenever I learn that another enquiry is going to be chaired by some Lord Ignoramus. They are supposed to be "independent", but he, or she, will be easily influenced by the loudest voice or deepest pocket. Then a year later, to the blast of trumpets, we get a report that has cost millions to produce and says precisely nothing. These investigations are just jobs for the boys and expensive ones at that. And what is even worse is that people are expected to act on the ill-conceived advice that comes out from them.'

Martin, who had heard Matthew pontificate on this subject several times before, decided to move the conversation on. 'What are we doing after we've finished with the lawyers, Matt?'

'We are seeing the insurance brokers, who have invited us to discuss what sort of cover we will need; over lunch, if we get there in time.'

'I assume that will be Cooper and Hartley, with whom we normally deal?'

'Bob Hartley will be there, but he is going to introduce us to another firm of Lloyd's Brokers that specialises in US liability insurance. Apparently it is not going to be easy to get cover, and it will almost certainly cost a packet.'

'Let's hope the lawyers don't delay us then. The last time we had lunch with Bob, he took us to the City Club, and they have a wonderful cellar!'

'Yes, I remember it well, but that was on a very relaxed occasion. This time we will need to keep a clear head to understand all the complicated details. In many ways the brokers will have more experience of liability claims than the lawyers. We need to be very precise about the extent of cover we will require.'

'Okay, Matt, you're quite right; just fizzy water at lunchtime. If you are staying in town, perhaps we could sink a few this evening?'

'Sorry Martin, I've arranged to meet my brother Philip, whom I rarely get a decent opportunity to see these days.'

'Oh, give him my regards, I don't remember when he and I last met. Where is he stationed now?'

'All over the place; I never know where to find him. He seems to spend a lot of time near Fréjus, in the south of France; you know, where the Foreign Legion has its headquarters.'

'He's getting mixed up with a rough crowd, then,' Martin remarked with a grin. 'Good job he's a bachelor, I wouldn't want to take a wife anywhere near that lot!'

'His mother is not too keen on his latest assignment either, but she's not told everything that goes on.'

'Did you say we are also meeting some bankers, Matt?'

'That's right, if we get time, but we can't discuss any ideas with them until we have the lawyers' advice. I'd like to have some concrete plans before the board meeting next month and I definitely want you to be there.'

'Like you said, you shouldn't table anything until you are sure of getting full support. I think the next meeting would be far too soon.'

Martin was distinctly nervous of Matthew's precipitate nature and wanted plenty of time to weigh up the pros and cons. Trading in America would require a great deal of careful planning and exhaustive preparation.

'You may be right, Martin, but we need to move things along as quickly as possible. David assures me that Bosteinex is far more efficacious than these poly-pills that are being sold, but I would hate to lose the market because someone else comes up with a comparable drug.'

Their conversation was interrupted by the captain announcing their anticipated landing at Gatwick in twenty minutes' time. He reminded passengers to adjust their watches to the local time in England which was ten minutes to nine.

Carrying only a small cabin bag each, they were able to leave the airport precinct without delay and were soon aboard the Gatwick Express to London. As the train was approaching East Croydon, Matthew's mobile phone rang. Several passengers in the compartment glared at him and he swiftly switched the sound off. There is an unwritten code in the first class carriage that mobile phones are no longer acceptable. He nodded an apology all round and looked at the phone to see who was trying to contact him, as only a few people had this particular number. It was Anna. He noticed that he had also received a text message whilst he was on the plane. This was also from Anna asking him to get in touch urgently.

'Anna is trying to reach me,' he said to Martin, 'I'd better give her a call immediately we get to Victoria. It's not like her to ring when she knows I'm travelling. I hope there is nothing wrong there – I've got enough to contend with.'

When they arrived at Victoria and passed through the barriers, Matthew looked for a place away from the rushing crowds and loudspeakers. Martin waited while he put in a call to Anna. In London the time was exactly ten fifteen.

Having sent the text message to Paris, Pierre and The Rook continued their drive north in the direction of Florence. They picked up the A1 motorway at the Orvieto junction and proceeded at a steady 100 kilometres per hour to remain well within the speed limit. This autoroute is the spine of Italy, running from Milan in the north, past Modena, Florence and Rome, and finishing near Naples in the south.

They had just passed the Arezzo turn-off when Pierre felt the mobile phone in his pocket vibrate. Once again, he tapped The Rook on the shoulder, who nodded his understanding. He turned into the next service station and pulled up by a pump.

Filling his open-top Lotus Elan, Sean Barker, MI6's senior agent, operating out of the British Embassy in Rome, watched as the motorcycle drew up. He was tapping his feet rhythmically to the smooth sound of Kid Ory playing 'Loveless Love' on the trombone. He noticed the pillion passenger get off the bike and turn his back on the security camera. He walked to one side of the forecourt and removed his crash helmet.

Pierre, unaware that he was under observation, took the phone from his pocket and returned the call to the Baron in Paris. He received the news that French agents had picked up police signals in Rome that there had been an attempted assassination. The police had reason to believe a motorcycle was involved as tyre marks had been discovered in the woods nearby.

'Where are you now?' the Baron enquired, and Pierre gave him their exact position. 'Then I suggest you keep to the minor roads from now on, although you are probably well away from scrutiny already.'

'We'll do just that, Baron,' he replied, 'and with a bit of luck I'll see you in Paris tomorrow.'

As Pierre reached for his helmet that he had placed on a low wall, Sean stiffened and stared hard. 'Pierre Lavalle,' he said to himself, 'I'd recognise that nose anywhere. I wonder what he's doing here. This is not his usual territory; and why the beard?'

Sean's natural reaction was to go over and slap the man on the back, but his training had taught him otherwise. He slipped quietly into the Lotus and continued to watch the men through a wing mirror. Pierre replaced the helmet on his head and lifted the visor to speak to his companion. The Rook, who had just finished filling the tank, also lifted his visor, and received the new instructions. Sean strained to recognise the other man, but the slit was too narrow and the dark beard concealed too much of his face.

Seam waited patiently in the car while The Rook walked over to the kiosk, paid the bill and returned to the motorbike. Pierre now moved on to the driver's seat and The Rook checked the map before climbing on behind him. Sean waited until they had gone out of sight before getting out to pay his own bill.

'Is anything the matter?' asked the blonde girl who was sitting in the passenger seat when he returned. She had been waiting patiently, wondering why he was behaving in such a peculiar manner.

'No, nothing at all,' Sean replied, 'just thought I saw someone I knew.'

'What, one of the motorcyclists?' she continued.

'Yes, but I couldn't see well enough to be sure,' he replied dismissively and started the engine.

'You looked as though you were hiding from him,' she persisted.

'Look, angel, if he was who I thought he might be, I didn't want to get involved, okay?' he replied irritably and slammed the car into gear. He regained his composure on hearing Jack Teagarden playing 'After You've Gone' on his trombone; he just loved that instrument and had brought a number of traditional jazz discs for the journey. Sean regained the motorway and continued on the long drive to Spain, where a three-week break awaited him and his new girlfriend. He had not taken a holiday for almost two years.

At the next exit Pierre paid the toll and proceeded along the back roads on the west side of Florence. Their next destination was to be a small lake near Maranello to the south of Modena. Pierre had previously checked out the site and it was perfect for the switchover. They would now have to drive through a mountainous region, which would slow down their progress, but up till then they had been slightly ahead of schedule.

Nearly two hours later, Pierre found the track that led from the winding road and passed through woodland down to the lake. He drove along it but was stopped by a woman who appeared suddenly from behind the trees and flagged him down. It was Michelle, who had originally taken him to Italy at the start of the mission.

'We have a little problem,' she informed them. 'There is a fisherman in full view at the lake. I suggest you switch off the engine and roll down the path to just short of the lake and conceal the bike for a while. I'll follow you down.'

Following her instructions, Pierre drove silently down the track, noticing on the way Michelle's Renault Mégane parked in a clearing. After a few hundred metres, he pulled off the track short of the lake and waited for her to catch up.

'Helga was already here when I arrived and she caught sight of the fisherman. That's why I'm parked back there,' she said.

'Where is Helga?' asked The Rook. 'Has she been spotted?'

'She's down by the lakeside; she has obviously been seen, but that is not a problem.'

Pierre thought for a moment but came up with no immediate solution. 'I suppose we will have to take him out,' he finally said.

'I could easily manage that,' offered The Rook with relish.

'There is no need for that,' Michelle interjected, giving The Rook a cold stare. 'Helga has a better idea: we are all just going to the edge of the lake and having a bit of fun. We discussed several alternatives and we certainly don't want any dead bodies around. That would only lead to the police taking an interest and possibly dragging the lake. Follow me.'

They joined Helga at the edge of the lake, where she was getting some sandwiches from the boot of an emerald green Volkswagen Golf. Michelle supplied a bottle of Pinot Grigio and the group sat enjoying the light picnic. The fisherman, who came to the lake every Monday for a bit of peace and solitude, glared aggressively at them from across the water.

When they had finished eating, Helga packed the remains back into the car and walked with deliberation to the edge of the lake. She was tall and slim with long blonde hair and sensuous lips. The fisherman watched as she removed her sweater, followed by her shoes and jeans.

A loud cheer from the other three rose as she slowly removed her red bra with lace edging and slid into the water. She swam, with a lazy crawl, past the fisherman and turned toward the shore about 20 metres further on. He had now forgotten his initial annoyance at the intrusion and was wondering what Helga's next move would be.

She swam to the edge and climbed out of the lake, stumbling a little as the soft mud clung on to her feet. She started to walk towards him, cupping her hands beneath her ample breasts. The cold water had made her large pink nipples protrude and he was unable to divert his gaze. Ten metres from him she came to a halt and began slowly to remove her matching red panties that were clinging to her wet body. The mesmerised fisherman continued to stare despite an apprehensive feeling beginning to come over him.

Out of his vision, the two assassins were gently lowering the motorcycle into the lake. The number plates had been removed and the tyres slashed to avoid any chance of an upsurge of bubbles in the water. They made sure it had sunk completely before rejoining Michelle at the lakeside. They had packed their leathers and helmets into the side saddlebags. The rucksack containing the remote controls and a few tools they had buried in the woods separately from the number plates. All incriminating evidence of their deed was now completely out of sight. Their exaggeratedly loud chatter on the side of the lake signalled to Helga that the task had been completed.

Helga continued her deliberately provocative walk towards the fisherman, put her arms round his neck and planted a long kiss on his cheek. When she released him, he toppled slowly backwards off his canvas stool.

'Thank you very much,' she remarked, 'my friends over there bet me fifty euros each I wouldn't dare do that.' She put the stool back upright and helped him recover his position. Once she had retrieved her panties, she dived triumphantly into the lake and swam back to the others. The fisherman watched as she climbed out of the water and received a towel from Michelle.

'Wait till I tell the lads back at the fishing club about this,' he said aloud to himself. But then it dawned on him: this would be just another fisherman's story that would never be believed!

The four secret agents climbed into the VW and left the lake behind. Michelle and Pierre got out by the clearing where she had parked the Renault. Hands were shaken and cheeks kissed before they set off, in their respective directions, for home.

10

The light-blue Lamborghini turned slowly into a lay-by off the A90 ring road. Paolo Medina, sitting in the driving seat, removed his crash helmet and turned to speak to the passenger. The bodyguard pulled off his own helmet, wiped a little sweat from his forehead, and grinned at Paolo. There was an obvious look of relief on his face.

'How long before the others get here, do you think?' Paolo enquired.

'The speed at which you were driving, sir, we could have quite a long wait,' his bodyguard replied with a hint of sarcasm. 'Considering that you usually insist on our chauffeur keeping to the speed limits, you're lucky the *carabinieri* didn't spot us today.'

'They wouldn't have managed to catch me,' Paolo remarked contemptuously, 'and even if they got the licence number or recognised the car, Rico would get the blame,' he added with a smile.

'Well, if they left just after us, they shouldn't take more than fifteen to twenty minutes to catch up. By the way, you must have forgotten the police have recently acquired a few Lamborghinis specially to catch speeding motorists, so you could have had quite a race.'

Paolo fumbled in his pocket and took out a cigar. He removed the band, rolled it gently between his fingers before clipping the end and lighting it with a match. He sat back contentedly.

'You know, Gino, this car is an absolute dream to drive. The handling is so light and she's so responsive to the slightest touch. I wouldn't mind getting one for myself,' he said, giving his bodyguard a mischievous look.

'That wouldn't do a lot for your image, sir. I don't think the factory workers in the north would appreciate your turning up to meetings in one of these.'

'They all worship Rico Orvetti,' Paolo pointed out with a laugh.

'I know they do, but it's not the same for a socialist politician. You know you shouldn't even be seen driving this car, let alone owning one.'

Paolo reluctantly nodded his agreement. Fast cars were his one weakness and he hated giving them up, even for his political ambitions. He glanced at his watch.

'We've been here over twenty minutes; they should be here by now. What the hell is keeping them? I bet that daughter of mine wasn't ready – she's never on time for anything!'

'I'll give Fredo a call and find out where they are, sir,' Gino said, pulling his mobile phone out of a pocket. He dialled a number and waited for a response.

'I can't seem to get through;' he said, checking that there was a strong signal showing on the screen. 'They must be in a dead zone. His phone isn't even ringing; he most definitely wouldn't have switched it off.'

'Try the chauffeur, then.'

'I'll see if his phone rings, but he won't answer it while he's driving.' Gino pressed some more buttons, but with no luck. 'They must be caught in a tunnel somewhere; don't worry, they'll be here in a minute or two.'

'I think I'll phone Bella and find out what time they left; they really shouldn't take all this time. They know damn well I hate being late,' Paolo snapped, beginning to get agitated. He snatched Gino's mobile and dialled the house number.

'Is that you, Bella?' he demanded brusquely. 'Whatever

time did Gina leave after me, assuming she's not still with you? There's no sign of them and Gino's not been able to contact the car.'

'They left only a few minutes after you,' Bella replied calmly, using her long experience in dealing with an irate husband. 'I expect they'll be with you any minute now.'

'But we've been waiting over half an hour; they should have got here ages ago.'

'Actually, I was quite pleased to hear your voice on the phone. There was a loud bang not long after you left and I said to Anna, "I hope Papà hasn't hit a tree, you know how he drives sometimes." But then I remembered they are blasting again at the old quarry.'

'I expect you are right Bella, and they'll be here shortly,' Paolo replied hurriedly. 'I'll get Gina to give you a ring when we've swapped cars, ciao.' He rang off and turned to his bodyguard.

'There was a loud explosion not long after we left, which she assumed to be from the quarry. I don't like the sound of it at all.'

Gino let out a low whistle. 'Neither do I, sir. What do you think we ought to do?'

'I think we had better go back and find out if there's been an accident,' Paolo replied, but he already feared the word 'accident' could be a euphemism. He started the engine, but Gino put a hand on the wheel.

'I think you had better let me drive, sir, your hand is shaking already.' For once, Paolo didn't argue and they exchanged places.

Gino set off and this time took the shortest route back towards Bracciano. 'Don't you think you should phone the police, sir, and find out if they have received any reports of an accident? They should at least be alerted.'

Paolo just sat motionless, with his head in his hands and the helmet rolling about beneath his legs. He made no response, so Gino drove as quickly as he was able along the twisting road. As he turned into the narrow lane leading up to the house, he could see the flashing lights of a police vehicle. He tapped Paolo on the shoulder and stopped the car.

Paolo contemplated the situation for a moment. 'We'd better go and find out what has happened,' he said, trying to brace himself for the inevitable shock. Gino eased the car forward until he was stopped by the outstretched arm of a police officer.

'I'm afraid you can't come through this way, sir,' he started, but then went silent on seeing Paolo emerging from the passenger side.

He stood up and straightened his back. 'What has happened here?' he questioned tentatively. The policeman took a step back as a more senior officer strolled towards the car. He also recognised Paolo and took him by the arm.

'Thank God you are safe, sir. It looks like someone has blown up a vehicle and I feared you might be the target, being so close to your house.'

Paolo slumped down on the front wing and shook his head in grief. 'I almost certainly was,' he said, 'and, God, I wish I had been in the car. Are you sure it was an explosion and not an accident or collision?'

'You may take a look if you like, sir, but there is nothing much to see but a huge hole in the ground and a lot of debris. Nobody could have survived; it wasn't an accident, that's for sure.'

Paolo was shaking visibly as he got to his feet and walked forward. The policeman held up the security tape to allow him to pass. He rounded the bend before he could see the massive hole and the scene of total destruction. The senior officer went with him and held his arm for support. Paolo stood for several minutes and then turned his back on the unbelievable devastation.

'I've seen enough,' he said to the officer, and his whole demeanour hardened. He returned to the car and got into the driver's seat.

'You won't be able to go through this way, sir,' said the officer. 'If you are going home you will have to take the long route round and enter from the other direction. And if you have any idea who was in the vehicle, we will need to know.'

'Come up to the house in half an hour and we will talk then,' Paolo replied and reversed the Lamborghini down the lane. He backed the car into a small clearing to turn round and set off for his house by the alternative route. He managed to leave just before several journalists, who had been listening in to the police broadcasts, arrived at the lane. As he reached the iron gates, he realised he had left his bodyguard behind at the scene.

Not having a remote control in the Lamborghini to open the gates, he pulled himself out of the car and rang the bell. He heard Maria asking who was there and replied in a voice cracking with emotion. The gates opened and he drove nervously up the drive, wondering what he was going to say to Bella.

He was greeted by Anna and Bella while Maria stood anxiously in the background. Bella was already in a state of deep concern, having tried unsuccessfully to contact Gina on several occasions after Paolo's phone call. She rushed over to him as he got out of the Lamborghini.

'What's happened; why have you come back; has there been an accident?' she gasped, as she grabbed him by the arm.

Paolo pulled her to him and hugged her for a moment. 'We had better go into the house,' he said, 'I think something terrible has happened.'

Anna came over and assisted her mother into the house. They insisted she sat down before Paolo tried to tell her

147

what he thought must have occurred. He sat on the arm of the chair and held her hand with both of his.

'I believe there was an attempt on my life down the lane this morning. There has been a massive explosion and the car is a complete wreck. If Gina was in the car...' but his voice trailed away as Bella let out a shriek.

She leaped to her feet. 'Oh, no! Not my girl, not my little girl!' she cried, and Paolo caught her as she stumbled towards a table.

'Dear God, not Gina,' Anna wailed, and collapsed sobbing into a chair.

Maria burst into tears and fled to the kitchen. Paolo held on to Bella for a while before gently easing her back into a chair; he had barely had enough time to get over his shock and he started to shake uncontrollably. He sat down and tried to pull himself together. The women were still crying and he felt helpless and inadequate. He put his head in his hands and finally the tears came.

Mark and Louise were staring through the patio doors. They had heard Bella's scream and come to investigate. On seeing the tragic spectacle inside, they had remained nervously in the garden. Maria, who had recovered a little from the shock, remembered the children and appeared on the terrace.

'Mamma's had some terrible news,' she told them, 'I think you had better stay in the garden with me for a while.'

'Why, what has happened?' Mark demanded. 'We want to know.'

Maria knew it was not her place to tell the children that their aunt had died. 'I don't know exactly,' she lied. 'I think you should wait until your mother knows a bit more.' She pulled them gently away from the windows.

Anna was the first to recover a little and she sat watching the desolation of her parents. She walked over to her mother and knelt down in front of her. She put her head on Bella's lap and allowed her mother to run her fingers through her hair. This seemed to give Bella some comfort and she slowly raised her head and attempted to dry her eyes.

Paolo removed his head from his hands and leaned back in the chair. 'I should have been in that car,' he whispered. 'God, why did I have to go off like that? It's all my fault.'

Anna moved over to his chair and sat on the arm. 'It's not your fault, Papà,' she said. 'Who would want to kill you?'

'When you are in politics you make enemies...' Paolo began, but was interrupted by the sound of the doorbell. Maria came into the room and waited for instructions.

'If that is the police,' Paolo said resignedly, 'you had better let them in to my study. I don't want to see anybody else,' he added.

Maria showed the superintendent into the study while Paolo washed his face and settled himself for the meeting. He walked into the study, shook hands limply, and invited the policeman to sit.

The two men sat facing each other, both waiting for the other to open the conversation. Finally, the superintendent spoke. 'I am Superintendent Carlo Vincenti from Bracciano,' he began, 'and I'm very sorry to see what has obviously occurred this morning. But thank God you were not in the vehicle. If it was your car involved, I assume you know who was; was it only your driver?'

Paolo, his right elbow on his desk and hand gently manipulating his forehead, shook his head. 'There were four people in the car,' he said, 'my daughter was one of them.' He continued to shake his head in despair.

The superintendent was more used to giving out bad news, for which he had made preparations, and found himself unable to reply immediately.

149

'I, I, I'm so sorry to hear that, signore,' he eventually stuttered. 'Would you prefer I leave now and come back later? I hadn't realised a member of your family was involved.'

'No, stay here and I'll tell you what you need to know. I realise you have a job to do.'

Superintendent Vincenti took a notebook from his pocket and looked enquiringly at Paolo.

'I believe the four people in my Mercedes were my chauffeur, Toni Ferrino, and a bodyguard, Fredo Poltera. My daughter Gina, and Rico Orvetti, the footballer, were also in the car.'

The Superintendent's eyes widened with disbelief; this was going to be even bigger than he originally suspected. He continued to utter his condolences before saying, 'I think I will have to get in touch with Rome for instructions. Do you think I could telephone from here? I don't want to use the police line; the press listen in to our broadcasts.'

Paolo motioned towards the phone on his desk and sat back as the superintendent dialled a number.

'Superintendent Vincenti here; I was talking to Commissioner Carlotta about half an hour ago and need to speak to him again. It is extremely urgent, tell him.' The operator went off the line and almost immediately the commissioner came on.

'What's the problem Vicenti? I thought you reckoned you could handle things when you discovered Signor Medina was not the target?'

'I believe now he was the intended target, Commissioner, and at this moment I am sitting with him in his study using his telephone for security. It appears that the car blown up was his official Mercedes and there were four passengers, including his daughter, Gina, and Riccardo Orvetti.'

The Commissioner let out a long whistle. 'I'd better get over there as fast as I can. What do we need?'

'Plenty of reinforcements, sir. We need to shut the site off completely from the media and all the public who will come pouring out to stare at the scene. Signor Medina will need his house protected from the paparazzi; we will probably require about a hundred men and I can't supply many of them from Bracciano.'

'Leave it with me, Vincenti, and in the meantime keep the press well away from the area. I would like to get all the men in position before we make any announcement to the media. My deputy will organise that and get on to the aviation authority to make sure the area is out of bounds to air traffic. We'll try to do as much as possible without using the police channels. There must be no mention yet of the names of the victims; I'm on my way.'

Superintendent Vincenti replaced the phone and turned to Paolo. 'The Commissioner is taking charge and will be here as soon as possible. If there is anything I can do in the meantime ... perhaps you would like us to get your doctor here?'

'Unfortunately, our family doctor is in Turin and we have not had any reason to call on one since moving here. I have a consultant for my heart in Rome, but he wouldn't be any use. I think Bella will need some medical assistance.'

'I know just the man to help you, signore; I'll send a car out to fetch him. Now, if you will excuse me I will get on. Anything you want, you just have to ask.'

Paolo remained in his chair as the policeman got up and left the house. He eventually plucked up the courage to return to the room where Bella and Anna were still consoling each other.

Bella turned on him. 'How could you let this happen? She was so happy, I've never seen her so happy,' she shrieked and she burst into tears again.

Anna, who had regained a little composure, went to her aid again. 'It's not Papà's fault,' she said in a placatory voice. 'It's not anybody's fault; we must all stick together now and help each other.'

Paolo slumped into a chair. 'The police superintendent is arranging for a doctor from Bracciano to come round,' he remarked, for something to say.

'Don't you have a doctor here...' Anna began to question, but stopped when she heard her mobile ringing. She searched round for her handbag and fumbled vainly inside. Paolo watched as she frantically tipped the bag upside down to find the phone. She recognised the number calling and went into another room to speak to her husband.

'Anna, is that you? Why are you trying to contact me; is anything the matter?' Matthew enquired.

'There has been a terrible accident and Gina has been killed. She's dead, Matt. Papà's car was blown up and she was in it.' Her voice trailed away and she burst into tears again.

'Oh my God, Anna, I'm so sorry,' said Matthew fumbling for something to say. 'How on earth did that happen? Was your father in the car too? Are you all right, darling?'

Anna took a deep breath and recounted the events of the morning. Matthew let it all pour out from her, although he was having difficulty hearing everything she was saying. She spoke for about five minutes without interruption until she started to cry once more.

'What about Mark and Louise?' he managed to ask. 'How are they taking it?'

'I haven't told them yet, although they know something awful has occurred. I shall have to tell them next and they are going to be terribly upset.'

'Of course they are darling; look, I'm going to catch the next plane to Rome and I'll be with you as soon as I can.'

'You may have trouble getting to the house as the police are throwing a cordon round the whole area. Keep in touch and we will let them know when you are coming.

I'm dreading telling the kids, Matt; they are going to be devastated.'

'I don't know what you are going to say, darling; Louise was getting quite infatuated with Gina. Perhaps it would be a good idea if I brought them back here; they could stay with my parents.'

'We can discuss that when you get here,' she replied, unable to get her mind round any immediate decision.

'Okay, I'm on my way to Heathrow now, ciao.' Matthew rang off and drew a deep breath; he found Martin waiting for him and gave him the news. 'I'm going to get a cab to Heathrow right now and get on the next flight to Rome. I suggest you go to the meetings and glean what information you can and report back to me. My movements from now on are going to be dictated by events, but I'll try to get to see the lawyers as soon as possible. I don't want to delay things any more than I have to.' Martin put an arm round Matthew and led him to the taxi rank outside the station. 'Just let me know if there's anything I can do, Matt. Look after yourself,' he added.

'Thanks, Martin; Anna says the press haven't been informed yet, but all hell will be let loose when they find out. Do you mind phoning David and telling him? He won't want to hear it on the news. I suggest you make sure you get your own flight back booked immediately; the whole world's media is going to be making a beeline for Italy this week.'

'You're right Matt, I'll get Jane on to it straight away.'

'Wait until I've spoken to her first. I want her to get me on the next flight out of Heathrow, whatever the cost.' He waved farewell as the cab pulled away.

Matthew sat in the back and called Jane first and then his parents. Gerald was on the golf course but Linda was there to take the call.

'My God, Matt, what a dreadful thing. How on earth are

the family going to take this shock? What was Anna like when you spoke to her? How are Mark and Louise going to take it? Did you say they are actually staying at the house where it happened? Is there anything we can do to help? We have nothing important on this week. Why don't you come and stay with us? You won't want to be all by yourself.'

Matthew waited, without interrupting, for his mother to finish; he was used to her nervous outbursts. 'I'm going straight back to Rome,' he eventually managed to say, 'I need to be with the family. I'll let you know what my next movements are when I know myself. I might suggest Mark and Louise come over and stay with you, if that's all right.'

'Of course they can, we can look after them. Your father is going to be terribly shocked when he gets back. I'll turn on the television to see whether there is any news coming through. What an awful thing to happen. Take care of yourself, darling. We'll be thinking of you all.'

'Okay Mum, I'll be in touch; cheerio.' He rang off, settled back in the cab and closed his eyes till he reached the airport.

As requested, Martin phoned David in Turin to give him the news. He was surprised to learn that David had already heard. 'Anna rang me earlier, Martin,' David explained. 'She wanted to talk to someone and Matthew wasn't answering his phone.'

'She knew damn well he was on a plane and couldn't use his mobile,' Martin replied. Like Linda, he had noticed a strong bond between Anna and David. 'I've got to go to these wretched meetings without the chairman now; I'll let you know when I'm coming back.' He rang off and went to the underground station to catch a Victoria line train to Oxford Circus.

*   *   *

At three o'clock in the afternoon, the Commissioner called a press conference. There had been wild speculation circulating since the media heard about the explosion. Once they had ascertained that Paolo Medina was not in the car the rumours began. If he was not the victim, then who was? There was already gossip at the Stadio Olimpico that Rico had not reported for training and could not be reached on his mobile. The press were getting frantic for information.

When the announcement from the police finally came, the whole of Italy went into a state of shock. It was one of those occasions when every Italian would remember where they were when the news broke. There was a sudden desire by everybody to go home, as though they felt themselves threatened by the news.

In Rome the roads quickly blocked up, and the entrances to the metro became a mass of people pushing for position. The railway stations were in complete turmoil as passengers, unused to travelling at that earlier time of day, milled around the indicator boards. The *carabinieri*, renowned for hanging around aggressively in large numbers, were not prepared to deal with the situation. They melted away and let chaos reign.

The police threw a large cordon around the area of the explosion. Roads were blocked and diversions organised. Press reporters screamed abuse at the officers in charge for preventing access to the site. Eventually a chosen few, including some television news cameras, were allowed to photograph the scene. They found there were already many forensic medical and scientific experts sifting through the debris.

Following the police announcement, Supt Vincenti arrived at Paolo's residence accompanied by a police doctor. They asked if they could see Paolo alone and he showed them into his study.

'I have to ask you a particular favour, Signor Medina, and I thought it better the ladies were not in the room. The doctor here needs to take a DNA sample from you to help identify the remains the forensic experts are accumulating from the explosion. We obviously would want to get as much of the remains as possible to the families for burial. If I could also have your permission to go into your daughter's apartment in Rome we should be able to get some DNA from there to verify your sample. We are naturally asking for the same help from the families of the other victims.'

Paolo slowly nodded his consent. The doctor took a swab sample from the inside of his cheek and checked whether he needed any medication. Paolo declined as the superintendent's recommended doctor had already prescribed a variety of drugs to help the family through their trauma.

'We will leave no stone unturned until we have found the perpetrators of this crime, signore,' the superintendent promised.

'I know you will, and I have already had that promise from the President, who was kind enough to phone me. I realise that I can be a little controversial at times, but I never expected an attempt on my life. I hope the politics in this country is not going back to the dark ages again.'

'It seems it could be, signore, but we'll get these bastards, I assure you.'

Paolo showed the two men to the door and returned to the lounge, where Bella wanted to know the reason for the policeman's visit.

'He just wanted a bit of information about my car,' Paolo replied, deliberately avoiding the truth. 'It seems it will be a few days before they can release Gina's body for burial as a lot of forensic work needs to be carried out on the vehicle. We can't make any arrangements for the funeral until we get police approval.'

'What about Mark and Louise?' Bella asked, trying to steady her mind and appear composed. 'Where are they now?'

'They were in such a state after I told them and they went to their rooms,' Anna replied. 'The doctor prescribed a light analgesic for them and they are sleeping peacefully now. I don't want to disturb them.'

'I knew Louise would be traumatised; she has become very close to Gina since you all moved over here. She is going to need a lot of care, you know,' Paolo remarked.

'She will probably be a little better when Matt arrives,' Anna remarked. 'She has become a real daddy's girl lately. By the way, did you warn the police to let him through?'

'That's all arranged, so he could be arriving anytime now,' Paolo replied. 'I shall be certainly be grateful for his help over the next few days.'

'If he agrees to stay,' Anna remarked acidly, 'provided he hasn't got something more important on with the business!'

Bella burst into tears again. 'I hope you two aren't going to quarrel,' she sobbed, 'I just can't bear any of that.'

An hour later, a call from the police confirmed Matthew's arrival at the gates and Maria went out to help with his luggage. The taxi driver muttered his condolences and, out of respect, refused payment of the fare. He reversed into the lane under police direction and took the long route back to the airport.

Sitting in a long traffic queue approaching the French border at Bordighera, Sean Barker was still tapping his feet to the rhythm of a traditional jazz number. His girlfriend was looking bored and irritated by the slow progress. He felt rather than heard his mobile phone ring and switched off the music when he recognised the caller.

'Is that you Barker, where the hell are you? I've been ringing for ages!' Alan Dewar, the deputy head of M16, shouted down the phone.

'I'm just off on holiday, sir, and I'm sitting in a bloody traffic jam. I did let head office know I would be away, and I haven't had a break for nearly two years.'

'Haven't you heard the news, man? We've been expecting you to contact us with some information.'

'I've been listening to CDs in my car on my way to the border. Why, what's been happening, sir?'

'I suggest you turn on your radio; there's only been an assassination attempt on Paolo Medina, that's all! You'd better cancel your leave and get back to Rome and find out what's going on. Get your contacts working, the DG wants to know who's behind all this.'

Sean reluctantly accepted the instructions and rang off. 'One day I'll get a bloody break!' he said to himself. He explained the situation to his girlfriend who, to his amazement, just shrugged her shoulders. He switched on the news station to get a full report and moved slowly along with the queue. 'That's why there's a queue, Martina,' he remarked, 'they are obviously checking every car at the border.'

As he edged forward, his back suddenly stiffened. The earlier event of the day shot into his mind when he heard the announcement that the police were interested in a motorbike. 'Give me that map, Martina,' he said excitedly, and pulled over on to the hard shoulder.

He studied the map and found the service station at which he had filled his car that morning. He worked out the timing and a satisfied grin came over his face. 'They could have done it,' he said out loud, but only received a blank stare from his passenger in exchange.

He phoned Alan Dewar at headquarters. 'I think I might have some interesting information, sir, but I wouldn't like to mention it over the phone. What I suggest I do is drive to Nice and get on a plane to London. Could you get me booked on an evening flight? Oh, and I shall need two tickets,' he added.

'I'm intrigued, Barker; yes, I can get that arranged. See you tomorrow morning then.'

Sean turned to Martina. 'Change of plan my lovely; we are going to London instead.'

Martina smiled at last. Having been brought up on the spectacular Adriatic coast of Croatia, Spanish beaches held little appeal. London sounded much more exciting.

11

The shock waves running through Italy were transmitted to the whole of the world by an over-zealous media. There had not been a political assassination in Italy for more than thirty years and the hideous death of a major football star only magnified the headlines. The European press was particularly outraged, filling both their political and sports pages with angry speculation.

The fact that Paolo Medina had survived presented the left wing with an immediate hero. His anguish over the loss of his daughter was totally ignored by those seeking to take political advantage. The fascists were initially accused of perpetrating the assassination, but after strong denial, the Mafia became the main suspects.

The news of the failure to kill Paolo had come as a huge shock to the Baron in Paris. His subsequent call to Albert Von Meissen was embarrassing and apologetic. They decided to delay their lunch meeting in Munich to a more suitable occasion.

'I've found a posting for Lavalle in Serbia, where he can contemplate his future,' the Baron informed Albert. 'Thank God we kept the operation between just the two of us.'

'I'm still wondering what to do with The Rook,' Albert replied, 'but, I agree, we will just have to keep things under wraps. As we anticipated the Mafia is right in the firing line, so there is little prospect of anyone else coming under suspicion. It is just as well I took your advice and didn't involve my government. I would also be out of a job by now!'

'A pity we didn't get our target, Albert; I have a nasty feeling Europe is going to regret our failure to get rid of that man. The signs of extreme left-wing insurgency are not diminishing. Goodbye, we will no doubt be in touch again.'

Albert Von Meissen put the phone down, regretting he had allowed himself to be party to what, in hindsight, appeared a very foolhardy plot. 'I must be losing my grip,' he said to himself, 'perhaps it's time for me to retire.' He got up and left his office, a very thoughtful man.

While the *carabinieri* searched tirelessly for the assassins, the families of the four victims were receiving very varied exposure. The media almost totally ignored the sufferings of the wives and children of Antonio Ferrino, the chauffeur, and Frederico Poltera, the other bodyguard. Five children lost their father that day, but all the publicity focused on the death of one footballer.

On hearing of the tragedy, hundreds of thousands of football fans decided to make a pilgrimage to the Stadio Olimpico. The perimeter of the stadium quickly became congested with mourners bearing all manner of contributions. The authorities decided to take the unusual step of opening the gates and allowing the fans' tributes to be placed inside the ground. Soon the entire pitch was covered in flowers, scarves and rosettes bearing the names of every football club in the Italian leagues. In addition, there were discernible tributes from the fans of major European teams. These, ironically, included teams from France and Germany, unaware of their own nations' involvement in the assassination.

It had taken more than a week before the bodies of the victims were released to the families for burial. The funeral of Rico Orvetti was scheduled to take place three days later on a Friday. This had been declared a public day of mourning by the Italian government, criticised by some as a cheap way of regaining the popularity that had rapidly been slipping away from them.

Paolo and Bella decided to arrange Gina's funeral for the day before. The shock of her death was already laying open some deep divisions within the family. Contrary to Anna's wishes, Matthew had insisted upon taking Mark and Louise to England. He had not wanted to expose them to the excessive daily publicity that was certain to continue for some time after the victims had been laid to rest.

Matthew's opinion was that the children would be far less affected by being away from the limelight and would recover from their mental anguish sooner under the protection of their grandparents in England. Anna had been unable to argue against the logic, but was intensely jealous of Matthew's influence on them. In particular, she had noticed their affection for their father had increased since, by living in Italy, they saw less of him. She was now deeply concerned that Matthew might attempt to re-establish the family back in England.

Anna returned to the family residence near Turin accompanied by her parents. A police cordon had been set up around the house to keep the press, well-wishers and the curious at bay. It had been arranged that Gina would be interred in the family mausoleum at the cemetery in Marentino.

Paolo walked from his study, where he had received a telephone call, and entered the sitting room.

'I have just had a call from the Bishop of Turin offering to conduct a full requiem mass for Gina at the cathedral before the interment,' Paolo began to say, but was quickly interrupted by Bella.

'I assume you declined,' she almost shouted out.

'On the contrary, Bel, I thought it a very kind gesture and I accepted.'

162

'But I don't want a lot of ceremony. I just want a quiet affair; just the family and a few close friends.'

'A lot of people have expressed a wish to attend and the local church is far too small. Many members of the government and our own party are expecting to come.'

'So you want to turn your own daughter's funeral into a political gathering, do you? Well, I'm not having it! All I want is a simple mass without a load of VIPs striving to position themselves for optimum publicity. You tell the bishop that!' With that she burst into tears.

Paolo looked awkwardly at Anna, who went over to console her mother. 'I'm sure Papà will do all he can to keep things under control, Mamma,' she said reassuringly.

'Explain to your mother that everything has got too big for us to have just a private funeral. The government, the press, television, in fact the whole country, are demanding the right to mourn. I will make sure that everything is kept in proper perspective.'

'What do they know or care about Gina?' Bella wailed. 'All they want is a spectacle! I don't want to mourn my daughter in public. Let them all go to Rico's funeral on Friday and leave us alone. He's the one they all really care about!'

'I'm sorry, Bella, but it is really out of our hands. I've agreed with the bishop that the service will be at the Cathedral of St John the Baptist and he is coming round later to discuss the service with us.'

'I won't see him,' said Bella flatly, fixing Paolo with a cold stare.

Paolo looked plaintively at Anna again before leaving the room, hoping she would talk her mother round. He knew there was no use saying anything; Bella still blamed him for Gina's death.

*   *   *

That evening Anna received a call from Matthew to say that Louise was running a high temperature and had been taken to hospital for observation.

'The doctor thinks it is just delayed shock, darling, but says it is sensible to have her watched, in case anything else goes wrong,' he informed her as casually as possible. 'Personally, I think the doctor is right, but it is better to have her in safe hands.'

'I want to be with her, Matt. Are you at the hospital now? Can I speak to her?' Anna cried despairingly down the phone.

'I am at the hospital, but about to leave for a while. Louise is asleep. I think they may have given her a mild sedative and she appears peaceful now. I'll give you the hospital's number and you can check in on her at any time. She has her own room and is quite comfortable. It is not looking likely now that I shall be able to attend the funeral on Thursday unless Louise is a lot better tomorrow. I'll obviously let you know how she is when I return to the hospital later.'

Anna rang off and burst into tears. Paolo went over to comfort her.

'Did I hear you say that Louise is in hospital?' he enquired.

'They think she's having a reaction to the tragedy, so they are keeping an eye on her,' Anna sobbed, 'and now Matthew says he probably won't be coming over. I feel so alone and helpless.'

'Tomorrow is Wednesday, Anna, you could take an early flight to London and return in the evening,' Paolo suggested.

'It is all getting too much for me; I don't think I could make the journey right now. I'll see how Louise is in the morning. There's still Mamma to think about.'

A week earlier Sean Barker had parked his car in the long-term parking at Nice airport. With Martina in tow he took the next flight to Gatwick, then checked in at the Park Hotel near East Croydon station for the night. The following morning they travelled to Victoria, where Sean took a cab to M16 headquarters, leaving Martina to spend the day as a tourist. Having passed the strict security, he made his way immediately to the office of the Deputy Head, Alan Dewar.

'We are intrigued by your secrecy, Sean,' Alan Dewar began. 'Do you really think you have some information about this assassination?'

Sean started to explain what had happened at the filling station the previous day, but was cut short when he mentioned the name of Pierre Lavalle.

'I really think the chief ought to hear all of this from the outset; I'll see if he's free at the moment.' He dialled a number and a few minutes later Stephen Johns, director general of M16, joined the meeting. Sean started at the beginning again.

'So you believe he was the assassin, do you Barker?' the director general asked after listening carefully.

'The two men were obviously keen not to be recognised. The driver didn't even remove his helmet or gloves when paying for the petrol. Usually drivers are desperate to get a bit of fresh air. What else would they be doing there?'

'So you got no opportunity to recognise Lavalle's accomplice?'

'No, sir; I took a couple of photos with my mobile, with which I think we should be able to identify Lavalle, but there's no chance with the other person. It's got to be someone highly skilled in explosives to create such a blast.'

'I don't see how we can assume anything on just this evidence, Barker; do you think there are ways to verify your suspicions?'

'It is going to be difficult, but I think we should try to get some CCTV films taken around the parliament buildings

165

for the past month or two. I can get my chaps working on that. The police will certainly be scouring them and we have some good connections there. We can offer to help.'

'But the press and everybody else are already blaming the Mafia; why should the police think MI6 could be of assistance?'

'Like I said, sir, we have our connections and we think we know what we are looking for. We have only to spot Pierre there once to confirm my view. I'll bet you dinner at The Ritz he did it.'

'We need to find out the identity of the other man,' Alan Dewar joined the conversation. 'Any ideas about who it could be?'

'I think we should ask our man in Paris if he has any information on who has been seen going into the offices of the DST lately. I assume we still keep a watch there on a regular basis.'

'Of course we do, but you will have to go to Paris yourself to look at the files. I don't want anybody to know a thing about this until we have more proof.'

Paris as well as London, Sean thought; Martina will be pleased.

'Very well, sir,' Alan Dewar added. 'I'll tell Paris that Sean is going to look at their files, without saying why. And we'll get the chaps in Rome to see how much CCTV they can drum up. This is going to be very interesting. I'll keep you informed personally every time we have any further information. If you hang around for a while, Sean, I'll decide on your instructions.'

Sean left the room while Stephen Johns and his deputy discussed this bombshell from their agent.

'I expect Sean is right about the assassins, Alan, he's not the kind of man to go into flights of fancy.'

'I agree, Stephen – so it looks like the French wanted Paolo Medina out of the way. I would not expect them to act without support from other agencies. The Baron hasn't been in touch with you, by any chance?' Alan enquired with a hint of suspicion.

'He certainly has not, which is just as well as I might have been tempted to offer some assistance. I would probably have needed to speak to the PM, who would have been horrified at the suggestion. I can assure you we are completely innocent here, for a change. I just can't believe the French attempted this. They must have some co-conspirators; let's find out who they are.'

'Are you going to tell the PM, Stephen?' Alan asked.

'Don't be bloody stupid, man!' came the retort. 'This could be political dynamite. We only tell the PM if it can be used on a very important occasion. If we tell him now he will probably feel we've got to tell the Yanks under the share of information agreement. Then we will have lost one hell of a trump card. We are going to keep this completely under wraps until it can be brought out at the right time. Let's get to work on it.'

The director general of M16 left the room with a satisfied smile on his face. If this turned out to be true, and he had little doubt that it would, he had a very powerful tool at his disposal. Sean Barker could be in for some promotion.

Paolo, of course, got his way and Gina's funeral service took place at the Cathedral of St John the Baptist in Turin. The president of Italy, the prime minister and most of the cabinet were present, creating huge media coverage, much to Bella's chagrin. She had at least managed to persuade Paolo to forbid any media presence at the private interment at the family vault.

The previous evening Anna had received a call from Matthew to say that the doctors were no longer worried about Louise and could find no physical problems. Her temperature was dropping and should come down completely when she had some more rest. He nevertheless felt he should stay with her and would not be attending the funeral.

Anna was getting in a terrible state. Paolo was going to attend Rico's funeral the next day and she felt she couldn't leave her mother. She was extremely worried about Louise, and Matthew was probably just using their daughter as an excuse to stay in England and carry on with his work. She had at least had David's support over the past week and a sympathetic shoulder to lean on at the funeral. She decided she would fly to London after the weekend. She was desperate to get the children back to Italy as soon as possible.

David's generous concern and support since Gina's death had brought him and Anna together again. Since their indiscretion a couple of years ago they had not managed to maintain a close relationship. David's feeling of guilt towards an old friend had prevented him from revealing his true emotions to Anna. For her part, she had felt David distance himself and was concerned that the children were very vulnerable in the event of a split with Matthew. But the chemistry between her and David had now been reignited; and she was glad.

Despite desperate attempts by the *carabinieri* to keep a clear passage for important mourners the Piazza IV Novembre, the main square in Perugia, was overflowing. Many younger citizens had climbed on to the Fontana Maggiore to obtain a better view, quite oblivious to the soaking they were getting from the beautifully sculptured thirteenth-century fountain. The crowd had spilled out from the square and along the wide Corso Vannucci, where the beautiful Palazzo dei Priori and Galleria Nazionale dominated the other buildings.

The skies were overcast, adding to the sombre atmosphere among the crowd. The police had managed to keep the Piazza Danti clear to allow the funeral procession to enter the cathedral of San Lorenzo, the unfinished facade of which overlooked the square.

The cathedral was filled to capacity with mourners awaiting the arrival of the coffin of Rico Orvetti. Like the day before, at Gina's funeral, the President, Prime Minister and the majority of senior politicians were present. There were also many representatives from the world of football. Chairmen of the major Italian clubs and many European clubs had arrived. The Presidents of FIFA and UEFA were in attendance. Many other dignitaries from sporting arenas had come to pay their respects.

The moment Rico's coffin was carried into the Piazza Danti, the hubbub ceased and the crowd went silent. As the coffin moved towards the cathedral, a large number of scarves bearing the names of countless football teams were raised aloft and waved gently in salute. Draped over the coffin was an Italian flag and jersey of the national team bearing the captain's armband. Only official photographers had been allowed in the Piazza Danti and they jockeyed with one another for the best positions.

The procession moved into the cathedral and slowly down the centre aisle. The service was to include *Requiem Mass* by Verdi and would be televised to the whole nation. In the square outside the service was relayed to a large screen, allowing the crowd to participate.

Cardinal Bertorelli spoke of the sadness felt by the Pope, that violence had returned once again to Italy's political scene. Without pointing a finger specifically, the implication was that the Mafia was once more interfering violently in the national democratic processes. He reminded the congregation of the time and effort given by Rico to his charitable work. He concluded his address with a plea for tolerance of all political persuasions, for national unity in these troubled times, and an end to all violence. The untimely death of this popular and gifted young man might help to make everyone aware of the tragic consequences of political hatred.

The coffin left the cathedral and was lowered gently on to an open hearse for the journey to the nearby cemetery at San Marco. Rico had risen from humble origins and the family had made clear their wishes to return to their simple lifestyle, out of the celebrity limelight. It would take a little time, but few stars are remembered for long as this frenetic world rushes ahead.

The crowd again fell to a reverent silence as the hearse pulled away, taking Rico on his final journey. Even the people present who had little interest in his fame had been moved by the service, and there was barely a dry eye in the square. When the coffin had disappeared from sight the mood of the spectators changed abruptly. Calls for the Mafia to be rooted out and obliterated from the face of the earth rang round the square. The police moved in to disperse the crowd before any rioting could get out of hand.

Cardinal Bertorelli looked out from the cathedral porch at the ugly scene, and shook his head in despair. Nobody, it seemed, had listened to a word of his address.

That weekend Anna took the early flight to London, having received the good news that Louise was better and out of hospital. Tom was there to meet her and drove to her mother-in-law's house in Northampton where the children were staying. She was anxious to get them home again to Turin and back to school as soon as possible. The doctor was convinced that Louise's illness was the direct result of shock and anguish. He had prescribed further rest for a while and her grandmother was using this as an excuse for keeping her in England. The children were happy to be back at their grandparents' house, where they always had fun.

On her arrival, Anna found that Louise was at the nearby stables renewing acquaintance with her favourite horse. Mark was playing tennis with a friend at the sports club owned by Boston and Wood. She was greeted by Matthew with the news that he was flying to Cincinnati on the Sunday to attend a meeting. She learnt with total indifference that he had found a US company willing to manufacture Bosteinex 1 under licence until he was able to set up their own factory.

Anna went upstairs to the bedroom to empty her holdall. She felt suddenly alienated and fearful of her place in the family. Matthew appeared to her distant and preoccupied but the children worshipped him. Whilst they seemed quite happy with their life in Turin, she knew their hearts were really still in England.

For the afternoon, Gerald had arranged to take his grandson and Matthew to the rugby stadium to watch the Northampton Saints play Toulouse in a Heineken Cup encounter. Linda had organised a few friends to come and play with Louise to brighten her up a bit, so Anna found herself stuck with her mother-in-law.

'I think Matt and I will take the children back to our house this evening,' Anna said to Linda once they were alone together in the drawing room.

Linda took a sip from her teacup. 'We have arranged a babysitter for this evening,' she stated in a commanding manner. 'We thought it would be nice for just the four of us to go out to dinner for a change. Gerald has booked a table at the Haddon Manor. Anyway, I think it would be better for Louise to stay with us until she is feeling strong again.'

171

Anna slammed her teacup on to the saucer in annoyance. It was no use arguing; she was trapped. She resolved there and then to book three flights back to Turin on Monday after Matthew left for America.

The following morning Tom arrived to take Matthew to Heathrow. Anna took him to one side to ask him to be available on the Monday. 'I'd rather you didn't mention it to anyone,' she whispered.

Matthew hugged the children and turned to give Anna a kiss. 'I won't be back before next weekend, but I expect you will still be here, darling; so I'll see you then,' he said, and climbed into the car.

Anna did not reply, but waved dismissively as the car pulled away. She had no intention of staying a week and, with Matthew out of the way, nobody could prevent her from taking Mark and Louise back to Italy.

12

Since the final ratification of the Treaty of Lisbon over three years ago by all the European States (as they were now called), the political face of Europe had altered dramatically.

There had been much controversy over the prescribed appointment of a President of the European Council, or President of Europe, as he was generally known. The larger states initially felt that a renowned political figure should be elected to be the face of Europe in order to set Europe on an equal footing on the world stage with the other major powers. Many of the smaller states were adamant that the role of the new president should be more inward looking and unify the thoughts and requirements of all the members. In other words, they felt uncomfortable with the idea of a figurehead strutting around the world like a peacock, on the misguided pretext of representing the whole of Europe.

As usual, the major countries were unable to concur on a suitable candidate. In the end, a compromise was reached. Raul Haitink, an academic from one of the smaller states and largely unknown to the political world, was duly elected. In fact, this benefited the powerful nations to a greater extent as they believed he could be more easily manipulated.

The terms of the treaty also allowed for the new appointment of a foreign secretary. The expectation here was that he or she would be able to show a united European policy on international affairs. But problems arose from the outset. Persistent disagreement among the major powers on foreign policy left the secretary far too often in a confused and impotent position. The United States became increasingly frustrated with what they had reasonably assumed would enable them to have a more positive relationship with Europe, but had resulted in a nightmare of indecision. Nevertheless the difficulties encountered did not stop the foreign secretary from building up a large and expensive bureaucratic empire.

The collapse of the banking system a few years earlier, culminating in worldwide recession, had left a much larger division between the rich and the poor in Europe. This economic gulf was just as wide among the various states as between the rich and the underprivileged. There was no doubt that the poorer nations were getting into major financial difficulties, in particular those which had gone into the euro currency.

The initial reaction, when faced with recession, was for the electorate to turn to the right of centre parties to sort out the problems. This was under the assumption that their better relationship with, and understanding of, the financial markets would enable them to kick-start the world economy again. First signs suggested that this policy was successful. Countries were soon reporting an upturn in their economies as they quickly came out of recession. But the full force of the financial crisis was yet to have its real impact.

Gradually, the onus put on the working classes and the deprivation on the underprivileged was rising to the surface. Unemployment continued to soar to unprecedented high levels. Taxation had increased to recuperate the large amounts distributed by governments to keep their banks solvent. The banks' practice of lending to those who were unable to show ability to repay the loans had almost completely dried up. It had taken over six years from the collapse of Lehman Brothers Bank to reach the stage where the working class people in many countries were beginning to rebel.

These rebellions were particularly aggressive in Italy and the other Club-Med countries of Europe. Paolo Medina now had the perfect forum for his political aspirations. The publicity surrounding the attempted assassination had thrown him into the foreground of his country's political arena. The left wing was growing stronger by the day and Paolo was taking advantage of the workers' anger. He had become an accomplished orator and was stirring up the proletariat at regular rallies. The militant industrial north was on the march.

Paolo was now receiving plenty of financial support in his own country. The media was beginning to sway in his direction and his play for the top was causing deep concern in the political corridors in Rome. Italian governments were traditionally unstable and the sexual scandals of a recent prime minister had left the parliament with little respect.

The depression of 1930 had created the perfect environment for extremism. During the decade that ensued, it was the aggressive movement of the far right that dominated. The rise of Hitler and Mussolini foreshadowed an era of unprecedented conflict. Dictators arose from the ashes of the smouldering depression, unchallenged by the cowardly politicians responsible for the economic disaster. Nationalism came to the fore as governments moved to protect their own economies.

The same attitudes were reappearing across the world. Globalisation, the watchword of the new millennium, was being shown up as fundamentally unstable. Politicians grossly underestimated the impact it would have as the capitalist society imploded. National interest was the paramount policy in the fight for economic and social survival. The laissez-faire tendencies of the past were quickly being discarded.

This time it was falling to the left-wing politicians to

motivate the beleaguered populations. The near nationalisation of many of the world's largest banks had put more of the financial power into the hands of governments and away from the free markets. The Socialists were intent on achieving widespread political domination and controlling world trade. In their encouragement to the workers, 'it was now or never'.

Socialist Europe was on the march as never before. Rallies were being organised across the continent to coincide with the annual May Day celebrations. Police forces were bracing themselves for the inevitable riots.

The vehemence of the rioters surprised even the most cynical observers. The scenes that followed had been sensibly anticipated in Italy, Greece and Spain where the police had organised their defences well. It was in Germany, Austria and France that preparations for the mob onslaught were found to be totally inadequate.

In France, the normally well-disciplined union marches had been hijacked by the New Anti-capitalist Party, which had strong communist infiltration. Fires and skirmishes in the streets of the northern outskirts of Paris had left three policemen and eight rioters dead. A similar situation occurred in Marseilles, with seven demonstrators dying in angry clashes. The number of wounded in both cities ran into hundreds.

Germany did not escape the wrath of the working class. Unemployment had risen to unprecedented levels and the old East–West divide reappeared. Whilst the standard of living in the East had practically caught up with the West, the number of people out of work was double. In recent provincial elections the extreme party of the left, known as Die Linke, had received almost forty per cent of the votes.

Under communist rule the East German state had been the employer of last resort and there was little or no unemployment. Now, market forces applied and the consequences of the downturn in trade were biting hard. Hamburg and Berlin were the main targets of the rioters and the police lost control. In all, over three hundred arrests were made and one police officer killed by a rock thrown from the crowd.

Linz in Austria suffered a similar fate as clashes with police during the traditional May Day parade turned violent. Four people lost their lives.

Social unrest was rising at a worrying pace in many of the Eastern bloc countries badly affected by the economic downturn.

Of the wealthier nations, only Britain was escaping the anger of the left. This was attributed to the fact it was a left-wing government that had led the country into the financial disaster. A weakening currency had helped the new right of centre coalition government avoid the levels of high unemployment being experienced in the eurozone.

The euphoria in the wake of the Olympic Games had concealed from the British public the rebellions erupting around Europe. As reality dawned, the United Kingdom again looked across the Channel at a Europe in severe turmoil, but foolishly ignored the warning signs.

The loss of life in the clashes across the continent only helped to promote Paolo and his socialist aspirations. The publicity surrounding the high-handed nature of the police only gave him more strength of purpose. He was about to take full advantage.

Sean Barker was staring out across the Thames from the window of his office at the MI6 headquarters. He was watching the flickering movement of the bright sunlight on the fast-flowing river. Paradoxically, he was listening to a Louis Armstrong rendition of 'A Foggy Day In London

Town' on his iPod. That was more suited to his mood as he reflected on his current situation.

The promised promotion for his actions had brought him back to London where he had joined the upper echelons of the service. He was now getting bored with his managerial and supervisory role and wished himself back in the field. A large craft floating downstream packed with waving tourists brought back memories of a joyous trip with Martina on the Seine in Paris. This, in turn, reminded him of his investigations there after the assassination of Rico and Gina.

On Alan Dewar's instructions he had flown immediately to Paris to see whether the agency there could reveal any evidence of Pierre Lavalle's recent activities. He had not been disappointed.

A regular surveillance was kept by the agency on the DST building. Sean sat down to go through the tapes. It had not taken long to recognise his old acquaintance, Pierre Lavalle, entering the building a few months earlier. From then there were several sightings of him in and out of the building, but what excited Sean most was the sudden appearance of a beard covering his face.

Further scrutiny of their surveillance tapes revealed another man who had visited the DST on several occasions. He too was photographed at a later date sporting a beard. Sean was not able to identify the face and, rather than ask questions of the staff in Paris, had couriered the photos to head office.

His next move, much to the annoyance of Martina who was accompanying him, was to return to Rome. He took a flight from Paris to Nice airport, collected his Lotus and drove back into Italy. His assistant in Rome had been charged with the task of getting information on any particular police interest in individual suspects.

For a substantial bribe they had managed to obtain copies

of police files that contained pictures of suspicious characters who had been photographed near Paolo's house in Via Gregoriana or in the piazzas around the parliament. One of these files contained photographs of a man Sean was able to identify as Lavalle. He had no doubt of the identity but was equally sure that the police would find it impossible to identify the man without his prior knowledge gained at the filling station. The rumours in Italy were still centred on the probability of a Mafia killing.

To complete his investigation, Sean hired a motorbike and retraced the route he presumed the assassins would have taken to get to the petrol station where he had first spotted Pierre. He wanted to make a note of the time they would have required to reach that point.

He was able, again with a bribe, to persuade the garage manager to let him sort through the recent recordings from the CCTV cameras. He surreptitiously slid the tape with the relevant date into his pocket, and left in a hurry.

Sean returned to London with all the evidence he had gathered. He now felt confident the jigsaw in respect to Pierre Lavalle's activities was both complete and damning.

In London Alan Dewar had been seeking information on the man Sean had been unable to identify. It had taken little effort to come up with the answer; MI6 had plenty of knowledge on this man's previous operations. He called Sean into his office.

'The man in these photos is Fritz Vogel, a well-known German agent, Sean. I'm surprised you didn't recognise him, with all your field experience.'

'The Rook himself,' Sean exclaimed. 'I have never met him, but I obviously know his reputation, as I'm sure you do. I think that says it all, don't you sir?'

'I'll pass all this evidence on to the guv'nor straight away; I don't think he'll need any further convincing. Good work Sean, what a coup; we'll be discussing your future in the next few days. In the meantime I suggest you take the break you were expecting.'

Sean maintained his concentration on the shimmering waters of the Thames. A small petroleum barge was sailing eastwards towards the mouth of the river and the open sea. Sean begrudged it its freedom.

Since the assassination attempt a few years before, Paolo and Bella had initially moved into the town house in Rome near the parliament. His main political motivation was now around Milan and Turin and so they decided to return to their property near Turin. This move had not suited Anna, who had been very comfortable living there.

Paolo was rarely home, but for Anna life with her mother was becoming acrimonious. Bella had found out about her affair with David, who was more than a regular visitor before the return of her parents. She had been horrified at her daughter's behaviour and made David's presence at the house unwelcome.

Anna decided she would have to find somewhere else to live. She would have to bite the bullet and admit her affair with David to Matthew; a move both she and David had been avoiding. The easiest thing to do, from her point of view, would be for David to return to England and she could follow him there.

David had long since lost any remorse over his affair with his best friend's wife. His argument with Matthew over the ownership of the patent had soured their relationship. Before the return of Bella and Paolo to the family home in Turin, David had practically had free run of the place.

Anna's initial suggestion of a return to England was not supported by David.

'I have made my home here, now,' he was now able to

tell her in fluent Italian. 'I have got the laboratory I want and I have complete freedom to further my own scientific experiments. And, on the social front, I am enjoying supporting your father in his political aspirations. Sorry Anna, but I intend to remain here.'

'You know I cannot possibly stay in my parents' house any longer, David. What else do you suggest I do?'

'Why don't I buy a house away from here, say on the other side of town, and you and Louise can move in? That would solve the difficulties with your mother.'

'Mamma is not the only problem; I'm not sure how Louise would react to living with you. I haven't told her about us.'

'Oh, come on Anna, don't kid yourself she isn't fully aware of our relationship. She is not that naive. Youngsters these days don't expect their parents to stay together ad infinitum.'

'I expect you are right, but I don't think Mark has noticed anything. Boys are far less observant but, when he finds out, I'm not sure how he will react either. He can apply a lot of influence over Louise and she is still very fond of her father, you know.'

'I still think it would be wiser for you to stay in Italy. At least it will continue to give the children two options and I believe they prefer life in Italy. I know Mark is away at the moment, but they are certainly very happy here whenever I see them together.'

'Okay, David, if that's what you think; buy a house and I will move in with you and we'll clear the air with Matthew. That's not going to be easy.'

'Of course not, darling, but I'm right with you and I'm not afraid of Matthew. I'll put my apartment on the market tomorrow and you can choose any house you want.'

Mark was now thirteen and, following the family tradition, had returned to England to further his education at the

Rugby School. Anna had been reluctant to let him go back, particularly as he would be so close to his father and grandparents. She was, however, obliged to keep her promise that he would finish his studies in England when she persuaded Matthew to take the children to Italy. She now had visions of losing Mark for good if he chose to remain in England. Louise, now eleven, was still with her but Matthew had tentatively arranged a place at Cheltenham Ladies College for her in a couple of years. Anna was determined to prevent that happening at all cost.

One thing that was annoying Bella was Paolo's indifference to the family's problems. In fact, he was more in favour of David, with whom he had greater empathy, than Matthew, whom he regarded as a bloated capitalist. It didn't really suit him at the moment to be related to such a wealthy man. He had been trying hard, with some success, to play down his own privileged background.

Mark was occasionally allowed to spend a part of the weekend with his father when Matthew wasn't travelling abroad. This particular Sunday he was having lunch with his grandparents, his father, and to his delight, Uncle Philip, who had arrived dressed in an unfamiliar uniform. Philip spent some time explaining to Mark the significance of the various attachments to his dress.

He was now a full colonel in the European Army and it was not long before the conversation centred on its successful formation. Mark had already decided he wanted to join the army as soon as he was able. Anything would be better than having to study hard for university, and old style nepotism was no longer on the agenda at Cambridge.

'I still don't understand how you managed to get twenty-seven countries together to provide the manpower to construct an army,' Gerald Boston said. 'As you know I was dead against this project in the first place, and it still seems to me an outrageous and unnecessary expense. How much is this bloody army costing the European taxpayer?'

Philip ignored the question as irrelevant, and proceeded to explain the various constituents of which the army comprised.

'It was obviously very difficult in the early stages to get agreement, both on the way the army would be constructed and also on its command. There has been a great deal of enthusiasm for a European Army ever since the collapse of the Berlin Wall. The idea was that it would be self-sufficient in protecting Europe's interests, instead of relying heavily on US forces within NATO.'

'Then why has it taken so long to establish this army?' Matthew interrupted. 'It must be at least twenty-five years since the Iron Curtain came down.'

'Yes, Matt, but what happened almost immediately after that was the break-up of Yugoslavia. At that time the Council of the European Union told the world that Europe, by itself, was going to sort out the problems in the Balkans. The President of the Council memorably announced that it was to be "the hour of Europe, not the hour of the Americans".'

'I certainly remember that well,' Gerald commented, 'and what happened next was a total disgrace.' It had ended badly in 1995, with the massacre in Srebrenica of over 7,000 Muslims by Serbian terrorists. The European peacekeeping forces, mainly Dutch, shouldered most of the blame. In reality, it was the lack of a unified and coherent military plan that lay at the bottom of the disaster, the problem being that the individual countries once again put their national interests above any common policy. Swift intervention was required by the Americans to broker a deal to end the fighting.

'You are quite right, Dad,' Philip added, 'and as we know, the disputes didn't end there.'

The following year, the US Air Force was again needed to stop the ethnic cleansing of Albanians by Serbian forces, led by Slobodan Milosevic. European leaders insisted on the right to approve American bombing targets, despite refusing to commit any fighting troops of their own to the cause. 'It was total humiliation for the European initiative,' commented Philip. 'That's why relationships with the US became so strained.'

'So what's going to be any different in the future?' Matthew enquired. 'Most of the knowledgeable Yanks I talk to when I'm over there are still extremely wary about getting any firm support from Europe. I've pointed out to them that at least we Brits make a firm commitment to them within our rather limited resources. They do appreciate that, but have little or no confidence in Europe as a whole, as a fighting force.'

'We are addressing the problem of our relationship and are definitely making progress. From now on the European Army will be under the command of one chief of staff, General Schweizer,' explained Philip. He will report directly to the President of Europe, who will have the authority to make a unified decision regarding the deployment of our troops. I'm sure the Americans will in future discover that it is possible for Europe to respond with one voice.'

'They are going to take a lot of convincing, brother. They are still sore about the lack of support from their so-called allies after the attack on the twin towers.'

'Under Article 5 of the NATO treaty, members were obliged to offer their support to another member nation that came under attack. But when it came to the crunch, very few were prepared to make a tangible military contribution to overthrow the Taliban in Afghanistan and Pakistan.

'Well, that's because in the past the accent has been put on the defence of the European Union rather than fighting against an outside adversary,' Philip countered. 'That policy is changing to become more embracing.'

'So how many troops do you now have under command, Philip?'

'We have not far off sixty thousand, in two training camps. One in the south of France, where I'm stationed, and the other in the Black Forest.'

'It must have been extremely difficult amalgamating the various nationalities,' Matthew remarked. 'How did you go about it?'

'There is quite a difference in thinking between Britain and most of the Continent regarding the structure of an army. Basically, we Brits tend to go in for the larger units, like regiments, and on the Continent they prefer smaller brigades or battalions. It has suited the European Army to have a mixture of both. There are four regiments, each comprising about five to six thousand men and twelve battalions of around two and a half thousand.'

'What about language difficulties?' Gerald asked. 'How on earth can you communicate in the field with all these different nationalities?'

'It's a long process, but we are winning. Obviously the language of the army has to be English; nobody on the Continent wants to learn French or German these days, as they are not widely spoken. The men in the three main fighting regiments are expected to be fluent in English.

'The twelve battalions have been put, as far as practicable, into national units. It is well known that fighting men respond better when they feel they have an identity. We have not put more than two nationalities together in one battalion. We have also avoided putting neighbouring countries together as they always seem to squabble.'

'You said three fighting regiments, Philip. What is the other one for?'

'The three fighting regiments are the tank regiment, the

airborne division and a naval command. The fourth regiment is the logistical division, which will supply the various troops on active service. They, of course, will also be trained fighting men.'

'So you are in command of the British battalion; are we partnered with anybody?' Matthew asked.

'There is no British battalion as such. My own job is Colonel in command of the tank regiment. All British troops have been placed in the various fighting regiments, apart from a few specialists who are helping to train some of the less experienced troops. Our government was reluctant to commit too many troops in the first instance to the cause. The French and Germans have been much more generous. I think they are hopeful of building up the army to a sufficient strength to enable them to drastically reduce their own domestic forces. Britain isn't yet prepared to go along that route. However, the troops we have committed are highly professional and are helping to make good progress in the training of troops from the lesser regions. I really believe we shall shortly have a fighting force capable of defending Europe against most opposition.'

'You are still far short of the estimates made a decade ago. Weren't you anticipating a rapid reaction force of something like one hundred thousand troops backed up by a massive fleet of aircraft and over a hundred naval vessels? The five thousand mariners you have at the moment aren't going to man many ships!' snorted Gerald.

'That is true, but fighting forces aren't put together in a few weeks. Believe me, we intend to achieve our targets.'

'What about atomic weapons?' Gerald wanted to know. 'Is Europe going to have its own nuclear arsenal?'

'We are in negotiation with the US and United Nations over nuclear capability. It may be possible if the British and the French are willing give up their stockpile to the European cause.'

186

'So you are saying that one day a European President, over whom we have no restriction, will have the power to press the nuclear button, Philip! Good God, man, whatever next?'

Philip decided to let the matter drop. He picked up his dessert spoon and continued eating.

'So you are in command of over five thousand men, Uncle Phil.' Mark seized upon the pause in the conversation. 'Will you take me for a ride in a tank during the next school holiday?'

The three men laughed, but his grandmother was less amused. She proceeded to change the subject of conversation to family matters that she considered more suitable for the ears of children.

13

Paolo had managed to find a soulmate in David and regularly visited him at his Turin apartment. He found himself able to share confidences with David that he preferred not to discuss even with his closest political allies. He feared that if some of his intentions were leaked to the media he could lose support from the less radical centre left.

'As you no doubt realise, David, it has taken longer than I expected to integrate all the left wing into a force that can seriously take on this government. I think I have now reached that stage and probably have a good majority of the electors on my side.'

'I have been watching the opinion polls swinging heavily in your favour, sir. So what is your next plan?'

'A general election is due in about eight months and, as you say, the polls are on my side. Seeing the amount of unemployment and the state of the economy I'm confident of winning, but I need a big majority.'

'The polls are suggesting that at least sixty per cent are likely to vote for you. Isn't that good enough, sir?'

'To push through some of my reforms I shall need well over seventy per cent of each House. And stop calling me "sir". It is Paolo from now on,' he cajoled, patting David roughly on the shoulder.

David smiled in acknowledgement of Paolo's suggestion.

'You could possibly get that much at a general election, Paolo' remarked David, with an emphasis on Paolo, 'the government is so unpopular.'

'I don't want to leave that to chance, so I have decided

to call a vote of no confidence in this government within a few weeks. I have been working on my speech.' Paolo pulled a sheet of paper from his inside pocket and waved it in the air.

'What does your deputy think? Or would he prefer to wait?'

'I haven't discussed it yet. I have a meeting of the shadow cabinet in a couple of days and I expect to get their support. If we can win a vote of no confidence, the President will have to dissolve parliament and call an early election. History tells us that people are even more reluctant to come out and vote for a humiliated party. That should be much better than waiting eight months. Anything could change in that time.'

'Not necessarily, Paolo; the problems are worsening by the day. It might be better to wait.' David cautioned.

'No, I'm sure it is better for the country to see this government totally disgraced. I intend to go for it now,' Paolo asserted.

'Let's hope it works then; are you going to let me in on your visions for the future?'

'That will depend a great deal on the size of my majority. I obviously need to maintain the support of the centre left. But if we completely control the finances, we can get this country back on its two feet.'

'Surely the government has that control already?'

'You must be joking, David. The banks, and in particular the European Central Bank, hold all the purse strings. In reality we have little or no management of our own finances. Just about all our directives come from the ECB.'

'Isn't there anything we can do to change the system?'

Paolo noted the 'we' and was pleased that David was taking a personal involvement in the politics. He had a few plans up his sleeve for the factory, and the drug, which he was not yet prepared to divulge.

'Simple, David; we nationalise all the Italian banks. So

189

much of the taxpayers' money has been put into them; in reality we already own a large proportion. We must take total control. I could even do that with a small majority; all the left thinks that is a step in the right direction, if you will forgive the pun.'

'Okay, so you nationalise all the banks; where do we go from there?'

'The nationalisation of the banks will just be a start. It will provide the finances to expand my programme to a lot of other areas. I tell you, we are going to change the face of Italy. Fifty years ago the left wing ruled this country, but its power has been steadily eroded by those capitalist bureaucrats in Brussels. It is time to fight back.' He banged his fist on the table.

David was warming to Paolo's ideas and enthusiasm. He wanted to learn more.

'Is it your intention to turn the government into a totalitarian authority; in other words a communist state, Paolo?'

'Look, David, I think I have said enough for now, but I enjoy our conversations. Anna tells me you are buying a house on the north side of town; how is that progressing?'

'Has she also told you she intends to move in with me, sir?' David asked cautiously, reverting to his previous manner of address.

'Not exactly, but Bella has her suspicions. You know she is not happy with your relationship with Anna. She has always been a big fan of Matthew.'

'That is the main reason why Anna wants to leave and persuaded me to get a house. It should be ready in less than a month.'

'Well, I'm not opposed to you, David, but you will have to square things up with Matthew as soon as possible. Then even Bella may accept the situation. The two women are at daggers drawn at the moment. A move is probably the right answer. I know it is some time since we lost Gina, but I don't like to see the family squabbling. We still need to stick together.'

'I'll look after her, don't you worry, and I'm sure Bella will come round once she realises Anna is much happier.'

'I know you will, David, and, as I say, from a personal point of view, the further I can distance myself from the Boston family the more pleased I shall be.'

'Yes, but I wouldn't want my relationship with them to become too acrimonious. The Bostons were always very kind to me. It is just Matthew I don't see eye to eye with any more.'

'Well, sort it out and let's move on. I'm flying back to Rome tomorrow to get cracking on the vote of no confidence. By the way, I know you will treat everything I said as confidential; I don't want the media getting a sniff at my intentions. I want to surprise the government and give them no time to organise a response. They are currently sleeping on the expectation of a general election much later in the year.'

'You have my word, sir, and thank you for your understanding with regard to Anna.'

For the past few years, Matthew had been spending a great deal of his time in America; just one more reason why he and Anna had become so alienated. It had taken quite a while for Bosteinex to become established there, but once its efficacy had been fully appreciated in all the states, sales had rocketed.

Initially, in order to control costs, the drug had been manufactured under licence by a company in Cincinnati. When it became a household name, Matthew decided it was time to acquire his own manufacturing plant and, for ease of distribution, built a factory in Chicago.

The success of Bosteinex had projected the name of

Boston and Wood across America and they were now able to sell many of their other brands there. The new factory began to manufacture a large range of products.

In order to raise capital to fund the expansion abroad, Matthew had successfully launched a rights issue on the London Stock Exchange. The issue had been heavily over-subscribed and a large premium was charged to purchase shares on the open market. Over two billion pounds was raised but the share price continued to increase. Boston and Wood was now firmly placed among the FTSE top 100 companies.

Those directors and members of staff who had held shares from the start were now extremely wealthy people. The only downside, so far as Matthew was concerned, was that he had lost some of his most experienced employees, who no longer needed to work. Such was the price of success, but as his father Gerald often pointed out to him, 'If you don't have problems, you are not in business.'

At the end of the day, nobody is indispensable, no matter who they are.

As the school holidays were about to start, Matthew decided to collect Mark and take him directly to Turin. They would arrive without notice and give Anna and Louise a pleasant surprise. Tom dropped them at Heathrow and was delighted to receive a week's holiday.

'I haven't booked a return flight yet, Tom, but I intend staying a few days. I could also do with a break myself. I'll be in touch.' The chauffeur tapped the peak of his cap and drove off.

'Was it Mark Twain,' Matthew mused, 'who said that if you didn't travel first class, your kids would.' Well, he certainly wasn't going to introduce his son Mark to first class travel at his age. Matthew was not in the habit of turning right when he boarded a plane but on this occasion they both sat in the rear seats.

Arriving at the villa near Turin, Mark jumped out of the taxi and pressed the bell at the entrance gate. Maria's voice answered.

'It's me and Daddy, Maria,' Mark shouted back, delighted to hear her.

'I'll open the gates, just hold on a minute.' Maria pressed the button and rushed off to warn Bella that she had visitors.

The gate opened and Mark rushed in, not thinking to help his father with the luggage. 'Hi, Maria; where's Mamma, where's Louise? Oh, there's Nonna,' he shouted, rushing over to Bella and receiving an overdramatic hug.

As usual, Matthew refused Maria's offer of help with the cases and set them down in the entrance hall. Bella waited for him to enter the lounge before greeting him with a kiss. This was going to be a difficult meeting; she knew Anna had not told Matthew about her move.

'Didn't you let Anna know you were arriving today?' she enquired nervously.

'No, we thought we'd give her a surprise. Has she gone out, then?' Matthew noticed the edginess in her voice.

'Didn't she tell you that she moved into a new house last week? I can't believe she hasn't contacted you.'

Matthew was stunned into a silence for a moment. Eventually he said quietly, 'I had no idea she intended to move. What has brought that about?'

'To tell you the truth, Anna and I weren't getting on too well together. Anna had got used to running the house on her own, and when I returned she found it impossible to readjust. So she decided she wanted to live elsewhere.'

'I know only too well she can be difficult, but she could have let me know. She hasn't asked me for any money; I assume she is renting a place.' Matthew raised his eyebrows in a manner of enquiry.

'Why don't you talk to her yourself, Matt. I'm sure she'll be delighted to hear you've arrived with Mark.'

'If you give us her address, Nonna, we could still surprise her,' Mark suggested.

'I'm not certain I have made a note of it in my address book yet;' Bella lied, 'you had better give her a ring.'

Matthew fumbled in his pocket for his mobile, but Mark was too quick. 'I'll do it Daddy,' he said, and pressed a few buttons on his own phone.

Anna answered without hesitation when she saw that it was Mark calling. 'Hello, darling, good to hear from you. Has the term ended now?'

'Yes, Mamma, we are at Nonna's house; we were hoping to surprise you, but you weren't here. Nonna says you have moved to another house. Where are you?'

'I'm sorry, darling, I should have let you know; I was just about to.'

'Daddy wants a word with you so I'll pass him over. See you later.'

'Wait, Mark, I've got something boiling on the cooker; I'd better see to it,' Anna lied. 'I'll phone back when I've dealt with it; it shouldn't take long.'

Anna rang off and immediately dialled David's mobile number.

'Anna, hello, I've got someone with me; can I phone you back?'

'David, don't ring off, we have a problem.'

'Just a minute,' David signalled to his assistant to leave the room. 'Now, Anna, what's the matter?'

'Matthew has turned up with Mark at my mother's, straight out of the blue; I've stalled him for a moment, but he is about to come over here. What shall we do? I've got to phone him back.'

'Couldn't you have told him you were out and wouldn't be back for a while?'

'I should have, but I didn't think quickly enough. Oh David, I don't want to confront Matthew by myself,' Anna said, the panic creeping into her voice.

'Okay, I had better leave work immediately and get back home as quickly as I can. That should be well before Matthew can get over to you. We always knew we had to face him one day. This will at least get matters into the open.'

'I suppose so, but I'm not looking forward to it; so get back soon, darling.'

Anna put down her mobile, thought for a moment, picked it up again and dialled her mother's number.

'Hi, Mamma, can we speak? Good; have you said anything to Matthew?'

'Only that you're not living here any more; I've been very discreet, though I don't know why I should have to be.'

'Mamma, I don't want to drive over to your house and see Matthew there. I think it would be better to speak to him here. Would you lend him your car and tell him how to get here?'

'I suppose I could. Is David with you?'

'He will be; he's leaving work now.'

'So you are too cowardly to see him on your own. I'm ashamed of you, Anna; he's such a lovely man. And what is Mark going to think?'

'It has got to be resolved some time, Mamma; things can't go on as they are. I'm sure Mark will understand. He's not a child any more.'

'Of course he is, Anna, and so is Louise. They are going to be very distraught.'

'Louise knows already and has not shown any particular signs of being unhappy. She likes David and has not seen a lot of Matthew for the last two years. He has spent so much time in America and hasn't come here very often.'

'I'll let Matthew have my car, then, and you will have to

sort yourselves out. You can tell him there is always a room in this house for him. He should be with you in less than an hour.'

Bella gave Matthew the car keys and directions to Anna's new home. She held on to Mark for a long time as they were leaving and burst into tears as the car went out of the gates. How often would she see her grandson in the future, she wondered.

Bella's directions could have been more accurate; Matthew eventually arrived in a rather agitated state. Anna came out to greet them; she gave Matthew a quick peck on the cheek and smothered Mark. Matthew had become accustomed to this treatment from Anna and paid little attention to her lack of warmth.

Anna led them straight into the lounge where David was sitting. He leapt up and crossed the room to shake hands with Mark and Matthew. The two friends eyed each other and Matthew pulled away to consider the situation. He had for some time suspected that Anna might be having an affair, but had not remotely considered David to be in the frame.

After a moment of indecision, he turned to Mark. 'Why don't you go and find Louise and play with her for a while?' he suggested in a voice that allowed no contradiction.

'She's in her room, Mark; upstairs, and then the third door on the right,' Anna added.

When he left the room there was an embarrassing silence. Matthew eventually broke the ice.

'So, who does this house belong to?' he barked out.

'Sit down, Matt, and let's discuss this thing in a civilised way,' David replied calmly. 'Anna felt she couldn't live with her mother any longer.'

'I can understand that, but what are you doing here?'

'David offered to buy a property that I could move into and get away from Mamma.'

'It seemed a simple solution, Matt, and as you can see, it has got Anna away,' David said, obviously playing for time.

'I could have bought a house for her just as easily. So what is really going on here?'

'Matt, darling, you have been away so much that we have become strangers. I have been very lonely at times and you don't realise how much I missed you at the start. I have been leaning on David for a long time now and he has been very supportive.'

'The fact is, Matt, that Anna and I have fallen in love,' David blurted out, not wishing to continue with the evasive conversation. 'I bought this house and Anna and I are living in it.'

'So my oldest friend wants my wife.'

'I'm sorry, Matt, I didn't plan for this to happen, but it just did. Anna and I got kind of thrown together after Gina's tragedy. Anna needed a lot of comforting and you just were not around to look after her.'

'Why didn't tell me about this before?' Matthew turned on Anna. 'I could have helped. You should have come back to England. Why did you want to stay here?'

Anna avoided giving him the real reason. 'The children were very happy here and I didn't want to interrupt their studies; surely you can see that.'

'I assume Louise knows about all this, seeing as you are both living here in this man's house.' Matthew had difficulty speaking David's name.

'She does, Matt, but don't take it out on her, she's not to blame.'

'I've no intention of blaming her, I just want to speak to her, that's all. Where is her bedroom?'

'I'm not letting you talk to her without me; I'll call her down.'

'No you won't! If I want to talk to my daughter alone,

I damn well shall, and you are not going to stop me. I don't intend to stay in this house a moment longer than I need to, but I'm not leaving until I've had a word with Louise by myself. Is that understood?'

'I think you should respect Matthew's right to do that Anna,' David tried a more conciliatory tone. 'We don't want a bust-up here in front of the children.'

Anna glared at David. She had expected to be playing the role of mediator between Matthew and David; she now felt vulnerable.

Matthew detected her weakness and pressed on. 'I'll go and talk to her and then we will leave. I need time to think.'

'What do you mean "we"? You are not taking the children with you!'

'I shall take Mark back with me; he won't want to stay in this house once he finds out what's been going on.'

'No you won't, Matt, he's down here for his holidays and Louise wants him here. You are not going to break up the children.'

'I'll go and talk to them and then I'll tell you exactly what is going to happen.' Matthew assumed his chairman's authoritative voice and made for the stairs.

When he returned to the lounge about an hour later he had learnt far more about Anna's indiscretions. Eleven-year-old daughters don't miss a lot.

'Okay, Anna, this is what I've decided we will do. Thanks to you two, by the way, I've just left both Mark and Louise in tears. I will leave Mark here with you for three weeks, then I will return and take both of them home for the remainder of the school holidays. They have both agreed to that.'

'Well, I haven't; there is no way I'm going to let Louise out of my sight.'

'I promise to bring her back before the start of the next

term, but I want her to spend some time with me. Otherwise I take Mark back with me now.'

'I think Matt's suggestions are reasonable, Anna,' David interjected, 'it's not sensible at this stage to start a tug of war; not when the children are so upset.'

Anna went silent for a while before nodding her head in resignation. 'If that is what you think, David, then I agree. But, Matthew, I don't want to go to Northampton. I insist that you terminate the lease on our house in London so I can use it when I want to.'

'I'll just go and say goodbye to Mark and Louise; then I'll get out of this house. I don't want to discuss anything else at this stage; I can't think straight. Make sure you bring them to London in three weeks' time and I will meet you at Heathrow – we can talk then.'

As he walked out of the house Anna turned away and said nothing. David held out his hand but Matthew brushed contemptuously past him.

'Once he had driven out of the gates, Anna and David embraced for a long time until she eventually pulled away.

'That wasn't anything like as difficult as I expected, darling; but I'm terribly worried about the kids. You never know how Matt will react. He can be quite vicious.'

'I probably know him as well as anyone, Anna, and I know exactly how he'll behave. In a few days he will be more concerned about the business again. Just let things run without provocation for the time being and he will soon have too many other problems on his mind.'

'He didn't seem particularly bothered that I was leaving him,' Anna remarked with a hint of disappointment in her voice.

'I was surprised at his lack of concern, too. Maybe he's having an affair with that secretary of his.'

'You mean Jane – do you really think so? Perhaps we

should make some enquiries. You must know some people to ask; there is bound to be some chat at the office.'

'I only said he might be, but I will see what I can find out about Matt's private life. There might be something there we need to have up our sleeves.'

'I had better go and have a chat with Mark and Louise, darling; just to see how they have taken it.'

'If I were you, I would leave them alone for a bit to talk between themselves. Don't interfere. In my opinion they are happier when they are here in Italy. I don't think you will lose them. Just don't try to influence them; that often has the reverse effect.'

'I suppose my real relationship with Matthew ceased a long time ago; when he took over the chair from his father. I seem to have gained out of this situation. I've got you, but I'm sorry you have lost a friend.'

'We haven't really been the best of friends since Matt tried to buy the patent for Bosteinex and I refused to sell it to him. It will be interesting to see how he behaves in the future. I still hold that trump card.'

14

The two Houses of the Italian parliament were populated by seven disparate parties. Several other parties existed, and fought in the elections, but had not achieved any parliamentary seats on the last occasion.

Five of the successful parties had formed themselves into two coalitions. At the last election the right-wing coalition of three parties had gained about forty-eight per cent of the national votes and obtained fifty-five per cent of the seats in each House. The left-wing coalition had polled about thirty-nine per cent of the votes and gained a little over forty per cent of the seats. The few remaining seats were with centrist parties that had minor support.

The extreme parties of both left and right were unable to achieve any representation in either House. The socialist Rainbow Left and the neo-fascist Tricolour Flame had polled over 2 million votes between them but were allotted no seats.

The three parties of the right coalition were The People of Freedom party, the Northern League and the small Movement for Autonomies. The PFP was by far the dominant partner controlling nearly three quarters of the coalition.

Before launching his attack on the government, Paolo needed to secure the support of the Northern League. Provided he could persuade them to swing their votes from the reigning right-wing coalition over to his side, he could expect to win a vote of no confidence.

The Northern League is a party supported mainly in the industrial north of Italy. Its original charter had been the secession of the northern region of Padania from the Italian state. This ambition had been toned down to a kind of fiscal federalism which would allow that region to set its own taxes and social reforms. Devolution rather than secession was now the party's major ambition.

The NL had, since its inception, variously changed its allegiance from one political wing to another. Paolo knew that the party's support was decreasing because of its current alliance with an unpopular government. The leader of the party, Aldo Bessino, was an old friend from the days when the NL was in coalition with the left. This friendship had ceased acrimoniously when the NL joined the right-wing coalition, but Paolo sensed it was time to put aside their old differences. He confided his intentions to Bessino, who, after extracting some promises for the future, agreed to vote with the opposition on the motion of no confidence. Paolo was now able to assure his shadow cabinet that they would defeat the government.

The following week he called a full meeting of his cabinet and set out his plan to take on the government. To his complete satisfaction, there were no dissenters; this was definitely an opportunity not to be missed. It was time to break up and depose the right-wing coalition that had led the country into this interminable depression.

Two days later, in the Senate, he put forward the motion of 'no confidence in this government'. He was particularly encouraged by a large number of abstentions from the government benches. With unmitigated support from the left-wing alliance plus the votes of the Northern League, the motion was carried by an unexpectedly high majority.

Paolo was now able to go to the President to demand the dissolution of parliament. Since the disillusion with the current government was so evident, the President had no option than to give his consent. He had won the first battle hands down.

A general election would take place within the time

prescribed by the constitution. Paolo set the party to work with his usual gusto and leadership. His own preparations were already well advanced. The surprise factor had wrong-footed the government who, as he had anticipated, were totally unprepared for an early election.

Paolo's manifesto understated his full intentions by pandering to the democratic left. Provided he achieved the large majority he desired in the two Houses, his own agenda could be implemented at a later date.

The normal socialist dogmas were prominent in the manifesto. Higher taxation for the rich, sweeping social reforms with increased benefits, more money channelled into education and welfare for the poor were at the top of the list. Much of the cost of these reforms would be met by a large reduction in the armed forces, particularly of those serving abroad. In Paolo's opinion, Italy's contribution to NATO and the European Army was out of proportion to other European nations.

Unemployment would be tackled by forcing the banks to lend more money to industry. Their selfish and defensive policies introduced since the collapse of Lehman Bros would be challenged. A socialist government would not allow the banks to gamble the nation's wealth in the madcap schemes of the past. In future, they would be made to invest in their own country.

Paolo announced that the main drive of his manifesto was to ensure that, in future, the nation's wealth would be used for the nation's benefit. Globalisation was a thing of the past; the protection of industry and jobs was paramount. This was what he was taking to the polls. This is what he expected the population to vote on. Italy's pride needed to be restored; only he, Paolo Medina, was capable of delivering Italy from this long and catastrophic depression.

*   *   *

After returning Bella's car and receiving a great deal of sympathy, Matthew had spent a solitary and distraught night at a hotel on the perimeter of the airport. Before leaving the following morning he telephoned Tom Bailey to pick him up at Heathrow. He cursed on receiving no answer and remembered giving his chauffeur a week off. He phoned his secretary, Jane, who at seven o'clock in the morning in Northampton, was only just out of the shower.

'Hello, Matt, what's so important at this hour of the day? I thought you were taking a few days' holiday.'

'Oops, I'm sorry Jane, I'd forgotten the hour's difference. Look, can you get someone to pick me up from the airport as Tom is not answering his phone. I foolishly gave him some time off.'

'Why are you coming back so soon; is there a problem with the business that somebody else can't handle?'

'No, nothing to worry about, Jane; just tell whoever is coming to be at Heathrow by ten o'clock.'

'What has made you change your mind then, Matt? I was hoping to take a few days off myself.'

'Jane, I can't talk now; please ring me back with the mobile number of the person who is going to meet me, so I can make contact when I land. You are welcome to take a break if you like, I won't be coming in for at least a couple of days.'

'So I won't be seeing you this afternoon, Matt. Where do you want the driver to take you?'

'I'm going home and then off to see my parents. I'd rather not be disturbed unless it's very important.'

'Okay, Matt, I'll ring you straight back with that number; let me know when you are coming back.' Jane rang off and stared for a minute at her mobile phone. 'Interesting,' she said to herself, 'very interesting.'

Matthew dropped his luggage off at his house, changed into some lighter shoes and went to see his parents.

Gerald and Linda were not used to a visit from their son during the week, and immediately noticed his troubled appearance.

'Is something wrong?' Linda was asking, almost before she had closed the front door.

'For goodness sake let him get inside the house, Linda; come on through, Matt, can I pour you a drink?'

'I wouldn't mind a beer, thank you Dad,' Matthew replied, sinking into one of the large armchairs.

'Coming right up. Why don't you go into the garden? We're sitting out there as it's such a lovely day.'

Matthew waited for his beer to arrive before carrying it into the garden. He noticed that his parents had already been enjoying a drink under the shade of a silver birch.

'What is the matter, darling?' Linda could contain herself no longer. 'I thought you were taking Mark to Italy. Where is he, by the way?'

Matthew recounted the events of the previous day to the obvious despair of his parents.

'I was certain there was something going on there a long time ago,' Linda remarked. 'This hasn't just happened, Matt: don't believe them if they say that.'

'Your mother mentioned to me ages ago that she had her suspicions, but I didn't take a lot of notice. I thought you were all just good friends together, and that was that,' put in Gerald, apologetically.

'I noticed them together even before they went to Turin,' said Linda. 'I reckon that little minx had been scheming the whole thing.'

'I was the one who insisted he worked out there, Mother. He didn't want to go in the first instance.'

'Then what do you think made him change his mind? Didn't it occur to you that something was going on?'

'Of course not – we were friends. In any case, I persuaded

him to go. Why didn't you tell me about your suspicions? It's no use telling me now.'

'I doubt it was really you that persuaded him. I suppose I should have spoken to you, but I doubt it would have made any difference.'

'Of course it would; I wouldn't have let Anna take the children off to Italy. Now I find myself in a much weaker position. How the devil am I going to get them back to England? She is going to make life very difficult, I've no doubt about that.'

Linda went very quiet; the possibility of losing contact with her grandchildren was too devastating to contemplate.

Gerald eventually broke the silence. 'Did you agree to anything while you were out there?'

'Not really, just that Anna would bring them over in three weeks to finish their holidays here. I was hoping they could stay with you as I can't look after them every day.'

'Of course they can, darling; perhaps we could persuade them not to go back.'

'Mark won't be going back as he will be starting a new term, but don't be silly, Mother, we can't keep Louise here. She has to go back to school too, you know.'

'Are you expecting to get a divorce?' asked Gerald. 'She is going to take you for a pretty penny.'

'I haven't even started to consider that yet; I've been far more worried about the children. I suppose Anna will want a divorce even if I don't.'

'I should go and see the company's solicitor,' Gerald suggested. 'Get him to recommend a top quality divorce lawyer to you; it looks like you are going to need one.'

The Italian constitution requires a general election to take place within seventy days of the dissolution of parliament. Paolo made strong representation for it take place within half that time, but the right-wing alliance demanded as much time as possible to rally its own troops. In the end the President of the Republic agreed to an eight-week period before the election date.

Paolo's well-planned preparations for an early election were quickly brought into play. He had outmanoeuvred his opposition from the start and intended to drive home his advantage. He immediately put the party machine into top gear.

Meticulous preparation had been made for three weeks of rallies across the whole country. These were to take place in the weekends leading up to the general election.

The first weekend of meetings was organised for the south of the country; many thousands of local workers and their supporters rallied in Naples, Reggio and Bari. In addition, thousands had travelled from all regions of the country to swell the crowds. In Naples it was estimated that over 100,000 people had joined the march. Paolo himself addressed a rally of nearly 80,000 in Bari.

The following weekend it was the turn of Perugia and Siena. Paolo felt that the people of Rome saw enough of him and were not so devoted to his cause. He would address a rally elsewhere.

A massive crowd had gathered in the Piazza del Campo in Siena where Rico and Gina had first met. Red banners, adorned with socialist slogans, were being paraded by a tumultuous mob. The cafes had wisely closed their doors and the police fought, with little success, to control the surging masses.

It was here that Paolo had decided to make his speech. In no time he had the crowd totally under his command. He spoke for over an hour; a speech loaded with venom, with expansive promises, with long pregnant pauses and majestic gestures. Paolo had become the complete orator and the population was eating out of his hands.

At the end of his speech he held his arms wide in a papal style gesture and the crowd gleefully copied the pose. Paolo took note of the response.

Two huge rallies had been organised for the final week. Saturday was the turn of Milan where an estimated 250,000 marched through the city. Paolo's momentum had gathered pace at a rate that finally set alarm bells ringing for the right wing. The animosity of ordinary people to the record of the current government was flooding out.

Paolo had reserved his final rally for the people of his home town of Turin. He had warned the police not to interfere in the proceedings. He, Paolo Medina, would control the masses; there would be no trouble.

The marchers appeared in even greater numbers; those who finally made it into the meeting point in the Giardino Reale were probably no more than half of the total. The party had wisely arranged a number of television screens scattered around the town in open squares. Everybody who had joined the rally would be able to see and hear him.

To tumultuous applause, Paolo climbed up to the podium erected in the park. He flung his arms wide to the crowd, who all returned the gesture. From that moment the open arms posture became the new symbol of the socialist movement in Italy. It would eventually spread to the left-wing movements across the whole of Europe.

Paolo decided on this occasion to dispense with political rhetoric; the people had heard enough from him over the past weeks. After a brief reference to the inadequacies of the existing government, he began to spell out names of those politicians who, he anticipated, would be making up his new cabinet.

As he introduced each name in person, the crowd responded with a cheer reminiscent of the individual team announcements made at many of the football grounds. He announced the intended appointments in ascending order of importance, causing the cheers of the crowd to increase with each nomination. By the time he announced the name of Luciano Aldini, his proposed Chancellor of the Exchequer, the noise had reached fever pitch.

Paolo saved his major spectacle for a grand finale. He called Bella to the stage. They faced each other with outstretched arms for a moment before embracing in front of the cheering crowd. The noise level grew in a massive crescendo as hats and other objects of clothing were flung in the air. There could be no stopping the momentum now.

Bella watched as the excited mob pressed forward. She felt a sudden surge through her whole body. She was back to the days of her youth when her political fervour had a real meaning. Her indifference and cynicism of the past years disappeared in a flash. She looked at the man she had fallen madly in love with so many years ago and wanted to be a part of him again. She would devote herself entirely to the cause; life was about to get exciting.

After the rally in Turin, Bella joined the party machine again and took over the organisation of socialist propaganda. Her past experience was invaluable as the newly named Movement of Light proceeded with its final preparations. So much new and unexpected assistance was being offered from all round the country that the mood of the electorate was easy to ascertain.

The opinion polls were giving Paolo a massive twenty point lead. If they were to be realised, he might achieve his target of over seventy-five per cent of the seats.

On the eve of the election some of the polls showed a decline in his popularity. He appeared for the last time on the main television networks to make his final appeal to the people. His charismatic personality came over the wavelengths as effectively as a live meeting. He finished his address with these words: 'These outstretched arms are a symbol of our unity. They are meant to embrace every one of you. This is not the aggressive one-arm salute of the fascists that seeks to divide. Come into the fold and together we will overcome the dark days of depression.'

The response of the right-wing coalition was pitiful to behold. They had needed to find a new leader in a short space of time. In their panic they chose a man who was drab and uninteresting; a trusted politician but with little punch. By the time he was halfway through his address to the nation, television sets were being switched off.

The press and bookmakers were already resigned to a foregone conclusion by the time the big day arrived. It had been impossible to place a bet on a left-wing victory since Paolo's rally in Turin. That did not stop the electorate turning out in record numbers. Paolo, who was convinced that a large turnout would benefit his cause, was able to take a composed position at the party's headquarters. He had voted earlier in the day in his constituency to the clamour of press reporters, paparazzi and television cameras.

The election was held over two days but as the early results came through it was obvious that a landslide victory was going the way of the socialists. By the time the papers were counted Paolo's party had received seventy-three per cent of the votes for the Chamber of Deputies.

The final results for the Upper House came through a short time afterwards. Paolo had secured seventy-one per cent of the Senate of the Republic and went immediately to the President to demand the right to govern the nation.

The President had originally been a member of the left of centre party in the senate before becoming a life senator. He was popular with the people, probably because his presidential role normally excluded him from the political debate.

Despite his left-wing sentiments, the President was reluctant to see Paolo Medina take over the government. The pair had clashed regularly in the past and Paolo's more extreme ideals were well known to him. But he had no choice; the nation had spoken. At least as president he would have the power to put a hold on any changes to the Italian constitution he suspected Paolo had in mind.

He confirmed Paolo's position as Prime Minister and President of the council of ministers. He sent, without comment, Paolo's recommendations for the new members of the cabinet to be approved by the two Houses; with such a huge majority the President knew they would be uncontested.

With all the traditional formalities completed, Paolo finally took up his position in the House.

In his inaugural speech to parliament, he repeated his determination to get the country back to work and improve the living standards of the poor and working classes. He started to unfold his socialist agenda by announcing his intention to nationalise the local and national banks, insurance companies and other financial services. This was the first body blow the conservatives had not seen coming. The Italian stock market plummeted at the news.

Paolo's final point concerned the *carabinieri* and the police. Their effectiveness had patently decreased during the term of the previous regime. Greater powers of arrest and prosecution were on the way to combat the waves of criminal activity that went unpunished.

To make his point, he recalled the tragedy of his daughter and Rico Orvetti. Nobody had stood trial for this heinous crime and the police were still nowhere near making an arrest. Renewed efforts would be made to identify the assassins; the Mafia was about to feel the full force of a disciplined socialist state.

Everything Paolo announced at the start of his regime

gained the approval of the majority of the country. His explanation for the nationalisation of the banks appeared to benefit the poorer people. 'If the country controls the flow of money, it can be directed where most needed and not into the hands of greedy capitalists,' was the reasoning that satisfied his supporters.

Such approval was not replicated in the offices of the European Central Bank. Italy is a member of the eurozone; how can it possibly nationalise its banks? Monetary policy is dictated by the European Central Bank. Member states may set their own taxes and organise their own welfare programs. They may not stop the free flow of money in the eurozone.

In the opinion of the president of the ECB, the Italian government did not have the power to nationalise the banks. Nationalisation was not even an option; it was completely against the spirit of the Treaty of Rome. In addition, taking into account the large international investment in the Italian insurance industry and other financial services, the outcry throughout the business world would be devastating.

Paolo was expecting this indignant reaction from the capitalist world. He had already planned his response.

15

Matthew was keen for Anna to have a place to stay whenever she came to London. He gave notice to the existing tenants at the house in St James's Square, who moved out after three months. A troop of cleaners and decorators was brought in to restore the property to its past glory.

The Pre-Raphaelite paintings and William Morris curtains were brought out of the vaults of the security company and the Victorian furniture reinstated in place of the temporary modern furniture.

When the restoration was complete, Matthew went to London to inspect the result. Perhaps the rediscovered beauty of the property might encourage Anna to rethink her life, he thought.

He was surprised to learn that his brother was also in town and they met for dinner at the Cavalry Club. Philip was taking a well-earned break after a spell of mock manoeuvres with his tank regiment. He wanted to offer his personal condolences to Matthew regarding the marriage breakdown.

'Mother wrote to me, but I've been away on manoeuvres and they don't always get round to sending the post on,' he explained. 'I was so sorry to hear about you and Anna. And I can't believe that David is the cause; you were such good friends in the past.'

'We had rather drifted apart after his refusal to sell me the patent,' admitted Matthew, 'but Mother thinks there was a liaison there well before that happened. I wouldn't be surprised if that was why he was so difficult at the time.'

'Well, I'm sorry it has come to this. What are your plans? Are you expecting to get a divorce?'

'Thank you for your sympathy, Phil, but I'd rather not discuss my marriage tonight. Why don't we just have a damn good time; like the old days. Tell me what you've been up to lately.'

'We've been having quite an exciting time. I don't think it got a lot of press over here but there was a lot of publicity in some of the continental papers; particularly the Spanish ones.'

'I wouldn't know, I've been in Chicago. Tell me about it.'

'In a nutshell, the chief of staff wanted to see whether we were capable of mounting an invasion by sea. Obviously we had to find somewhere in Europe for our mock invasion; anywhere else it would almost certainly have been taken as a hostile act.'

'There are parts of Europe I wouldn't invade either. Glasgow, for example; you'd get a pretty hostile reception there,' Matthew joked.

'We finally picked on Valencia, on the east coast of Spain. A lot of our equipment is down near the Mediterranean. In any case, we didn't want to try an Atlantic port as we would need some much tougher equipment, and that is still awaiting delivery.'

'Did it all go according to plan? I presume you were the officer in charge?'

'Not completely; the vice admiral of the naval command was in charge up to the landing point. I took over once we were docked.'

'Didn't you get fired upon by a reception party?'

'Certainly not; we hadn't arranged any mock opposition. It was designed to be a total surprise to the local inhabitants. Only the barest number of people were informed in advance about the invasion. We obviously needed permission.'

'So who did know about it?'

'We got the go-ahead from the Spanish Prime Minister, of course, and the King. The Chief of Staff of the Spanish Army and a few of the senior officials at the port of Valencia were in on it. But that was all – we didn't want a welcoming committee from a lot of banner-waving locals, hostile or not.'

'I assume it all went smoothly. How many men were involved?'

'It was mainly just my regiment of five thousand plus some back-up from the Dutch battalion. They were to come ashore after the main assault to secure access for additional ordnance. But to answer your question, no, it didn't all go smoothly.'

'What went wrong, Colonel?' Matthew enquired in a sceptical voice.

'I won't tell you Matt, if you are going to use that mocking tone. I think you are getting as bad as Dad in your disdain for my army. What actually happened was that some of the light-armoured vehicles unloaded too quickly and got ahead of the tanks along the dock wall. The tanks couldn't get through to break through the heavy security gates as arranged, so we had to push four of the trucks into the water to allow passage for the tanks. It probably wouldn't have mattered in a serious attack; the armoured trucks would have just blasted their way through regardless.'

'So the tanks had to crash their way through the closed security gates. What about the damage?'

'That part was all pre-arranged. The port authority already had a new set of gates ready to put back in place. We had to pick up the bill, of course.'

'So did you learn anything; it all seems pretty innocuous to me.'

'What we need to find out is the discipline and reaction of the men, from disparate backgrounds, working as a team. If you don't have these trials, the occasion when it's for real becomes your only test. The men learned a lot, though doing things under fire will be another matter. That will hopefully be the next thing on the agenda, if we can arrange a mock opposition.'

'Oh, well, I expect you had fun,' Matthew added in a patronising manner.

'We paraded the tanks out of the port area and all the way to the centre of town, with an amazingly small amount of interest from the locals. That was at least ten kilometres. The whole operation only took a couple of hours from landing. We were just grateful there were no casualties; usually some idiot gets in the way and gets hurt. The men went straight back to the port to reload the vehicles back on to the various assault craft. The Vice Admiral and I had a goodwill lunch with the Mayor in the delightful council building.'

'If nothing aggressive happened it is not surprising there was little in the press over here. You know they are only interested in disasters. If you wanted publicity, you should have shot a few of the locals,' quipped Matthew.

'The Spanish media was more than a little concerned that their soil had been violated, as they put it. Searching questions were asked in Madrid about the implied power of the European Army and who really has control over it.'

'And were any satisfactory answers given?'

'Of course not Matt; difficult questions are pushed to one side, unanswered, until forgotten. The big Brussels bureaucracy continues to grind on unchallenged. I'm a soldier, I just do as I'm told. It's not my concern.'

'Well, I'm afraid I am concerned about the Big Brussels Bureaucracy; but I enjoyed the alliteration.'

The brothers clicked glasses before downing their drinks in one.

* * *

216

Paolo and his government moved quickly to control the banking system. A bill of nationalisation for all the Italian banks was rushed through parliament. By arrangement with the Holy See, only the Vatican Bank escaped the legislation, on the understanding it would respect the spirit of new banking regulations about to be imposed.

The exchequer had already forbidden the removal of money from the country without prior consent. In order to retain control of the movement of currency a number of measures needed to be installed. A predetermined limit on all cash withdrawals or transfers would prevent the wealthy inhabitants from removing their funds and sailing off into the sunset. Personal loans were to be limited with tighter controls on mortgages. Credit card companies were made to lower their ceiling levels to €4,000 irrespective of the financial position of the client. Government policy in the future would be to place even more restrictive measures on them.

Import controls on goods from outside the European Union were also quickly imposed. To bring goods into the country it would be necessary to obtain import licences from the government and pay new taxes and customs duty. Border patrols at all exit points were reinstated to control the movement of merchandise by land, sea or air. For the time being, only goods produced or manufactured within the European Union would remain untouched by the import restrictions.

The decision to nationalise the banks had come as a total shock to stock markets around the world. International banks and trading companies with large investments in Italy saw their shares plummet as panic took over. The ECB responded with the offer of immediate loans to the Italian exchequer, provided the government reversed its nationalisation programme. Justification for the proposed loans was to kick-start the economy and get Italy out of recession.

Paolo's problem was that the Italian debt already exceeded 130 per cent of the gross domestic product. It was out of the question to accept any further credit. He turned down the offer and started to use the money taken from the shareholders of the banks to pay for his new welfare schemes.

The reaction of the ECB and other creditors was to attempt to call in the debts to slow down Paolo's socialist agenda. The Italian government refused to pay the creditors and maintained the embargo on any unauthorised movement of money.

Paolo's policies started to have the effect on the euro he desired. The financial press began to highlight the weaknesses of the currency as opposed to its strengths. Predictions of potential disaster made at the time of its launch continued to be disregarded despite the warnings created by the earlier banking disasters. The euro began to weaken against a basket of the world's currencies. The reduction in the value of the euro suited the member states as it would make their own exports cheaper. The situation was not welcomed by the Chinese who saw their markets threatened. With the vast resources created by their huge annual trade surplus they decided to purchase more euros and push its value up again.

There was an angry reaction across the eurozone. The inflexibility of the currency, predicted by the governor of the Bank of England at its introduction, was holding back growth. It had not been the intention when the euro was first floated that it should become a reserve currency. The one-size-doesn't-fit-all warnings, unheeded at the time, were being restated by the currency's critics.

The return of the overvalued euro forced Paolo to move more swiftly to his next plan. He called a meeting with his economic advisor, Martino Lippi, and Chancellor of the Exchequer, Luciano Aldini. The meeting was advised to the press as an informal weekend lunch. It was held at Paolo's villa near Turin as he no longer trusted the committee rooms at the senate. Too much information seemed to get to the ears of the media ahead of official announcements. The walls in both parliamentary buildings appeared to have ears.

To add to the appearance of informality no secretaries were invited to the meeting; Bella was the only addition to the group. Paolo had the property checked daily and surrounded with tight security; he was confident there were no bugs in any room.

He opened the meeting by coming right to the point. 'I'm sure we all know why we are here. I don't think we can delay our next move any longer.'

'How are the arrangements in Singapore progressing?' Lippi enquired.

'We have been in government now for almost a year,' Paolo continued, ignoring the question, 'and in that time we have made wonderful progress. Unemployment has already been reduced from twenty per cent to sixteen. We have managed to get a lot of factories working towards full production. Using the country's own money to stimulate growth is very popular with the workers but I fear the strong euro will halt the progress and reverse what we have achieved so far.'

'I agree, Prime Minister,' Aldini interrupted. 'If we are to maintain the decrease in unemployment we will need to introduce the next part of your plan as soon as possible.'

'I intend to get unemployment under ten per cent within another twelve months. We won't achieve that without a change of currency.'

Bella had not been informed of this latest plan and spluttered a gasp of surprise. 'What did you say? You are not seriously thinking of ditching the euro, darling? Surely the country can't afford such a change at this moment.'

'The country can't afford not to, Bella. We cannot

continue to live in the eurozone any longer. The euro is too strong and we are in danger of seeing the economy decline again.'

'There are plenty of signs of that and some factories are already reporting a reduction in orders,' the Chancellor added.

'How long do you expect it to take to introduce a new currency? What are you going to call it?' asked Bella.

'We shall go back to the lira, of course; we estimate it will take about six months to reintroduce. It won't be too complicated either, now we have complete control of the banks.'

'Do you really think the population will want to return to the days of needing thousands of lire just to buy an ice cream?'

'Don't worry about that; the new lira will be struck at parity with the euro. It will be a simple swap; one for one.'

'Then what's the benefit if it is worth the same as the euro?'

'The parity is only there for swapping your euros into lire. Believe me, on the day of the exchange the value of the lira will drop at least fifteen per cent against other world currencies.'

'So we will all be fifteen per cent poorer; that doesn't sound very beneficial, darling!'

'Not in this country we won't; only if you want to go abroad. We must have a currency over which we have total control, and can manipulate its value according to our own requirements, that's all.'

'So it's obvious you have already decided. What's the next step?'

'Getting it through parliament. That won't be a problem. The main trouble will come from the European Central Bank. They are not going to like this one little bit. I actually think I'm going to enjoy watching their discomfort.'

'Are you going to have a cabinet meeting next week to decide on the tactical approach, Paolo?' the Chancellor wanted to know.

'The sooner the better. I'll get the cabinet secretary to arrange one. Bella, would you get him on the line right now?'

'How is the printing and stamping of the new currency getting on?' Lippi pressed, trying to get an answer to his initial question.

'The printers in Singapore are almost ready to go. They tell me they can get it all here within two months once we give them the thumbs-up. They have been very secretive and inscrutable, as you would expect. Not a single rumour has come out.'

The party returned to Rome that evening to prepare the draft bill to be put to parliament. The meeting of the cabinet was arranged for the Tuesday. This would be D-Day, so far as Paolo was concerned. It would be impossible to keep his intentions under wraps once the cabinet was in possession of the proposal.

When the financial world heard the news, the speculators rushed in. The euro took a dive in initial trading, but made up ground again on suggestions it could actually benefit from the departure of a weak economy.

The chairman of the European Central Bank was beside himself with rage. He made a statement to the financial press:

'It is not possible to leave the eurozone without the permission of all the member states. No mechanism was put in place at inception for coming out of the currency. No consultation has taken place with me and the board of the ECB. We should have been kept fully informed from the start. We would be happy to put in place a number of measures immediately to assist the Italian economy. The board and I strongly advise the Italian parliament to throw out this mad proposal. It cannot possibly be the best way forward for the Italian people.'

Paolo pressed ahead regardless. Now the intention was made public there was no sense in delay. The parliamentary debate took place at the end of that week.

The leader of the opposition attacked the bill with vehemence. 'The nation,' he said, 'cannot afford another currency change in such short time. The cost of the changeover would be disproportionate to the benefits. Has the Prime Minister given any consideration to the massive price of altering all the cash machines, the toll booths, the ticket machines and hundreds of other mechanical operators?'

'Of course I have,' retorted Paolo, 'and the production and installation of new equipment will provide many jobs for our beleaguered workers.'

'What you obviously haven't taken into account, Prime Minister, is the reputation of Italy around the world. We will be accused of protecting our own industries, contrary to European law. In addition, by the introduction of our trade restrictions, we are totally disregarding the international code for the free movement of goods.'

'I don't give a damn about accusations of protectionism! And I don't give a damn about globalisation! This government was elected to look after the well-being of the Italian people, and that is what I intend to do.'

'When I was young,' Paolo continued, 'we made our own television sets, we made our own washing machines and we made most of our own clothing. Now many of our old factories are deserted.

'Look at this,' he shouted, waving a comb in the air, 'I went to use this today and what does it have stamped on it? "Made in Taiwan"! Now it seems we can't even make our own combs! It is time for a change of attitude! It is time to get this country back on its feet! It is time, once again, to be the masters of our own destiny!'

The bill was passed by a large majority. Paolo went on the air to inform the Italian people they would soon be free of the restraints placed on them by the European Central Bank, which he described as being heavily influenced by the strong economies of the northern states.

The European Central Bank started a war of attrition. Member states were encouraged not to acknowledge the new lira. All euro credit and investments would be called in. The Italian economy would be sidelined.

These pronouncements were deeply unpopular in the financial quarters of the English-speaking Western world. The United States was particularly critical of the ECB's stance. America would support Italy, and if it did, the rest of the world would have to follow.

In reality, it suited America to take this decision. The US had found it difficult to accept that Europe as a whole now had a larger economy than its own. A setback for the euro might reduce the strength of the European economies.

The ECB was forced to back off and accept the Italian desertion from the euro. The big worry now was that other member states might wish to reconsider their involvement. Greece, Spain, Ireland and Portugal were all suffering similar problems to those that had brought Italy to the point of sovereign bankruptcy. Was the euro about to disintegrate?

Six months later, Italy changed its currency back to the lira. Despite the immediate drop in its value against the euro and most other currencies, the move was greeted with enthusiasm across the whole population. They had their old currency back; they were Italians again, and no longer the puppets of the bullying northern economies. If the British could survive quite happily without the euro, so could they.

* * *

Paolo's global headlines came swiftly off the front pages. Russia had invaded Georgia. The persistent border disputes had broken out into open warfare.

For several years Russia had illegally occupied the north Georgian territories of South Ossetia and Abkhazia. These territories had been taken over in 2008 by Russian troops despite international recognition that they belonged to Georgia. The Western world and in particular NATO had been deeply suspicious of Russian intentions. Fear was rising that Russia was returning to its old imperialistic designs.

The United States was at last beginning to wake up to the swell of discontent in the whole of Europe. A destabilising gulf was running throughout the continent. Whilst Georgia was situated in the extreme south-west of Asia, it was closely allied to Europe and was even intending shortly to join NATO. Had she already joined, all other NATO members would have been committed to defend her.

At his regular meeting in the Oval Office with his chiefs of military staff, the newly elected President Lipatti expressed his concern over the political instability of the whole region.

'We have two particular situations that I find worrying,' he opened the discussion. 'Firstly, there is the eruption of socialism in the Mediterranean regions of Europe that is rapidly spreading north. Secondly, we have an imperialistic move by Russia which has no doubt been timed to coincide with Europe in disarray, and also to pre-empt Georgia's application to join NATO.'

'There is little we can do about it now, Mr President,' General Piton, the chief of army staff replied. 'We should have acted more forcefully when the Russians first walked into South Ossetia.'

'We did protest strongly at the time; as did the European community. There really wasn't much else any of us felt we could do.'

'I think there was, Mr President; we and the Europeans should have threatened to cut off diplomatic relations if Russia did not withdraw its troops. The world was in recession and the Russians could not have afforded a trade embargo.'

'We could think along those lines now, but I really wanted to ask whether there could possibly be a military solution to the problem.'

'Absolutely not – we will just have to try the diplomatic approach, though I can't see how we can make any inroads there either.'

'I don't see that Georgia is very important to us, anyway,' Sandra Pullen, the Secretary of State interjected. 'I think the problem we face is Russian imperialism manoeuvring in the Caucasus and some neighbouring regions of Eastern Europe. But if we turn a blind eye again to what is happening in Georgia, we will undoubtedly regret it in the future.'

'I totally agree with Sandra's opinion, Mr President, but it is no use looking to the military for a solution here. We have no standing in that region whatsoever. The Ukrainians are always in some conflict or the other with Russia, but they are deeply suspicious of any American involvement.'

'It is the Ukraine that really worries me, Dino,' Sandra Pullen added. 'The Russo-Ukraine deal over the Crimean Peninsula is due to run out shortly. I think the Russians are not going to let their naval concessions there become obsolete. If they can walk into Georgia with no fuss, they will probably do the same to the Ukraine.'

President Lipatti thought hard and long. 'I want a full report on the events in the Caucasus from both the foreign office and the military. Something needs to be done without delay.'

'Straight away, Mr President,' voiced the chiefs of staff.

'Now, let's get back to Europe. As you no doubt have read, the press is accusing me of ignoring what has been going on in Italy because of my ancestry. My family came to America over one hundred and twenty years ago to find work, so I think the comments are quite ridiculous. Nevertheless, I have a degree of sympathy with the struggle to remove their economy from the overpowering influence of the rest of Europe. It is also not in America's best interest to see Europe continuing as an economic region stronger than we are.'

'No need to take any notice of the media, Frank; they are only trying to stir things up for a headline. But I agree that we must take a serious look at what is happening over there. We cannot sit back and watch the increasing influence of communism again. Why the hell can't Europe have a sustained period of political stability? Something will need to be done to stop this socialist momentum, and that means taking Paolo Medina to task.'

'He is not a man, I think, who will take any notice, Sandra; not even of me. He relishes deliberately snubbing the other heads of state and it gets him lots of sympathetic votes. I am arranging a private session at next week's G20 summit with the Brits, French and Germans to discuss the Medina problem. They are as anxious as we are to put a stop to the left-wing revival, so we should get some consensus on how to deal with it.'

16

The hopes Matthew had when restoring the London house to its former glory proved to be misguided. Although its availability had initially been her request, Anna refused to return to London at any time. In addition, she no longer allowed Louise to travel to stay with either Matthew or her grandparents.

The end of summer term at the Rugby School was imminent and Matthew had been phoning Anna to arrange the holiday schedule. He had tried several times but Anna would not answer her phone or return his calls. She was only prepared to speak to him when it suited her. She finally returned his call on the last day of term.

'I assume you have arranged to bring Mark to Turin once the term finishes, Matthew.'

'That was my intention, Anna, and I would like to bring Louise back with me.'

'But the children like to be with each other during the holidays; you know that.'

'I would like her to come with me for a couple of weeks. You realise my parents haven't seen Louise for over a year. I'm sure she is dying to see them.'

'We'll discuss it when you get here Matthew; when do you expect to arrive?'

'Not until the day after tomorrow; Mark is going to spend a couple of nights with me.'

'Let me know when you are about to board the plane and I'll pick you up at the airport.' She rang off abruptly to prevent Matthew extending the conversation.

The faithful Tom Bailey dropped father and son at Heathrow. Matthew rang Anna to give her the flight details. As they were clearing passport control, Mark started to pocket his passport. Matthew suddenly snatched it from him and read out loud the writing on the front cover.

'Unione Europea Repubblica Italiana ... Passaporto. Where the hell did you get this from, Mark?'

'Mum got it for me when my old one ran out earlier this year.'

'But why didn't you just renew your British passport?'

'Mum said it doesn't matter what passport I have.'

'Of course it bloody matters! Just wait till I speak to her!'

Anna collected them at the airport as arranged. She got out of the car to give Mark a hug but gave Matthew scant recognition.

'Where is Louise?' Matthew enquired. 'I thought she would want to come to meet us.' Anna muttered something deliberately unintelligible and they continued the journey in silence.

Arriving at the new home, there was no Louise to greet them. 'Where is she?' Mark wanted to know.

So did Matthew. 'What's the game, Anna – where is Louise?'

'She wanted to go and stay with a friend for a few days.'

'Don't tell me that, Anna. You have arranged this deliberately. I was expecting to take her back with me tomorrow.'

'I never promised she could do that. She wants to spend her holiday here with Mark.'

'You obviously never told her I was coming with Mark. What the hell are you playing at? I can't even reach her on her mobile; I suppose you've taken that away!'

'She bought a new one; hasn't she let you know? Now that's a surprise,' Anna replied sarcastically.

'I expect you have forbidden her to contact me; is that what's happening?'

'Listen, Matthew, she won't be going back with you and she doesn't want to spend any time in Northampton – is that clear?'

'Where is she? I'm not going back until I've seen her.'

'She is staying with a friend on the coast, a long way from here; I'm not telling you exactly where.'

'How long before she gets back, Mum?' Mark wanted to know.

'Not for a few days, darling; and I told you to call me Mamma.'

'And that's another thing, Anna; how come Mark has got an Italian passport? He is not an Italian citizen.'

'He is now,' Anna confirmed in a taunting voice, 'and so is Louise.'

'I haven't agreed to this. You can't get them dual nationality without the permission of both parents. You need my approval.'

'We didn't need your permission, Matthew. When your father is prime minister it smoothes the way to many things, believe me.'

'Well, I'm going to make sure their British passports are properly renewed. They were born in England, and brought up most of their lives in England. As far as I'm concerned they are British and always will be. I'm not going to let you try to change that; is that clear?'

'They will be proud to be Italian. We are a much more famous family.'

'Notorious, you mean,' Matthew huffed, then changed the subject. 'I need to see David over a certain matter; I assume he is at his laboratory?' Anna nodded.

'I'll come back tomorrow morning to discuss Louise. I'm not letting this matter rest. I expect you will warn David I'm on my way. Mark, a word with you outside while I wait for a taxi.'

'If you have something to say to Mark, you say it in front of me,' interrupted Anna.

'Anna, if I want to speak to my son I shall do so where and when I like.' He put his arm round Mark and pulled him outside, slamming the front door behind them.

'Mark, I want you to promise me you'll get Louise to phone me as soon as you see her.'

'I think Mum has forbidden her to contact you.'

'In that case will you ring and give me her phone number? You might also let me know when it is a good time to contact her.'

'I promise I'll try, Dad. I do wish you and Mum could at least be friends.'

'So do I, Mark, I don't know why she is being so aggressive. Ah, here's the taxi; I may see you tomorrow. Say goodbye to your mother for me.'

Matthew arrived at the laboratory, where David was expecting him. The two avoided shaking hands and went into the private office. There was a short silence before Matthew broke the ice.

'Have you made any progress with the insulin, David?'

'Every time we think we've cracked it another snag arrives,' David answered, glad to be talking about something other than the situation with Anna. 'The reaction to the drug is still too unpredictable to think of marketing it yet.'

'You mean people are reacting badly to it?'

'No, we haven't had any worries in that respect; it's just that it sometimes works okay for a while and then suddenly stops for no apparent reason. You can't have that happening to a diabetic. It's still too unreliable. I'm getting a bit frustrated and you know how patient I am normally.'

'It's disappointing, David, especially as we have an opportunity to acquire larger premises for the factory in Northampton.'

'You told me that a couple of months ago, Matt; why did you really come here?'

'All right, David, I'm obviously not very happy with the way you and Anna are behaving. I can't seem to talk to Anna at all these days and so I'm coming to you.'

'Look, Matt, I cannot sort matters out between you and Anna. She is not in the mood right now for compromise. There is nothing I can or would even attempt to do. You will have to work it out between the two of you.'

'David, she is trying to alienate me and the kids; won't you have a word with her? Surely she will listen to you, won't she?'

'It is not a good time, Matt; she is boiling up inside. Don't you know what she has gone through all her life?'

'Come on, David, she hasn't had a bad life.'

'That's what you think; she has always been brushed aside. She was bullied and belittled by her overpowering father. She was completely overshadowed by her vivacious sister, who was always in the limelight. And then there is you; you just treated her like an appendage who was only there to look after the children and be available when required. You didn't cherish her. You didn't even know she was there half the time. And your parents ignored her unless she had the children with her. Now she's fighting back; she wants to be noticed.'

'And I suppose that's where you think you come in, is it?' Matthew barked.

'Don't get aggressive, Matt, you know what I'm saying is true. Anna is relying on me now and I'm not about to persuade her to do anything she doesn't want to; particularly with regard to her children.'

'So you won't get her to see sense over Mark and Louise. Okay, but just let her know that she will force me to resort to the law, and I don't really want to take that route.'

'Like I said, Matt, I'm staying right out of any of your negotiations regarding the children.'

Matthew got up to leave. 'I'm staying in a hotel overnight; tell Anna I won't bother to look in tomorrow morning.'

Sitting in the taxi, Matthew suddenly had the idea that Bella might be willing to help. He dialled the number at the villa but got a poorly recorded voice in Italian. He was just able to make out that the line had been disconnected. He scrolled down his screen and found her mobile number. This time he got no reception; the line was dead. In frustration, he gave instructions to the driver to take him to the villa; it was the weekend, she might be there.

As the driver turned into Bella's lane, four *carabinieri* sprang out and surrounded the car. They physically pulled the two men out and slammed them against the side of the taxi. They were frisked in a very rough manner while Matthew tried to explain who he was. He was left with his arms outstretched across the top of the car while the officer made a phone call.

Several minutes later the policeman returned, offered an apology and allowed the two men to stand normally. 'I am informed Signora Medina is in Rome; we don't know when she will be here again.'

Matthew glared at the officer, made no response and motioned to him to open the car door. The officer duly obliged and Matthew slumped heavily into the seat.

'Fuck Anna! Fuck David! Fuck the Medinas! Fuck the police! Fuck everybody!' he shouted out.

The ruffled cab driver wisely looked straight ahead.

Paolo's energy knew no bounds. He travelled tirelessly from the tip of the country to the toe to promote his visions of the future. He was now invariably accompanied by Bella, who was enjoying her new found enthusiasm for the political environment. She had a new pride in her appearance, had lost weight and made a major overhaul of her wardrobe. Italy was going to be proud of its new First Lady.

Media coverage of their travels was carefully organised by the party and their popularity increased. The new Movement of Light socialist coalition had the nation behind them and Paolo was able to press ahead with his intended reforms.

His next move was to nationalise some of the major industries. The targets this time were the motor manufacturers, the oil industry and mining companies.

The centre of the car-manufacturing industry was in the north, particularly around Turin, Paolo's own constituency. He had the complete confidence of the workforce there and there were no demonstrations of dissent. Shareholders were offered little or no compensation.

The mining industry was more spread across the country. Paolo promised the underpaid workforce 'an opportunity for greater equality', as he put it. The local unions had been well briefed and, again, the move was greeted with banner-waving enthusiasm.

Nationalising the oil companies proved to be more contentious. The general workers were more disparate, better paid and conservative. The unions were less powerful and a ripple of discontent spread throughout the industry. In addition, the international nature of the business made their assets more difficult to capture.

The oil industry also contained a number of smaller companies manufacturing components for exploration and drilling overseas. The weak lira had enabled these companies to thrive in a competitive market. Profits were good and the shareholders and staff reluctant to see government interference.

Paolo and his cabinet had not anticipated such strong resistance from the oil companies and their widespread international shareholders. For the first time he was getting criticism from the United States, which forced him to consider offering a fair price to shareholders. The cost would inevitably lead to a slowdown in his programme, so he braved the political pressures from overseas, refused to pay any form of compensation and pressed ahead regardless.

A number of EU members were beginning to get extremely concerned over the dismissive arrogance of the man. In the past, Italy had always acquiesced over the creeping movement towards federalism. Now Paolo was rocking the boat and questioning the pervasive march of capitalism that had catapulted the Western world into an enduring recession. He was invited to a summit meeting with other major EU powers in Berlin to discuss the debt which, they submitted, Italy owed to the rest of Europe following his programme of nationalisation.

Before attending the meeting Paolo decided to have a quiet weekend with his family. Anna and David were now regular visitors to the family villa since Bella had come to terms with Anna's change of circumstance. Bella's eventual acceptance of David pleased Paolo who enjoyed their discussions.

After dinner and with Louise safely off to bed, Paolo wanted to obtain David's opinion on several topics he knew were to be discussed the following week in Berlin. Since Bella was fully committed to any political debate, Anna was obliged to take an interest.

'We are a generation apart, David,' Paolo began, 'but I value your views, particularly as they have generally been sympathetic to our cause. I would like to think you believe we are still taking the best way forward.'

'I'm very relaxed about your reforms so far, sir. What's the next step?'

'Let me tell you what the other heads of state at the summit are going to say to me. They are going to threaten this country with all kinds of sanctions if we don't pay adequate compensation to the shareholders of the companies we have nationalised, and that includes the banks.'

'I got the impression from our last conversation that you have no intention of paying anything to anyone.'

'Quite right, David, we need all the money to fund our domestic reforms. The EU is getting precisely nothing and, if we won't pay them, we can't possibly be expected to compensate the Yanks either.'

'So why bother to go to a meeting with them? Wouldn't you be better off ignoring them?'

'No, I'm going to make sure they understand the real reasons why they can't expect any payment.'

'I'm not sure you should be discussing this with David,' Bella interrupted, 'only a few members of the cabinet have so far been informed of your proposals.'

'I'm not going into my solutions in the event of the EU getting difficult, Bella; I just want to run this particular argument past David as to why they should not be expecting us to pay out.'

'I'd like to hear your argument,' David replied, but Anna started to yawn and shuffle her feet.

'By the time Greece, in the first place, and then several other countries had problems with the euro, they had already run up massive debts. They should have done what we eventually decided to do, and changed their currency back out of the euro. Instead, they were persuaded to accept further credit by the European Central Bank to tide them over, in return for stringent measures imposed on their economies.'

'It appears to have worked, sir; they are still struggling on.'

'Struggling is the right word; the reality is that now they have even larger debts and no way to repay them. Their economies are about to collapse and their creditors will get no reimbursement; what is known as sovereign default. Instead of tightening their belts when the recession began they were given credit. The common people, quite rightly, in my opinion, were not prepared to accept the harsh disciplines and the national debt has just soared.'

'So what you are saying is that Italy has done the only sensible thing by getting out of the euro and nationalising the financial institutions?'

'Exactly that, David; we may owe a number of shareholders money they will never get, but this economy is not about to collapse, leaving massive worldwide debt. If the financial summit meeting next week doesn't understand that, they are fools. What we have done was by far the least expensive option both for us and our international creditors.'

'I have no problem with that argument either, though you may have a lot of difficulty selling it to those thick capitalists. Which are the other countries going to this meeting?'

'It is restricted to the original six members of the EU, that is, beside ourselves, France, Germany, Holland, Belgium and Luxembourg. I understand the prime minister of the United Kingdom and his chancellor of the exchequer will also be there.'

'So it is a pretty high-powered meeting. Why are the British invited? They are not part of the eurozone.'

'The British had a large interest in some of the companies we seized. I think they are also likely to have something to say on behalf of the Americans. A lot of the credit deals in the past were arranged through the London Exchange.'

'My God, you are going to have some hefty opposition; I'd love to be a fly on the wall.'

'One other thing, David; this will give those capitalist bastards a jolt, so I'm going to announce it before going to the meeting. The cabinet, by the way, is right behind me on this; we are going to legislate to force all the credit card companies into lending with much greater caution.'

'This will really shake them up,' Bella added with glee, 'I'm right behind this idea.'

'What we intend doing,' Paolo continued, 'is to limit the interest rate they can charge to no more than double our base rate set by the Bank of Italy. This way they will be very careful to select the amounts they are prepared to lend to prospective borrowers. The base rate, as you know, at the moment is only three and a half per cent.'

'So they will be limited to charging no more than seven per cent APR, if I understand you correctly.'

'That's right – and that will put a stop to them making unsolicited offers of credit, considering they are now charging around twenty-five per cent. Anyway, I'm going to make it an offence to offer unsolicited credit.'

'Are you going to keep the four-thousand-lire ceiling limit imposed at the moment?'

'I don't think it will be necessary to keep that in place; the credit card companies will impose their own ceilings. Believe me, they won't be over generous considering the restrictions.'

'Sounds like the press are in for a few days of excitement, sir. This is such a sensible move, but the capitalists are going to be up in arms. Your supporters will be delighted with this policy. Just a note of caution, though; won't this have a bad effect on poorer people?'

'That's what I've been saying,' Bella added, 'it will make borrowing almost impossible for them.'

'We have considered that very carefully,' Paolo replied. 'Don't forget this is a proper socialist society we are determined to put in place. Where there is real hardship, the government will step in and lend money at very favourable terms. The poor will be far better served by the state than by those bloody loan sharks.'

David got up to leave and Anna woke from her reveries.

'David and I are going home, Mamma,' she yawned, 'we'll leave Louise here with you for the night if you don't mind.'

Maria appeared from nowhere and pressed the button to open the front gates.

Not all of the government's measures had proved entirely popular with the nation. Some of the criticisms coming through the media were openly hostile. The nationalisation of the oil industry had created a platform for the right wing. Demonstrations were taking place in the oil-producing and importing areas, stirred up by those who had lost financially.

Paolo had foreseen the possibility of riots and taken early precautions. He had been gradually removing the chief officers of the police and *carabinieri* across every region and replacing them with his 'own men'. Any attempts at sustained anti-government demonstrations or insubordination were quickly, and if necessary, aggressively stamped on.

On the streets the whole atmosphere was changing. In the past the *carabinieri* were seen loafing around in small groups with little sense of duty or purpose. Under the new directorship they were parading in large numbers with their armoury on full display. The public no longer stopped for a chat but hurried past for fear of being questioned.

The managing directors of the various television channels had also been replaced with left-wing sympathisers. Criticism of the government was kept to a minimum in what Paolo risibly referred to as 'the only true democracy left in Europe'. Television coverage of the private lives of senior politicians was no longer permitted and all political broadcasts had first to be channelled through a government controlled agency.

Government supporters had also infiltrated the newspaper industry. The right-wing press was struggling to maintain its previous stranglehold over the business. Several editors had been arrested under trumped-up charges of subversive journalism. The independence of the media was gradually being eroded by the bullying tactics of the socialist regime.

Paolo wanted a sustained but orderly move toward a socialist society, not only in Italy, but over the entire continent of Europe. He was nevertheless becoming concerned that communist-inspired terrorism was sweeping across many of the poorer regions. His name and position were being used as a focal point by the emerging militant left wing.

The extremists were not just confined to the southern states and Eastern bloc; riots were occurring on a regular basis in Germany, France and the Netherlands. The centre right parties were still in control of northern Europe, but the recession had left governments weakened and open to attack. No single nation had yet managed completely to shake off the effects of the recession, even after several years.

After what was tantamount to the theft of shareholders' funds, Italy was at last producing a trading surplus month on month. Credit-rating agencies, like Standard and Poor's, had reinstated Italy to its triple A rating, whilst Greece, Spain and Portugal were still heavily downgraded. The cost of the credit required to keep these countries afloat had soared to unsustainable levels. The European Central Bank, backed by the German chancellor, was dictating a number of stringent measures to avoid the potential collapse of the euro. This was seen by many as a repeat, in financial rather than military terms, of the jackboot-style brutality meted out in the last century.

Paolo's defiance of the 'Old Europe Brigade' at the Berlin meeting gained huge publicity and increased his popularity. As he anticipated, there were threats of even tighter economic sanctions – but he stuck to his guns. No party at the discussions conceded anything and no compromises were in the offing. It seemed there was no common ground to be covered and the meeting broke up without any agreement. At the concluding press conference given by the host nation, Italian obduracy was blamed for the lack of any resolution.

Paolo avoided any interview with the media and returned to Rome for an emergency cabinet meeting. He laid out his plans for approval before calling his own press conference. He made sure the sympathetic newspapers and television held the front of the conference hall. The European press were seated to the rear.

He climbed on to the podium, raised his hand for silence and made the following announcement.

'Two days ago,' he began, 'I attended a summit meeting in Berlin with the heads of most of the powerful states of Europe. I was disappointed that they were unable to understand the Italian position regarding the economic future of our nation. Our current economic position, I might even say our economic success, is due to a disciplined and positive approach to the problems my government inherited on winning the last election.

'Various members of the European Union are now attempting to impose impractical and disproportionate measures on the people of Italy. They are even threatening further sanctions if we do not respond. I have made it clear that we are not prepared to comply with their demands.

'I therefore have to inform you that the government has reluctantly come to this decision.' He paused to achieve the full anticipation of the eager journalists. 'I shall be asking the people of Italy, by way of a referendum, whether they wish to remain members of this obsolete club. I think I know how they are likely to vote.'

17

The world's media began suddenly to take an enthusiastic interest in Italian politics. Not since the highly publicised sexual exploits of a previous prime minister had there been so many foreign correspondents flying into the ancient capital. The controversial exploits of the current incumbent were creating a wave of debate across the board; even the centre democratic parties were watching the evolving events with concern.

Support for Paolo's stance was coming from places as widespread as China, Venezuela, Africa and even Russia. On the other hand, his policies were being roundly condemned in northern Europe, Canada, the Middle East and Australasia.

The United States was more circumspect in its criticism. The socialist upsurge was anathema to the inbred capitalist mind of an American, particularly those raised under the influence of McCarthyism. However, with a presidential election approaching, the White House considered it unwise to offend its domestic Italian vote. Washington looked across the Atlantic itching to interfere but reluctant to take a partisan position.

The European President knew the writing was on the wall when he was handed a copy of the ballot paper for the Italian referendum. The voting form could hardly have been more biased. It read:

Please place a cross in the box adjacent to your preferred choice. Do you:

A. Want your government to withdraw from the European Union and return to a free and democratic Italy?

Or

B. Want your government to comply with the onerous demands of the European Council and remain a member of the European Union?

The President called the Foreign Secretary into his office. 'At least we know the outcome of the referendum before it takes place. The Italian government is urging everybody to vote for (A) so it's a done deal. We must prepare ourselves for a sensible response.'

The day following the ratification of the referendum in Rome, Paolo gave formal notice to the European Council of Italy's intention to secede from the union. He cited Article 49A of the Treaty of Lisbon as the terms under which the withdrawal should be agreed.

'What is the next step?' Bella wanted to know. Maria placed a bowl of iced soup in front of them. They were pleased to get time for a little relaxation away from the parliament building.

'In the first place,' Paolo replied, 'the treaty dictates that our seat on the European Commission will be terminated; we will no longer have a representative there. The commission will determine the terms under which we may leave the EU. These, of course, will need to be accepted by us.'

'Do you mean to tell me, darling, that we are not allowed to have our own representative at the meetings when the terms are being drawn up? We get no chance to negotiate? That's bloody ridiculous!'

'I agree it's a ludicrous regulation, Bella, but we don't have to accept their terms; they can't force them on us.'

'Supposing, by some chance, we are able to agree to them, what next?'

'We can withdraw any time thereafter; we could be out in just a few months. Think about it, Bella, no more heavy dues from Brussels, no more jurisdiction from Luxembourg; we can breathe freely again without breaching someone else's regulations.'

'And what happens if we can't agree to the council's terms? Knowing you, Paolo, that is the more likely scenario.'

'The Lisbon Treaty puts a time limit of two years from the time we gave notice to withdraw for negotiations to be completed. If we haven't reached an acceptable compromise by then, we can secede without agreement.'

'Two years, Paolo! We can't possibly wait that long. Anything could change or go wrong. A week in politics is a long time; you know that!'

'That is what the EU is hoping for, I suspect. The situation would probably be more advantageous for us if it weren't for the new formula for withdrawal prescribed by the treaty.'

'So it looks like a long wait.'

'We will just have to see what the European Commission demands and then respond in our own way, Bella; but you are right, I'm certainly not going to be bullied by that lot.'

After his frustrating experience in Turin, Matthew decided to pay a visit to the Boston and Wood factory in Chicago... For the first time he invited his secretary, Jane, to travel with him. She readily accepted and arranged the flights.

'If you are staying in the company suite, Matt, where should I check in; at the Trump International Hotel, perhaps?'

'I assumed you would stay at the suite with me; there is plenty of room.'

'Oh … and how many bedrooms are there?'

'Don't worry, Jane, there are three, so you have a choice of all three.'

'A choice of the other two, you mean?'

Matthew gave her a cheeky grin before walking out of her office. It was nearly six years since he had taken over the chair. His soft spot for Jane hadn't gone away, but his work, new responsibilities and marriage had precluded any advances he would have liked to make. He was still curious to know whether Jane had ever had an affair with his father in her younger days, but had never had the courage to broach the subject.

It had become routine for Matthew to visit the Chicago factory every six weeks. The expansion of business there had been beyond his wildest expectations. The infeasibility of expanding the Northampton factory had forced him to move the manufacture of some of their popular products to America. The company now had in excess of 6,000 employees based outside the United Kingdom, but Matthew was getting very worried about the political upheaval in Italy that could potentially affect his operations there. This concern was also noted by stock market analysts and was being reflected in the share price.

The flight to Chicago takes around eight hours and Jane and Matthew made themselves comfortable in the business class cabin. They were not expecting to arrive at the O'Hare International Airport until early evening and Matthew decided to take the opportunity to discuss his marital problems.

'I suppose there have been some rumours floating around the office concerning me and Anna,' he began.

Jane had heard some comments but preferred to deny any knowledge in order to get him to expand more fully.

'I don't listen to rumours. Are you saying that your marriage is in difficulty?'

'She's been having an affair with David Steinberg; I'm afraid it has been going on for quite some time.'

'It must be very awkward for you with Anna so far away. What do you intend doing about it?'

'I've come to the conclusion there is nothing I can, or perhaps even want, to do to reconcile the situation with Anna. But I am very worried about the children; I certainly don't want to lose contact with them, which she is trying hard to manipulate.'

'Then what are you doing on this plane when it's the school holidays?'

'You know jolly well I have to chair the board meeting of our American subsidiary.'

'No you don't, Chairman, it's time you slowed down and handed more responsibility over to others.'

'What are you suggesting?'

'I think you are obviously spending too much of your time on the company and too little on your private life. You can't expect to have the love and support of a wife and children unless you give them their share of your attention. Your father knew how to combine the two aspects of his life without any trouble.'

'It was much easier for him in those days, the company was only a quarter of the size.'

'So you should find yourself another deputy chairman who could take a lot of responsibility off your plate. Why didn't you replace Peter Woolidge when he retired several years ago?'

'I guess I just preferred to do it all myself. He was very experienced but I wanted to discard the old ways and modernise the business in my way alone.'

Jane shook her head at this. 'For goodness sake, Matthew, can't you see your personal life is crumbling around you?

If you want to stay in touch with Mark and Louise, you will have to drastically change your lifestyle. They won't come visiting if you are always too busy to keep them amused. What they want is your time and you should make yourself available.'

'Okay, maybe you're right, Jane,' he relented, 'but I will have to go outside the family to find a deputy; I'm not sure what Dad would think about that.'

'I know your father well, Matthew, and he would want you to look after your family first. He must be totally devastated by your problems with Anna.'

'And exactly how well did you know my father?' he asked, giving Jane a hard stare.

'If you are insinuating by that remark you think we were having an affair, then you are barking up the wrong tree.'

'There were suspicious comments made at the time by some of the staff, even in front of me.'

'Look, Matthew, I was only in my early twenties when he took me on, and very impressionable. I'm prepared to admit that I was probably infatuated a little then, and he was a lovely man. I loved being his secretary, but I can assure you our relationship was never more than professional. If you really want to know, it was probably his devotion to his wife and family that prevented our relationship going any further. His devotion to his wife and family,' she repeated pointedly.

'Then I'd better take your advice and find a deputy,' Matthew said, satisfied with the answer. But Jane had more to say.

'I'll admit it was probably Gerald's fault that I never got married; I so much enjoyed being his secretary and spent so much of my time at the office, that I just didn't get around to looking seriously for a man.'

'There were plenty of takers around the office, from what I remember.'

'Yes, but the truth is I was really in love with Gerald and the importance of my job. I suppose I was too aloof to get involved with subordinates. I sometimes look back and realise how stupid I was.'

'Dad left nearly six years ago – you've had plenty of time since then to find someone.'

'And I still have, Matthew, but first we must get you sorted out.'

'And what, may I ask, do you mean by that?'

'I'm going to take you in hand from now on, and make sure you don't lose all your family. We are going to start by getting you on the first plane home after the board meeting and straight off to Italy to see your children.'

'But there are bound to be meetings that have been arranged for me with clients over the week; it is not that easy.'

'Oh yes it is, I'm sure they can get on quite well without you; nobody is indispensable, you know. Then, when we both get back to head office, we can start looking for a deputy chairman.'

'Aren't you flying back with me?'

'No, I have arranged to stop off in New York before going home, to do a bit of shopping.'

Matthew looked hard at Jane and suppressed a grin. He had grown accustomed to her strong personality, but she had never been this bossy before.

The flight arrived on time at Terminal 5 and they were able to stretch their legs a little on the long walk to passport control. Having finally passed through a frustratingly slow immigration desk and collected Jane's luggage, Matthew made a call on his mobile.

'We are ready to be picked up, Arlene; see you at the usual place.' He turned to Jane, 'I always get her to pick me up here; the queue at the cab rank can take forever.'

A Rolls-Royce Silver Cloud pulled in just past the parked

taxis and Arlene jumped out to help place the luggage in the spacious boot. Matthew opened the rear door for Jane, and then, much to her annoyance, climbed into the front seat next to Arlene.

'I didn't realise the company had a roller here, chairman; what's wrong with a good old Jaguar like you have back home?'

'Nothing whatsoever; but I wouldn't dare have this car in England where a demonstration of success is considered ostentatious. Over here success is appreciated; the sight of me in a Rolls-Royce probably adds a dollar or two on to the share price.'

Jane had already noticed Arlene's hourglass figure. She was in her mid twenties, with long, naturally blonde hair and deep blue eyes. Her tailor-made short black skirt and matching jacket fitted perfectly, and contrasted with a white lacy blouse. Only the stubby-heeled shoes she needed for driving prevented a perfect appearance.

Leaning forward, Jane was able to see that the short skirt had ridden a long way above her knees, which was attracting Matthew's full attention.

'Little hussy,' she thought to herself. By the time they had driven the 17 miles to the company suite in the centre of town, she had decided she didn't like Arlene one little bit.

Paolo pressed ahead with his various objectives designed to create a single-party dictatorship in Italy. In order to fulfil his target he still required total domination over the newspapers and the armed forces.

Nationalisation of the press was comparatively straight-forward as the senior executives were socialist supporters Paolo had already positioned in the top places. All national newspapers were immediately amalgamated into a single unit. This was then subdivided into two sections. All political and international news was distributed as one newspaper under the title of *La Nuova Repubblica*. Every article in this paper was first censored by a special government agency before publication. *La Nuova Repubblica* was circulated throughout the country free of charge.

The other permitted newspaper, *La Nuova Epoca*, contained all the sports and social columns. Non-political local news and sundry items also appeared in these pages. *La Nuova Epoca* was allowed greater liberty provided it made no criticism of the government. This newspaper was also permitted to display advertisements from commercial enterprises, local or foreign. *La Nuova Epoca* had a normal selling price.

Taking control of the armed forces proved to be a much harder proposition. Traditionally, the overall chief of the armed forces was the president of the republic. He was extremely unhappy with the policies introduced by the government since it was elected, but was unable to intervene with the normal political process. The rumours that Paolo intended taking control of the armed forces put the two men on a collision course.

Paolo called together his closest advisers and discussed the possibility of removing the president from office. The advice came that anything was possible but at least a two-thirds' majority would be required in both Houses to force the president to step down. He called a cabinet meeting to see whether they considered it possible to achieve that majority.

'It might be possible,' the Chancellor, Luciano Aldini, affirmed, 'but who do you propose to put in his place? He would need to be popular with the people.'

'I'm not proposing to put anybody in his place,' came the reply, 'I intend combining the job of president with that of prime minister.'

The cabinet fell silent while they absorbed the implications. A number of them started fidgeting in their chairs.

'It might be easier to start with, Prime Minister, if we found a new president who was totally sympathetic to our cause and liked by the people.'

'Are you suggesting the country would not want me as its president?' Paolo glared round the room.

'I don't think that is the point, sir,' the Home Secretary intervened nervously. 'What I think we are trying to say, is that it will be very difficult to get rid of a president and combine the two jobs, in one fell swoop.'

'Prime Minister, we have had practically total support from the centre left since we got into power, but I fear they would not all vote with us on this issue. Might I suggest a different approach?'

'Can't we get the whips to force this through?' Paolo replied, completely ignoring the Chancellor's words. 'If everyone on our side votes, then we win. Will anybody dare vote against me?'

'It's unlikely that anyone will vote specifically against, but I can think of quite a number who would probably abstain. They could certainly add up to a sufficient number to prevent us achieving the required majority. I doubt the whips will be able to pressurise them as they will come from the centre left. We wouldn't want to lose a vote in the House when everything else has been going so smoothly.'

Paolo noticed a lot of nodding heads around the table and sat back in his seat to give himself time to think. He was not used to having warning voices at his meetings and his anger was rising. He turned sharply towards the Chancellor. 'You implied a while ago that there could be a different approach; perhaps you would care to spell it out?'

The Chancellor noted the anger and frustration in Paolo's voice and attempted to be as conciliatory as possible. 'I think it is just a matter of patience, Prime Minister; we

251

just wait until the president's term of office expires and then refuse to put another up for election. We could easily combine the two offices at that stage.'

'But that's nearly two years away; I thought you had something more immediate to suggest!' He glowered round the table but most heads were looking down at their notepads. 'Very well, I suppose we shall have to wait!' he barked out. 'Meeting over!' He snatched up his pen and thrust his large frame through the nearest door.

The Chancellor and Home Secretary left the room together. 'We'll probably get the sack for opposing him at a cabinet meeting,' Aldini whispered, 'but I wish he would sometimes ask our opinion before trying to force things through.'

'In this case he will have to learn a bit of patience; Rome wasn't built in a day.'

'I once tried saying that to him and what do you think his response was?'

'I won't try guessing.'

'He said that if he were the foreman on that job, it would have been.'

The following morning Paolo was having his daily meeting with Bartoli, the head of the government censorship agency. 'There were strong rumours circulating in the senate yesterday, Prime Minister, that you intend to get rid of the President. The opposition are reported to be outraged by the idea. It is out in the open, so what do you want me to say in the newspaper?'

'First of all, you deny that there was any intention to usurp the presidency. Secondly, you tell them that there is no immediate plan by this government to change the constitution. Finally, you may imply that there are some very good reasons for combining the offices of president and prime minister in the future.'

'What is the President likely to think about that, signore?'

'I don't know, and frankly, I don't really care. We hardly speak to each other these days, as you are fully aware. I've no doubt he will be trying to find ways to undermine my authority, but he is just a powerless figurehead now. Nobody takes any notice of him any longer.'

'I think I understand how you want this reported, Prime Minister; we'll play the matter down, but make sure the people get used to the idea there may be changes necessary in the future.'

'That's exactly what I want, Bartoli. I know I can trust you to get the right expression for your pages. See you again tomorrow morning.'

At the company suite, Matthew had a bedroom reserved solely for his use. He was therefore able to keep clothing, shaving equipment, etc. in the apartment and travel light. Waiting at the airport carousel for Jane's luggage to arrive had been just another aggravation on the journey.

Arriving at the suite, Jane found she had a choice of two rooms, both with en suite bathrooms. She chose the one with pale green furnishings and a superb view overlooking Lake Michigan. They were both exhausted after the long flight and decided to remain in the apartment for the evening. Jane ordered some food to be delivered, which they ate in relative silence, and then they went their separate ways to bed.

Arlene had made sure there were plenty of breakfast ingredients in the kitchen and the following morning Jane went to explore. Matthew suggested they went out for coffee and bagels, but Jane wanted to whip up some scrambled eggs and bacon. The smell of the bacon cooking quickly changed Matthew's mind and he sat down to enjoy a hearty breakfast.

'I thought you should have a proper meal before the board meeting, Matt,' she said. 'You operate better on a full stomach.'

'I agree, and that was very tasty,' he replied, noticing she was using the familiar form of his name for the first time. 'I thought you might like to attend the meeting this morning and meet some of the people who haven't yet come over to head office.'

'That sounds fine to me; what happens after that?'

'I've arranged for Arlene to pick us up at half past eight; it is a bit of a drive to the factory. I thought that after the meeting I would get her to take you round town, show you some of the sights of Chicago.'

'Oh, well, if that's what you think, I suppose it would be quite nice,' Jane lied.

'I'm bound to have a number of things to sort out, so I thought we could meet back here before going out to dinner.'

'Fine, Matt. Now, I'm going to get you on tomorrow's flight to London and then on to Turin the following day. You can stay overnight in St James's Square.'

'I was really expecting to stay here a lot longer than that.'

'You must put your relationship with Mark and Louise first,' Jane emphasised. 'You told me you wanted to get Louise over to England. If you don't move promptly the school holidays will be over and it will be too late.'

'I suppose you are right,' he replied meekly, surprised at the commanding tone in her voice, 'but don't worry, I'll get Arlene to sort all that out.'

'No you won't, I'll do it; I know what needs to be done. What is her job anyway? I thought she was just the company's chauffeur, or should I say chauffeuse.'

'She not really a driver at all, she just looks after me when I'm in town, does all my secretarial work and the

254

like. She's very good and, I'm reliably informed, is going a long way with the company.'

There was a ring on the bell in the hallway. 'That will be her now; I'll tell her we are on our way.'

'I'm not quite ready yet, Matt. She could come up and tidy away the breakfast things.'

'Don't worry, she'll be happy to wait downstairs; and in any case, we have a maid to come and clean things up.'

It was a half-hour ride to the factory and Jane sat quietly in the back taking in the views. Matthew, in the front seat again, talked shop with Arlene as she weaved in and out of the busy traffic.

Jane was pleased to note that the board agenda was not too extensive; she was only there to show herself off. Matthew had learnt the art of chairing meetings and progressed through the agenda with consummate ease, allowing the barest of discussion. The meeting eventually reached the last item on the agenda: 'Any Other Business'. Matthew looked round the table and the laboratory director gave him a nod.

'I'm sorry to have to tell the meeting, chairman, that we have received notice of a possible court action concerning Bosteinex. It appears that a man in Augusta, in his early thirties, has just died from kidney failure and the family is blaming our drug.'

'Do we know how long he has been taking it?'

'We believe just over two years, but at the moment the information is scanty; we only received notice a couple of days ago.'

'When did he die; do they have any scientific evidence?'

'He died about three weeks ago. We will obviously be trying to find out if they have any real evidence or are just trying it on.'

'I assume you would have told me before if there had been any previous intimation in the US that the drug was unsafe?'

'This is the first, Chairman, and we obviously don't want to start any unnecessary ripples. There are always rumours that some drug or another has caused problems and the public don't take a lot of notice initially. But sometimes these rumours entice others to come forward in the hope of getting compensation; then you can get a class action going and things start getting out of hand.'

'Have you let our attorneys know? They must be able to give us some immediate advice.'

'Of course, Chairman, and we have arranged a meeting with them for tomorrow morning at their office.'

Matthew glanced over at Jane, who gave him a determined stare back. 'I'm afraid I am returning to London tomorrow,' he said apologetically. 'Try and rearrange the meeting for this afternoon.'

'That shouldn't be difficult. Is there anything else you want done?'

'Yes, we obviously need to get in touch with the pathologist as soon as possible; get some samples of the kidney tissue at least. I think the best thing is to get David Steinberg over here immediately – he will know exactly what to look for.'

Matthew glanced at Jane again. 'Would you get straight on to that please? Make sure he understands the urgency and gets on the next available flight.'

With the meeting concluded, Matthew was due to meet a potential new client who had flown in from Chile. Jane went off to contact David and spent the afternoon reluctantly with Arlene.

'Did you have a nice day at the office?' Jane asked mockingly when they met up again in the evening.

'You should know – you were there half of the time,' Matthew replied, ignoring the sarcasm. 'How did you get on with Arlene?'

'She's very pretty, isn't she?' Jane remarked casually.

'Is she? I hadn't really noticed,' he pretended.

'She took me around a few places. I'm a great fan of Sinatra's song, but I'm afraid Chicago isn't my kind of town. So while I was booking your flight home tomorrow I took the opportunity to reschedule my flight to New York. I'm also leaving tomorrow; our flights are roughly about the same time, so Arlene can drop us both off together.'

'Okay, but you'll be going to a different terminal. I must say I'm extremely concerned about this potential action; we haven't had any suggestion before that the drug could be unsafe. The attorneys weren't particularly helpful, either. This could go on a long time.'

'Forget it, Matt, it is just someone attempting to extract some money from you. Let's just have a pleasant evening out, shall we?'

They had a quiet dinner in Taverna Salamanca on the lakeside. The cosy Spanish restaurant had been recommended to Matthew that morning by his new Chilean client. They washed the gourmet meal down with a fine Rioja and returned to the apartment in a giggly mood.

As they squeezed together in the small escalator going up to the suite, Matthew put his arm round Jane and gave her a long kiss. She responded by pressing her groin into his. It was quickly apparent that only one room would be required that night. 'My bed or yours?' he whispered in her ear.

The next morning Arlene dropped Jane off at Terminal 2. She checked in her luggage and went for a cup of coffee. She sat staring out of the window at the runway where a small executive jet was manoeuvring for take-off. A thought suddenly struck her and a wry smile crossed her face; she had fallen for the oldest trick in the book. Matthew had cried on her shoulder about his marriage, flirted with a beautiful younger woman in front of her, and then taken her for a romantic candlelit dinner. The wry smile turned into a spontaneous laugh; she was perfectly happy with the situation.

18

David's emergency summons to Chicago gave a clear advantage to Matthew when he arrived in Turin; his absence made Anna more vulnerable. Matthew hired a large Mitsubishi four-wheel drive at the airport and drove to David's villa.

He arrived at the security gates and rang the bell, which he was pleased to hear answered by Anna herself. 'Anna, it's me, Matthew, would you mind opening the gates, please?' he requested politely.

There was a long pause. 'David told me you were in America,' she replied, playing for time.

'I was, but I'm here now. Let me in, please.'

'Did you call David over to Chicago under false pretences, just to get him out of the way?'

'No I didn't, we have a definite problem there. For the last time, will you open the gates please?'

'I haven't got anything to say to you, Matthew, please just go away.'

'I haven't come here to talk to you specifically, Anna, I want to see my children.'

'They are not here; they are staying with friends.'

'Don't lie to me, Anna; David told Jane they would be here for the rest of the holidays.'

'Well, you are not coming in and that's final!'

'Anna, I'm going to count up to ten; if you haven't opened the gates by then, I'm smashing this car straight through them. Have I made myself understood?'

'Don't be foolish, Matthew, I'm going to call the police.'

'I'll be through these gates long before they arrive; one … two … three … four…'

There was a buzzing sound as the lock released and Matthew waited while the wrought-iron gates swung open. He motored slowly up the drive and Mark opened the front door to greet him. He allowed himself no more than a nod of recognition in Anna's direction.

'Where's Louise?'

'I sent her up to her room; she doesn't want to see you.'

'Mark, go up and fetch her; what I have to say concerns all of us.'

Mark did as he was told and shortly reappeared leading a nervous Louise by the hand. Matthew walked over and gave her a long hug.

'Now, that didn't hurt, did it?' he said. Louise gave him a sheepish smile, not quite knowing how to respond in front of her mother.

'Anna, I've come here to take Mark and Louise back to England for the rest of the school holidays. They have plenty of friends there they haven't seen for a while and my parents are dying to see Louise again. This time I won't take "no" for an answer.'

'They are quite happy here, aren't you?' Anna said looking at the children. They stared back, expressionless.

'I'm sure you'd like to come back with me and see Granny and Grandpa and play with your old horse,' Matthew suggested, smiling at Louise, who looked to Mark for support.

They both nodded their heads and Anna rushed from the room in tears. She reappeared after a few minutes, having wiped her eyes, and went over to the children.

'I will only agree to this if you stay at Granny's house; I don't trust your father to look after you properly. I know him; he will leave you all day with some friend or another while he clears off to the factory.'

'No I won't, Anna, I'm taking the whole time off to look after them myself.' Matthew noticed her look of disbelief and decided it was better to concede to the demand. 'Okay, they can stay with my parents, but I assure you, I am also taking a holiday.'

'How is my horse, Daddy? I bet she's missed me terribly.' Louise finally had something to say.

'You will find out tomorrow – I've already booked your air tickets. Tom will pick us up at Heathrow as usual; we're going to have a lot of fun.'

'I'm not sure they can be ready by the morning, Matthew. By the way, where do you intend to stay tonight?'

'I might as well stay here; there must be a spare bedroom or two.'

'David won't want you staying in his house. You will have to find somewhere else to go.'

Matthew was not certain he could trust Anna not to usher Louise away from the house before he could collect her the next morning. 'I'm sure David won't mind under the circumstances; I'll camp down here on the sofa for the night if you don't have a spare room.'

Anna realised she was on the losing end. 'Okay, Matthew, I'll make up a bed, but I'm not cooking a meal. You can take us all out to dinner.'

'That's better, Anna – so much more civilised.'

'I shall want them both back in two weeks' time;' she added sharply. 'We have arranged to spend a week in Positano, on the Amalfi coast. I hope you are not going to keep David in Chicago for long.'

'Won't it be too hot down there at this time of the year? Mark is due back at school in less than a month – it seems to be asking too much of him. All that travel could wear him out.'

'He's young and fit, Matthew, and look at all the travelling about you do. If you like, I could come to Heathrow myself and collect them. That would at least save you the extra journey.'

'All right, as you wish, I'll make sure they are back again in time for your trip. I'm afraid I can't tell you how long David will need to stay in Chicago. It will be up to him to make that decision.'

The next morning, Matthew sat on the other side of the gangway to the children on the flight to Heathrow. He glanced across at them and smiled contentedly. 'I have Jane to thank for this,' he said to himself, 'she was absolutely right to insist on my flying back.'

While he waited for the proposed terms from the European Commission for Italy's secession, Paolo attempted to complete his programme of social reform. In what he expected to be his final move, he gave instructions for almost all the rest of the commercial enterprises in the country to be nationalised. Any enterprise with an annual turnover exceeding 10 million lire or with a staff of more than fifty would be automatically subjected. This included supermarkets, household retailers, construction companies, telecommunications and pharmaceutical companies. Only companies with strong overseas connections, like shipping, travel and hotels, were excluded. The farming industry and wine trade, both highly subsidised by the Common Agricultural Policy, were also left temporarily to their own devices.

Matthew heard the news that his factory had been taken over while he was with the children on a short holiday in Scotland. In the past he would have hurried to the trouble spot to take control of the situation. On this occasion he realised his promises to the family had left him helpless. Jane was right again – he needed somebody to deputise for him.

Gerald and Linda had joined their grandchildren in Scotland for a few days at a hunting lodge near Perth, by the River Tay, owned by a family friend. Matthew and Mark had arranged to go trout fishing while Linda took Louise riding. Gerald was trying to organise a game of golf as fishing was too placid for his fidgety nature.

'Why don't you come riding with us, Grandpa?' Louise asked. 'We're going over the hills and the views are stunning.'

'No thank you, Louise, have you ever seen me on a horse?' He gave a shudder.

'There's always a first time, Grandpa; don't worry, I'll look after you.'

'It wouldn't actually be the first time; I tried it once before in my younger days. I ended up terribly bruised round the buttocks and couldn't sit down for a week. I had to have my breakfast off the mantelpiece. Never again, Louise, never again.'

The holiday in Scotland was followed by a few days' walking in the Lake District. Luckily, the weather was warm and sunny and they followed the well-worn paths through Borrowdale and Watendlath. By the time they returned to Northampton the whole family was tired but contented. Matthew began to regret how much he had allowed to pass him by on the road to commercial success. He was going to hand his children back to their mother in a couple of days; when would he get another chance to take them away and enjoy their company, he wondered.

Matthew had left strict instructions with Jane that he should not be contacted during his vacation. The news of the nationalisation of his factory had reached him via Mark after a conversation with his mother. He telephoned Jane to check that David had returned to Italy before contacting Anna.

'Anna, don't worry about coming to London; I obviously have to talk to David about the factory and I can't seem to get through. Nobody's answering the phone – what the hell's going on over there?'

'Don't ask me. All I understand is that the trade union steward has taken over the factory. So there's a change of plan, you will come here and bring Mark and Louise with you?'

'Yes, meet us at the airport the day after tomorrow, and bring David. Tell him to get Martin Ford to come to the airport, too; we can have a meeting there and you can take the kids home.'

'Okay, I'll organise that if I can; even David is not very comfortable with this latest development. See you on Wednesday.'

Anna, in fact, knew more than she wished to divulge to Matthew. She and David had been invited to lunch the previous day at her parents' house and the nationalisation programme had been discussed at length.

On arrival, David had received the expected hearty thump on the back and had a gin and tonic thrust into his hand. 'Well, my lad, how do you think we are progressing? We've got those capitalist bastards on the run, haven't we? There's no turning back now,' Paolo added.

'That latest move was a bit sudden, sir, even for me to take in.'

'If you are going to do something that won't please everybody, it is best done quickly. Don't look over your shoulder, it only slows you down; something I learnt in the army.'

'I'm a little annoyed that the shop steward, who seems to have taken complete control of the factory, is interfering with my laboratory. I get the feeling he is wary of me and would like to get rid of me. I'm inclined to set the monkeys on him.'

'I'll get that sorted for you, David; one word from me will suffice. Let us have some lunch and then I have a proposition for you.'

In the past, Bella would have left the table after lunch to escape Paolo's political banter. She now stayed put and entered enthusiastically into the conversation. Anna, rather against her will, felt impelled to do the same.

When they were all replete and Maria had brought in the coffee, Paolo decided it was time to make his proposition. Bella was already aware of his plans and wanted to be fully supportive.

'David, you are practically family now and I'd like you to feel you can be of use to my government,' he began, in a tone unusually soft. 'I believe, with your help, we could expand the Turin factory into the largest pharmaceutical producer in Europe. Now we have total control between us, we could make it ten times the size; employ thousands more workers.'

'What do you mean by "we have control", sir? The union boss has completely taken me over. I don't think I'm going to be allowed any say.'

'Of course you will, David. You have the patent for the Bosteinex drug that will be the basis of the expansion. As far as I'm concerned you would be the senior executive at the factory.'

'But I'm a scientist, a laboratory buff – I don't want to be a manager or chief executive officer. Up till now I've been left alone to operate as I please, and that's all I ever want.'

'David, you can have anything you want; what I want is for you to hand the patent over to my government. We can then afford to invest in a much larger factory; you will be well looked after, I promise you.'

'It is just not possible for me to do that immediately; Boston and Wood have at least two years to run on their exclusive right to manufacture. I also agreed to give them first option to renew the licence when it runs out.'

'The hell with Boston and Wood; you're not tied to them any longer, is he Anna?'

'Time moves on, David,' Bella gently intervened, having noticed Paolo's exasperated tone of voice. 'We can't always stick to old promises. I'm sure you would prefer to see the community here benefit from your endeavours. You are one of us now.'

'Are you suggesting I cancel my arrangements with Matthew just like that? He'll sue me.'

'Not if I'm the owner of the patent,' Paolo interrupted. 'Have you given any undertaking not to sell it?'

'Not that I know of, but I hardly bothered to read the small print in our contract. I'm sure it must at least be implied that I wouldn't sell during the period.'

'Well, that would be all right; if it's only an implication we can easily get round it. So you agree to let me and my government have the patent then?'

'I can't decide anything, sir, without first checking the terms of my agreement with Boston and Wood. You realise, of course, that they offered me a great deal of money for the patent several years ago.'

'If it's a question of money, that's no problem. I'll see you get properly reimbursed once the factory has been fully expanded.'

'Thank you for lunch, Prime Minister; I'll let you know what I can do once I've made some inquiries,' said David, getting up to leave.

'Don't take too long, David, I'm relying on you.' Paolo gave him another hearty slap as he and Anna went out through the front door.

On the drive home Anna was anxious to find out how David felt about her father's proposal.

'Are you really going to let Papà have the patent?' she

enquired. 'I don't understand why, but he seems very desperate to get hold of it.'

'Your father has just put me in a very difficult position. If I refuse to let him have it, I will be put under enormous pressure at the laboratory. That pig of a shop steward will make my life a misery. If I give in to him, I shall lose most of my friends in England and totally alienate the Boston family, who have given me so much support.'

'I think we've already alienated them, *caro*; that shouldn't bother you anymore. Anyway, your life is here now, with me.'

'I can't just let your father take the patent off me. Didn't you notice how bullying he was? Bella had to step in and calm him down.'

'That's just his natural manner; he's used to getting his own way all the time.'

'Yes, but you know only too well what the patent is worth. I would be stupid to let the government take it off me. They can't actually nationalise me, thank God.'

'But I heard Papà say he would pay you for it.'

'Yes he did – when the factory has been expanded. Do you honestly believe he will keep to his word?'

Anna didn't answer so David continued. 'I wouldn't trust him to pay me anything. Nobody with any sense trusts a politician these days, and you can't say your father's record is whiter than white.'

'So you intend to hang on to it yourself, then? I suppose you should do what you think is best; you realise, of course, it will probably lead to another family altercation.'

'Are you implying I should let your father have his own way, just to keep the peace?'

'No I'm not; I'm used to having arguments with Papà, don't let that influence you.'

'In that case, Anna, if you're not bothered, I won't rush into any decision.'

* * *

267

As arranged, Anna met Matthew at Turin airport and took charge of the children. 'Do you want me to collect Mark for the start of the new term,' Matthew offered, 'or will you bring him over?'

'I'll get in touch with you when we get back from Positano and we can sort things out then.' David had arrived with her in the car and she left the two men together at the terminal. They had not met since the encounter at David's house and didn't attempt to shake hands. They were joined by Martin Ford, the local company director, and went to find a quiet corner.

'Do you know I had to get a taxi here today?' complained Martin. 'That bloody shop steward has commandeered my company car. What are you going to do about that, Chairman?'

'That's your problem, Martin – you're the man on the spot. I don't suppose there is much I can do about anything at the moment; that's why I wanted to have our meeting here at the airport. I doubt whether they will even let me through the factory gates right now.'

'You probably guessed right – the whole place is a mess. I'm thinking of requesting a reassignment back in England; I am going to be surplus to requirements out here very soon.'

'I had a feeling you might say that, but I'd like you stay around for a bit if you can stick it. Something tells me this government has gone a bridge too far. There could be some sharp reprisals coming. The right wing in Italy is getting very restless.'

'Forget the right wing,' David remarked, 'they are absolutely powerless. Paolo has them right where he wants them. I know, I had lunch with him the other day; he is still on a roll and I don't believe he can be reined in. The factory is just another casualty so far as he is concerned. You know my political persuasions, Matthew, but even I am beginning to worry about his ambitions now.'

'So what do you think our next move should be, Martin? How do we protect our interests?'

'I've been concerning myself with that ever since nationalisation was announced,' Martin said, with a grave expression. 'The very next day, that bastard just walked straight into my office, without even knocking, and announced he was taking over. I didn't even get a chance to get all our records out of sight.'

'I was thinking,' mused Matthew, 'all our overseas clients currently pay for the drugs you manufacture direct to our subsidiary company over here. Suppose in future we debit them from head office, couldn't we avoid the government grabbing all our cash?'

'We might get away with it for a short time, but once the locals work out what's happening they will put a stop to it,' disagreed Martin.

'Might still be worth a try; these union officials are not necessarily very bright when it comes to financial arrangements. So long as we make sure all the expenses, salaries and the like are paid in good time, they may not understand the intricate accountancy.'

'Okay, but if they introduce their own accountant, you can expect big trouble. By the way, another thought I had was to halt all production here and increase the output in Chicago. Just walk away from Turin – that would stymie them.'

'I wouldn't agree to that,' David chipped in, 'you would be putting thousands of workers here out of a job.'

'Surely that's the chairman's decision, David. I think it would serve Paolo Medina right. I'd love to see his face if we just walked out.'

'I think I do have a say in the matter, Martin; it's my drug, don't forget.'

'I think we will have to pass on that suggestion for the moment,' Matthew said, immediately understanding the meaning behind David's sharp retort. 'Now, David, what's going on at the lab? Have you made any further progress with the diabetes drug?'

'We've had some positive results recently and I'm finally getting quite optimistic that we are on to a winner. As I said, I spoke to Paolo on Sunday and he has at least promised to give instructions that there must be no interference with my laboratory.'

'That's good news,' Martin remarked, 'it's unlike him to be so protective. What induced him to make that offer?'

David was not prepared to admit to receiving a proposition from Paolo about the patent. 'It's useful sometimes to have intimate connections,' he replied, before realising how tactless the remark was. 'I'm sorry, Matthew, that wasn't appropriate,' he stuttered. 'My apologies.'

'When it comes to Paolo Medina,' Matthew snorted, 'you are welcome to him.'

When the meeting finally broke up, Martin suggested they all went for a few drinks in the town for old times' sake. David declined, much to Matthew's relief, stating that he had some unfinished work at the laboratory. As he got up to leave he held out his hand to Matthew and, after a moment's hesitation, was pleased to receive a positive response.

Matthew flew back to England and eight days later phoned Anna about Mark's travelling arrangements for his return for the next term at the Rugby School.

'I have decided, Matthew, that it would be far better for Mark to continue his studies over here. I have therefore arranged for him to attend a college in Milan, starting next week.'

'You can't do that, Anna, he loves it at Rugby; that's where all his friends are. What does he think about it?'

'He can take the international baccalaureate in Milan,' Anna continued, ignoring the question, 'and then go on to any university he chooses.'

'This is completely out of order, Anna. I bet you didn't even give the requisite term's notice to the school, did you?'

'No, I forgot; we will just have to pay for a term, that's all.'

'You didn't forget, Anna, you arranged this ages ago. What does Mark think about it? Let me speak to him.'

'He's not here, Matthew, and I don't want you talking to him anyway. From now on I'm arranging his life, not you.'

'I'm not going to let you get away with this, Anna; you'll be hearing from me.'

'I'm not afraid of you any more, Matthew, and believe me – there is nothing you can do.'

Matthew heard the line go dead and sat staring at his mobile phone for several minutes. 'The bitch is absolutely right,' he said out loud, 'there's bugger all I can do about it.'

The Italian government had to wait over three months to get a response from the European Commission. A sub-committee had been set up by the commissioners to draw up the terms for the withdrawal of Italy from the union. The document was over sixty pages long and written in English, with a translation into Italian. When it arrived, Paolo took plenty of time to understand the full implications of every requirement, down to the last detail, before calling a cabinet meeting.

'You have all had time to read the document,' he began, 'but I think these are the salient points.'

The cabinet secretary passed a sheet of foolscap paper around the table to each member. Although Bella was not a cabinet member, it was quite usual for her to attend the meetings. It was she who had drawn up the précised version of the commission's demands for Paolo to circulate.

271

'I have listed the items in what I consider to be an ascending order of importance' Paolo continued. "Basically, the political aspects are straightforward and we can probably agree to comply without further clarification. As I suspected, the main contention is going to be financial. So let us deal with the political requirements first and get them out of the way.

'You might just give everybody a couple of minutes to read this through properly, Prime Minister,' Bella suggested, and Paolo sat for a while drumming his fingers impatiently on the table.

'I'll read them out to you and then we won't have to wait for those of you who have difficulty reading,' he said impatiently, and allowed the titters to die down before continuing. 'It would appear that the time limit to which we shall be working is six months from the agreement date to secede.'

'How do we determine an agreement date, Prime Minister?' Luciano Aldini, the Chancellor asked.

'From the time we agree to comply with all their requirements, but under the circumstances that is likely to be irrelevant. Now, these are the main bullet points.'

Paolo read out the points one by one:

One. Full Citizenship of the EU will terminate after six months. From that time all rights and privileges of Italian nationals working in the EU are to be withdrawn.

Two. Italy will cease to be an automatic member of the Schengen agreement. We would be eligible to reapply, if so desired, under separate application, as it is not confined to EU members.

Three. All border restrictions with contiguous EU countries are to be reinstated.

Four. The EU will allow a more gradual withdrawal

272

of EU subsidies to communities that rely on them, e.g. agriculture and wine producers, to minimise hardship in those areas.

Five. To help pay for the exceptional expenses attributable to Italy's secession and the cost of maintaining subsidies incurred by the EU, Italy will be obliged to continue its contribution to the EU exchequer for the two years following the agreement.

Six. Italy is to provide full and proper compensation for the commercial properties of companies domiciled within the EU that have been nationalised. The valuation of these properties is to be agreed by independent assessors appointed by the president of the European Central Bank.

Seven. EU nationals who held equity in Italian companies that have been nationalised are to be acceptably reimbursed. The London Stock Exchange will be instrumental in computing a fair price.

'Taking each one in turn,' Paolo continued, 'I think we can have no argument with number one. It is exactly what should happen. On the one hand it will mean an influx of Italians returning home jobless. On the other, it means we can expel EU nationals working in Italy if we wish. I see that as a very fair exchange, don't you?'

'It might mean a glut of chefs and restaurateurs turning up looking for work, Prime Minister.'

'I'd already thought of that, and decided it was no bad thing,' Paolo replied to a ripple of laughter.

Attention now turned to the second item on the list. As a member of the EU, Italy was an automatic member of the Schengen agreement, which allowed citizens to cross European borders without a passport. It had recently become more of an obligation; certainly any new applicant for EU membership would have to comply. However, the

United Kingdom and Ireland, wishing to retain their security, had refused to sign up.

'So we can reapply to join Schengen if we wish,' noted one member of cabinet. 'Is there a good reason why we shouldn't?'

'I'm of the opinion that, like the British, we should protect our borders against all comers in the future, but it's not a subject that needs immediate attention,' said Paolo, dismissively. 'I suggest we move on to number three which is really the same topic; control of the borders. As you know we have been charging import duties on non-EU imports for some time now. After secession it will be our intention to add goods coming from the EU to our list of dutiable items. So we are going to need border controls with France, Austria and Slovenia, our EU neighbours. We will also need to set up controls on our borders with Switzerland as they are one of the few non-EU nations to sign up to Schengen.'

'I think we all accept, Prime Minister, that secession means we shall be going back to greater restriction of movement for both foreigners and our own people,' the Home Secretary intervened.

'Okay, let's move on; I think we can look at numbers four and five together. For once I think the EU commissioners are trying to be reasonable in offering to maintain subsidies to areas that would be hard hit. But look at the payback they are demanding for this gesture; two years' subscription to the EU coffers. I can't see any real advantage to us; in fact, it is quite ridiculous. If we don't pay the EU dues, we can use the money to help our own farmers without receiving subsidies from the Common Agricultural Policy.'

'Would you propose putting some money aside for that purpose immediately, Prime Minister?' the Minister of Agriculture and Rural Affairs asked hopefully.

'Possibly, but I don't want to discuss that right now.'

Paolo moved on to the next item. 'Number six is already becoming an insoluble argument with the EU. The commissioners know damn well we are not going to compensate foreign companies that operated in Italy. I've told them time and time again that is just not going to happen. As far as I'm concerned, that was a risk they took when they invested here. A change of government can lead to a change of policies and regulation. Nationalisation was in our manifesto and they got caught up in it; it's as simple as that.'

'We all know your views on that, Paolo,' Bella butted in, 'I don't think anybody disagrees with your stance.' He glared round the room to see if anyone dared to deny Bella's remark.

'The last item, then; should we compensate EU shareholders of nationalised Italian industries? I say a very definite NO to that. We haven't given any compensation to Italian investors; why should we compensate EU members? If we offer them something, we will have to extend it to people here; we can't afford that. So I say we refuse this demand point blank.'

Paolo looked round the meeting to see all heads nodding in agreement. 'Well, that's it in a nutshell, comrades; I don't believe there is any real progress we can make with these demands.'

'Don't you think we could ask for some compromise on the financial requirements, now that we are finally able to have some part in the discussion?' Aldini suggested.

'I am not prepared to compromise or give an inch to the commissioners. Nationalisation means taking control away from the capitalists and giving it to the state; and I mean taking, not purchasing. I can't see the commissioners wanting to compromise either. They have drawn up this agreement to get compensation from us for all those who have lost out in our programme of nationalisation. If they offer any compromise, who are they going to pick out to disappoint?'

'So who will take the next step?' the Home Secretary wanted to know.

'I will; I will hand the agreement back to them and say, "no deal". We will put the ball right back in their court and see how they react.'

'If they don't come up with any changes we can accept, then I understand we can secede after two years without agreement,' Aldini announced.

Paolo scowled at him. 'I don't intend waiting that long,' he bellowed.

19

The EU commissioners accepted the Italian government's swift rebuff to their terms with equanimity; it was entirely as they expected. Much to Paolo's annoyance, they put out an understated press release designed merely to diffuse any suggestion of conflict. They decided unanimously that there was no sense in putting forward alternative or ameliorated terms; they would play for time.

Paolo eventually received a response stating the EU's disappointment with his reaction to their proposals and promising to reconvene the sub-committee and consider the matter further in due course.

'What the hell do they mean by that, Bella? What do they expect me to do now; just wait until they come up with more unrealistic demands?'

'They are trying to calm things down, darling; probably hoping you or the government might have a change of mind. They had most likely worked out in advance what your immediate reaction to their proposals would be.'

'Well, I suppose we also knew in advance they wouldn't come up with any acceptable terms, so everything is progressing along anticipated lines.'

'Exactly – and if there is going to be any real progress, we will have to initiate it. It's quite obvious they are just going to wait for us to concede.'

'You're right, Bella, we mustn't let things stagnate. It took three months for the commissioners to draw up their terms in the first place. We replied in two weeks, and then it took them over a month just to acknowledge our response. We are getting nowhere; I'm calling a cabinet meeting.'

'Only another twenty months to go until we don't even need an agreement,' Bella teased.

'Bella, you know bloody well I'm not prepared to wait that long. For your damn cheek, you can get hold of the cabinet secretary for me! Get him to arrange an emergency meeting for next Tuesday; I'm determined to press on with this matter.'

At precisely nine o'clock on Tuesday morning the cabinet stood up respectfully as Paolo and Bella entered the ornate committee room. There was only one item on the agenda and Paolo got straight down to business.

'May I take it you are all as angry and disillusioned as I am by the EU's complacent reaction?' He peered around the table and noted a line of determined faces. 'Good, then we need to agree on what steps to take next.'

'Isn't the ball still in their court, Prime Minister?' a junior minister dared to ask. 'Shouldn't we wait for a proper response? We ought to make them formulate new terms. Surely they are obliged to come up with something we can reasonably accept. Wasn't that section of the Lisbon treaty designed to provide an orderly exit?'

'Can't you see they are just using the treaty as a political weapon?' Paolo riposted. 'We must make up our own minds on how best to progress; I'm looking for a resolute decision from this cabinet.'

'I agree, Prime Minister, we are getting nowhere fast with the commissioners. It is time for firm action,' Luciano Aldini said, adding his weight to the point.

'I want an agreement on what I'm about to propose reached by the time I close this meeting today. Nobody is going home till I have a decision,' Paolo declared.

The members of the cabinet shuffled in their seats to get more comfortable and refilled their water glasses. They could be in for a long session. 'What I'm suggesting is this,' he began, 'and I have already put some senior members here in the picture. They tell me they are completely behind my proposals.

'I don't think we should delay any further our complete secession from the European Union. We have made our intentions clear and the EU is deliberately procrastinating. At the end of the day it must be our decision as to how we go about it. I believe we have nothing more to achieve by prolonging negotiations; it is time for action.

'Let me make one thing clear; I want a unanimous agreement from this meeting. Your total loyalty to me and the party is paramount. I have prepared a document to be sent to the commissioners stating that it is our intention to secede from the union without further negotiation. I have set a timescale of three months to complete the various political actions required to terminate our membership; for example, closing our borders and restricting the movement of people and goods.'

'Can we really organise that in so short a time, Prime Minister?'

'I have been carefully drawing up plans with the chief commissioner of police. He confirms we can have the right personnel in place and be capable of action within the prescribed period; it is the bordering states that are more likely to be ill prepared.'

'And the Schengen agreement; have we decided about that?' a cabinet minister asked.

'My opinion is that we come out and stay out. I want to make our position very clear to the commissioners; we are making a total withdrawal from the European capitalist society. In future Italy will be an independent socialist state.'

'Won't that leave us too far out on a limb, Paolo?' Bella had always had her concerns; she felt more comfortable sharing them in the meeting than tackling Paolo at home by herself.

'It may do initially, but I've been in touch with a lot of friends around the Continent. I am certain we can expect a lot of supportive action. Just look at how much stronger the left-wing parties have been growing lately in the European parliament itself. I know several other countries are watching our stance with interest. If we act boldly, you will probably see others following in our footsteps.'

'Do you really believe our defiance could start a mass exodus from the European Union?' A junior minister asked in an incredulous tone.

'I've no doubt about it; I have had a number of calls from senior politicians in other countries sympathising with our position. The EU is about to have a big shake up. I'm now going to ask the Chancellor of the Exchequer to take us through the financial implications.'

'Thank you, Prime Minister, I will try to be as brief as possible,' said Aldini, getting up to speak. 'Our offer to the commissioners is this: we will offer to pay our normal annual dues to the EU exchequer pro rata up to the date of secession, i.e. in three months' time. We will demand in return our due subsidies up to that date but expect to get nothing thereafter; that seems equitable.'

'They already pay our subsidies very late,' the Foreign Secretary pointed out pointed out. 'Once we have withdrawn, I bet they won't pay up at all.'

'You are quite right; but I had thought of that. We will just hang on to our subscription and subtract anything we are owed before making a final settlement. If it turns out they actually owe us money, we will probably have to write it off.'

Food and a little wine were brought in at lunchtime and the discussion continued across the table in a more leisurely fashion. At the end of the meal Paolo stood up and brought the meeting back to order.

'We have all had time to consider our position;' he began, 'this is going to be a momentous decision. I want a straight answer from each of you. The question is clear: do we take the decision to secede immediately from the EU, or do we continue to get nowhere with the negotiations? You obviously know my opinion or we wouldn't be having this meeting. Remember, I am demanding a unanimous decision today. Anyone who is opposed, and I perfectly respect his or her right to be, will have to resign from the cabinet. I therefore put this proposal to the meeting today; that we give notice to the European commissioners that we intend to withdraw our membership forthwith. Now, Luciano, I will start with you.'

'I'm with the proposal, Prime Minister, but there's just one thing I meant to ask earlier: will we need to take our decision to the House for ratification?'

'Not in this case, Luciano; the voters gave us the go-ahead in the referendum. All we are dealing with here are the means for withdrawal and the timescale. Now, who's next?'

Paolo continued round the table in an anti-clockwise direction. One by one the cabinet members confirmed their support for the motion with total conviction; there were no dissenters.

'Thank you everybody, that gives me a great deal of confidence in dealing with the media exposure we are about to receive. On the expectation of your decision, I have already prepared a press statement which will go out immediately after this meeting. I have also prepared a full statement of our final intentions to be passed concurrently to the EU commissioners. I think we are in for an interesting few days.' The members of the cabinet rose to their feet again as Paolo and Bella left the meeting.

* * *

The first indication from the Italian government that Italy intended to secede from the union had come as a complete surprise to the commissioners. Their initial reaction had been tempered by incredulity and the desire to play down the potential consequences. The new announcement from Rome came as a total shock.

The commissioners' original expectations were that the harsh terms imposed on the Italian government would make them retract their decision to withdraw. The media began immediately to speculate about whether general support for the future of the union was disintegrating. Some of the old divides reappeared, coupled with fresh concerns from newer entrants. The EU was now over sixty years old. Had it run its course? Had it outgrown its strength? Had it usurped national sovereignty to unacceptable levels? The journalists were having a field day.

The French President and German Chancellor requested an urgent meeting with Raul Haitink, the long-serving President of the European Union. The pressure from the media to make statements on the impending crisis within the union required a uniform response. The anodyne announcement from the meeting stated that every effort would be made to keep Italy in the fold.

In reality, the meeting had discussed more drastic measures. After some deliberation, it was decided to invite the original six members of the EEC, apart from Italy, for further discussions, and to include the United Kingdom. The President offered to go to see the prime ministers of these states to ascertain their opinions. He visited Holland, Belgium and Luxembourg in that order, and finished his series of meetings in London.

He was entertained in Downing Street by the Prime Minister, Neville Aitchison, who gave him a tour of the main state rooms within the building. He was impressed with the relative simplicity of the cabinet office which had only a single painting placed above a marbled fireplace, a portrait of Sir Robert Walpole, the first prime minister to occupy the building. Three ornate brass chandeliers hung from a high ceiling, shedding light on to a boat-shaped table top, introduced by Harold Macmillan. At one end of the room, two pairs of Corinthian columns gave support to the extension completed at the end of the eighteenth century. The columns created an attractive ante-chamber that had been turned into a small library.

The Prime Minister's private office was in an adjacent room and he invited the President to join him for an unofficial working lunch. Raul Haitink had already requested an informal private meeting, with no other people present, and no minutes taken.

The appearance of the two men could hardly have been more different. The sixty-three-year-old President was short, slightly built and with sleek grey hair. He had hazel brown eyes that portrayed a piercing intelligence, but the crow's feet at the corners gave him a benign look. His prominent white teeth contrasted well with his olive skin. Despite his slight stature, his presence in a room was always apparent.

Neville Aitchison was in his early fifties, with thick brown hair showing no signs of grey. He was heavily built, just under six feet tall, but gave the appearance of a very large man, which owed much to his robust personality and exaggerated swagger. He had light grey-green eyes above a nose misshapen by years of playing in the front row of the scrum. His ample mouth, set above a square jaw, displayed a neat row of crowned teeth. Despite his over-powering appearance he could easily switch to a gentle diplomatic demeanour.

'I have been asked to sound you out,' the President began, 'by Guy de Valbien and Hermann Kranz on the question of where we go now with Italy.'

'What do the French and Germans want this time?' Aitchison asked bluntly.

'They believe the commissioners have gone as far as they can go with Paolo Medina and much stronger action is now required.'

'Of course we need to take a firm stand with him, but nothing we've tried in the past has had any effect. We are wasting our time on him; I say let him go, and to hell with him. Italy will come snivelling back in due course; they have no alternative in the long run.'

'That's not the view of the others that I've been talking to, Neville. They think the EU needs to fight back hard; Medina has got to go.'

'Don't be bloody stupid, Raul; we can't change the duly elected government of another European country.'

'The others think a regime change would not be inappropriate here. Medina has torn up all the rule books; he needs to be brought to task.'

'So what have they asked you to suggest to me, Raul?'

'I think they would rather explain that to your face, Neville. All I can say is that it's pretty radical. Would you mind sparing the time to come to a joint meeting next week if it can be arranged?'

'I suppose I could if you really think it's that urgent,' Neville agreed.

'Thank you, Neville; I won't take up any more of your time for now.'

Having completed the round tour to his satisfaction, the President proceeded to organise a discreet meeting attended exclusively by the heads of state of France, Germany, and the other countries he had visited; only the Prime Minister of Luxembourg declined to be present. The meeting took place in Bonn at the invitation of Hermann Kranz, the German chancellor.

The President opened the meeting. 'As you can see I

have allowed only my private secretary into the meeting; whatever is discussed here must not go beyond these four walls. Chancellor Kranz assures me there are definitely no bugs, so we can say exactly what we like. I am going to hand over the meeting to him to give you his views on where we stand with Italy. After that I will get everyone's opinion in turn and hope we can get a realistic consensus.'

'I have made a point,' the German Chancellor began, 'of talking to most of the senior politicians of our member states. I included some experienced MEPs in this survey as well as the various heads of state. Almost without exception they are concerned about a possible break-up of the EU. There were several countries that sympathised with the Italian stance and I suspect you all know who they are. However, I don't believe that even they would want to see a complete rupture in the EU.

'As you know, Italy was one of the founder members of the union, or the EEC as it was then known. It is therefore even more distressing that this country has voted to secede. Were we looking at a more recent entrant there would be far less of an impact. In my opinion we cannot afford to allow Italy to withdraw. I believe it will greatly weaken the powerful unit we have built up over these past sixty years. All our foreign competitors are looking for chinks in our political and financial armoury. I believe our prosperity has come from our unity. Of course we have our differences, that's healthy, but Europe as a whole has developed into a combined force that is respected around the globe.'

'I agree, Chancellor,' Guy de Valbien, the French President added, 'there can be no doubt the Americans, the Chinese and the Russians will revel in our discomfort if the EU starts to disintegrate.'

'As I was saying,' Kranz continued, ignoring the interruption, 'we cannot afford to allow a breakaway. We deliberately made the terms for secession as harsh as we could in order to frighten Paolo Medina into withdrawing his application. I know the Italian people voted to secede, but we felt they would come to their senses once they understood the potential costs.'

'That policy might now appear to have backfired on us,' Haitink added, 'but frankly there was no alternative. It would have been impossible to backtrack on our previous demands for full compensation with regard to his programme of nationalisation. That would have made us look weak and opened the gates to other members to take advantage.'

'Quite so, Raul, but we didn't expect such a quick rebuff, even from Paolo Medina. We need to make an even quicker response. It looks as though we will have to go ahead with our contingency plan without delay.'

'I have spoken to all of you in turn,' the President added, 'that a plan was being put forward. It was agreed to hold this meeting to discuss the joint proposition by France and Germany. We all know what we are talking about today; the invasion of Italy by our own armed forces. We all agreed to limit the decision to the few of us round the table. It is time to make that decision. I have already asked Chief of Staff of the European Army, General Schweizer, to draw up a plan of attack, so we could proceed without delay.'

'One moment, Raul,' Neville Aitchison intervened, 'I thought I was coming to this meeting for a discussion, not to be presented with a fait accompli.'

'And I thought I made it quite clear, Neville, we would need to act swiftly, otherwise it will get out somehow and there will be no element of surprise.'

'I accept we need the element of surprise or we can't proceed, but I am going to find it very difficult to justify invading another European nation to the British people.'

'We realise the British are overwhelmingly Eurosceptical,' de Valbien pointed out sarcastically, 'but we need your support on what could turn out to be a very important time in the history of Europe.'

'How dare you keep calling us Eurosceptical or even anti-Europe, just because we happen to disagree with a lot of your political aspirations? You can accuse us of being anti-federalists; we don't want to see the whole of Europe controlled by a President and a bunch of unelected commissioners in Brussels.' Neville Atchison glared at the German Chancellor. 'We've fought war after war to stop dictators from dominating the entire continent,' he pointed out angrily.

'The British can hardly claim innocence when it comes to military conquest,' the President intervened, hoping to dampen down the argument.

'It may be true that we've tried to dominate the rest of the world,' Atchison replied, with a smile, 'but we've never had any designs on Europe. We haven't produced a Napoleon or a Bismarck or a Hitler!'

'Maybe not, Neville, but we are having this meeting to decide on what to do with another potentially lethal dictator,' Kranz responded in a conciliatory tone. 'Let's stick to the point.'

'I still don't see how I am going to justify an invasion of Italy to the British public.'

'I don't understand your reticence, Neville; we have all had billions of euros stolen from us since Medina took over. In my opinion we have every right to take it back by force. We have given him plenty of opportunity to be reasonable, but he just mocks us. The EU cannot survive if members are allowed to steal from one another with impunity.'

'I'm already under a lot of pressure from those industries back home that have suffered financially to take drastic action. Nevertheless, it seems anathema to me that we could actually use our own European Army to attack a member state. I almost can't believe this is happening.'

'Are you saying you won't support this initiative, Neville?' de Valbien demanded impatiently. 'I think I can safely say the rest of us are completely in favour. It would be disappointing if you felt unable support us.' The other men in the room nodded their heads and looked at the British Prime Minister for an answer.

Neville Aitchison took time to stir his coffee; he was wondering what the others would do if he declined to support the proposal.

'Another thing that has been worrying me is the number of casualties we might expect. I am obviously concerned about civilians in particular. Is it possible to get General Schweizer in here to explain to me the plan of attack?'

'He is unlikely to be available at the drop of a hat, Neville. Anyway, it wouldn't be a good idea for journalists to see him entering this building; there would be all sorts of wild speculation.'

'Okay, I accept that, but I still need something to persuade me there won't be any casualties. Before I came here I decided to educate myself again on what actually happened when Texas and other southern states of America decided to secede from the USA. I don't have to remind you it turned into a gigantic bloodbath.'

'Yes there was a very bloody war,' Haitink agreed, 'but then there were two opposing armies and the conflict lasted over four years. What we are planning is really no more than a quick political coup.'

'You can hardly call it a political coup if you're using the European Army, Raul.'

'General Schweizer is certain he can act so quickly that the Italians won't have time to retaliate before our tanks are surrounding the parliament buildings. He assures me there is no reason to assume there will be any loss of life. I have to accept his professional advice.'

'But what happens if the Italian Army does fight back? You can't tell me there won't be any loss of life then.'

'I am giving the General instructions that any retaliation is not to be defended. We will withdraw our troops immediately; there is to be no fighting. However, the General is convinced that the Italian Army will have insufficient time to mobilise.'

'The reasoning behind that, Neville,' the Chancellor added, 'is that it's the Italian President himself who controls the armed forces and not Paolo Medina.'

'I see where you are coming from; I know the Italian President is not very friendly with Medina. And that's putting it mildly. So it's your intention to warn him before the invasion occurs, is it?'

'We've discussed this possibility and decided against it,' Kranz continued. 'Quite frankly, if he were to be told in advance, he would be obliged to inform his government; failure to do so would be regarded as treason. We can't put him in that position, but we think he'll be quite happy to see Paolo Medina thrown out of office.'

'We also believe there will be rejoicing in the Vatican,' the president added. 'Although Medina is known to be a practising Catholic, the rise of communism is a big thorn in the Pope's side. In addition, Catholic countries like Spain and Portugal are beginning to get in the grip of left-wing extremists; we think we can guarantee his support after the event. He will not wish to see communism taking over in his other faithful territories.'

'You make it all sound very straightforward, Raul,' Neville Aitchison responded, sitting back thoughtfully in his chair. 'I can see that on balance the odds are in our favour. If it all goes wrong I shall probably have to resign, but I'm willing to go along with you and take a chance.'

A look of relief came over the faces of the other men. 'I think that probably applies to all of us,' de Valbien voiced his agreement.

'Thank you, Neville, and in fact I can tell you we had decided we could not possibly go ahead without your consent,' the President confided.

'I don't know whether I find that comforting or not, Raul,' Neville Aitchison remarked as the President signalled the end of the meeting by packing his briefcase. As they left the room Aitchison took the President to one side. 'By the way, I assume you mentioned to Kranz and de Valbien the stipulations I made before agreeing to come to this meeting?'

'I did, of course, Neville, and I have their assurances you will get all the support you need from them when the time comes for me to retire.'

20

Jane entered Matthew's office to be met with a tirade of abuse which, she thankfully realised, was not directed at her.

'That bloody bitch has done it again; I can't get hold of Mark. I've got no idea where he is.'

'I thought you told me he was at a college in Milan?'

'He is, but I don't know which one. I phoned Anna, who actually deigned to answer, but she refuses to tell me. She took his mobile phone away, so I can't contact him and I'm upset that he hasn't tried to contact me. She has obviously threatened him with dire consequences if he attempts to do so.'

Jane thought for a moment 'Leave it with me, Matt; I have to talk to David about a large shipment of chemicals he wants sent over. I've got it here in the warehouse, and he wants it before the deadline for payment of this new import tax to the government. I'll get chatting to him and see if I can wheedle the information out of him. His mind is usually up in the clouds somewhere when he's in the lab, so I might catch him off his guard.'

'Good thinking, Jane; would you mind getting on to it straight away?'

'I'll do it from my office, Matt.' Jane didn't want him interfering while she was making the call.

Every call to the factory was now being monitored and Jane had to go through a tedious rigmarole before she finally got through to David. 'This is quite ridiculous, David; do you realise it has taken me over ten minutes to get hold of you?'

David was not in a position to agree with her and just apologised diplomatically. 'I'm sorry, Jane, it's just the new system; for security reasons, I'm told.'

'I'm phoning about your shipment of chemicals. Oh, by the way, how's Anna?'

'She's fine, thank you. So are the chemicals in your possession now?'

'They are in the warehouse at the moment, ready for shipment. Do you want them sent by air, or would it be better to put them on a boat? I understand Louise has been taking some exams; how did she get on?'

'I don't think she's due to take any exams until next week. Perhaps it would be wiser to airfreight the shipment. If the sea journey takes too long, we could be in danger of having to pay the import duty.'

'I'll get the boys straight on to that then; you should hopefully get it within a week. How is Mark enjoying his new school in Milan? I've forgotten its name already.'

'San Bartolomeo's,' David said unwittingly, 'and so far as I know he's settled in okay. Will you let me know which flight it's on, please, so I can try to speed it through customs.'

'Of course I will – don't forget it will arrive at the cargo terminal.'

'Thanks for ringing, Jane. I hope to see you sometime soon, ciao.'

Jane rang off and went directly to Matthew's office. She tapped on the door but entered without waiting for an invitation. She walked up to his desk, unable to conceal a self-satisfied grin. 'It's San Bartolomeo's,' she announced triumphantly, 'I got it out of David, no trouble at all.'

'Well done, you!' Matthew leapt from his chair and gave Jane a hug and a kiss before pulling sharply away, 'Did you verify they have a pupil there called Mark Boston?'

'I'll get on to it immediately,' Jane replied. She returned

an hour later. 'I got the number from international directory enquiries and rang the college secretary, who fortunately speaks good English – but they have no student of that name.' Matthew's face fell at this news. 'Then I thought; I bet Anna has entered him under another name,' Jane continued. 'I made a lucky guess – they have a Marco Medina who only started this term,' she said triumphantly.

'Book me on the first flight to Milan tomorrow, darling,' Matthew replied jubilantly, 'I'm going out to see him, but I won't be calling him Marco.'

Tom Bailey dropped Matthew at Heathrow early the next morning. He was getting fed up with the drive. 'I hardly ever had to make this awful journey under the old chairman,' he muttered to himself, 'I hate Heathrow and no doubt I'll have to come back again in a couple of days.' On that assumption he was wrong.

Matthew flew directly to Milan; it was not an airport to which he was accustomed and he followed the signposting through to passport control. He gave his passport to the controller, who fed it through a scanner. '*Un momento, signore,*' he said, picked up the passport and left the booth.

Matthew started to protest but was forced to watch as the controller walked through the door marked 'CARABINIERI'. A few minutes later he came back, accompanied by two police officers. 'I am sorry, Signor Boston,' the senior officer said in a polite but firm tone, 'but I am not able to let you enter the country.'

Matthew rocked back on his heels. 'Don't be stupid, man,' he barked, 'don't you know who I am?'

'No, signore, I don't; I just have my orders that you are an "undesirable" and are not permitted entry.'

'But I'm your prime minister's son-in-law; I'm married to his daughter, for God's sake!'

The two officers exchanged a look and returned to their office, still retaining Matthew's passport. When they reappeared, one of them took Matthew by the arm and led him away. 'Our instructions are that you may not enter Italy; we will be putting you on the next plane to London. You will wait in this office until we have made the necessary arrangements.'

'May I at least make a phone call?'

'You are permitted to make just the one, signore,' the senior officer replied officiously, 'from this desk. You may not use your cell phone.'

Tom Bailey was sitting comfortably in a chair at home, watching cricket on the television, when the call came through; he was required to go back to Heathrow. He received a stern rebuke from the lady in the kitchen for his choice of language.

Since he was the Commander-in-Chief of the European Army, it was not unusual for the European President to visit army headquarters in the south of France. His arrival there created no special comment, and he was taken immediately to the office of General Schweizer. Seated with the general were Colonel of the Tank Regiment Philip Boston and Albert Walewski, the major in charge of the ordnance corps. The General introduced the two officers to the President before getting down to the matters in hand.

'I knew you would wish to look over the plans, Raul,' the general began. 'May we assume from your visit that you have obtained full approval from the men that matter?'

'Yes, only Luxembourg decided not to give their national consent, but they are not going to oppose either. So the invasion can go ahead if you are sure you can pull it off without any fighting.'

'As I told you before, Raul, the plan of attack is relatively straightforward. We believe we can create sufficient surprise that it will be all over before the Italians wake up to what is happening. Philip, will you take the President through the detail, please.'

'The initial invasion will be through the port of Civitavecchia,' Colonel Boston began, 'which is the nearest port to Rome capable of taking our vessels. In the first wave there will be four vessels, each carrying fifty armoured vehicles of various sizes, and twenty-five tanks. We will need to pick a day when we know there will be no more than one cruise boat in dock. It is almost impossible to find a day when the port is empty.'

'The weather will also need to be calm,' the General interrupted.

'Yes, we can't exactly set a date, but we will be ready to go when the time is right,' Philip continued. 'From previous manoeuvres we know we can unload the vessels in less than fifteen minutes. The armoured vehicles can come off in pairs in six minutes, and it takes about nine to offload the tanks in single file. We are allowing no more than forty minutes to unload, and exit the port after docking.'

'Are you sure you will be able to dock?' the President queried. 'Couldn't the port authority close the port if they suspect an attack? When they detect four naval vessels bearing down on the port, won't they get alarmed?'

'We've thought of that,' Philip replied. 'We intend sailing from the French naval port of Toulon and the voyage will take around twenty hours. We will sail across to Livorno, on the Italian north-west coast and then turn south-east down the coast towards Civitavecchia. We will inform the Italian coastguard that we are bound for Cyprus, and request permission to pass through the Strait of Messina, way down south by Sicily. That should be sufficient to prevent any suspicion and we can slip into Civitavecchia before they realise what we are doing.'

The President nodded his understanding so far and looked at Philip for the next step in the plan.

'Once we are safely ashore, sir, the difficulty will start. We are planning to dock by three-forty-five, about two hours before sunrise. Civit, as we are calling it for short, is nearly eighty kilometres from Rome and we want to arrive at the parliament buildings by seven-thirty at the very latest. That means the operation is expected to take no more than three and three-quarter hours.

'The tanks are obviously the slowest vehicles, but are still able to roll at over thirty kilometres an hour; provided, of course, that they are not held up. We must keep all the roads we intend using free of traffic and this is how we plan to do it. The first fifty kilometres will be covered along the A12 autoroute, after which the convoy will split in two. One group will take this route,' Philip pointed out, showing the map to the President, 'it's called the Aurelian Way. The other group will stay on the A12 as far as the major orbital road.'

'As you can see, Rome has a motorway known as the GRA that encircles the city, about fifteen kilometres from the centre. There are around twenty-five roads that feed into this ring road, about half of which are major arterial roads. We think that if we block the entrance routes to the GRA early in the morning, we can practically close Rome down to busy traffic. This will enable our convoys to get into the city centre with little impediment. We would expect to be well inside the GRA before seven and up to the parliament buildings on schedule.'

'How will you block the slip roads leading on to the GRA?' President Haitink wanted to know.

'We have already got our hands on a few dozen lorries that are currently parked in a pound we've hired exclusively, near the orbital road. We will get our drivers there by five-thirty, with instructions to drive them into blocking positions before immobilising them. The minor roads leading on to the GRA we can block off with some of our own armoured vehicles; the rest of the vehicles will plough ahead, to open up the two separate routes we will be taking into the centre.'

'Okay, I'm with you so far, Colonel,' the President said confidently, 'but there will still be the police to contend with. Won't they attempt to blockade the roads into the city?'

'Almost certainly there will be a reaction from the *carabinieri*, but our armoured cars should be able to deal with that pretty quickly. Don't forget that, apart from the few vehicles we will be leaving behind to block off the GRA, there will be almost two hundred of them paving the way for the tanks. In any case, the police don't possess anything that the tanks can't easily roll over; only the Italian Army could do us any damage, and we are betting on them staying in bed.'

'What is to stop us getting attacked from the air?'

'Again, President, we don't think the air force will have time to react. By the time we're inside the orbital road they won't dare bombard us; the civilian houses are too dense.'

'So we have the tanks rolling through the city and surrounding the Senate and the Chamber of Deputies. Let's say we have won the military battle without a fight; presumably the next move has to be political. I suppose that's where you want me to come in?'

'Exactly, Raul,' General Schweizer replied, 'you will need to be ready to appear on behalf of the European Union as soon as possible. We have planned for you to arrive in the Piazza Navona in a helicopter immediately after the tanks have secured our position. We are arranging for a second wave of two vessels to dock in Civit. One of them will contain more tanks and armoured cars, in case they are needed for additional support. The other will, with your approval, contain you and your helicopter.'

'It all sounds feasible, General; almost too straightforward. Will you be leading the attack?'

'No, I shall be orchestrating the invasion from the dockside at Civitavecchia. I will, of course, be in constant communication with all the section commanders, including those organising the blockades. Colonel Boston will be leading the attack through the city.'

'Who will be with me in the helicopter? I would like, at least, to have my foreign secretary on board for support.'

'Once I get the confirmation that we are in control of the parliament buildings, we can all fly in,' the general explained. 'The Piazza Navona will be cleared and we will land there, right by the senate. I anticipate coming with you, Raul, in the first helicopter, but you may also take whomsoever you choose; provided, for reasons of secrecy, they are not briefed before the invasion.'

'The Foreign Secretary is already aware of the plan, General, and I don't think I need anybody else with me to start with. On second thoughts, it might be sensible to have our own photographer and reporter with us to record the proceedings. You know how the press can misrepresent any occasion.'

'That can easily be accommodated, and the army will also be recording everything as it happens,' the general agreed.

'I would also prefer to be put in touch with the Italian President before I arrive at the senate. Presumably you will have the communication system in place in case he tries to make contact with me?'

'I've no doubt he will be desperate to speak with you as soon as he is made aware of the invasion, Raul. We will make sure you can be easily contacted from Brussels by your private secretary.'

'You will make it quite clear to your troops, Colonel,'

Raul Haitink turned towards Philip, 'that there is to be no fighting. If the Italian army retaliates you are to withdraw immediately; is that quite clear? We want no bloodshed.'

'That is perfectly understood, Mr President, but believe me, the Italians won't have anything like enough time to mobilise. It is going to be a piece of cake.'

'In that case, I'll share your optimism. If we pull this off without a hitch, it will help to stabilise the European Union at a very difficult time. If we fail, we will suffer an enormous embarrassment, so the future of a lot of senior politicians depends on your success. By the way, how many days' notice do you expect to be able to give me?'

'At least three, Raul, but if the weather is set fair, we might be able to give you up to a week. I thought you would like to know that the code name we have given the invasion is Operation Caesar.'

'That sounds appropriate,' the President replied, smiling. 'Well, I suppose that just about wraps everything up, gentlemen – so good luck!'

'Thank you, sir, and would you care for a fresh cup of coffee before you leave?' Major Walewski spoke for the first time.

'No thank you, Major, I must be on my way; but I look forward to seeing you, in due course, on the steps of the Senate House.'

When General Schweizer had shown the President out of the barracks he returned to his office, where Colonel Boston had remained seated. 'Haitink appeared to like the plan, Philip, and seems comfortable with our assertion that there will be no bloodshed. What did you think?'

'I expected him to go away happy with the plan, Karl, but there is no way there won't be any bloodshed. It's bound to happen on a manoeuvre like this; something invariably goes wrong when some idiots get in the way. We can't afford to slow down for anything.'

'I know, Philip, but we can't let that worry us. That weasel Paolo Medina deserves to get everything that's coming to him. I must say I'm looking forward to the operation and, as far as I'm concerned, the sooner the better.'

A very sullen Tom Bailey went to Heathrow, for the second time that day, to pick up his chairman. On the journey home, Matthew telephoned Jane, who wanted to know why he was back in England so soon.

'You won't believe this, Jane, but the bitch has actually managed to get me thrown out of Italy. She must have persuaded her father to put me on the list of undesirables and they wouldn't let me in. I felt like a bloody terrorist!'

'Good God, Matt, I can't believe she would go to those lengths; is there anything I can do to help?'

'I thought up an idea on the plane that might work; perhaps we could have dinner out tonight and see what you think of it.'

'You must be worn out, darling; I think it would be better if I cooked you a meal at home. I'll see you in about an hour; we can discuss things more peacefully in your house.'

Jane was not living with Matthew and had preferred to keep her apartment in the centre of Northampton. This reduced the inevitable gossip at the office, but she regularly spent several days at his house and was used to the kitchen there.

Matthew arrived home in an aggressive mood and threw his holdall across the entrance hall. Jane heard the clatter and came out to greet him. She gave him a long hug before finally breaking the silence. 'I'll fix you a large gin and tonic while you change into something more comfortable. You can relax and tell me exactly what happened.'

She was pleased to see him reappear looking more casual;

by the time he had taken a large swig of his drink he was able to give her a pleasant smile. He related the earlier frustrating events of the day and how he had been put back on the plane.

'You don't know how embarrassing it is, being practically frog-marched round Milan airport. I was livid and I'm sure the police just loved doing it; pompous bastards!'

'Well, you're back here with me now. Sorry you've had such a harrowing day. I don't understand why Anna is going to ridiculous lengths to keep you away from Mark and Louise. Now, you were saying you had another idea'

'I'm going to fly down to Nice tomorrow and hire a car. The border with France is still open and I can drive to Milan without being asked to show a passport. I thought you might like to come with me; I might need your help to get into Mark's college.'

'I'm happy to help, Matt, but wouldn't it be better if I were to travel separately in case we get stopped at the border? If I fly to Milan, at least one of us should be able to make contact. I can't possibly be *persona non grata* yet.'

'I see your point, Jane. Here's what we'll do: I can get on a flight from Luton to Nice, so I'll get Tom to drop me there for the early morning flight. He can then take you on to Heathrow for a flight to Milan.'

'He won't like that, darling; he told me that if he has to take you to Heathrow once more this month, he'll hand in his notice.'

'He's just a grumpy old man these days,' Matthew said, brightening up at last, 'don't take any notice of him. He's got a very cushy number and, anyway, it's you he's taking to Heathrow, and he likes you.' He walked across the room to where Jane was sitting and bent over to give her a kiss. 'But not as much as I do,' he added, lifting her out of the chair and running his hand up the inside of her thigh.

'Later, Matt,' she whispered, squeezing out of his grasp, 'I think our dinner must be ready.'

As predicted, Tom was in a better mood with Jane as his passenger on the airport run the next morning. 'Just let me know when you want to be collected;' he said, as he lifted her case from the boot and pulled up the handle. 'I'm delighted to have a lovely lady sitting with me in the car for a change.'

'I hope to be on the evening flight tomorrow, Tom, if all goes well. The chairman will probably take a little longer to get home.'

Matthew landed at Nice airport's Terminal 2 and took the short walk through the long-term parking area to the Avis car hire office. He showed his shareholders' card at the 'preferred' desk and was on the road within a few minutes. It took an hour to reach the Italian border, which he crossed with no complications. He anticipated the onward journey to Milan would take him less than three hours to complete. It would be a drive of about 270 kilometres, all along motorways, and with nearly a hundred tunnels through the rock formations to negotiate.

Jane had no difficulty entering Italy at Milan airport and took a cab to the Hotel Manzoni, in the heart of the fashion district. She would have plenty of time to do some shopping before Matthew arrived. He had wisely elected not to stay at the same hotel, and would find a small *albergo*, where the police would search last in the case of trouble.

The couple made contact in the early evening and had dinner in a small restaurant recommended by the manager of the *albergo*. The proprietor turned out to be the manager's brother and they were greeted, in typical Italian style, like long-lost friends. After some delicious wild sea bass ('caught in the Mediterranean only this morning, signore') and a bottle of Pinot Grigio ('from my father-in-law's own vineyard') they sat contentedly discussing the plan for the following day.

'It wouldn't surprise me, Matt, if there isn't an order preventing you from getting into the college and seeing Mark. I think it would be more sensible if I were to enquire after him; that would be less likely to arouse attention.'

'You are probably right; you must try to get him out and I'll wait in a restaurant nearby.'

'If I do it at the start of the lunch break, he will hopefully be allowed to come out with me.'

'Surely they won't prevent him from coming out of college in his lunchtime; I must see him.'

'Don't worry, darling, I'll get him out. But if not,' she added with a note of caution, 'I'll make sure he at least gets the mobile phone. Give it to me now and I'll put it in my handbag, so I can't forget it.'

At twelve o'clock the following day, Matthew waited in a cafe around the corner from the impressive San Bartolomeo College. Jane went to find Mark. She passed through the ancient portico entrance to the lodge where the concierge had a small office.

She introduced herself as an aunt of Marco Medina and said she was hoping he would be allowed to see her and have some lunch. The porter made a phone call which resulted in her being asked to provide identification. He studied her passport carefully before returning it and leaving the office.

Jane found a plain wooden chair in the corner and sat down. She was surprised to find her heart thumping in her chest whilst she waited for the next move. Ten minutes later, the door opened and the porter appeared with Mark following. She leapt to her feet and cried, 'Marco! It's lovely to see you! Can you come out for some lunch?' She looked enquiringly at the porter, but he hadn't completely understood.

Mark explained that he would be allowed out, but would need to sign the register book indicating his whereabouts. He performed that task under the watchful eye of the porter and Jane breathed a sigh of relief as they left the lodge.

'I've a lovely surprise for you, Mark,' she said as they walked past the front of the cathedral and into the back street where Matthew was waiting. She did not notice a man come out of the shadows and follow them as they left the college gate.

She led Mark into the cafe and he fell gleefully upon his father. The tears welled up in both of them as they hugged for a long time in the middle of the floor. They eventually sat down and Matthew called up the waiter to order some food and a drink.

'Mark, I've been trying to get in touch; why haven't you rung me?'

'I haven't got a mobile; Mum took it away and in fact it's the college's policy to ban their use by students.'

'Did you know that I'm not supposed to be in Italy? Apparently I'm an enemy of the state. Your mother has obviously organised my ban. What's going on, Mark? Louise has only managed to phone me on one occasion.'

'Mum found out about the phone you gave her and stamped on it.'

'Well, at least it wasn't because she didn't want to get in touch, I suppose. Now, tell me, how are you getting on at your new school?'

'I don't like it at all, Dad; I've made a couple of friends, but it's not the same as Rugby. I suppose I'm beginning to understand why I'm being forced to stay in Italy, but I really miss my old friends; it's not fair.'

'That's exactly what I told your mother would happen,' Matthew remarked, and followed Mark's gaze as a man entered the cafe and sat down at a table near the door.

'I can't go anywhere without that man following me. He's obviously some sort of bodyguard, so I guess it's something you just have to put up with if you happen to be the prime minister's grandson.'

Jane looked at the man as he held up a cell phone and took a couple of photographs. He then dialled a number and began a conversation. 'Matt, I think you had better go quickly before he summons up some reinforcements. If you get caught here you will be in a great deal of trouble.'

'Okay, I'd better get going; have you given Mark the mobile?'

'They make me turn out my pockets every time I go back into school.'

'It's only small; stick it in your shoe and try not to limp. Jane, I'll stand in front of the man on the way out, and block his view for a minute, while you slip the phone to Mark. Oh – and slip him some money.' He got up and put his arm round his son, 'I'll get you out of this mess one day soon, that's a promise. Tell Louise I love her; sorry I can't stay any longer.'

He stopped in front of the man on the way out and spoke to him. 'I presume you speak English as you are looking after my son. Keep a careful watch on him, he's very precious to me.'

The man gave a wry smile, nodded, but made no reply. Matthew decided he had given Jane long enough to pass over the mobile, and strolled out of the cafe. He increased his pace outside, jumped into the first available taxi and directed the driver to the street where his car was parked. Having already checked out of the *albergo*, he drove away immediately.

Jane was able to enjoy the meal and update Mark with news of his grandparents and local gossip. Eventually Mark had to return to the college and she walked with him as far as the portico. This time she noticed that the man had been joined by another, who proceeded to follow her after she kissed Mark goodbye. She walked the 500 metres back to the Manzoni, deliberately stopping to watch, with a degree of amusement, the evasive antics of her pursuer.

She collected her case from the hotel concierge, spent fifteen minutes in the ladies' powder room, and then took a cab to the airport. As she attempted to go through passport control she received the same treatment experienced by Matthew earlier in the week. She was led off to a side room where a senior police officer attempted to interrogate her.

'You realise you were breaking the law when you helped a banned person enter this country, and then told lies about your relationship with the prime minister's grandson,' he spoke sternly in perfect English, trying immediately to put her on the back foot.

'I didn't help anyone to enter the country and I've always been practically an aunt to Mark. I was secretary to his English grandfather and have known him since the day he was born,' Jane replied defiantly.

'I have to insist that you tell me where your accomplice is at this moment. You are not leaving this airport until I have that information.'

'I have no idea where he is at this moment,' Jane replied, annoyed with herself for finding the officer, and the lilt in his voice, very attractive.

'You have a mobile phone, I presume, signora? You will please contact Signor Boston and ask him exactly where he is. If you refuse you will be put in a cell. I have known us to forget people are there for quite some time,' he added forcefully.

Jane fumbled laboriously in her handbag, playing for time as she searched for her mobile. She finally retrieved it and scrolled down her list of contacts until she came to David Steinberg. She dialled the number, held the phone tightly to her right ear, and waited for a response. When she heard a 'hello' come over the line she jumped in quickly.

'Hi, it's Jane speaking; how are you? Where are you right now?' she continued, not waiting for a reply.

'I'm in the laboratory, Jane, why do you want...'

'Oh! good, you're there already,' Jane cut in, 'and have you checked that the chemicals I sent out arrived safely?'

'I thought you knew they were here, Jane,' David replied, getting very puzzled at the conversation.

'I think you should leave the factory very quickly, Matthew, ciao,' and she rang off, leaving David staring at his mobile in bewilderment.

'Well, signora?' the officer enquired.

'He's at the Boston and Wood factory in Turin,' she said, with a resigned tone in her voice. 'Now, if you don't mind, I have a plane to catch.'

'You will remain here, signora, until I have checked the call. I'm not very happy you warned him to leave, but we will soon catch up with him.' He walked out of the room, leaving Jane with her heart pounding for the second time that day. He returned after ten minutes, sat down purposefully, and fixed her with his piercing brown eyes.

'My technicians have confirmed the call was indeed made to a location in Torino, signora; thank you for being sensible and cooperating. You may leave now; I will get one of my men to escort you to the aircraft. You will please note that, in future, you will be required to get permission from the Italian Embassy in London before being allowed entry into Italy. Do you understand what I am saying?'

'Perfectly!' Jane said, gathering up her belongings. She had no desire, whatsoever, of ever setting foot in Italy again. She suffered an agonising wait for the aircraft to take off, expecting to see the reappearance of the officer at any moment. When the plane was finally airborne, she gave an audible sigh of relief and burst into tears.

Matthew put his foot down hard on the pedal as he sped along the A7 motorway towards Genoa. He went on to the A26 to avoid the Genoa traffic, and eventually turned right along the A10 toward the French border. He had just passed the turn-off for Savona when a glance in the mirror showed a police car flashing at him. He reduced his speed; the police car overtook and waved to him to draw on to the hard shoulder.

A policeman got out of the car and walked warily towards Matthew, who apprehensively wound down the window. '*Vous roulez trop vite, monsieur,*' he said in a poor French accent. '*Vos papiers, s'il vous plait.*'

Matthew handed over his driving licence. 'Ah! *Inglese,* you are English, yes?' Matthew nodded. 'You drive too fast, sir; you exceed speed limit going one hundred sixty kilometres, and you not reduce speed in tunnels, as demanded by law.'

Matthew did not argue the point; he was just relieved to find the man was only a traffic controller. He paid the 150-lire fine with cash on the spot and was even relieved at getting no receipt. With a bit of luck the money would just go into the policeman's pocket and the offence would not be reported. As he continued his journey at a more careful pace, he began to worry that his escape route might be detected if his name did get registered, and decided to change his plan for re-entry into France.

About 10 kilometres before the border, he turned off the motorway to the town of Ventimiglia. He left the car in a side street and walked to the railway station. He had remembered that there would be a large market there on that day, as it was a Friday. Hundreds of people crossed the border from France, to find cheap bargains; he would just be another shopper heading home after a day at the market. He bought a ticket to Nice and waited for the next train.

308

The train barely slowed at the border crossing and a relieved Matthew arrived in Nice too late, unfortunately, to catch the evening flight home. He checked in at the Hotel Negresco on the Promenade des Anglais and phoned Jane. Receiving no reply, he concluded she must be on a plane, and went to the bar for a large drink.

The next morning he took a cab to the Avis office and handed in the car keys. He told them where they would find their vehicle in Ventimiglia, before boarding the plane for home in a relieved and happier mood.

21

A little over three weeks after the strategic meeting in the south of France, Raul Haitink received a call at the weekend from General Schweizer.

'We have a window of opportunity for Operation Caesar next Thursday morning,' the General informed him.

'Okay,' said Raul, trying to ignore the increase in his heart rate. 'Where do you want me to be and when?'

'The naval commander invites you to spend Tuesday evening as his guest in Toulon,' said the General, deliberately not giving too much away over the phone. 'One of my officers will contact your secretary on Monday to confirm.'

'I'll be there, Karl,' replied Raul.

'Oh, and one more thing,' the General put in, 'don't forget your seasickness pills.'

'Thank you, General, but I'm actually a very good sailor. Till Tuesday night, then.'

This was going to be another historic event in the course of European conflict, the president thought to himself as he hung up. Since he would be relying on his secretary as a line of communication to the Italian President when the time came, he had had to take him into his confidence. Raul made a mental note to make sure his appointments weren't cancelled until the last minute; he didn't want anyone enquiring in advance where he might be going.

At 4 a.m. on the following Wednesday, four heavily armed vessels slipped anchor and sailed silently out of the harbour of Toulon in the south of France. Raul would be in the second convoy of two leaving at 7 a.m. The convoy headed eastward, past the Iles d'Hyères and into the Ligurian Sea. A strong but hot southerly wind was blowing and a sharp thunderstorm left the vessels covered in a coating of red Saharan dust. They sailed to the north of Corsica before turning south towards Civitavecchia. Before midnight they could clearly distinguish the lights on the coast of the island of Elba to the port side. The pre-arranged message of deception was sent to the coastguard at the Strait of Messina, requesting passage through to the Aegean Sea with an intended destination of Nicosia.

The calm Mediterranean waters were shimmering under the light of an almost full moon as the four vessels eased their way past the Civitavecchia lighthouse and into the harbour, exactly to time early on Thursday. As anticipated, there was only one scheduled cruise ship moored, belonging to the Italian Costa line.

There was plenty of docking area for the naval vessels and they tied up on the western mole. The men were at their stations and poised to disembark. They had only been given a full briefing during the journey and were naturally surprised at the target. They had supposedly been training for an exercise in Cyprus, but now realised that the format fitted perfectly with the operations ahead. An air of excitement pervaded the ships as the bow doors were opened to release the armoured cars. This was the first time the European Army was going seriously to war.

The unloading of the vessels went neatly to plan and the first armoured cars broke through the security gates of the port. Philip Boston had been amazed at how unmanned the docksides were at that hour of the morning. A fleet of fifty fast vehicles was sent on ahead, to organise the blockades at the motorway slip roads and to deliver the drivers to the compound where the lorries were stored. The remainder of the convoy moved out of the port area and proceeded, in an easterly direction, through the town.

The noise of the tanks woke the entire population along the road and doors and windows were flung open. The armoured cars were all flying the European flag; the tank commanders, with their heads and shoulders above the turrets, were waving energetically at the people. The spectators naively waved back. After 4 kilometres the convoy joined the A12 motorway and turned south towards Rome.

During this time the Civitavecchia police had been frantically trying to determine the purpose of the sudden activity. They had been contacted by the surprised port security, but had few officers on duty. Most of these were fully occupied in dealing with inebriated vagabonds and dockside prostitutes. It took more than an hour to get a senior official out of bed and into the local head-quarters. He decided to travel along the coast road to the next motorway entrance in the hope of heading off the convoy.

General Schweizer had foreseen this move and sent a couple of armoured cars in that direction to block the access. The police inspector drove up to the corporal in charge of one of the vehicles and demanded to know the object of the exercise.

The corporal's Italian was not good, but he eventually persuaded the policeman that it was just a training exercise and that the police headquarters in Rome were fully aware of the operation. The officer seemed satisfied with the answer and returned to the local station. There, he began to feel uneasy and decided to telephone Rome.

His call was treated initially with derision and he had difficulty persuading the desk sergeant to put him through to the Superintendent.

'What are you trying to tell us, Inspector? Do you really expect us to believe that we might be being invaded?' the superintendent snapped down the phone.

'I don't know what to think, sir, but we have not been advised here to expect an army exercise; I'm just checking that you are in the know.'

'If it is one of the EU Army's mock exercises, and I know they have them, I would not expect the information to be passed down to my lowly position. I suppose I had better get in touch with the chief commissioner; he won't be very happy to be woken up at this hour. See what extra information you can get at your end, and I'll ring you back after I've contacted the chief.'

The Superintendent chewed on the end of his pencil for a moment before making up his mind. He picked up his phone and asked to be put in touch with Chief Commissioner Carlotta, the officer who, a few years earlier, had overseen the unsuccessful investigation into the assassination of Rico Orvetti.

The convoy travelled along the A12 at a steady pace and by 6 a.m. the first vehicles were approaching the exit on to the Aurelian Way, where it divided in two as planned. Colonel Philip Boston decided it was an opportune moment to report his position to General Schweizer back in Civitavecchia.

'We are at the dividing point, sir, on time and all's well. The blockade is obviously working. Major Wright has taken over command of the other half of the convoy. I shall be slowing down a little as the Major has further to go.'

Philip's unit continued along the Aurelian Way and crossed over the GRA orbital road. He was now less than 15 kilometres from the Senate. He was directing operations from the leading armoured vehicle and had arranged for several tanks to come forward and form up directly behind him. They might be required to batter the way through once the road into the centre ran out of dual carriageway.

*　*　*

313

Chief Commissioner Carlotta was not pleased to be pulled out of bed at daybreak and answered the phone gruffly. 'What is it, Superintendent, that can't possibly wait or my deputy can't handle?'

'I thought this situation needed your immediate attention, sir, or I wouldn't have roused you. I have been informed that an army convoy waving the EU flag is advancing rapidly on Rome. My initial reaction was that it was an exercise, but the Civitavecchia Port Authority has not been informed, nor have we any record here of a mock invasion. I am assuming you've been advised and are waiting to see how the capital reacts to an emergency.'

'Good God, man, I know nothing about this! How big is this army?'

'I am getting reports coming in now from the field. It appears there are over a hundred armoured cars and tanks on the Aurelian Way and a similar number on the A12 approaching the ring road.'

Carlotta shook his head in disbelief, but thought quickly. 'We must put up some road blocks immediately. Get as many men out there as you can find and tell them to blockade all the routes into the city.'

'As you say, sir, but I doubt that our cars will have much effect against an army of tanks. I'm told the convoy is moving at about twenty-five kilometres an hour; it could be here in less than ninety minutes.'

'Then commandeer anything you can lay your hands on. I'm going to phone the prime minister straight away; this does not sound good.'

Carlotta managed to get immediately in touch with Paolo Medina at his private residence in the Via Gregoriana. The prime minister listened with complete incredulity to the commissioner's assertions. At 6.15 a.m. he was already dressed and ready to breakfast before going to parliament, where he was invariably at his desk before seven. He thought quickly. 'Get on to the President for me and put him in the picture. I'm going to get our army mobilised as quickly as I can. This is outrageous; we've got to stop these invaders getting right into the centre of town.'

'Very good, Prime Minister, and I've decided to send some men to your residence as extra protection.'

'Don't worry about me, I'm going straight to the senate once I've talked to the army chief.'

Paolo for once in his life felt disorientated and uncertain. He sat for a moment in an armchair before picking up his phone and dialling his secretary. 'We have a state of emergency here,' he shouted down the phone. 'I want you to get me General Hugo Montefiori on the line immediately, and then get hold of as many members of the cabinet as you can find. Tell them to meet me at the senate in double quick time.'

'May I ask what the emergency is, sir?'

'We're being invaded by the bloody EU, man; now just get on with it,' Paolo screamed before slamming the phone down.

As predicted by General Schweizer, communications between the top Italian officials at that hour of the morning took time to organise. It was twenty minutes before the Italian army chief responded to Paolo's call and listened dumbfounded to his assertions that the country was under attack.

'Are you certain nobody has received any advice from the European Army that they were mounting a mock attack on Rome?' was his first reaction.

'No we haven't!' Paolo retorted, 'make no mistake, General, this is definitely an invasion. You must get mobilised immediately and come to defend the capital.'

'I can't possibly get a force organised in such a short time. Did you say they are inside the ring road already?'

'No, I don't think they are quite that far yet, but I

understand they are mounting a two-pronged attack from the north. There is a mass of tanks – surely you have plenty of anti-tank missiles?'

'Of course we have, but we stand no chance of getting into the centre in time to launch them.'

'Then launch them from helicopters. You must be able to do something immediately to stave off this attack. I insist you get some helicopters in the air.'

General Montefiori gave a resigned sigh at Paolo's lack of military sense. 'I'm sorry, Prime Minister, I can't do that. We cannot have missiles flying around in populated areas.'

'I am not concerned with the number of casualties, I'm concerned about our sovereign security. Get some helicopters armed and over the city now.'

'You know perfectly well I cannot mobilise our army without permission from the President himself. If you like I will try to contact him and see what action he expects me to take.'

'Can't you see that will be too bloody late?' Paolo shouted. 'Don't bother yourself, General, I'll speak to the President myself. Just wait there for his instructions,' he barked, putting an abrupt end to the call.

Sitting in his office at the Senate, where he had gone early to deal with some important papers, President Carlo Salvatore received a frantic call from his Prime Minister. His immediate response was incredulity. 'This can't be true, Medina, the European Union isn't going to invade Italy. It must be some sort of exercise; if you like I'll get in touch with Raul Haitink and find out what it's all about.'

'I think you should mobilise our army first. General Montefiori is waiting desperately for immediate orders.'

'No, I'll call Haitink now and I expect we can put a stop to all this nonsensical speculation. What do you intend doing now?'

'I'm coming straight over to the senate for an emergency meeting of the cabinet.'

'Come straight to my office – I should have a reply from Haitink by then.'

It was now seven o'clock and the two convoys had crossed the ring road and were heading at a steady pace toward the city centre. Colonel Boston received confirmation from his tank commanders that no resistance had so far been encountered; he relayed the positive news to General Schweizer.

'We are exactly on course, sir and should be in position around the parliament buildings within half an hour. The population are still waving cheerfully back at us, and there appears to be no panic.'

'Good work, Philip, and just to let you know, Raul is currently in conversation with President Salvatore. I'll keep you informed of the outcome of their discussion. It should be very intriguing.'

President Salvatore had immediately phoned Brussels and Raul Haitink's secretary forwarded the call to the dockside at Civitavecchia.

'Is that you, Raul?' he began. 'Can you explain to me what your army is doing in Rome? I've received no warning of this exercise and Paolo Medina is going wild. He believes you are making a genuine invasion. What the hell is going on?'

'I can confirm that this is not an exercise, President. It is a serious response from Europe to your government's decision to secede from the union. I can assure you this is a benign attack; we knew you would not be able to respond militarily to this invasion in time to prevent us from reaching the city. I am asking you not to mobilise your troops; we don't want any unnecessary bloodshed.'

Carlo Salvatore sat back in his chair and pondered the situation. 'What do expect me to do, then?' he finally asked, in a resigned tone, just as Paolo Medina burst through his office door.

'Are you speaking to Haitink?' he demanded. 'What is he saying? Let me talk to him!'

Salvatore waved an arm at Paolo, motioning him to sit down, and waited for a reply to his question.

'In a matter of minutes, Carlo, I'm told that our tanks will surround the parliament building and the senate; in other words, the entire political centre of Rome. I am, at this very moment, waiting by a helicopter at the dockside in Civitavecchia to fly into the city. I would like you to meet me when I arrive, and I will inform you of our wishes.'

'Just a moment, Raul,' Salvatore replied. Paolo could contain himself no longer and tried to snatch the phone from his grasp but was pulled away by the President's secretary. 'I suppose I have no choice in the matter,' Carlo continued. 'I will be at the senate when you get here.' He replaced the receiver and looked at Paolo.

'It seems you were right, Medina; the European Army has indeed mounted an attack on Rome. I just can't believe they would have such audacity.'

'You sound very calm about it, Carlo; what the hell do they expect to achieve? I've instructed General Montefiori to organise a counter-attack, but he refuses to do anything without your instructions.'

'It's far too late for to defend the position; I never thought for one minute this was a serious invasion. We have been caught napping here; lessons will have to be learnt.'

'If you're not even prepared to defend parliament with our army, what bloody use are you?' Paolo shouted, rising from his chair. 'I've always said you and your position were obsolete and you've just proved it!'

'Sit down, Medina, and listen to some common sense for a change. I am not prepared to have a war with the whole of Europe at this stage. I have agreed to talk peacefully with Raul Haitink when he arrives.'

'And when will that be? We can't sit around waiting for him to appear at whatever time he chooses. We must get this fucking EU army out of Rome, right now.'

'He is about to board a helicopter and will be here in less than an hour. I suggest that you and your cabinet get out of the building, before the tanks arrive, and go into hiding while I sort this problem out.'

'I shall do no such thing, Salvatore! What the hell do you think I am? I'm not going to flee at the sight of a few amateur soldiers. I'm going out to meet them face to face. What would the Italian people think if I were to run away from these bastards?'

'I've given you my best advice, Medina; so on your head be it.'

The two columns were homing in on the city centre. Philip Boston was passing the Vatican on his left flank and preparing to cross the Tiber by way of the Vittorio Emanuele II bridge. The mighty dome of St Peter's Basilica looked down once again at the arrival of a foreign army.

The second column had already crossed the river; Major Wright stared with admiration as the mighty Colosseum came into view. He proceeded along the Via dei Fori Imperiali, leaving the ruins of the old Roman forum on his left, and entered the Piazza Venezia.

To his horror, Philip received a message from his Number 8 tank commander. 'Colonel, I've just witnessed an awful tragedy. A young girl ran out in front of my forward tank and disappeared under the caterpillar wheels. A woman I take to be her mother saw the accident and is screaming in the street. Are there any instructions?'

'Nothing we can do about it,' he told his commander,

'just keep on going, but it's not going to enhance our popularity.' He looked ahead to see a line of cars belonging to the *carabinieri* blocking the entrance to the bridge. He signalled to his leading tank to halt and drove forward to confront the police blockade. As he approached a salvo of bullets thumped against the windows of his armoured vehicle. He decided to pull over and summon his tanks to clear the path.

The *carabinieri* watched with astonishment as the leading tanks rolled without difficulty over the police cars. Two officers had remained defiantly in their vehicle. One, seeing the danger, flung open his passenger door and dived to safety. The driver attempted to do the same, but he had parked too close to the adjacent vehicle. A loud scream went up as the tank crushed the car and continued relentlessly on to the bridge. Two larger security vehicles, designed for transporting prisoners, were merely pushed aside and overturned in the gutter.

Major Wright's column rounded the Piazza Venezia and met a similar blockade in the Via del Corso. Once again the tanks demolished the police vehicles and pressed ahead with little delay. They continued up the Corso before turning left by the Palazzo Chigi toward Piazza del Parlamento. Within a few minutes they had surrounded the Palazzo Montecitorio where the Chamber of Deputies is housed. The Major phoned in his final position to Colonel Boston.

'I have totally surrounded the parliament and await further instructions. I can report we encountered no resistance other than a minor blockade, and have no casualties.'

'Thank you, Major, stand firm. You are a few minutes ahead of me; I am just turning into the Piazza Navona now. We should all be in position in five minutes. I'm amazed at the welcome from the citizens of Rome. They obviously have no idea of our real mission.'

'I thought that myself, sir; it was as though we were Pompey returning from the battlefields and receiving a hero's welcome.'

'I'll confirm your position to the General and leave you to deal with any local problems.'

Colonel Boston drove into the Piazza Navona and watched as his tanks alternated their movements to surround the Palazzo Madama. There were now over twenty tanks positioning themselves in the Piazza Navona and Philip was anxious to ensure that no damage was done to Bernini's beautiful Fontana dei Quattro Fiumi. He leapt from his armoured car and personally directed the tanks to avoid any mishap. He knew from experience that most tank commanders paid little respect to property.

With all his troops in position, both at the Chamber of Deputies and the Senate, he contacted General Schweizer.

'It is twenty to eight, General; I apologise for being ten minutes behind schedule. All our equipment and men are in position; you may inform President Haitink that we have arrived without any casualties to ourselves. As you know, we believe there have been two mortalities to civilians on the way.'

'Thank you Philip; not your fault, I know, but I had hoped to keep a clean sheet in that respect. I am about to get into the helicopter with Raul and should be landing in the Piazza Navona in about half an hour. By the way, the good news from our intelligence division is that Paolo Medina is in the Senate at this very moment. I want you to station men in every exit so that he can't leave the building. You know my instructions; no military personnel are to enter the parliament buildings before the President and I arrive.'

'I will pass on that reminder to Major Wright, sir, and await your arrival.'

'Okay, and now that the tanks are in position don't

forget to send a number of armoured vehicles round to the Italian television headquarters and the head office of *La Nuova Repubblica*. We must control the media until the two presidents have reached agreement.'

'That has just been arranged, general, and we will start handing out our propaganda leaflets to the local people straight away. We must reassure them that this is a peaceful operation.'

For the past half hour members of the cabinet had been arriving and a dozen men, headed by Carlo Salvatore and Paolo Medina, were gathered in the prime minister's office. The President was the first to speak.

'I understand now that our two Houses of Parliament have been completely surrounded by forces of the European Army. We have been taken completely by surprise; nobody, in the wildest stretches of their imagination, could possibly have foreseen such an event. I refused to involve our own forces as I believe the outcome could have been catastrophic for the city. No doubt the invaders were relying on that assumption but I couldn't take the chance. I have just been speaking, for the second time, to Raul Haitink, who is due to arrive shortly by helicopter. We have no option but to hear what his demands are.'

'I disagree entirely, sir,' Paolo intervened with impatience. 'I think we should ignore him completely. He has no right to invade our soil; we only give him credence if we sit round a table with him and his cronies.'

'I agree with your sentiments, Medina, but do we honestly have any choice?'

'Yes, we lock ourselves in and refuse to meet him. If we shut the doors of the Senate to him, he wouldn't dare force his way in. It would be totally unacceptable to the whole world for a European army to usurp our parliament.'

'Look, Paolo,' President Salvatore replied in conciliatory tone, 'they haven't come this far to be kept out by a few doors. Our only immediate option is to talk to them and find out what their demands are. They are not going to go away empty-handed.'

'And I am not going to give them the privilege of entering the Senate. I insist that we all go outside when Raul Haitink arrives and offer to talk to him in the Piazza Navona, in front of the citizens of Rome.'

At that moment, Paolo's secretary entered the room to inform him of the arrival of President Haitink's helicopter in the piazza. Paolo got up, removed his jacket from the back of the chair, and slowly put it on. 'Is everybody coming with me?' he enquired, and strolled out of the room.

The nine men and one lady representing the cabinet followed the President and Prime Minister down the wide staircase and out through the main doors. On reaching the piazza they were immediately surrounded by armed soldiers. President Salvatore was taken aside from the group and allowed to watch the proceedings unguarded. He saw Paolo Medina and the Chancellor of the Exchequer separated from the others, handcuffed and pulled to one side. The remaining members of the cabinet were shepherded away into several armoured vehicles.

It took a few minutes for Paolo to regain his composure. He raised his handcuffed wrists in the air and shouted at the soldiers lining the piazza, in the vain hope that his voice could be heard by the people who had gathered to stare at the tanks.

'You are witnessing here,' he bellowed, 'an act of aggression, in fact an act of war, committed by the European Union that has ceased to have any semblance of true democracy. The army that you see before you was never intended to...' At this point, he was roughly hauled away in the direction of the helicopter that had brought Raul

Haitink and General Schweizer to the city. On seeing Philip Boston he stopped, pulled himself away from his escort, and stood facing him defiantly. He stared hard for a moment at the man he recognised as Anna's brother-in-law, but for once, words failed him. Philip stood unflinching as Paolo spat contemptuously in his face before being dragged away.

Paolo and his Chancellor were put into the helicopter and flown to the dockside at Civitavecchia. They were taken on board one of the naval vessels and retained in a locked cabin.

President Carlo Salvatore had been left to deal with the invading party alone. He greeted them stiffly, holding his head high as he led them into the Palazzo Madama. Raul Haitink was accompanied by his PPS and the European foreign secretary; he had invited General Shweizer and Colonel Boston to join the discussions. They all returned to the room recently vacated by Paolo and his cabinet, where President Salvatore offered them a seat. He remained standing while he enquired about the nature of the invasion.

'I will start by reiterating the words of my Prime Minister. This is an unacceptable act of aggression. You have no right to bring this army to our shores and invade our capital. I can tell you in advance that I have no authority from the Italian people to offer any form of agreement to the demands I assume you are about to make.'

'Let me first apologise to you, Mr President,' Raul Haitink replied, 'for what we feel is a necessary response to your government's disdainful treatment of our member states. We decided it was impossible to deal in a politically sensible way with Medina and no other option was open to us. In addition, he was stirring up a great deal of trouble in a number of countries and in danger of destabilising the union. Quite frankly, we came to the conclusion that he needed to be removed before he got out of control.'

'I understand your concerns, Raul, and I probably share some of them, but invading a member state is an act of war. There can be no other term for it.'

'I beg to differ, Carlo, we have no intention of remaining in Italy – we are not an army of occupation. We have merely come here to ensure a change of regime, that is all. We have already achieved that target; Paolo Medina is under arrest.'

'And what do you intend doing with him? As far as I know he has committed no crime.'

'That will be up to the European Court of Justice to decide. In the opinion of many members, stealing from the balance sheets of businesses and taking shareholders' money are punishable offences. He will have to stand trial.'

'So where do you think that leaves me, Raul, now that you have removed my Prime Minister and half the cabinet? Don't tell me you are suggesting the introduction of European MPs into my parliament?'

'Certainly not, Carlo, you are free to make your own decisions up to a point. What we would suggest is that you appoint an emergency coalition government, of your own centre right and left MPs, whilst we sort out our differences. On the one hand, the European Union is not prepared to be plundered. On the other, we would not wish to stand in the way of your secession, if that is what Italy really wants.'

'I think I understand what you are saying, but I obviously need a great deal of time to discuss this matter with the other political leaders.'

'Of course, but we will not be moving our tanks out until we have a reasonable undertaking from you that our demands will be met.'

'I don't want your army on Italian soil any longer than necessary, so I will press ahead with your suggestions. May I have your assurance that all members of parliament will have full access to the chamber and the senate?'

'Of course, Carlo, that is easily arranged.' Raul Haitink looked over to Philip Boston. 'You will please make sure, Colonel, that all MPs can come and go freely. I assume you will be staying in charge of the troops here?' Philip nodded his assent.

'In that case, gentlemen, I will leave you to find some refreshment, while President Haitink and I arrange a press conference.' President Salvatore started to wind up the meeting. 'By the way, Colonel, I apologise for the disgraceful action of my prime minister. Spitting in someone's face is not acceptable behaviour.'

'I can understand his feelings, sir, but when he stopped in front of me, and gave me such a stare, I thought he was going to say "Et tu, Boston" and fall in a crumpled heap at my feet.'

'That would certainly have been a fitting finale to Operation Caesar,' General Schweizer couldn't resist adding.

Laughter rippled round the table and even the Italian President had difficulty concealing a wry smile.

22

Bella was going frantic. She had been woken up by Paolo telling her of the invasion, and that he was going directly to the senate. Despite showering and dressing quickly, she had not managed to beat the arrival of the tanks. She managed to slip between a couple of the moving vehicles and get as far as the Chamber of Deputies before the net closed completely.

In the Chamber she encountered several MPs who were also trapped and unable to comprehend the events happening outside. Bella took them to the prime minister's office and explained what she believed the situation might be.

'If the attack is only on the Chamber, because that is where they would normally expect the Prime Minister to be, it's possible that Paolo has escaped the invaders. I have been trying desperately to get in touch with him, but he no longer carries a cell phone for security reasons.'

'Why don't we try the RAI, Bella, and see what information they have?' someone suggested.

'Good idea. I'm regularly in touch with the senior journalist, and I'm pretty sure I have his number,' Bella replied, relieved to be getting some friendly assistance.

The RAI is the Italian state television network. Unlike the BBC, which is run by an independent trust, the RAI is totally controlled by the government. This was the case even before Paolo became prime minister, but there were also a few independent companies operating. As these happened to be owned entirely by a wealthy ex-prime minister, Paolo promptly nationalised them and integrated them with the now exclusive RAI network, giving the state total control of the television waves.

Bella managed to get a response from her contact, who was trying desperately to make sense of the reports coming in.

'We have sent a helicopter up, Bella, and I am getting some pictures coming through right now. I regret to tell you that the senate is completely surrounded. I can also see a military helicopter parked in the Piazza Navona.'

'Has anybody at the RAI managed to talk to my husband?'

'No, and all attempts at speaking either to him or the president have failed. Oh my God! I can see a number of armoured vehicles approaching this building. I'd better get out while the going's good. I am in constant contact with our helicopter on another line, so I should be able to keep you informed of any developments outside the senate.'

'Okay, get out quick and get back in touch with me on this number.'

Bella reported her conversation to the others. 'It seems both we and the senate are separately surrounded and cut off from each other. Get a television in here as fast as you can.' Just then her mobile rang; it was her contact at RAI again.

'I managed to get out of the building in time and have just been talking to the pilot. He tells me that the Prime Minister and President are just coming out into the piazza.'

'Thanks, someone is just fixing up a TV in this room, we can watch that for a time.'

It took several frustrating minutes to get the television operational. Bella was just in time to see her husband and Luciano Aldini being escorted across the piazza and bundled into the military helicopter, which took off immediately and banked towards the north. As the camera from the RAI helicopter swung back to the president, left standing disconsolately by himself, the whole network went blank.

Bella kicked the television off the coffee table. An MP placed a comforting arm round her shoulder.

'Who was that on the phone just now?' Linda Boston asked her husband Gerald.

'It was only Matthew wanting to know if he could have lunch with us on Sunday.'

'Of course he can; we haven't seen him for ages. Why didn't you let me answer the phone? You know I like to speak to people.'

'I was standing right by it when it rang. Anyway, I told him we'd love to see him.'

'Did you ask him how things are with him and Anna?'

'No, but he did say he wanted to come over and talk to us about Anna and the children and Jane.'

'I do hope they have patched up their differences; I do miss seeing Mark and Louise. Did you say something about Jane?' Linda suddenly realised what Gerald had said.

'There has been a rumour that Matt is having an affair with Jane.'

'What? Why haven't you told me about this? How long have you known about it?'

'It's only a rumour; I heard about it when I bumped into Jack Edwards at the Wheatsheaf in Crick a few weeks ago. You know what he's like; anything for a bit of gossip. I didn't take it very seriously.'

'Do you mean to tell me that I've been worrying myself sick about Matt and his marriage, and all the time he's having an affair with Jane?'

'I really don't know, darling; just calm down. I expect he'll tell us all about it when he comes round.'

'Why don't you men ever pass on important information? I'm going to phone him right now and find out what's going on.'

'He was in a rush to get off. I believe he's still having problems with Bosteinex in America. So don't bother him now; you'll see him on Sunday.'

'I suppose I shall have to wait then. I wish I'd answered the phone,' Linda added in a frustrated voice. She started to leave the room but an idea struck her. 'I think I'll ask Maggie to come round and do the cooking so I'm not stuck in the kitchen while you men are having a conversation.'

'Good idea, darling; so long as she's available on her day off.'

'She has plenty of days off; not that you would notice, of course.'

'And another thing he said was to switch on the telly; apparently there's some amazing news coming in at the moment from Italy.'

'Now thanks to you, I shan't get a wink of sleep tonight wondering what the hell is going on in my son's life!'

Gerald gave an exasperated sigh, slumped into his favourite armchair, and turned on the television.

The blacked-out television network and exchange of photographs up and down the country were leading to wild speculations. Eventually the whole of Italy stopped work as people gathered together and waited for an explanation to the events. At one o'clock the television returned to life with the announcement that the President would speak to the nation in an hour's time.

At precisely 2 p.m. a grim President Carlo Salvatore was filmed, seated in his ornate office, beside the European President, Raul Haitink.

'What I have to say to you,' he began, 'has been agreed between me and the President of the European Union. We have been invaded by the European Army and our Prime Minister, together with several members of the

330

cabinet, taken away. I decided it would be foolish to try to counter this attack with our own forces for fear of a major loss of life and damage to our capital city.

'The European Union has not invaded Italy without reason, and I have been discussing various demands with President Haitink. I have decided, having considered his concerns, to exercise my constitutional rights and dissolve this parliament. Until a general election can take place I intend to form a temporary coalition government, composed equally of responsible left and right wing politicians. They will manage the affairs of the country while we sort out our differences with the European Union.

'I have made the following points quite clear, and they have been accepted by the European President. Firstly, that I have no authority to take decisions unless they are ratified by your parliament. Secondly, that no political decisions will be made while a foreign army remains on our soil. Thirdly, that any decisions made by the Italian government, with regard to our future relationship with the European Union, will not be directly influenced by the recent demands of the European commissioners.

'President Haitink understands perfectly that only your parliament has the authority to determine the future for Italy. He has also assured me that, once I have formed an emergency coalition, the European troops will withdraw. Provided I obtain the cooperation from your elected members of parliament, I expect to complete this task within a week.

'Whilst I have this opportunity, I would like to ask the whole country to remain calm. I refused to allow our troops to enter any battle with the invaders for fear of heavy loss of life. It would be foolish, at this stage, for any citizens to attempt to take the law into their own hands and create an atmosphere of civil unrest.

'As you already know, Paolo Medina was determined to

tear up the Italian constitution for his own political ends. He has been attempting to get support for my removal, as your President of the Republic, and to incorporate the presidency within his own spectrum of power. He has been moving to turn parliament into a one-party organisation; in other words, to give him complete dictatorship.

'President Haitink informs me that Paolo Medina and Luciano Aldini will be taken to Luxembourg and put on trial for the embezzlement of money and property belonging to fellow Europeans. I shall insist on being involved in the validity of all accusations made against them. Whilst my differences with your prime minister were well publicised across Europe, I still intend to question the authority or constitution under which the EU feels able to put an elected member of our parliament on trial.

'We have discussed the question of secession and I have informed President Haitink that the decision of the Italian people will not be reversed, unless we determine to hold a further referendum. I have made no undertaking in that regard as it can only be decided by your future government. In the meantime, I expect the coalition to extend the timescale announced unilaterally by Paolo Medina, to enable renewed dialogue and conciliation.

'It was the wish of Raul Haitink to speak to you at this moment about the reasons behind the European decision to attack Italy. I did not consider it to be appropriate for the commander–in-chief of an invading army to be given free access to our media. I have, therefore, persuaded him to allow me to read out a prepared statement at the end of this address.

'The action by the European Union will have come as a shock to this entire nation. I doubt whether any member state ever considered the possibility of the European military forces, for which we have actually supplied our own troops, being used against a fellow member. I intend to find out which of the powerful member nations were behind the approval of this invasion.

'I intend to speak to the nation every day at six in the evening, whilst the emergency exists, and until the EU army withdraws all its troops.

'In conclusion, I will read out the prepared statement from the EU, signed by President Haitink: "The European Union regrets the necessity to instigate the removal of the Prime Minister, Paolo Medina, and to demand a change of regime in Italy. There has been concern in the European Commission regarding the swell of communism on the continent. This has been exacerbated by the influence of Paolo Medina and his government. We realise that the long global recession, following the collapse of the banks, has inevitably led to the increase in extremism. It should be remembered that this also happened, with dire consequences, following the great depression of the early 1930s.

' "The EU is determined to avoid history repeating itself. On the last occasion it was the extreme right that dominated Europe. Today we are in peril of a repetition, this time from the extreme left. Paolo Medina has been leading this movement, which is spreading to all corners of Europe. He has been using funds, embezzled from member states and their citizens, to further his political aspirations. That is why we have intervened. We will be working with your president to restore the reputation of your country within the European Union. This invasion is not meant to be seen as an act of aggression. We have come in peace to help retain the integrity of Italy in the world of international politics. We shall withdraw our troops the moment your president advises us of his new political appointments." '

President Salvatore paused for a minute to allow the statement to be digested. 'I will just finish by adding that it will take some time for the Italian people to be convinced that this is not an act of aggression. I would nevertheless repeat my request for calm while I proceed with the reorganisation of the government. I shall speak to you all again tomorrow.'

The President's first act was to take control of the police and the media. He discharged Chief Commissioner Carlotta and reinstated his predecessor, who had been forcibly retired by Paolo. He decided to retain the services of the chief executives of RAI television and the two national newspapers, but with strict instructions for them to be unbiased in their political reporting.

It was late afternoon before he found the time or inclination to return the persistent calls from Bella Medina.

'I suggest you come over to my office now, Bella. Where are you at the moment?'

'I'm still at the Chamber, where I've been stuck all day,' she replied in a sharp voice. 'I want to know where they have taken my husband.'

'I'll send an escort round to collect you and bring you over to the senate.'

Bella duly arrived at the president's office, where she was offered a comfortable chair and coffee.

'Let me first say I'm sorry that our country has got itself into this argument with the EU. I am, nevertheless, of the opinion that Paolo's contempt for the European Commission is mainly to blame. As such I am concerned for your own safety for the time being. I am withdrawing your pass into the parliament buildings and would ask you to let me know where you intend to reside until these problems are sorted.'

'What do you mean you are concerned for my safety? I have nothing to fear, and I want to be around here, where I can be of assistance to Paolo.'

'Bella, I suggest you leave Rome as soon as possible. You probably don't realise the amount of animosity towards your husband by the Mafia and other right-wing factions.

I have placed the police on full alert for the inevitable demonstrations we are going to witness over the next few weeks. The trade unions, on the one hand will be demonstrating against the EU. The fascists will seize the opportunity to riot, now that the police are no longer under Paolo's dictatorial influence. We are in for a period of civil unrest.'

'In that case, I suppose I could go back to Turin for a while, where my family is. I shall want to be kept informed daily about my husband's situation.'

'I think that is the best for you, Bella. I will arrange for you to have an armed guard at the villa for protection. Please don't do anything to expose yourself to danger. Don't forget the attempt on Paolo's life by the Mafia a few years ago.'

'How can I forget it, Carlo, I lost my daughter – and now the European Army has taken my husband. And you expect me to isolate myself and take no action. On second thoughts, I'm not so sure I agree to that.'

'Bella, what I am suggesting to you is not optional. I have a state of emergency to deal with and don't want you involved in stirring up trouble. I'm not putting you under full house arrest, but the security guards will not allow you to appear in public. You may see your family and friends, go to the shops and so on, but you are not to attend or speak at public meetings. I promise to get a daily bulletin to you on Paolo's position. Tomorrow I intend to send a top lawyer to Luxembourg to ensure all Paolo's rights are properly protected. Despite our differences, the sovereignty of Italy is in dispute. That must be defended at all costs.'

'You must do more than that. You should get a delegation together immediately, to go to Luxembourg and get my husband out of detention.'

'Bella, I advised him to leave the senate early this morning, before the army arrived. He foolishly refused and is suffering the consequences. I will do all I can to see that he is properly treated; that is the limit of my power at the moment.'

'Thank you for that, at least; but don't presume I won't be doing everything in my power to get Paolo back. I assume I will be permitted to visit my husband in Luxembourg very shortly?'

'I will do all I can to help. However, permission from Luxembourg for you to enter the country may not be automatically forthcoming.'

Matthew was greeted by an agitated Linda Boston when he arrived for Sunday lunch. She didn't know which subject to tackle first.

'How are you darling? How are Mark and Louise; have you talked to them lately? Have you been watching the events in Italy? Do you think Philip is in any danger? Did you see the pictures of that horrible man spitting in his face?'

Gerald arrived in the hall and rescued Matthew by pulling him into the lounge. He poured three glasses of champagne and handed them round. 'Sit down, Matt, and let's first catch up with your own news. It has been a long time since we had a chat. How are things at the factory?'

Linda interrupted, 'I want to know about the children first and how you and Anna are getting on.'

'Okay, Mother,' Matthew finally got a word in, 'the situation has not improved one little bit since we last spoke. I still can't get to see Mark, but I have had the occasional call from him, when he can use the mobile Jane managed to pass over to him. He's not very happy at the college, which probably means his schoolwork is suffering. He gives me news about Louise, and I think she's probably more settled than he is. I'm desperate to see both of them; I've talked to David, who, believe it or not, is sympathetic. But he won't go against Anna's wishes, and she is being even more awkward.'

'Do you think that, with Paolo removed, you might be able to get your ban reversed?' Gerald asked.

'I thought about that already and I've been trying to get in touch with Philip. He might be in a position to help.'

'We've tried to phone him, too, but his mobile seems to be permanently switched off.'

'I sent him a text this morning, telling him I'd be with you today; if he gets it, he might, with a bit of luck, phone us here.'

'Wasn't that a fantastic move by the European Army?' Linda exclaimed. 'It really took the wind out of that nasty man's sails. He's going to get everything he deserves. Well done Philip, I say.'

'I don't like this at all, Matt,' Gerald intervened. 'What has happened is exactly what I feared would happen, when Europe agreed to form an army. Didn't I warn you all about it? The old pretenders to the throne of Europe were bound to misuse the power; that was inevitable. It's just happened sooner than even I predicted.'

'You did say that, darling, right at the very beginning,' Linda admitted, 'but what they have done cannot be said to be bad. They have got rid of an aggressive communist, who was leading his country into very troubled waters. I think the EU has done the right thing.'

'Then you are very wrong, Linda; even though our own son was in the foreground. Unfortunately, I can't say I am proud of his involvement. I never believed in the formation of this army. You do realise the commander-in-chief, in other words the European president, is an unelected politician who can easily be manipulated by the powerful states? No person should be accorded that amount of power or responsibility, especially an unelected one.'

'Well, the deed is done now,' countered Linda, 'and both

337

Italy and Europe will be better off without Paolo Medina. I'm very proud of Philip's participation, aren't you Matt?'

'Of course I am, but it's going to make life with Anna even more impossible. I haven't dared contact her since, and I suspect she will become even more intransigent, now that her father has been so humiliated.'

'As you know, I never liked the man,' Gerald added, 'but he was, at least, democratically elected by the Italian voters; the EU should not be allowed to interfere in the internal politics of another country. There are going to be some major adverse reactions around the world. It seems incredible to me that our government was actually in favour of this invasion; we are in for a lot of criticism.'

'We are already getting some. Today's papers are pointing to the fact that the European Army was commanded by a German and led by an Englishman. They have already ascertained that the French, Dutch and Belgians were also behind the attack. I wonder how many other EU countries were consulted before they decided to invade?'

'That, Matt, is the sixty-four thousand dollar question. Who is entitled to make these decisions on behalf of the whole of Europe? I understand the Spanish are already threatening to withdraw their troops from the EU army; others are bound to follow. This will just prove what a terrifying policy this has been. If you keep an army unoccupied for a length of time, it will eventually go looking for a fight. That is the intrinsic nature of the military.'

'Your father tells me you are having an affair with Jane,' Linda burst out, unable to contain her curiosity any longer. 'Is that true?'

'I suppose you could say that, Mum; Jane has been very kind and supportive since I told her about my problems with Anna.'

'I'll bet she has,' Linda snapped, 'she's always had her eye on the main chance, hasn't she Gerald?'

'I think that is a little unfair, darling,' Gerald replied, unwilling to get pulled into the discussion.

'I'm sure she had her eye on you at one time. I was watching her very carefully.'

'Were you really, darling?' Gerald feigned surprise. 'Actually, it was the other way round; I had my eye on her,' he added mischievously. 'I wouldn't blame you Matt, she's a thoroughly decent girl. You won't get any criticism from me.'

'You men are all the same. Just because she's pretty, you don't see through the make-up.'

'She helped me to get to see Mark in Italy and her reward is that she's also banned from entering the country. Anyway, you thought Anna was the bee's knees when I first brought her home. Now what's your opinion of her?'

'I'm really sorry that you and Anna are so estranged. I'm desperate to see my grandchildren again; is there no way of mending fences with her?'

'You know I tried, Mum. I loved Anna and was devastated when I found out about her and David. I'm trying to hang on to Mark and Louise, but she is being so difficult. I'm going out of my mind here, and Jane is being so supportive. Please don't take against her,' Matthew pleaded.

'All right, Matt, I apologise for what I said. It's just that I worry about you and whether you are happy, that's all. Of course we will welcome Jane.'

At that moment the phone rang in the hallway. 'I hope that's Philip,' Linda cried and rushed out to answer it.

23

The news of the invasion of Italy provoked a strong reaction from the international community. The nations of the Far East were divided in their opinions.

China condemned it as an attack on the democratic rights of a communist controlled country. The Chinese president noted that it would severely damage the relationship between the European Union and the People's Republic of China. 'It was,' he announced, 'an old-style imperialist intrusion into the affairs of an independent nation.' He called for the immediate release of Paolo Medina and total reinstatement of the pre-existing government in Italy.

The Indian government was more circumspect in its response. India had been vociferously denouncing the heavy import duties imposed by Paolo, which had greatly reduced its export trade with Italy. The Japanese were of the same opinion. Their economy was still suffering from the deflation experienced in the nineties and their export markets continued to dwindle.

Elsewhere, the Catholic countries of Latin America were desperately waiting for an announcement from the Vatican. The Pope had been noticeably silent since the invasion, and rumours were circulating that his silence indicated he was not dismayed by the events. In fact, the Pope was wisely watching to see how the tightly sprung political coil would unwind. The Vatican was concerned that Paolo Medina's outward allegiance to the Catholic church did not sit comfortably with his communist ideals.

The media was at first surprised that no statement had

been received from Russia. However, the reason for the unusual silence from that quarter became apparent before even a week had passed. Using the cover of the political furore over Italy, Russian tanks had rolled into the Ukraine. For several years the relationship between the two countries had been deteriorating, owing mainly to disagreement over the costs of natural gas supplies and distribution to Western Europe.

Europe had been dreading this possible action by Russia. There were now even greater fears that gas supplies could be squeezed. The warning signs had been there for quite some time; the predictions by many of impending troubles had not been properly addressed. Now, by its action against Italy, Western Europe had left itself unable to criticise, on moral grounds, the Russian attack on the Ukraine. Eastern Europe began to feel uncomfortable again with the imperial might of Russia menacing their neighbourhoods.

The reaction in the United States was explosive. With a presidential election due at the end of the year, both the Republicans and Democrats were vehemently critical of the invasion. The President, Frank Lipatti, was forced to take an open stand against the powerful nations of the European Union. His first move was to invite the British prime minister for discussions at the White House. The invitation was, in reality, more in the form of a summons, and Neville Aitchison flew to Washington the next day.

He had requested a private meeting at the Oval Office, during which he planned to explain his position to the president. The President opened the discussion with a direct attack on him and the other heads of state involved in the invasion.

'You have all put America in an impossible situation, Neville,' he began. 'How could we have responded if Italy had requested military support from us, as is their perfect right under the NATO agreement?'

'We had determined there would be no fighting; we just wanted to get Paolo Medina out of office,' Neville replied. 'You must have seen how his communist influence was spreading across Europe. In reality you will surely agree that we needed to take some action.'

'Look, you know full well that America was totally opposed to the formation of a European Army. We made it quite clear at the time that it would conflict with NATO. Now look at the mess you have made. Everybody knows we have an agreement that if a member country is invaded, we are committed to go to their defence. Nobody dreamed that one member might attack another. This has turned NATO upside down. Why weren't we informed of the intended invasion in advance? That's what we expect our friends to do.'

'Yes, it was one hell of a gamble that the Italian President would decide not to come to you for immediate support,' Neville conceded, 'but we gauged his mood correctly. I'm sure he's secretly quite pleased with the outcome.'

'Well, I have spoken to him, and I can assure you, he is not at all happy that the European Army has been used in such a way. Neither are the American people,' said Frank, frowning. 'I don't see how we can continue to keep NATO together while Europe decides to go its own way militarily, whenever it suits them.'

'I am entirely in agreement with you – and that is why I wanted a private audience. The British have never really been in favour of this army.'

'But one of your men actually led the attack,' the President interrupted. 'You've been supporting the growth of this army since the outset.'

'That's true, but we intend to demand a change of policy in the future. We want to throw all our military resources solely behind NATO, as before. Let me explain why I agreed to support the invasion of Italy.

'We have, for a long time, been opposed to the creeping move towards federalism in Europe. There are many aspects embodied in the treaties of Maastricht and Lisbon which are being used by the European parliament in Brussels and the judiciary in Luxembourg and Strasbourg to completely remove the sovereignty of the member states. It is the British desire to reverse this trend before matters get out of hand. In our opinion, nothing is more likely to stir up another war in Europe than the attempted demolition of individual democracy by this new bureaucratic empire.'

'But that's exactly what you have just done – invaded the rights of a sovereign nation,' Frank maintained.

'And that is exactly what I wanted, in my own peculiar way, to achieve. I wanted to highlight the potential dangers when a redundant army is in the hands of an unelected president who, in turn, is under the influence of a few ambitious statesmen.'

The President contemplated this for a moment, before replying, 'You certainly managed to highlight that situation, but don't tell me that was your sole reason.'

'It certainly was not. I believe that the best way to reverse the trend to federalism is to get a British person to take over the European presidency when Raul Haitink's term of office expires in a few months' time. What I managed to extract from the other heads of state involved, before I would consent to the invasion, was a promise to support a British person for the position when it becomes vacant,' Neville revealed.

'Very interesting – and may I ask who your candidate will be?'

'I'm really not in a position to say yet, but I will be announcing it within the next few weeks. I think you may see some sparks fly on the Continent when our proposal hits the headlines.'

'I look forward to it, but you realise I can only join in

the total condemnation of the action of all the European superpowers, including the British. Believe me when I tell you America is appalled at this attack on one of the very founders of the EU. I know the newspapers are prone to exaggeration, but there's been talk that this could start another war over your side of the pond.'

'That's not going to happen, Frank, I assure you. I think in the long term you will be happy with the outcome. I know the United States is not keen on the idea of a United States of Europe, and with very good reason. A hundred and fifty years ago, you managed to tame your dissenting states, but only after a very bloody civil war. We don't want to see Europe getting in the same mess. I hope you will be satisfied, if not in complete agreement, with the explanation for my action.'

'So what you are saying is that, in reality, the invasion had nothing to do with communism; it was more a matter of secession. You all feared that Italy's secession would herald the eventual break-up of the EU. Am I right?'

'Not entirely; I don't think the British people care one way or the other. I do believe some of the other countries were more concerned that the EU is about to crumble. Maybe their motives were different from mine,' suggested Neville.

'I understand, and possibly sympathise, with your position here, but will not be saying so in public,' the President stipulated. 'You and your friends on the Continent can anticipate a torrid time from the American media.'

'I am expecting that, but it will pass. I do have a strategy that I think will be appreciated, in due course, in Washington.'

'Thank you for coming over so promptly and explaining your position,' said Frank, rising to his feet to signal the end of the meeting. 'I should have realised that the British, or should I say "Perfidious Albion", would not have gone along with an invasion of Italy without a definitive political plan. I will reserve judgement until I discover what those plans are.'

'At least by speaking the same language we understand each other, even if we don't always agree. I hope you will give some verbal support to my candidate for Europe's presidency when I announce it shortly,' said Neville, shaking the President's hand.

'I'll see what I can do,' replied Frank, without obvious commitment. 'Safe journey home.'

Bella had been trying desperately to get news of her husband but military intelligence had gone completely silent. It was not until the following Monday, four days after his removal, that Carlo Salvatore contacted her.

'I'm sorry that it has taken so long, Bella, but I have just received confirmation from our embassy in Luxembourg that as we anticipated, Paolo is now under guard there. I understand he was taken by ship to Calvi, on the island of Corsica, and held there for a couple of days. He was then flown in a military aircraft to Luxembourg. He is still under military supervision, but there is a move to hand him over to the civil authorities before he can be charged.'

'How can I get to see him?' Bella asked urgently.

'There is a flight from Rome on Wednesday and I took the liberty of getting you booked on it. The ambassador will meet you at the airport; we would expect, by then, to have arranged his release from military custody. I should from now on be able to give you a daily update on his position.'

'Thank you, Carlo, at least now I know where he is. I will be on that plane on Wednesday. Would you ask your secretary to get a seat for my daughter Anna, as well?'

'Of course; she will confirm that and pass on any new information regarding Paolo as it comes in. Ciao.'

Bella turned to Anna, who had been listening to the conversation. She had moved in with her since Paolo's arrest to support her mother. 'Did you hear that, Anna? Papà is in Luxembourg; I hope you will come with me on Wednesday.'

'It's not very easy, but I'll try to arrange something. David is in America, so I'll have to find somebody else to look after Louise.'

'Maria can do that.'

'Yes, but she doesn't drive, so we will need to ask someone to take and fetch her from school. Don't worry, she can stay with a friend.'

'Why don't you bring her with us? She will want to see her grandfather.'

'She's very confused at the moment. I don't want to take her away from her friends. They were very supportive last Friday after all the publicity.'

'She's very worried about Papà; she told me so.'

'Of course she is, she's very upset, but I don't think you realise how much her feelings are being divided. She is also very fond of her Uncle Philip; she doesn't like the way the family is being torn apart. You and I don't care if we never set eyes on the Boston family again, but the children don't see things that way. Mark is even worse, he practically idolises Philip.'

'I know it's going to be very difficult for you, darling. How are the children getting on with David?'

'Fortunately, they quite like him now. They used to find him a bit distant, but he has made a big effort to get on to their wavelength. I think they have accepted him now. With a bit of luck, they might gradually become less connected to their father.'

'I've noticed that Mark is very anglicised; there's going to be a lot of difficulty persuading him to stay in Italy once he is eighteen and leaving college.'

'I know, but I can't think about that now. At least, at the moment, he has no contact with Matthew. I spoke to him yesterday, and suggested he comes home for the weekend; I hope we will be back by then, Mamma.'

'I may not be, but you can always take a plane back whenever you like. Mark needs his mother at a time like this. I hope he isn't being ragged at the college about his grandfather; boys can be so vicious in these circumstances.'

'So can girls, but Louise has only had a few small problems. Mark's big enough to look after himself. One thing I can say about his public school education in England, it taught him to be tough.'

'Don't forget we will have to fly to Rome tomorrow so we can catch the Luxembourg flight on Wednesday. I hope to God we will be allowed to see him. You know how the military behave; they don't stick to the laws of habeas corpus.'

Bella was relieved to get a call from Carlo Salvatore once she and Anna arrived in Rome, advising her that Paolo was being held at a private detached villa.

'I can tell you that he is under house arrest, but is being very comfortably looked after, in the manner his status merits,' Carlo reassured her. 'You are at liberty to visit at any time and may stay with him indefinitely at the house, if you so wish.'

'Thank you – and is he still under custody of the army?'

'So far as I know, he is.'

'Then what are you doing to get him away from those bastards?'

'I have sent a lawyer to handle that. When you get to Luxembourg, the embassy will fill you in with all the details. At the moment I'm too busy trying to form a government and getting the EU army out of Italy.'

'And I think you should order the Italian army to throw them out by force and get our prime minister back here.

347

Why not turn the tables on them; invade Luxembourg and demand Paolo's release?'

'From now on everything is going to be done through diplomatic channels,' Salvatore replied, startled by her suggestion. 'I will complete my new government by the end of the week and the EU army has promised to leave immediately once that is achieved. There will be no bloodshed instigated by me.'

On the day Anna flew to Luxembourg with her mother, Matthew received a welcome call from Philip.

'I have good news for you – I have managed to talk to the president's secretary and he has agreed to act with regard to your ban. He says if you go to the Italian Embassy in London, they will sort matters out for you. It shouldn't take more than a couple of weeks.'

'Thank God for that. Do you realise I haven't seen Louise since well before last Christmas, nearly seven months ago? And I only saw Mark for a few minutes before I had to flee the country. I do speak to him from time to time when he has the opportunity to phone, but that is either more difficult than I think, or he just doesn't bother; I'm not quite sure which.'

'Well, you should be able to see them shortly. I'm hoping I can start to move the troops out of Italy by the beginning of next week. The natives here are getting less and less friendly; I can see some trouble brewing if we don't move out soon.'

'I should stay in the south of France if I were you; the press here is giving our government an absolute roasting over the invasion. It might be better not to show your face or you'll be surrounded by reporters.'

'Thanks, Matt, I'll take your tip; something will soon crop up to divert their attention elsewhere. Surely they're not concerned about Paolo?'

'No, but the PM is getting slated for the abuse of Italian sovereignty by your army. It hasn't helped him that you were taking such a prominent role. I think you might find yourself demobilised from the EU Army and recalled by your old regiment. There is definitely a media demand to pull all Brits out.'

'Thanks for the information; I'm not getting much news here. I get to talk military affairs to General Schweizer and that's about it. I'm not really supposed to talk to anybody, although I sneaked a call through to Mum and Dad at the weekend.'

'I know, I was there; Dad's not very happy with your involvement.'

'I didn't expect him to be. I've always been the black sheep of the family by not going into the family business.'

'I don't think he minded that, but he's always been a bit of a pacifist. You know, in his cosy world, fighting is suppose to cease when the referee blows for time. He probably never thought of you going to war.'

'Well, if this was as bad as it gets, then he hasn't got much to worry about. I'll buy him a pint when I come home and we can be pals again.'

'I know he can be a lot of bluster, but he's always had strong views against the EU Army. Believe me, he won't change his mind, not even for your sake.'

'I wouldn't expect him to; don't forget you can go at any time now to the Italian Embassy and get yourself reinstated. Best of luck, and love to Mark and Louise when you catch up with them.'

Bella and Anna were met at the airport in Luxembourg and driven straight to the villa where Paolo was being held. Bella leant forward and tapped the ambassador, who was seated in front of her, on the shoulder.

'What sort of mood are we going to find my husband in?' she enquired.

'Don't ask; I've visited him twice and got one hell of a tirade on both occasions. If you say nothing, he gets through it quicker. Then he calms down, when he realises who you are and that you might be a friend. But don't expect him to ask after your health.'

'That's precisely how I would expect him to be. Thank God I've got Anna with me; she can usually calm him down.'

'I stroke his hair, which infuriates him, but then he sees the funny side of things and relaxes,' Anna explained.

'That will do him a lot more good than all the lawyers he's been screaming for,' the ambassador replied. 'Well, good luck; excuse me if I don't come in with you,' he said as they pulled up at the villa.

The sergeant of the guards recognised the car and went over to check the occupants. Satisfied, he waved them through the gates of Paolo's prison.

To Bella's surprise, as she and Anna were led into the drawing room, Paolo was sitting calmly reading a book. He got up with a slow deliberation and stood steadfast as the two women fell on him. He received their embraces, but responded with little warmth before slumping back down in the armchair.

Anna broke the silence. 'Don't worry, Papà, we're going to get you out of here, one way or another.'

Paolo waved to them to find a seat before replying. 'And where could I go if you did get me out?'

'We have been talking to your lawyer; not the one sent by Carlo Salvatore, but the party's chief adviser, Luigi Bertorelli. He will come to see you anytime you wish.'

'He won't be any use, Bella; what I need is a really slick attorney who can run rings round the European courts. See what research you can do; it will most likely be someone with a practice in Paris or Berlin. There must be someone who can help me take on these bastards.'

'We were thinking we could try and get you out hidden in the boot of a Land Rover,' said Anna. 'You remember how they got that journalist, Donald Woods, out of house arrest in South Africa in the boot of a car and off to freedom. I'm sure David would help.'

'That did cross my mind for a moment, but where could you take me? I couldn't even hide in my own country; that bastard president would just hand me back. I'll bet he's rubbing his hands with glee.'

'I suppose you're right,' sighed Bella. 'So what do you want us to do?'

'Like I said – go and find me a first class lawyer. The one Carlo sent is bloody useless. No doubt that is deliberate.'

'You're looking very weary. Are you being properly looked after?' Anna asked, concerned.

'I have this manservant to do the housework and a chef who comes in to do the cooking. Otherwise there is a guard who checks up on me every hour. The whole thing is so bloody tedious.'

'Well, I'm going to stay and look after you from now on, darling,' Bella said forcefully.

'No, Bella, just stay till the weekend and go back with Anna. I need you to be active on the outside. I've just realised that there is nobody I really trust any more, apart from the family. Go and find me a lawyer who knows his job. I know that if I can have my day in court, I can make the EU regret their actions.'

'I'll bring Mark and Louise to see you when the term finishes; they are both very worried about you. They've been having the odd problem at school since the invasion, with other pupils taking sides. I thought of withdrawing them, but I think it will pass and they both said they can handle it.'

'And what about Matthew; have you spoken to him? What does he have to say about his brother's involvement in my arrest?'

'He can't contact me any more, since I changed all my phones. I don't want to speak to him and he still can't get to Italy to see Mark and Louise. I'm not allowing them to go to England, so as far as I'm concerned he's out of all our lives.'

'The press got hold of some photos of you spitting in Philip Boston's face; I suppose that has really highlighted our disdain for that family,' Bella added, having decided to change her past support for Matthew.

'Yes Papà, we now only use David to find out how Matthew is reacting.'

'Well, I advise you to be on the alert; he is a very rich and powerful man now. He will find a way of getting to his children.'

'So you want me to go back with Anna at the weekend, darling,' Bella said, changing the subject. 'Do we have any contacts who could advise us about finding this lawyer?'

'I think I will leave that to your ingenuity. Just stay away from any links with the party; our old advisers wouldn't go down well in an EU court.'

'David is due back from the States, where he has been dealing a lot with attorneys. He might be able to make a few suggestions. Maybe an American, with good international law experience, would have a lot of influence. I'll phone him now and get him to make some enquiries.'

'Good thinking, Anna; an American taking on the Luxembourg mafia might be just the answer. The power they have insidiously assumed over the legal systems of all the member nations needs to be challenged in their own courts by an attorney accepted as being completely unbiased.'

'Is there anything else you need, while we're here?' Anna asked.

'You might pop out and get me a case of a good Barolo. The stuff the guard brought in yesterday is practically undrinkable.'

24

David drove Louise to the airport in Turin to collect her grandmother and Anna. Louise's concern for Paolo resulted in a spate of questions. 'What's going to happen to Grandpa in the European court? Could he end up in prison? Will he be allowed to come back and do his job in parliament?'

'We can't know for sure, Louise,' Bella responded, 'but I have no doubt this politically motivated manoeuvre will backfire on the perpetrators. I really believe they won't dare to take Paolo into the courts of justice.'

David, who had up till then refrained from entering the conversation whilst concentrating on the road, intervened. 'I'm afraid I disagree with you. I think they will throw everything they can trump up against him. They will be determined to make an example of him. He was a thorn in the side of their capitalist ideals. These people in the European Commission are determined to control the whole of Europe. I don't think you understand the threat that Paolo made to them.'

'He was only trying to get Italy out of their clutches, David,' Anna replied.

'Yes, but they were already infuriated by us leaving the euro. They can't bear the thought of secession. They will attempt to throw the book at him. Northern Europe wants to control the whole of the continent. Look at the stranglehold they maintain over Greece, Ireland, Spain and Portugal, after six years of financial restraints.'

Bella had heard enough of the argument by the time they arrived outside her house. 'I think I'd rather be by myself now, Anna,' she remarked emphatically. 'I've got a lot of things to attend to; I suggest you go home with David and I'll keep you posted on what is really happening to your father. No doubt the press will have a lot of sensational columns. Don't take any notice of them.'

'Okay, Mamma, and David promises he will continue to make enquiries with some more American attorneys. I'm sure they will come up with the right man to defend Papà.'

When they reached home and Louise had gone off to play with a friend, Anna at last felt free to relax with David.

'I'm so glad Mamma decided she didn't need me to stay any longer, *caro*; we can still only take so much of each other. Did you have a successful trip to the States?'

'Yes, thanks, all the flights were on time for a change. But the really good news is that no medical reaction has been found by the experts out there to link Bosteinex with kidney failure, or any other problems. I never thought it could be the drug, but I've been on tenterhooks ever since the initial accusation. You don't know how relieved I feel. I doubt I could have survived the agonies of knowing my drug had been responsible for the death of a number of people.'

'I thought there was only one person dead.'

'Oh no, the moment it got reported on the internet, a lot of relatives of dead people tried to jump on the bandwagon, obviously hoping there might be some payout. But there's no positive proof of Bosteinex causing permanent harm, so that should be the end of any potential litigation. I've been advised not to worry any more; this kind of thing is happening all the time out there.'

'So you can relax, forget all about it, and there's no need to go out there again; is that right?'

'Yes, but I've been thinking; this scare has made me come to my senses and I've made up my mind. I'm going to let Matthew buy the patent from me, and then I am no longer responsible if anything does goes drastically wrong in the future.'

'You wouldn't sell it to my father – isn't it a bit hurtful to him at this time to let Matthew have it?' Anna asked, sounding put out.

'Look, Anna, I just want to get over this particular scare, shake off the responsibility and get on with my other researches. Don't forget I always promised Matthew I would give him first option to buy. I'm a man of principle and I intend to stick to my word.'

'But retaining the ownership of the patent keeps you in such a powerful position, David. I still think you should hang on to it and to hell with Matthew.'

'I'm sorry but I have made up my mind. The money will enable me to set up my own exclusive laboratories somewhere else. I don't think you realise how much I hate being dictated to by that bloody shop steward. And your father was supposed to have protected me from him!'

'And where, may I ask, is "somewhere else"?'

'I don't know, but we will be able to afford to go anywhere we like; make a new start.'

'You realise you will have to go to England to see Matthew; he can't come over here, thank God.'

'Yes, I know that and I'll phone him next week for a meeting as soon as I've found time to speak to some business advisers.'

'I think you should make some conditions in the sale of the patent; keep Matthew away from Mark and Louise for a start.'

'Are you suggesting I use the sale of Bosteinex to prevent Matthew from seeing his children?'

'Why not? It would solve a major problem for us. Don't forget, Matthew was always more interested in the business than he was with his immediate family.'

'You realise that will put me on a collision course with

the whole Boston family. I wouldn't like that; they have always been very kind to me, as you well know.'

'But they haven't been kind to me or my family!' Anna screamed back. 'How can you even think of taking their side after seeing what Philip Boston did to my father? I hate the lot of them and their arrogant English manner.'

'Of course I understand your feelings,' said David, trying to calm Anna, 'and I accept that what was done to your father was inexcusable. But Philip is a soldier; he was presumably only acting on orders from above.'

'David, I really can't bear discussing this any further. Some day you are going to have to make a choice between your feelings for me and the Bostons. What is it going to be?'

David leant back in his armchair and took a long time to reply. 'I suppose I will need to be seeking legal advice over the sale of the patent. I will enquire whether it is at all possible to draw up an agreement along the lines you are suggesting.'

Matthew was intrigued to get a call from David stating that he had been in consultation with lawyers and would like to meet to discuss the patent.

'I'm happy to discuss the patent at any time, David; is tomorrow convenient?'

'Can we meet at your house in Northampton, rather than at the factory? I would prefer a more informal atmosphere, with nobody else present. Not even Jane,' he added pointedly.

'I'll see you tomorrow at ten, if that's okay.'

David arrived promptly and Matthew offered him coffee before the two sat down. 'I'm all ears,' said Matthew eagerly. 'Have you at last come to the sensible decision to let the company have the patent?'

'To be honest with you, the problems in America have made me realise the potential risks involved in the world of big business. I no longer want the responsibility of owning Bosteinex. So yes, as promised, I'm giving you first option'

'Of course I want it; what are you proposing?'

'I have been talking to lawyers and accountants and they have come up with a market price of five hundred million pounds. As you know I am not a greedy man; money has never been my motivation. I would be happy to take four hundred and fifty.'

Matthew laughed at the apparent gesture, but was not in the least bit fazed by the amount demanded.

'I will have to take any offer to the board, of course, but I assume that would be within our range. Our accountants will also have to scrutinise the figures, but I accept that Bosteinex has greatly increased in value since we last discussed a sale. I think I can persuade the board to agree your proposal.'

'I have to tell you one thing, Matt; this offer does not come without certain conditions. Please believe me, I don't like doing this; but Anna has put pressure on me. One condition of sale depends on an undertaking from you that you will not make any contact with Mark or Louise until they are eighteen.'

Matthew leaped to his feet and charged over to David, grabbing him by the lapels and hauling him to his feet. 'Don't be crazy, man; you can't possibly prevent me from seeing my own children,' he shouted. 'That's inhumane; in fact, it's got to be illegal.'

David pulled Matthew's hands away and took a step back. 'It's not illegal, Matthew, I've had confirmation from my lawyers. It's no use us fighting; calm down and let me explain to you how the sale agreement will operate.'

'Is this the only condition you intend to impose?'

'No, there is one other, but I'll come to that in a minute. What the agreement will stipulate is this. Boston and Wood will pay one hundred and fifty million to me on day one. The remainder will be payable plus agreed interest in five years' time. To be more precise, in a little less time than that; when Louise reaches the age of eighteen.'

'What about Mark when he's eighteen? That's less than three years.'

'Anna realises he will be able to do whatever he likes when he gets to eighteen. I've no doubt he will be dying to see you after so long. As I was saying, the agreement will stipulate that no member of the Boston family will contact the children before the contract is completed. If Mark chooses to contact you, then we will have to accept his wishes.'

'David, a public company can't fork out all that money without a definite deal. How do I explain this to my shareholders?'

'You'll find a way, you always do; they trust you. I promised you first option and that is what I am giving you. If you break the conditions, I will put the patent on the open market and refund your initial payment. So Boston and Wood will not suffer financially if the deal falls through. It's entirely up to you to explain the conditions to the board and give them your assurances.'

'This is all so ridiculous; why is Anna being so vicious? What am I supposed to have done to alienate her so much?'

'In the first place she thought you were not interested in her or the children. Boston and Wood took up all your time, and probably always will. She wants to get completely away from you and your family and any influence you might have on Mark and Louise. She doesn't want Mark to get involved with the business and become another you.'

'That's Mark's decision to make, not hers.'

'Maybe, but she doesn't see it that way. She wants her

children to become Italian, live out there and be more a part of her family. She thinks Italians are much nicer people than the British and they will all be happier there.'

'And is that your view, too? Why are you going along with all this?'

'I would not have contemplated agreeing with Anna over this, had the EU Army not invaded Italy. I found the sight of your brother standing aside while your father-in-law was being hauled away deplorable in the extreme. It was also very much the last straw for Anna; she was beside herself with rage. She will never speak to you or your family again; believe me, the rift is irreparable.'

Matthew sat down and rubbed his eyes wearily. 'Well, what about your own socialist principles – where do they fit into this?' he demanded. 'You surely realise that if you take the patent away from the company, I will have to make thousands of my workforce redundant. Don't you care about that? Because believe me, I bloody well do!'

'If the patent goes elsewhere, it will create jobs elsewhere. Why should I concern myself with which set of workers gets the job?'

'Because you know a lot of the staff at Boston and Wood.'

'That's true, but my work was always separate; that was the agreement. I was never employed by the company.'

'I'm not sure I can carry the board with me if there are conditions. Did you say there were others?'

'Yes, one other, and this is just as much my condition as Anna's. Until you are the full owner of the patent, you will maintain the factory in Turin fully operational.'

'I suppose I could reluctantly agree to that; but why are you worrying about the Italian workers when you are so disdainful of the people here? I thought you were pretty unhappy with the circumstances in Turin.'

'I certainly intend to move my laboratory out of the

factory when I have the money for the patent. However, I am sympathetic to Paolo's problems; the factory was very much his baby. I reckon it would destroy him personally and politically if it were to close immediately. Believe it or not, I'm actually thinking about him.'

'Well, I don't think that poses any difficulty for me, David, although I can't say I'm personally worried about hurting his feelings. He knew damn well he intended to nationalise that factory if he got into power. He just used me and the company.'

'It's a pity relations between the two families have become so resentful – and I'm stuck right in the middle. So I'm going to look after myself first in future, and at the moment my relationship with Anna is the most important thing in my life.'

Matthew was quiet for a moment, as he mulled this over. 'This leaves me in an impossible position. I will have to go away and think about it. I would definitely like to talk to my father and get his advice.'

'Well, that's the deal; the ball is in your court. But if you cannot accept my terms, I will be offering the patent to other prospective buyers straight away; and I'm told there will be no shortage of contenders.'

Matthew spent the next few days speaking to his legal advisers and contemplating the complications of doing a deal with David. Having satisfied himself that he would be unlikely to win a legal battle over the children, even if the courts were sympathetic, he contacted his father and explained his dilemma.

'I think you had better come here to discuss this,' said Gerald gravely. 'Your mother won't want to be excluded from the conversation. Come and have some dinner this evening.'

Seated round the table, Matthew gave the full details of David's demands to his parents.

'You cannot possibly agree to such preposterous conditions!' Linda almost screamed. 'Don't be blackmailed into giving up your children like this. And what about us? We want to see Mark and Louise again.'

'One of the problems with having sons is that you are more likely to lose your grandchildren,' Gerald pointed out. 'The kids invariably stay with their mothers, so the father's family can so easily get excluded.'

'Not all women behave like Anna. What right has she to persuade David into taking these draconian measures?'

'The fact is, Mother, she has, and there is nothing we can do about it.'

'Oh yes there is; you can tell David exactly where he can stick his patent!'

'Let's look at this more sensibly,' Gerald remarked, attempting to pacify his wife. 'Getting wound up won't solve anything. Have you made any decisions yet, Matt? What do you intend to do?'

'I obviously wanted to discuss this rationally with you both, although I knew Mum would only see things one way. Personally, I don't think I have any alternative but to accept David's terms.'

'Of course you have, Matthew,' Linda shouted again. 'As usual, this is all to do with money and the company and the bloody shareholders again. Why did you open a factory in Turin? It was just to get a cheaper deal, wasn't it? You allowed Paolo to entice you there for his own political ends and Anna took full advantage to take the kids away. What about thinking of your family for a change; how are Mark and Louise going to feel? You and your father are both alike.'

'That's hardly fair, darling,' Gerald replied softly, trying to defuse the atmosphere. 'What you have always refused to accept is when you own a business you do have a responsibility to others.'

'And that is precisely my conundrum, Mum; do I break up my family for the sake of the business? Or do I put my children first and put thousands of jobs at risk?'

'How can you possibly worry about the company where your children are concerned? That woman is a venomous bitch! You can't let her get away with this and give them up just like that!'

'Maybe, at this moment, it seems that the Bosteinex drug was the worst thing to happen to us, but even you, Linda, were ecstatic about it at the beginning,' Gerald added. 'It just goes to show how a wonderful success story can so easily have a tragic consequence.'

'I know what this is all about,' Linda interrupted, ignoring Gerald's comments, 'it's Anna attempting to get back at this family over the demise of her father. She should accept the fact that it wasn't at our instigation the European Army took him out.'

'No, but Philip was in the forefront of the attack. I always said no good would come of this bloody army; perhaps now someone in the family will believe me!'

'The fact is,' Matthew continued, 'if I put Mark and Louise first, I will almost certainly have to put nearly ten thousand workers out of a job. I know the company has successfully expanded many of our other brands, particularly here and in the United States. Nevertheless, about half of our workforce is solely employed with the manufacture and distribution of Bosteinex. How can I tell so many people they are going to be made redundant?'

'Haven't you explained all that to Anna and David?'

'They are only concerned about the factory in Turin. That's merely an attempt to save Paolo's face when the European courts let him out. Anna doesn't give a toss about the British and American workers.'

'David has always shown strong left-wing tendencies. What's his excuse for endangering people's jobs?'

'I did put that point to him, but as he sees it, all those jobs will inevitably be transferred elsewhere, so there won't be a net loss of workers. Anyway, he is particularly disillusioned with the litigation obsession in America. I don't think he wants to see the drug manufactured there any longer.'

'That's not sensible thinking, Matt,' Gerald remarked. 'Whoever buys the patent will need to retain the American market. That's where most of the turnover is now.'

'Yes, but as you see, David doesn't think sensibly when it comes to business. I'm afraid he is completely letting his emotions rule his mind at the moment.'

'So when are you going to make up your mind what to do, Matt?' Linda was anxious to know.

'After our chat I think I have, Mother. I always knew what your opinion would be but I'm sorry that on this occasion I can't go along with you. It is obvious that Dad understands my situation more readily. His reluctance to express a firm opinion only adds weight to my own decision; I have to put the welfare of my workforce above my own emotions and family commitments. I never expected to be put in this situation, but I don't really have a choice in the matter.'

'Then I shall never see my grandchildren again,' Linda cried out, and burst into tears.

'That's not quite true, darling,' said Gerald, coming round the table to comfort her. 'We will just have to wait until Louise is eighteen.'

'I might be dead by then,' Linda cried and rushed for the door. 'If you do this Matthew, I'll never speak to you again,' she added, slamming the door behind her.

Gerald returned to his chair and looked at Matthew, who had his head buried in both hands. 'Don't worry Matt,

I'll talk her round. I won't let our family be destroyed by this. She won't really want to lose you as well. Would it help, do you think, if I were to have a word with David? We always had a very good relationship.'

'I don't think so, his mind is made up; Anna has got at him. He's had the sale agreement drawn up already by his lawyers. Mine are going through it now. By the way, Anna and David are insisting that I'm not even to contact Mark or Louise while these negotiations are taking place. This is all very frustrating since I've just managed to get my ban into Italy rescinded.'

'I'm no doubt going to be in a lot of trouble for not fully supporting your mother, but I can weather that storm. I'm sorry I said very little to help you either, but I thought it better you made up your own mind, without any persuasion from me. If it's any consolation, I think I would have made the same choice, but I can't be certain. It's a brave decision you've made; I only hope Mark and Louise will understand when they finally learn the full facts.'

'That's what I'm relying on, Dad; I think this perverse act by Anna could eventually rebound on her. I can't see Mark wanting to be Italian; he was really enjoying his life in England. I would just like the opportunity to explain my position to him right now. I think he is old enough to understand my predicament.'

'Louise may be more difficult to deal with, though. By the time she's eighteen, she will have spent more than half of her life in Italy and her roots will be there. I can unfortunately foresee a two-way split in your family, the way things are going.'

'I've learnt an awful lot of lessons since taking over the chair from you, Dad. This current trend towards both commercial and political globalisation is becoming far too complicated. If I had foreseen the ramifications, I would have kept my family and business much closer to home.'

'I was always a little concerned when the business expanded so quickly,' Gerald admitted, 'but I understood you had little choice. The shareholders are no longer content these days with a nice little dividend from the profits; they demand constant capital growth as well. The City is so bloody greedy. But I agree, we should probably have kept the company in our own private hands.'

'Perhaps it's all my fault and I've reaped what I've sown; I've let things get out of my control. When I eventually get full possession of that patent, everything is returning back here. I don't care what it costs, we'll find the space in England to expand. Never again will I deal with the Americans and their mania for litigation. Never again will I allow communist shop stewards to get a foothold in my factories. And never again will I allow myself to be manipulated by ambitious politicians like Paolo Medina. That man has cost me my wife and kids. If I had any influence in the European courts, he would rot in a Luxembourg gaol for a long, long time.'

25

The announcement by the President of the European Union of his impending retirement provoked a stream of cynical articles in the press. 'Here is the man,' they were quick to point out, 'who presided over a most unpopular military coup of Italy. He now proposes to divest himself of all responsibility. Shouldn't he be forced to remain in office and face the consequences when Paolo Medina is taken to court?'

Raul Haitink's response was that he had no choice in the matter. His term of office was due to expire before Paolo could possibly be brought into court. It was going to take a minimum of six months for all the potential claimants of financial loss to lodge their complaints.

In fact, it was more likely to take a year to compile the full list and the President was doubtless grateful to retire ahead of the proceedings.

In the meantime, Paolo continued to be retained under house arrest while a petition for his release was being prepared. The European courts had no precedent on how to deal with this situation and were concerned that they would find it difficult to get Paolo back to Luxembourg if they gave him total freedom ahead of the trial. David had managed to secure the services of an eminent American attorney, well versed in international law, to plead Paolo's case.

Paolo's cult image with the socialist groups around Europe had not diminished. The EU commissioners were determined to get him into court before he could create a concerted uprising. The harsh financial restrictions imposed on the Club Med countries had led to deflated economies. The left-wing parties were exhorting their governments to follow Italy out of the euro and into flexible currencies in order to be competitive. This would hopefully get their workforce on the move again in those areas where unemployment had risen to unsustainable levels.

The reality was that Europe had become a political cauldron. Trouble had been boiling up from all sides. The German taxpayers were incensed that they had, for too long, been asked to bail out those profligate members of the euro. This also applied, although to a lesser degree, to the other wealthy nations of northern Europe. Deflation in the southern countries, caused by the loss of jobs, was creating a loss of trade around the whole of the continent. This was even detrimental to the industrial northern states as manufacturing slowed down and unemployment increased.

It was in this uncertain climate that Neville Aitchison decided to announce his proposed candidate for the vacant position of European president. With the support of France and Germany already assured, the British Prime Minister was able to call a press conference with confidence.

'I have secured the support of the majority of European heads for the appointment of a British citizen as the next President of Europe. He is Sir Henry Willington and we will be announcing our proposed agenda for the future of the EU imminently.'

A concerned German Chancellor phoned the French President, Guy de Valbien. 'We don't know much about this man Willington,' he commented, 'do you have any details?'

'I've been making some enquiries and it seems he's a former British ambassador to Washington and is now their senior representative at the United Nations. We haven't a full dossier on the man as he hasn't been very active or outspoken.'

'I'm surprised Neville has put forward a diplomat rather than a politician,' Hermann Kranz responded, 'but that's probably to our advantage. We obviously don't want somebody too controversial; we should be able keep him in check.'

'Absolutely. There's a rumour the British have some radical new plans for Europe – I wonder what they're up to, don't you?'

'It can't be much, if they are putting up a lightweight candidate for President.'

'So we let him stand unopposed?'

'We did give an undertaking to accept a British appointee. As far as I'm aware, this man doesn't appear likely to be a problem.'

'Let's leave it like that, then,' Hermann resolved. 'By the way, I did have the Spanish ambassador sounding me out about putting Jose-Maria Jimenez in the frame, but I was non-committal about that.'

'I had a similar approach from the ambassador in Paris, and took the same line. Jimenez is very popular in Brussels and might make a perfect standby if Willington drops out. In some ways I would prefer to have him.'

'So would I, Guy, but maybe having a British president will help to make the Brits more friendly towards the European Union. The Eurosceptic attitude prevalent in the UK is catching on too much for comfort in a lot of the other countries.'

'I can't say it's totally absent in France these days,' Guy confessed. 'We are going to need to fight hard to keep the EU together.'

'That was why I was a little concerned when I phoned you. The thought of a British president doesn't exactly fill me with confidence.'

'Nor me, but we did give Aitchison our word, so we will just have to wait and see what his agenda is.'

'Okay, I agree; auf Wiedersehen.'

After a long and gruelling board meeting, Matthew made a call to David at his laboratory in Turin. 'I have permission from the directors to purchase the patent at your price. Believe me, they were astounded at the conditions you are imposing on me. They couldn't believe someone could be so vindictive.'

'It's not really me, Matthew, you know that. So I've decided to sweeten the pill a little, if that's possible.'

'I don't believe you would really invoke the conditions if the children and I were to meet by chance,' Matthew continued. 'I mean, what would happen if Mark or Louise needed medical treatment in England?'

'Look, Matt, I expect you to abide by the spirit of the agreement. Obviously if anything unexpected crops up, I wouldn't want to be unreasonable. You can always talk to me; you know that.'

'You mentioned a sweetener; I was hoping you would agree to my seeing the kids once more before the conditions kicked in.'

'No, Matt, I'm afraid that's not going to happen. What I had in mind is to offer you the patent on the diabetes drug. That would be first option to purchase, with definitely no conditions attached, I promise you that.'

'So you are expecting a breakthrough with your research?'

'I'm pretty certain I've got my breakthrough. The latest results are all positive. We could have the drug on the market quite quickly, particularly as it operates on the same principles as Bosteinex. Also, of course, the basis of the drug is insulin, which is as safe as houses.'

'Yes, David, all that will no doubt put you in a better

light with the board, but personally I would have preferred to see Mark and Louise. I presume I can at least discuss them with you without Anna's permission, and find out how they are getting on?'

'Yes – if it's only you. I don't want to be contacted by either of your parents.'

'That's it, then; I will see you get your money. I deeply regret that our old friendship has come to this. And yes, I will accept your kind offer on the new drug,' Matthew added bitterly.

'You were the one who always used to say "business is business",' David remarked in a sarcastic voice, before switching off the phone.

Neville Aitchison decided to take Sir Henry Willington to Brussels to introduce him to the European parliament. The journalists from the press and television were anxious to hear the thoughts and expectations of the proposed president elect. Speculation had been running high that the British were intending to introduce a radical agenda.

The British Prime Minister spoke first. 'I intend to let Sir Henry introduce himself as I realise he is less known in political circles. I and many other heads of state thought that the position of president would be better represented by a man of diplomatic skills. We are convinced that radical change is necessary to overcome the political dissent penetrating the EU at the moment. He will need all his skill to persuade the majority, or hopefully all, of the twenty-seven member nations represented here that his agenda for a democratic and progressive EU is the best way forward. I will now ask him to set out his proposals to you for a revised European Union.'

Sir Henry Willington replaced Neville Aitchison at the podium, accompanied by the sound of murmurings of anticipation and rustling notepaper. He was fifty-eight years old, but an unlined face gave him a much younger appearance. He had silver grey hair swept back over an almost imperceptible parting. Soft brown eyes gave him a sympathetic look, and a row of perfect white teeth a charismatic smile. When the hubbub had died down he began his speech.

'I have come to offer my services to you as your next president,' he began. It was instantly apparent that a man of strong personality was addressing the meeting and greater concentration appeared immediately on all the faces in the auditorium. His deep resonant voice was of particular attraction to the large number of ladies seated around the hall. 'I am aware that at this time the European Union is deeply divided,' he continued. 'The causes are diverse, but I think we can single out the three main areas of concern.

'In the first place, the euro currency has caused financial inequality across the continent. In attempting to deal with this imbalance, harsh restrictions have been loaded on some, while the cautious feel they have been forced to bear the brunt of others' profligacy. Dealing with the financial problems of the single currency is not the specific role of the president, so I mention this merely to identify the difficulty, as it inevitably leads to the next.

'It became apparent that the only way to make the single currency survive was to accelerate the steady movement towards federalism. This has greatly added to the powers of the wealthy nations and those with the largest share of the weighted votes. Indeed, the smaller countries are in danger of having their individual identities swallowed up completely.

'Lastly, and possibly the most worrying, is the continuing upsurge in Europe of extreme politics. The strength of the response we give to these extremists, from both the right and the left, will determine the outcome to the threat they pose to our democratic society. It is also evident that the financial and political stranglehold that a small minority has over the rest of the nations is in danger of provoking another major strife on our continent.

'If you will accept me as your next president, I intend to introduce the following agenda. It has long been my experience that weighted voting is undemocratic in any society. Every member, whether large or small, rich or poor, should have an equal voice. Ask yourselves; why should a German be worth more than a Czech? Or why is a British vote worth more than the combined Danish, Swedish and Finish votes? Are the French really more important than the Dutch? Is a Spaniard of greater value than a Portuguese? I am therefore proposing to abolish the weighted vote in favour of each nation, i.e. member, having only one vote. I hasten to add that my country, the United Kingdom, is one of the countries with the largest number of votes, but is willing to give up this position for the general good.'

A ripple of astonishment went round the auditorium, but silence resumed immediately Sir Henry continued. 'The next item on my agenda is the continuous and, it seems, unstoppable increase in the powers of the European Court of Justice. It would be my intention to reconstitute their powers, so that they deal solely with the legal interpretation of EU treaties. In other words, the courts should not be able to interfere with, or overrule, the laws of the sovereign nations. I know that all over Europe citizens are concerned that their national laws are being disregarded by a legal system that is often petty and irrelevant and has quickly become self-perpetuating. We need to put a stop to the ever increasing onus of legislation that is out of touch with individual reality.'

This time a ripple of applause greeted the speaker before he came to his next point. The press reporters in particular were warming to the speech, while a number of MEPs were shifting nervously in their seats. 'I now come to the question of expenditure. Criticism has been coming from many quarters about the ever increasing costs of bureaucracy. I intend to tackle this problem in two ways.

'A large additional expense has arisen since the introduction of a foreign office and a Foreign Secretary. The experiment of having one person to represent the entire continent has not been a success; our individual opinions are too diverse. In addition, enormous expenditure has been wasted in the formation of EU embassies in many non-EU countries. This has resulted in confusion and controversy when EU ambassadors purport to represent a concerted opinion or policy of every European state. Each nation is entitled to have separate and special relationships overseas; we cannot allow a third party to voice our disparate views. I would therefore propose to terminate this portfolio forthwith.

'I now come to the question of the vast numbers of bureaucrats working in Brussels. The push towards federalism has greatly increased the functions performed here. I think most Europeans believe this move has gone too far. National sovereignty has been usurped in the drive to expand the centralised powers.

'My plan is to revert to the spirit of the original Treaty of Rome. Europe should be a continent of free trade, not a slave to federal idealism. We must not allow ourselves to be inveigled into a political reconstruction of the expansionist and dictatorial dreams of Napoleon or Hitler. Europe is not one nation, and those who are determined to force a federal government on us will only bring strife. As an example, the terms of the Treaty of Rome would never have provoked the attack on Rome we have recently witnessed. With that incident in mind, I am determined to demobilise the European Army without delay. There is

374

no useful work for it to perform, and the high costs to our budgets of maintaining an army are prohibitive.'

This time, the applause from the media was joined by a large number of delegates.

He waited for the applause to die down. 'Finally, I know many of you are concerned at the increase in crime since the freedom of movement between European states was introduced. I think this policy needs revising to at least allow the deportation of offending criminals to their native countries. It may be necessary to consider the closure of borders in the future to control indiscriminate or undesirable immigration.

'The European Union,' Sir Henry began to wind up his speech, 'was an inspired conception that has helped to keep the continent in peace for over sixty years. We should never forget that. However, we should not permit the aspirations of a few ambitious and power-hungry politicians to disturb this peace. The warning signs are there for all to see, but have been intentionally ignored. It is time to reappraise the past agenda and take appropriate action. Unless we introduce a radical and democratic formula into the future organisation of the Union, we will continue unwittingly along this current course of self-destruction.'

The room fell silent for a moment as Sir Henry stood back from the podium. Then pandemonium broke loose. The journalists scattered around the auditorium started clapping, waving their notepads and shouting their support. Some members of the European parliament stood up to cheer, but the majority looked decidedly nervous. Some senior bureaucrats stared at each other in disbelief. Could it be possible their gravy train was about to reach the terminus?

In the Luxembourg court, Paolo's new American lawyer had failed to get his release. The three judges had decreed that he should be detained under emergency regulations allowed in the constitution. He would therefore be retained under house arrest until the date of his trial.

A frustrated Bella visited him at his guarded villa. 'I have been talking to Carlo and, believe it or not, he assures me he's in negotiations to secure your release.'

'I don't believe it, Bella; he must have something up his sleeve. Why on earth would he be looking to help me?'

'He tells me that the EU is considering the removal of charges against both you and the Italian government, provided we withdraw our request for secession and fulfil some new requirements. In other words, some of the previous demands are to be ameliorated.

'And I suppose you think that traitorous bastard will accede to their demands. What are they, anyway?'

'It seems there are five main conditions and, in my view, it could be argued they make some sense, darling.'

'I wouldn't want to see us agreeing anything with the EU commissioners.'

'Firstly,' Bella proceeded regardless, 'the EU are happy to accept the continued nationalisation of Italian banks. Considering so many of the European banks have needed to be bailed out by their governments, there would be no requirement to compensate past shareholders.'

'I could accept that, Bella; that is merely maintaining the status quo as I arranged it.'

'Secondly, they propose that we denationalise immediately all those foreign companies that were taken over by the state. All their assets are to be returned but with no compensation for lost revenue.'

'We can't agree to that; there could be a large loss of jobs if the foreign companies then decide to withdraw. For a start, Boston and Wood would almost certainly run off.'

'Actually, that's one factory that will continue to operate,

Paolo. Anna assures me that David has insisted on a five-year deal at least.'

'That's only one small mercy – I can assure you the majority will pull out. The President can't possibly be allowed to sign up to that condition.'

'Thirdly, there must be a gradual denationalisation of Italian-owned industry. All previous shareholders will be allotted their previous participation. As you know, a lot of Italian-owned businesses had large shareholders from EU countries; they want their investment back.'

'Again, Bella, Italy can't afford to revert to the old capitalist ways. The whole of southern Europe, except us, is in the grip of the northern capitalists. The others have all got to get out of the EU and stay out.'

'Next, overseas banks are to be readmitted,' Bella continued, ignoring his protests, 'but this time under strict control of the Italian government.'

'But why the hell do we need overseas banks setting up in Italy? If we are to remain a socialist country, we only need one nationalised bank to control all our transactions.'

'You will probably be happy with the last condition. There is to be no pressure put on Italy to rejoin the euro currency.'

'Oh, so they have finally woken up to the disastrous effects on some countries the euro has managed to achieve.'

'I think the President will try to talk the coalition round to accepting the EU's proposals. If they do I believe you will be released without trial.'

'Bella, we all know this invasion was really all about regime change. And if the new government accepts these terms, we will have lost our individual status, in Europe and the rest of the world. We will just become puppets of the bureaucratic beasts of Brussels again.'

'Maybe not. I assume you read Sir Henry's manifesto for democratic change that is causing such a stir. He even wants to disband the European Army.'

'Believe it or not, I quite like his agenda. Maybe, on his terms, Italy could reasonably withdraw the application and remain in the union. I could accept that situation, if the EU really does revert to the spirit of the original Treaty of Rome we signed up to sixty years ago.'

'That's what I was thinking, darling; and if we then feel able to withdraw the secession, we wouldn't be obliged to accede to all the demands.'

'Quite right, and if this man Willington gives the army the boot, that bastard Philip Boston will be out of a job,' Paolo added with relish.

'So is there anything you think you can do about your removal, darling?' Bella asked. 'Is there any chance of getting your position back?'

'Yes there is – I'm going to take this fight to the European courts myself. I've decided I'm not going to allow myself to be tamely released. If Carlo Salvatore is prepared to ignore the electorate, and capitulate to the capitalists, I'm going to challenge the whole chain of events. I had a legal government and the EU Army had no authority to intervene. I had a mandate from the people to take Italy out of the clutches of the EU. The commissioners had no right to impose such onerous conditions for our secession. I will take my case to the UN and the international courts, if necessary. I've arranged everything with my attorney; I'm staying here and we are going to have a massive legal battle.'

'Are you sure we can afford one?'

'The party will be behind me and there is a lot of support from other parts of Europe. Also, Anna phoned me to say that David would give me all the financial help I need, now that he has sold the patent. In other words, Matthew Boston will end up paying for my legal battle!' Paolo remarked gleefully.

'You and Anna certainly have a hate campaign against that family,' Bella observed.

An irate German Chancellor contacted Guy de Valbien, the President of France. 'Have you had a chance yet to absorb the outrageous propositions of this man Henry Willington?' he almost shouted down the phone.

'Of course I have, Hermann, and I've had some further research done on him and his policies.'

'He's dynamite – he had the media eating out of his hands. We've got to stop this man before he's able to drum up too much support. We've already had the ambassadors of several of the smaller nations making contact to say how much they agree with his policies and wanting to know our position.'

'That offer to give each state equal voting rights was damn clever and a very tempting carrot to the smaller nations.'

'It's not just the small countries; nearly every member nation would benefit to some extent. Do you realise that now Italy is precluded from voting, there are only three of us left with highest number of weighted votes?'

'Yes and the UK is one of them; so why the hell does Neville Aitchison want to rock the boat?'

'The British are determined to stop the federalisation of Europe at any cost. I know we promised to back up Aitchison but this is a bridge too far. We must tell him our support is not there for this man. I suggest we ask him to find another candidate.'

'He won't do that, Hermann; that would be seen as a climb-down for him. Anyway, I expect he thinks he can get enough support without us if he really needs to.'

'We don't traditionally vote on this presidential election, though,' Hermann pointed out. 'We normally have a general consensus of opinion. If we say we won't give our support, that should be enough.'

'I don't think Aitchison will agree to that,' Guy disputed. 'He has his candidate and a lot of approval already. I think he's prepared to take us on.'

'So what are our chances if he pushes for a vote?'

'That's the research I've been doing since yesterday; I naturally assumed you'd be with me. With Italy unable to vote there are now a total of three hundred and sixteen weighted votes. To outvote Aitchison we need more than thirty-five per cent; in other words, one hundred and eleven votes.'

'It could be difficult to achieve that, Guy.' Hermann Kranz was already having his doubts.

'I know we can manage it,' de Valbien replied confidently. 'We both have twenty-nine votes, so that's fifty-eight already. I have been speaking to the Spanish prime minister this morning and have offered to back his candidate, Jose-Maria Jimenez, in return for Spain's twenty-seven votes.'

'Good thinking, Guy. I assume he was happy to agree?'

'Exactly, so that takes us up to eighty-five. I contacted our old friends in Belgium, Holland and Luxembourg who have a total of twenty-nine votes between them. The Dutch were a little reticent at first, but in the end agreed to add their support. Belgium and Luxembourg are right behind us as they fear big redundancies in their own countries if Willington gets elected.'

'So that adds up to one hundred and fourteen votes; enough to stop Aitchison in his stride. And, if need be, I can probably lean on the Greeks; they still rely heavily on our financial aid. Well done, Guy; are you going to tell him or am I?'

'I reckon we both tell Aitchison now, and spell it straight out to the media after giving him the good news,' de Valbien suggested with a chuckle.

'Okay, I have a sinking feeling this will not make us very popular, but that will pass. We can't possibly sit back and allow Sir Henry Willington to introduce such a radical agenda.'

'The press aren't going to like it one little bit,' Guy agreed. 'They were definitely warming to his manifesto; he's got a very magnetic personality. But we must stay firm. As you know, Jimenez is very popular, so we should be able to get our preferred candidate through eventually.'

'Okay, let's give him and the media our decision and wait for the eruptions.'

Neville Aitchison received the news from France and Germany with utter disbelief. 'How dare they,' he demanded of his deputy, 'renege on a gentlemen's agreement? They promised to support my candidate; no restrictions were placed on my choice. This is tantamount to war!'

'And one, it seems, we can't win if it goes to a vote. Unfortunately, this ridiculous weighted voting system is still in operation.'

'Well, I'm not changing my chosen candidate for anybody. Let's see how they get on with the rest of Europe if they try to put Jimenez in the frame.'

The journalists' headlines the following day were explosive, and not only in the UK. Sir Henry's manifesto was receiving widespread acclaim across the continent. The political leaders of old Europe sat back to ride out the storm. They were not going to allow the move to federalism to be blocked by one man.

26

Seated in his office overlooking the Thames, Stephen Johns, the Director General of MI6, was alternating his gaze between the slow movement of the London Eye and the headlines of the daily newspapers. He stiffened involuntarily, leaned back in his padded leather chair and pondered his sudden idea. After a few minutes, he made his decision, picked up the phone and spoke to his deputy.

'Alan, I was just thinking, do you know where Sean Barker is stationed at the moment?' he asked.

'I believe he's in Eastern Europe; do you want me to get in touch?' Alan Dewar replied cautiously. He preferred not to let the DG deal directly with his agents.

'I want to have a word with him about that assassination business in Italy.'

'I have the file locked away in my personal cabinet, Stephen. I obviously didn't get it downloaded on to the computer as it's far too sensitive. Do you want to see it?'

'Yes, bring it in right away if you would.'

Dewar arrived a few minutes later carrying a thick buff file under his right arm. He placed it on the desk and turned it towards his superior. 'Do you need me to stay?' he enquired.

Stephen Johns waved him towards a chair in reply and opened the file. 'Is it really six years ago since this took place?' he muttered incredulously. 'Perhaps it's time to take advantage of our well-kept secret before the full impact can wear out. I hadn't realised how long the file has been gathering dust.'

Dewar raised his eyebrows questioningly, but allowed Stephen to continue without comment.

'You must have seen the headlines today, Alan. What do you think of the French and German refusal to support Sir Henry?'

'Didn't come as a great surprise to me, Stephen. The PM surely didn't expect them to accept Willington's agenda.'

'It says in this paper here, and I happen to know it's true, that the PM had an agreement with them to support a British citizen as the next president; and they have reneged.'

'So what's the problem? The PM can find somebody else.'

'Don't be naive, man, this isn't Willington's agenda, it's the prime minister's. He won't be bullied into changing it, and he certainly couldn't find a better man than Sir Henry to sell it to the rest of Europe.'

'So what's on your mind, Stephen?'

'I'm seeing the PM tomorrow for my usual weekly meeting. I'm going to whisper in his ear that maybe we have the ability to put a little bit of pressure on these bastards who are double-crossing him.'

Alan Dewar needed no further explanation. A wry smile crossed his face. 'Would you like me to get in touch with Barker?' he offered.

'That may not be necessary as you seem to have all the details here. I'll just read through the file and remind myself of all of the circumstances.'

'Okay, I'll leave it with you. If I'm fully in touch with your train of thought, it looks like the PM could be extremely grateful to us for keeping our past intelligence under wraps.'

Stephen Johns requested that the meeting with the PM the following morning be private; just the two of them.

'You've never asked for a private meeting before, Stephen,' Neville Aitchison began. 'Are you worried that our state security is being threatened in any way?'

'No, sir, I've no evidence of that; it's just I think that what I'm about to tell you is too sensitive for the ears of lesser mortals. If this information leaks out it could make us look very bad in the eyes of the world.'

'You'd better go on,' the PM invited.

'To cut a long story short, we found out who the assassins were that murdered the Italian football captain, Rico Orvetti, six years ago.'

'I remember the incident well; and you've only just managed to find out?'

'No, sir, we discovered the culprits almost immediately.'

'Good God, man, why haven't you passed the information over to the Italian police?'

'Because we felt the information was even more explosive than the deed. It was highly political and we considered it could be more usefully employed by our government at a time best suited to our own needs.'

'And nobody else has this information, Stephen?'

'Only us, sir, and I think it's time to use it.'

'How do you mean, use it? Who did it, anyway? I thought everyone accepted at the time that it had to be the Mafia.'

'That's why all the investigations went dead, sir. By chance, we uncovered a plot between the French and German secret agencies to assassinate Paolo Medina. As you will recall, the attempt went horribly wrong. We managed to compile all the proof we need.'

'And you've known who really did it all this time,' Neville Aitchison mused. 'I presume you handed all the information over to my predecessor?'

'We feared he might waste the information on some triviality, sir, if we just passed it over to him at the time. We thought we'd hang on to it, till a suitable moment arrived.'

'And in what context do you think there is a suitable occasion now?' the Prime Minister was curious to know.

'If this ever comes out, the French and Germans are going to be more than embarrassed. The whole world will jump on them.' The PM nodded as Stephen Johns continued. 'I thought I might have a word with my counterparts in their secret services; let them know that we've found out who was really responsible for the murder of Rico Orvetti and Medina's daughter, Gina. I intend to imply to them that the whole world will hear about it unless they can persuade their bosses to withdraw their objection to Sir Henry.'

Neville Aitchison sat back in his chair and stared meaningfully at the head of M16. 'But that's blackmail, Stephen,' he finally remarked.

Stephen Johns stared back at the Prime Minister. Slowly, a wicked grin appeared on both of their faces.

It was normal on a Monday evening for Gerald and Linda Boston to be at home. After dinner, Linda switched on the television to watch a pre-recorded episode of *EastEnders*.

The sound of the programme's signature tune is invariably the signal for most men to leave the room. Gerald was on the way to his study when there was a ring at the doorbell. Opening the door he was surprised to find Matthew and Jane in the porch.

'Lovely to see you both,' he exclaimed, helping Jane over the threshold and giving her a kiss. 'You didn't say you were coming, did you?'

'No, Dad, we assumed you'd both be here as it's a Monday, so we just dropped in. We have some good news.'

'Well, come through; your mother's in the lounge watching TV. She'll be delighted to see you.'

Matthew was not so sure; Linda had not spoken to him for several weeks since his decision about the patent. They entered the room with Gerald bringing up the rear. Linda looked up, saw who had come in, and immediately refocused her attention on the television. Gerald perceived the frosty atmosphere and made a brave decision. He walked purposefully over to the television and switched it off. Linda glared at him, said nothing, and picked up a gardening magazine.

The two visitors stood awkwardly until Gerald offered them a chair. 'Matthew and Jane tell me they have come over with some good news, sweetheart,' Gerald began. 'I think it would be kind to hear what it's all about.'

Linda made no attempt to reply, and pretended to continue reading.

'Let me get you all a drink,' Gerald suggested, trying to break the ice.

'That's just what I need,' Matthew replied, glad for something to say. 'I'll have a glass of whisky and water; a malt, if you've got one.'

'What about you, Jane?'

'I'll just have an orange juice, thank you, Gerald,' she answered, looking nervously at Linda.

'How about you, Linda, are you going to join us?' Gerald was beginning to show his irritation with his wife. Linda shook her head and continued to say nothing.

With a drink in his hand, Matthew decided to open the conversation. 'I'm glad to say that my and Anna's solicitors are now going ahead with divorce proceedings. What is surprising is that she seems content to have a pretty straightforward agreement. I understand she is prepared to accept a reasonable cash settlement without resorting to valuations of the company shares and all my other assets.'

'That could be David's influence,' Gerald conjectured. 'He probably feels that he and Anna have pushed you far enough.'

'That's almost certainly the case, Dad; he is feeling guilty about the children. So he has offered to give the company first refusal on purchasing his new drug. He tells me it's ready to be marketed when the approval is through.'

'By the time he's got the money for that as well, he will be extremely rich,' Gerald observed, 'so they obviously don't need to squeeze you over the divorce.'

'Good news! You call all that good news?' Linda could contain herself no longer. 'Is that all you've come to interrupt my evening for? I don't give a damn about your financial dealings!'

'Actually, we do have some more news for you,' Matthew answered in a conciliatory tone. 'You are going to be a grandmother again.'

Linda looked shocked for a moment and remained speechless as she tried to regain her composure. She was in a predicament of her own making. She got out of her chair, walked over to Gerald and held his hand for comfort.

Gerald broke the silence. 'That's wonderful news, Jane! How long have you known about it?'

'It is coming up to nearly eighteen weeks,' Jane replied, able to involve herself in the conversation for the first time.

'But that's over four months, Jane,' Linda could contain her excitement no longer. 'Why haven't you told us before?'

'I tried to a couple of weeks ago,' Matthew pointed out, 'but you slammed the phone down on me, if you remember?'

Linda let go of Gerald's hand, rushed over to Jane and gave her a kiss. 'I wouldn't have, if I'd known why you rang,' she remarked illogically. 'So the baby is due early next year – do you know whether it's a boy or a girl?'

'We decided to leave it as a surprise,' said Jane, smiling. 'We probably won't be having any more; not at my age.'

'Well, I'm absolutely thrilled, Jane. Gerald, I think I might have that drink you offered me now. How about opening a bottle of champagne?'

'Jane's not drinking,' Matthew pointed out.

'I don't think one small glass will hurt her, 'Linda observed. 'This calls for a proper celebration!'

As the prospective parents were leaving to go home, Linda made a point of giving Matthew a long hug. 'I'm so glad you've got something to look forward to, darling,' she said. 'I've been really worried about your behaviour over Mark and Louise.'

'I'll make sure I get them back one day, Mother, I promise,' he replied, giving her a kiss on the forehead.

As they were preparing to drive away, Gerald stuck his head through the window of the car and whispered in Matthew's ear. 'It's amazing how the prospect of a baby in the family can change a woman's attitude. I'm sure your mother has been looking for an excuse to bury the hatchet,' he added, trying to defend her previous behaviour. 'And you two have found the perfect one.'

Returning to his office, the director general of M16 got down to the task of contacting Baron de Courcy in Paris and Albert von Meissen in Munich. The two men were naturally intrigued at their invitation to an urgent meeting in London.

They both asked the same question. 'Can you give us some idea what this meeting is all about, Stephen? Why is it so urgent? Do we need to bring any papers with us?'

'No, I have all the necessary documentation,' came the reply. 'The subject of this meeting is both secret and highly sensitive. I don't want to discuss it over the phone or even outside of my office.'

Two days later, the chief officers of the French and German secret services arrived together at the headquarters of M16 on the Thames embankment. They were immediately escorted to Stephen Johns' office and offered a seat round an informal coffee table. After the initial greetings and the arrival of some refreshment, Stephen opened the buff file in front of him.

'I want to talk about the failed attempt on the life of Paolo Medina six years ago,' he began.

The two guests glanced quickly at each other before regaining their composure. Stephen noted their reaction with amusement before continuing.

'We obtained evidence at the time that your two agencies were involved in the assassination.'

Albert and the Baron shook their heads simultaneously, but neither made any response.

'It will be no use you denying the facts, gentlemen, I have them all before me.' He spread the papers across the table for them to see, placing the photographs to one side.

'One of my agents recognised Pierre Lavalle at a certain service station and we started our enquiries from there. We have photos of him in the square by the Italian parliament on several occasions prior to the incident. We have photos of The Rook coming in and out of your headquarters, Baron,' he said, passing them across the table. 'I really don't think you need me to go into all the evidence, but believe me, it's all here.'

The two men sat uneasily back in their chairs. Albert looked to the Baron for support. He had been due to retire several years earlier, but was persuaded by the new administration to remain in office. He was now regretting his decision to stay. The Baron noted Albert's reticence and took charge.

'You obviously didn't bring us here just to embarrass us, Stephen, so what exactly is your motive?'

'My Prime Minister is very disappointed that France and Germany, along with a couple of their friends, have reneged on a firm promise to support Sir Henry Willington for the European presidency.'

'I don't think my President promised to support Willington

in particular,' the Baron protested sharply. 'We are surely entitled to vet any candidate first.'

'According to Neville Aitchison, at the time no conditions were applied to his proposal. Now suddenly your heads of state are trying to preclude Willington because you don't like his agenda.'

'Let's not get into a political argument – just come to the point.'

'I think you are already getting it. Unless you can persuade your governments to support our man, this information will be handed to the Italian authorities.'

The Baron thought for a moment before replying. 'You won't come out very well in all this, Stephen. You should have told the Italians long before now.'

'I accept we may get a little criticism, but we will argue that it took a long time to accumulate and piece together all the facts. Believe me, it will be nothing like the criticism and indignation your governments will receive from all around the world.'

'Life has moved on since then,' Albert intervened. 'Paolo Medina is practically in gaol; who is going to care about a bungled assassination six years ago?'

'Possibly very few people would care if we were talking about Medina, but you ended up murdering Rico Orvetti, a star footballer. Football players are much more worshipped than any politician, and he was probably the most popular player in the world at that time. When the media finds out who was responsible for his assassination, all hell will be let loose. You've barely got over all the criticism regarding the invasion of Italy,' Stephen added.

'I don't know how my President is likely to act in these circumstances,' the Baron remarked, shaking his head. 'What you don't realise, Stephen, is that Albert and I never got consent from our bosses. They could quite correctly say they were not involved in the plot.'

'They could, but who is going to believe them? I can understand that not getting their consent makes your position even more untenable; but what's it to be? Are you going to talk this over with President de Valbien, or do we publish the facts?'

'So if we fail to persuade them to support Aitchison, you will publish your file, Stephen? I thought the British secret service was more honourable than that.'

Stephen Johns gave a cynical chuckle. 'Just let your bosses understand they are in a no-win situation here. If they force us to reveal this information, they will be deserted by all their friends in Europe and Sir Henry will get elected regardless. For my part, I promise to shred the file immediately we have confirmation that France and Germany have withdrawn their objections. Is that honourable enough for you?'

'You leave us no option, and you've put both of us in an invidious situation. Don't expect to get an invitation to my resignation party. I think it's time to leave, Albert,' he suggested, helping the venerable gentleman out of his chair.

'Nor to mine,' von Meissen added gruffly.

It took a whole week of waiting before Neville Aitchison received a call from Hermann Kranz.

'I have been in discussion with Guy de Valbien at the Elysée Palace and we have come to the decision to withdraw our objections to Henry Willington,' he said.

'I hoped you would come round to our way of thinking. I honestly believe Europe needs a complete change of course. If we continue down the same road much longer, there will inevitably be a major conflict. We cannot possibly maintain an army that has no nationality.'

'Guy and I have reluctantly come to the same conclusion, Stephen. We are behind you there.'

'I know you don't like the idea of one nation one vote, but I am confident it will help to hold the EU together. The bigger countries can't continue to bully the others. Democracy isn't about power; it's about equality and freedom of choice.'

'We are prepared to listen to the arguments, Neville. It is unquestionably true that the members are too divergent. We politicians should have learnt by now that, in human terms, closer relationships invariably lead to greater conflict. In the end, we have to admit that the aspirations of a totally united Europe, both politically and economically, were just a pipe dream.'

'I realise you didn't want to support Willington in the first place, so I'm both surprised and delighted to hear your conciliatory response.'

'Well, Guy and I have decided that maybe it's time for a change. To be frank, we are tired of shouldering the burden of financial responsibility while half of Europe squanders the benefits. Our electorate is fed up with being the paymasters for the profligacy of the Club Med countries. We only needed a federal Europe to make the euro a success, but it's obvious it never will be.'

'That's not been a British problem, I'm glad to say. Sir Henry has no specific plans for the euro; those decisions are up to you.'

'We accept there is a lot to be applauded in his policies, in particular the restraints on the courts in Luxembourg and Strasbourg,' Hermann admitted. 'But we won't be agreeing to everything when it comes to a vote. Believe me, we will fight Sir Henry tooth and nail if we think he's overstepping the mark.'

'That sounds like democracy working, Hermann. I think it only fair to acknowledge that in so many ways the EU has been a success. But it is time for some radical reforms. We would like this to be introduced without bloodshed.

When would that have been achievable in Europe in the past? So long as we accept that every nation is entitled to retain its own identity and sovereignty, we can still hope to progress in peace and prosperity.'

Neville Aitchison replaced the phone on its cradle and leant back thoughtfully in his chair. He called his secretary and asked to be put in touch with Stephen Johns.

'Stephen, I thought you would like to know that France and Germany are withdrawing their objections to Sir Henry, thanks to your intervention. That was a master touch on your part.'

'I knew our intelligence would come in useful one day Prime Minister; it was just a matter of waiting for the right occasion. Thank you for letting me know.'

The head of M16 replaced the phone and strolled over to his window. His eyes fixed, in a mesmerised stare, at the heavy traffic jockeying for position on the embankment. 'Pleased to be of service,' he said out loud and allowed himself a satisfied smile.

As was his custom at six o'clock in the evening, Gerald Boston was pouring a drink for Linda and himself. Relaxing in their armchairs, they clinked glasses and simultaneously downed a mouthful. A contented look spread over their faces.

'I expected to have a nice quiet retirement, Linda,' he began, 'but it hasn't quite worked out like that. We've had a fairly turbulent time ever since I handed over to Matt.'

'I know what you mean,' Linda replied, 'and it doesn't look likely to end here. God knows how I wish Matthew hadn't married into that family. Mark my words, we haven't heard the last of them.'

'Maybe, but if Matt could just get the children back here, we could forget all about them.'

'That's not going to happen in a hurry, darling; and then we've got all this business with Paolo's trial to contend with.'

'I was rather looking forward to that, except it's going to put the family name back in the headlines again. I knew nothing good would come out of Philip's participation in the coup. Hooray for Sir Henry, I say.'

'But when you think about it, a lot of good has come out of Paolo's demise, so don't pick on our son.'

'Such as, Linda?'

'Well, a dictator has been prevented from leading a major European country again. Don't forget how easily Mussolini stirred up the Italians.'

'True.'

'And it highlighted the extremism that has been increasing all over Europe. The hatred of communism is breeding fascism, and vice versa.'

'Paolo's time in court should be very intriguing,' Gerald pointed out. 'But believe it or not, I rather hope he wins his case; even if that embarrasses Philip.'

'You can't mean that, Gerald. He's an ogre!'

'Yes, but he'll never get back into power again, Linda; he's finished. Don't forget he's also Mark and Louise's grandfather. We must respect their feelings or we will definitely lose them.'

'Paolo Medina wouldn't see it that way. If you fell under a bus, darling, he'd just laugh.'

'Yes, Linda, but then he's a politician.'